ALESSANDRO AND THE CHEERY NANNY

AND

VALENTINO'S PREGNANCY BOMBSHELL

BY
AMY ANDREWS

GW00691742

⊙ ™MILLS & BOON®

ITALIAN SURGEON TO DAD!

On call for the hospital—and the nursery!

Welcome to Amy Andrews' enchanting
new **Italian Surgeon to Dad!** duet, introducing
the two devastatingly gorgeous Lombardi surgeons

ALESSANDRO AND THE CHEERY NANNY

Bubbly nanny Natalie has put the smile back
on single dad Alessandro's little boy—
but can she win over the brooding surgeon's heart?

VALENTINO'S PREGNANCY BOMBSHELL

Single mum Paige has a young daughter
who needs a great deal of special care—
find out how she'll find the courage to tell
playboy Valentino she's expecting his baby in:

ALESSANDRO AND THE CHEERY NANNY

BY
AMY ANDREWS

MILLS & BOON

**This book is dedicated to all good fathers and their sons.
Little boys need their daddies too.**

First published in Great Britain 2010
Harlequin Mills & Boon Limited,
Eton House, 18-24 Paradise Road, Richmond, Surrey TW9 1SR

© Amy Andrews 2010

ISBN: 978 0 263 87914 8

Harlequin Mills & Boon policy is to use papers that are natural, renewable and recyclable products and made from wood grown in sustainable forests. The logging and manufacturing process conform to the legal environmental regulations of the country of origin.

Printed and bound in Spain
by Litografia Rosés, S.A., Barcelona

Dear Reader

What is it about Italian men? Is it their dark, brooding looks, their seemingly effortless charisma, or that accent? Why are they so popular in our books? Why do we love to read about them so much? I'm not sure I know the reason myself, but I'm sure my two heroines Nat and Paige do!

When my editor suggested I write two linked books with Italian heroes I didn't hesitate. I've had such fun writing them in the past, how could I resist? And what fabulous men my muse presented to me!

Cousins Alessandro and Valentino Lombardi have so much in common—both specialist doctors, both compassionate and honourable men, growing up like brothers in Italy and forging new lives for themselves on the opposite side of the world. But also, in many ways, they are complete opposites. Alessandro, so strained and serious, failing to cope with the death of his wife and raising his four-year-old son. And Valentino, the fun-loving, easy-going Lothario.

It seemed only right to give them women they needed. Or who needed them. Nat, so bright and peppy, and determined to forge a bond between Alessandro and his son. And Paige, single mother of a deaf child, so fragile and shut down—a combination a hot-blooded Italian male like Valentino finds hard to resist.

I hope you enjoy their stories as these four special people find their way to love. I know I certainly enjoyed writing them.

I miss them already.

Love

Amy

Amy Andrews has always loved writing, and still can't quite believe that she gets to do it for a living. Creating wonderful heroines and gorgeous heroes and telling their stories is an amazing way to pass the day. Sometimes they don't always act as she'd like them to—but then neither do her kids, so she's kind of used to it. Amy lives in the very beautiful Samford Valley, with her husband and aforementioned children, along with six brown chooks and two black dogs. She loves to hear from her readers. Drop her a line at www.amyandrews.com.au

Extract from
ALESSANDRO AND THE CHEERY NANNY:

Alessandro pulled up short in the doorway as the sound of his son's laughter drifted towards him. It had been months since he'd heard the noise. He'd almost forgotten what it sounded like. And after an arduous day it was a surprising pick-me-up.

His midnight gaze followed the sound, widening to take in the picture before him: his son, cuddled up next to a woman with blonde hair and blue eyes.

His welcoming smile froze before it had even made an indent into the uncompromising planes of his face.

CHAPTER ONE

NAT DAVIES was instantly attracted to the downcast head and the dark curly hair. There was something about the slump to the little boy's shoulders and the less than enthusiastic way he was colouring in. He seemed separate from the other children laughing and playing around him, and it roused the mother lion in her.

He was the only stationary object in a room full of movement. And he seemed so...forlorn.

'Who's that?' she asked, bumping Trudy's hip with hers to get her boss's attention.

Trudy stopped chopping fruit and followed Nat's gaze. 'Julian. It's his second day. Four years old. Father is ooh-la-la handsome. Italian. Perfect English. Just moved from London. Widower. Recent, I think. Doesn't smile much.'

Nat nodded, well used to Trudy's staccato style of speech. 'Poor darling.' No wonder he looked so bereft. 'How awful to lose your mother at such a young age.' Not that it mattered at any age really. She'd been eight when her father had left and it still hurt.

Trudy nodded. 'He's very quiet. Very withdrawn.'

Nat's heart strings gave another tug. She'd always had

a soft spot for loners. She knew how it felt to have your perfect world turned upside down while life continued around you. How alienating it could be. How it separated you from the bustle of life.

'Well, let's see if I can fix that,' she murmured.

Nat made a beeline for the lonely little boy, stopping only to grab a copy of *Possum Magic* off the bookshelf. In her experience she found there was very little a book couldn't fix, if only for a short while.

'Juliano.' Nat called his name softly as she approached, smiling gently.

The little boy looked up from his lacklustre attempt at colouring in a giant frog. His mouth dropped open and he stared at Nat with eyes that grew visibly rounder. She suppressed the frown that was itching to crease her forehead at the unexpected response. Surely he was used to hearing his name spoken in Italian?

He was looking at her with a mix of confusion and wonder, like he was trying to figure out if he should run into her arms or burst into tears.

She kept her smile in place. '*Ciao*, Juliano. *Come sta?*'

Nat had learnt Italian at school and spent a year in Milan on a student exchange after completing grade twelve. Given that she was now thirty-three, it had been a while since she'd spoken it but she had been reasonably fluent at one stage.

Julian's grave little face eked out a tentative smile and Nat relaxed. '*Posso sedermi?*' she asked. Julian nodded and moved over so Nat could share the bench seat with him.

'Hi, Juliano. My name's Nat,' she said.

The boy's smile slipped a little. 'Papa likes me to be called Julian,' he said quietly.

The formality in his voice was heart-breaking and Nat wanted to reach out and give him a fierce hug. Four-year-olds shouldn't be so buttoned up. If this hadn't been St Auburn's Hospital crèche for the children of hospital staff, she might have wondered if Julian's father had a military background.

Maybe Captain Von Trapp. Before Maria had come on the scene.

'Julian it is,' she said, and held out her hand for a shake. He shook it like a good little soldier and the urge to tickle him until his giggles filled the room ate at her.

She battled very uncharitable thoughts towards the boy's father. Could he not see his son was miserable and so tightly wound he'd probably be the first four-year-old in history to develop an ulcer?

She reminded herself that the man had not long lost his wife and was no doubt grieving heavily. But his son had also lost his mother. Just because he was only four, it didn't mean that Julian wasn't capable of profound grief also.

'Would you like me to read you a story?' Nat pointed to the book. 'It's about a possum and has lots of wonderful Australian animals in it.'

Julian nodded. 'I like animals.'

'Have you got a pet?'

He shook his head forlornly. 'I had a cat. Pinocchio. But we had to leave him behind. Papa promised me another one but…he's been too busy…'

Nat ground her teeth. 'I have a cat. Her name's Flo. After Florence Nightingale. She loves fish and makes a noise like this.'

Nat mimicked the low rumbling of her five-year-old tortoiseshell, embellishing slightly. Julian giggled and it was such a beautiful sound she did it again. 'She's a purring machine.' Nat laughed and repeated the noise, delighted to once again hear Julian's giggle.

As children careened around them, immersed in their own worlds, she opened the book and began to read aloud, her heart warmed by Julian's instant immersion into its world. Page after page of exquisite illustrations of Australian bush animals swept them both away and by the end of the tale Julian was begging her to read it again, his little hand tucked into hers.

'I see you've made a friend there,' Trudy said a few minutes later, plonking a tray of cut-up fruit on the table in front of them and calling for the children to go and wash up for afternoon tea.

Julian followed the rest of the kids into the bathroom, looking behind him frequently to check Nat was still there. 'I hope so, Trude,' Nat replied.

If anyone needed a friend, it was Julian.

An hour later the chatter and chaos that was usually the kindy room was filled only with the beautiful sounds of silence as the busy bunch of three- to five-year-olds slumbered through the afternoon rest period. Nat wandered down the lines of little canvas beds, checking on her charges, pulling up kicked-off sheets and picking up the odd teddy bear that had been displaced.

She stopped at Julian's bed and looked down at his dear little face. His soft curls framed his cheeks and forehead. His olive complexion was flawless in the way of children the world over. His mouth had an enticing bow shape and his lips were fat little cherubic pillows.

Unlike every other child in the room, he slept alone, no

cuddle toy clutched to his side. With the serious lines of his face smoothed in slumber he looked like any other carefree four-year-old. Except he wasn't. He was a motherless little boy who seemed to carry the weight of the world on his shoulders.

More like forty than four.

He whimpered slightly and his brow puckered. Her heart twisted and she reached out to smooth it but he turned on his side and as she watched, his thumb found its way into his mouth. He sucked subconsciously and her heart ached for him. He seemed so alone, even in sleep. It was wrong that a boy who had just lost his mother should have nothing other than a thumb to comfort him.

She made a mental note to talk to his father at pick-up. Ask him if Julian would like to bring along a toy, something familiar from home. Maybe she could even broach the subject of counselling for Julian. Something had to be done for the sad little darling. Someone had to try.

It may as well be her.

It was early evening when Nat found herself curled up in a bean bag with Julian in Book Corner, reading *Possum Magic* for the third time. The room was once again quiet, most of the children having gone home, their parents' shifts long since finished. The few remaining kids had eaten their night-time meals and were occupied in quiet play.

Despite her best efforts to engage him with other children, Julian had steadfastly refused to join in, shadowing her instead. Nat knew she should be firmer but in a short space of time she'd developed a real soft spot for Julian.

His despondent little face clawed at her insides and she didn't have the heart to turn him away. He looked like he was crying out to be loved and Nat knew how that felt. How could she deny a grieving child some affection?

She didn't notice as she turned the pages that Julian's thumb had found its way into his mouth or that one little hand had worked its way into her hair, rhythmically stroking the blonde strands.

All she was really aware of was Julian's warm body pressed into her side and his belly laugh as she mimicked Grandma Poss and Hush on their quest to find the magic food. As ways to end the day went, it wasn't too bad at all.

Dr Alessandro Lombardi strode into the crèche. He was tired. Dog tired. Emotional upheaval, months of no sleep, moving to the other side of the planet and starting a new job had really taken their toll. He wanted to go home, get into bed and sleep for a year.

If only.

He pulled up short in the doorway as his son's laughter drifted towards him. It had been months since he'd heard the sound and he'd almost forgotten what it sounded like. And after an arduous day it was a surprising pick-me-up.

His midnight-dark gaze followed the sound, his eyes widening to take in the picture before him. His son cuddled up next to a woman with blonde hair and blue eyes exactly like Camilla's. His fingers absently stroked her hair while he sucked his thumb, just as he used to do with Camilla.

His welcoming smile froze before it had even made a dent into the uncompromising planes of his face. He crossed the room in three strides. 'Julian!'

Nat felt the word crack like a whip across the room and

looked up startled as Julian's thumb fell from his mouth and he dropped his hand from her hair as if it had suddenly caught fire.

She didn't need Trudy to tell her Julian's father had arrived. They were carbon copies of each other. Same frowns, same serious gazes and brooding intensity, same cherubic mouths.

But where Julian's appeal was all round-eyed childhood innocence, his father's appeal was much more adult. There was nothing childish about his effect on her pulse. He looked like some tragic prince from a Shakespearean plot to whom the slings and arrows had not been kind.

Put quite simply, at one glance Julian's father was most categorically heart-throb material. A tumble of dark hair, with occasional streaks of silver, brushed his forehead and collar, a dark shadow drew the eye to his magnificent jaw line and that mouth…

She knew without a doubt she was going to dream about that mouth.

She suddenly felt warm all over despite the chill that blanketed her as cold dark eyes, like black ice, raked over her. Nat was used to men staring. She was blonde and, as had been pointed out to her on numerous occasions, had a decent rack. She was no supermodel but she knew she'd been blessed with clear skin, healthy hair and a perfect size twelve figure.

Until today she'd thought living in Italy had immunised her against being openly ogled. As an eighteen-year-old blonde with pale skin in a country where dark hair and olive complexions were the norm, she'd certainly attracted a lot of interest from Italian boys.

But there was nothing sexual about this Italian's

interest. Rather he was looking at her like she was the wicked witch of the west.

And he was definitely no boy.

'Julian,' he said quietly, not taking his eyes off the strange woman who was eerily familiar. From the way she folded her long pale legs under her to the blonde ponytail that brushed her shoulders and the fringe that flicked back from her face, she was just like Camilla.

His gaze strayed to the way the top two buttons of her V-necked T-shirt gaped slightly across her ample chest. They lingered there for a moment, unconsciously appreciating the ripe swell of female flesh. It had been a long time since he'd appreciated a woman's cleavage and he quickly glanced away.

His gaze moved upwards instead, finding the similarities to Camilla slapped him in the face again. Same wide-set eyes, same high cheekbones, same full mouth and pointed chin complete with sexy little cleft that no doubt dimpled when she smiled.

Hell, he must be tired, he was hallucinating.

He held his hand out to his son. 'Come here.'

Julian obeyed his father immediately and Nat felt the beads of the bean bag beneath her shift and realign, deflating her position somewhat. She looked up, way up, at a distinct disadvantage in her semi-reclined state on the floor.

From this angle Julian's father looked even more intimidating. More male. His legs looked longer. His chest broader. He loomed above her and she was torn between professionalism and just lolling her head back and looking her fill.

She couldn't remember ever having such an immediate response to a man.

His pinstriped trousers fell softly against his legs, hinting at the powerful contours of his quadriceps. The thick fabric of his business shirt did the same, outlining broad shoulders and a lean torso tapering to even leaner hips.

Unfortunately he was still staring down at her like she was one of those insects who ate their young and reluctantly professionalism won out. She floundered in the bean bag for a few seconds, totally annihilating any chance of presenting herself as a highly skilled child care worker before struggling to her feet.

Snatching a moment to collect herself, she smiled encouragingly at Julian. She noticed immediately how, even standing next to his father, Julian still looked alone. They didn't touch. There had been no great-to-see-you hug, he didn't take his father's hand, neither did his father reach for him. There was no affectionate shoulder squeeze or special father-son eye contact.

It was obvious Julian wasn't frightened of him but also obvious the poor child didn't expect much.

Nat returned her gaze upwards. Good Lord—the man was tall. And seriously sexy. She smiled, mainly for Julian's benefit. 'Hi. I'm Nat Davies.' She extended her hand.

Alessandro blinked. He'd braced himself when she'd opened her mouth to speak, half expecting a cut-glass English accent. But when the words came out in that slow, laid-back Australian way, still unfamiliar to his ear, he relaxed slightly.

The similarities between this woman and his dead wife were startling on the surface. Same height, same build, same eye colour, same blonde hair worn in exactly the same style, same facial structure and generous mouth. Same cute chin dimple.

No wonder Julian had taken a shine to her.

But looking at the fresh-faced woman before him, he knew that's where the similarities ended. This woman exuded openness, friendliness, an innocence, almost, that his wife had never had.

Her hair had been dragged back into its band, rather hurriedly by the look of it, with strands wisping out everywhere. It hadn't been neatly coiffed and primped until every hair was in place.

And Camilla wouldn't have dared leave the house without make-up. This woman…Nat…was more the girl-next-door version of Camilla. Not the posh English version he'd married.

Even her perfume was different. Camilla had always favoured heavy, spicy perfumes that lingered long after she'd left the room. Nat Davies smelled like a flower garden. And…Plasticine. It was an intriguing mix.

Most importantly, her gaze was free of artifice, free of agenda, and he felt instantly more relaxed around her then he ever had with Camilla.

Alessandro took the proffered hand and gave it a brief shake before extracting his own. 'Alessandro Lombardi.'

Nat blinked as the fleeting contact did funny things to her pulse. His voice was deep and rich like red wine and dark chocolate, his faint accent adding a glamorous edge to his exotic-sounding name. But the bronzed skin that stretched over the hard planes and angles of his face remained taut and Nat had the impression he wasn't given to great shows of emotion.

No wonder Julian rarely smiled if he lived with Mr

Impassive. Nat looked down at Julian, who was inspecting the floor. 'Julian, matey, would you like to take *Possum Magic* home? It's part of our library. Maybe your papa could read it to you before bed tonight.'

Nat watched as Julian glanced hesitantly at his father, his solemn features heartbreakingly unhopeful.

Alessandro nodded. *'Si.'*

Nat passed the book to Julian, who still looked grave despite his father's approval. Did he think perhaps his father wouldn't read him the book? She had to admit that Alessandro Lombardi didn't look like the cuddle-up-in-bed-with-his-son type. 'Go and find Trudy, matey. She'll show you how to fill out the library card.'

They watched Julian walk towards Trudy as if he was walking to his doom, clutching the book like it was his last meal.

Nat's gaze flicked back to Julian's father to find him already regarding her, his scrutiny as intense as before. 'Senor Lombardi, I was—'

'Mr, please,' he interrupted. Alessandro was surprised to hear the Italian address. Surprised too at the accuracy of her Italian accent. 'Or Doctor. Julian knows little Italian. His mother…' Alessandro paused, surprised how much even mentioning Camilla still packed a kick to his chest. 'His mother was English. It was her wish that it be his primary language.'

It was Nat's turn to be surprised. On a couple of counts. Firstly, Julian knew a lot more Italian than his father gave him credit for if today was anything to go by. And, secondly, what kind of mother would deny their child an opportunity to learn a second language—especially their father's native tongue?

But there was something about the way he'd faltered when he'd talked about his wife, the hesitation, the emptiness that prodded at her soft spot. He was obviously still grieving deeply. And maybe in his grief he was just trying to do the right thing by his dead wife? Trying to keep things going exactly as they had been for Julian's sake. Or desperately trying to hang onto a way of life that had been totally shattered.

On closer inspection she could see the dark smudges and fine lines around his eyes. He looked tired. Like he hadn't slept properly in a very long time.

Who was she to pass judgment?

'Dr Lombardi, I was wondering if Julian had a special toy or a teddy bear? Something familiar from home to help him feel a little less alone in this new environment?'

Alessandro stiffened. A toy. Of course, Camilla would have known that. There was that mangy-looking rabbit that he used to drag around with him everywhere. Somewhere…

'I've been very busy. Our things only arrived a few days ago and there's been no chance to unpack. We're still living out of boxes.'

Nat blinked. Too busy to surround your child with things that were familiar to him when so much in his world had been turned upside down?

'This is none of my business, of course, but I understand you were recently widowed.'

Alessandro saw the softness in her eyes and wanted to yell at her to stop. He didn't deserve her pity. Instead, he gave a brief, controlled nod. '*Si.*'

If anything, he looked even bleaker than when he'd first entered but despite his grim face and keep-out vibes Nat was overwhelmed by the urge to pull them both close and hug them. Father and son. They'd been through so much and were both so obviously still hurting. She couldn't bear to see such sadness.

'I was wondering if Julian had had any kind of counselling.' *Or if the good doctor had, for that matter.* 'He seems quite…withdrawn. I can highly recommend the counselling service they run here through St Auburn's. The child psychologist is excellent. We could make an appointment—'

'You're right,' Alessandro interrupted for the second time, a nerve jumping at the angle of his jaw. 'This is none of your business.' He turned to locate his son. 'Come, Julian.'

Nat felt as if he had physically slapped her and she recoiled slightly. Alessandro Lombardi had a way with his voice that could freeze a volcano. He was obviously unused to having his authority questioned.

She'd bet her last cent he was a surgeon.

She watched Dr Lombardi usher his son towards the door. Julian partially lifted his hand, reaching for his father's, then obviously thought better of it, dropping it by his side. He turned and gave her a small wave and a sad smile as he walked out the door, and Nat felt a lump swell in her throat.

They left side by side but emotionally separate. There was no picking his son up and carrying him out, not even a guiding hand on the back. Something, anything that said, even on a subliminal level, I love you, I'm here for you.

Nat hoped for Julian's sake that it was grief causing this strange disconnectedness between father and son and not something deeper. There was something unbearably sad about a four-year-old with no emotional expectations.

Having grown up with an emotionally distant father Nat knew too well how soul destroying it could be. How often had she'd yearned for his touch, his smile, his praise after he'd left? And how often had he let her down, too busy with his new family, with his boys? Even at thirty-three she was still looking for his love. She couldn't bear to see it happening to a child in her care.

But something inside her recognised that Alessandro Lombardi was hurting too. Knew that it was harsh to judge him. As a nurse she knew how grief affected people. How it could shut you down, cut you off at the knees. He had obviously loved his wife very deeply and was probably doing the best he could just to function every day.

To put one foot in front of the other.

Maybe he was just emotionally frozen. Not capable of any feelings at the moment. Maybe grief had just sucked them all away.

She sighed. It looked like she'd also developed a soft spot for the father also. Yep, it was official—she was a total sucker for a sob story.

The next day Nat had finished her stint in Outpatients and was heading back to the accident and emergency department for her very late lunch. She'd been sent there to cover for sick leave and was utterly exhausted.

She didn't mind being sent out of her usual work area and had covered Outpatients on quite a few occasions since starting at St Auburn's six months ago but it was a full-on morning which always ran over the scheduled one p.m. finish time. There hadn't been time for morning tea either so her stomach was protesting loudly. She could almost taste the hot meat pie she'd been daydreaming about for the last hour and a half.

Add to that being awake half the night thinking about

Julian's situation, and she was totally wrecked. *And then there'd been the other half of the night.* Filled with images—very inappropriate images—of Julian's father and his rather enticing mouth.

She'd known she was going to dream about that mouth.

'Oh, good, you're back. I need another experienced hand,' Imogen Reddy, the nurse in charge, said as Nat wandered back. 'It's Looney Tunes here. Code one just arrived in Resus. Seventy-two-year old-male, suspected MI. Can you get in and give the new doc a hand? Delia's there but she was due off half an hour ago and hasn't even had time for a break. Can you take over and send her home?'

Nat looked at the bedlam all around her. *Just another crazy day at St Auburn's Accident and Emergency.* And they wondered why she kept knocking back a full-time position. Nat's stomach growled a warning at her but she knew there was no way she could let a seven-months-pregnant colleague do overtime on an empty stomach.

She smiled at her boss. 'Resus. Sure thing.'

Nat stopped just outside the resus cubicle and pulled a pair of medium gloves out of a dispenser attached to the wall. She snapped them on, took a deep breath, flicked back the curtain and entered the fray.

'Okay, Delia. You're off,' she said, smiling at her colleague who happened to be the first person she saw amidst the chaos. 'Go home, put your feet up and feed the foetus.'

Delia shoulders sagged and she gave Nat a grateful smile. 'Are you sure?' She turned and addressed the doctor. 'Are you okay if I go, Alessandro? You're getting a much better deal. Nat here is Super-Nurse.'

Alessandro? Nat swung around to find Alessandro Lombardi, all big and brooding, behind her. The bustle, the sounds of the oxygen and the monitors around her faded out as she stared into those coalpit-black eyes.

They were alert, radiating intelligence, but if anything he looked more tired than he had yesterday. He stared back and Nat felt as if she was naked in front of him.

She dropped her gaze as some of the images from last night's dream revisited. *Bloody hell. He* was the new doctor? Working part-time generally kept Nat out of the loop with medical staff rotations and she'd just assumed Imogen had meant a new registrar. Surely Julian's father was a little too old to be a registrar?

So much for her surgeon theory.

Alessandro took in the woman who had been the cause of another sleepless night. A new cause, granted, but still a complication he didn't need. She was different today, out of her shorts and T-shirt. Very professional looking in the modest white uniform with the zip up the front. Her hair was a little neater in her ponytail and in this environment he felt on a more even keel around her.

Still, his gaze dropped to the zip briefly and before he could stop it, an image of him yanking the slider down flitted across his mind's eye.

He looked at Delia briefly. 'Yes. We've met.'

Then he turned back to the patient and Nat felt thoroughly dismissed. If only he knew what he'd done to her in her dreams last night…

Had she had time she might have been miffed but her patient caught her attention. 'Super-Nurse, hey?' he croaked behind his oxygen mask.

Nat dragged her gaze away from the back of Alessandro's head to look at the patient. He was sweaty and grey with massive ST changes on his monitor.

Multiple ectopic beats were worrying and as she watched, a short run of ventricular tachycardia interrupted his rhythm.

His heart muscle was dying.

He was also in pain despite the morphine that she noted had already been administered, but there was still a twinkle visible in his bright eyes. He was obviously one of those stoic old men who didn't believe in complaining too much.

'Yes, sir.' She reached for his hand and gave it a squeeze. 'That's me. To the rescue.'

The patient gave a weak chuckle. 'Ernie,' he puffed out. 'Looks like I'm in safe hands, then.'

Nat glanced at Alessandro. She hoped so. She hoped he was better at doctoring than he was at communicating. At fathering. 'The very best.'

'What's the ETA on the CCU docs?' Alessandro asked no one in particular.

Seeing Nat Davies from the crèche was a bit of a surprise but he didn't have time to ponder that, or her damn zip, now. He had to focus on his patient, who needed that consult and admission to the coronary care unit pronto.

Ernie's ECG was showing a massive inferior myocardial infarction. They were administering the right drugs to halt the progress of the heart attack but these patients were notoriously unstable and with age against him, Alessandro worried that Ernie would arrest before the drugs could work. Or that his heart was already too damaged.

'Couple of minutes,' someone behind him said.

As it turned out, Ernie didn't have a couple of minutes and Alessandro's worst fears were realised when the monitor alarmed and Ernie lost consciousness.

'VF,' Nat announced as the green line on the screen developed into a series of frenetic squiggles. Her own heart rate spiked as a charge of adrenaline shot through her system like vodka on an empty stomach.

Alessandro pointed at Nat. 'Commence CPR. I'll intubate. Adrenaline,' he ordered. 'Charge the defib.'

Nat hiked the skirt of her uniform up her thighs a little as she climbed up onto the narrow gurney. She planted her knees wide and balanced on the edge of the mattress, a feat she'd performed a little too often, as she started compressions.

Any ill will she may have been harbouring towards Dr Lombardi fizzled in an instant at the totally professional way he ran the code. It was textbook. But that wasn't doing him justice. It was more than textbook. He didn't see a seventy-two-year-old man and give up after a few minutes. He gave Ernie every chance. It wasn't until the down time reached thirty minutes that he finally called it.

He placed his hands on Nat's, stilling their downward trajectory. 'Thank you,' he said. Then he looked at the clock. 'Time of death fifteen twenty-two hours.'

Nat looked down at his hands. She could just see her own through the gloved fingers of his. She noticed for the first time his sleeves were rolled back to reveal the dark hair of his bronzed forearms and she absently thought how strong they looked. How manly.

She glanced at him and their eyes locked, a strange solidarity uniting them. She could see the impact of this loss in his bleak stare. As she watched, his gaze drifted briefly south, lapping her cleavage, and she felt her nipples bead as if he'd actually caressed them. When he looked back at her, all she could see was heat.

Two beats passed and then as quickly as the heat had come it disappeared and he was removing his hands, extending one to help her off the gurney. Dragging her gaze from him, she accepted, easing back to the floor.

Her knees nearly buckled and Nat snatched her hand away, grabbing for the edge of the trolley to steady herself.

'Are you okay?' he asked as he watched her wobble slightly.

Nat rubbed her at her knees. 'Fine'

Except, staring down at Ernie, she knew it wasn't. Ernie was dead. And whatever was going on between her and Alessandro didn't matter next to that. Neither did it matter that she'd only known Ernie for only a handful of minutes—he was still dead. Gone. The twinkle in his eyes extinguished for ever. In fact, it made it worse that she didn't know him. It was wrong that a person should die surrounded by strangers.

She felt as she always did, overwhelmingly sad.

Alessandro nodded. 'We need to talk to his family.'

His cold onyx gaze bored into hers with an air of expectation, no trace of the heat from a moment ago.

Looked like she was going with him.

Confronted with the businesslike professional, she wondered if she'd imagined the fleeting glimpse of sorrow and passion she'd seen. Her tummy growled again and she bargained with it for another half an hour.

Alessandro strode briskly ahead and Nat worried as she followed him. Sure, the view was good. His trousers hugged the tight contours of his butt and each stride emphasised not only the power of his legs but pulled at his shirt, emphasising the broadness of his back.

But none of that meant this man was remotely equipped

to talk to grieving relatives. He was still grieving himself. Had Ernie's death resonated with him? Had this death reminded him of his dead wife, of his own grief?

He was obviously a consultant, she didn't think for a moment this was his first time. But if he was as emotionally disconnected with this family as he was with his son, it could be disastrous for them. As a nurse she was used to being involved in these conversations but did he only want her there to fill in the emotional gaps for him? Was she going to be left to pick up the pieces like she'd done too many times before in her career because too often doctors were ill equipped for this sort of situation?

She contemplated saying something. But despite the brief flare of desire that had licked her with heat, his terse *This is none of your business* from yesterday still rang in her ears and she didn't want to annoy him before this heart-wrenching job. But he seemed as tense as yesterday, as distant, and not even the growling of her stomach could override the foreboding that shadowed her as she tried to keep up with his impossibly long stride.

Telling someone their husband/child/mother/significant other had died was always dreadful. As a health-care worker, Nat would rather clean bedpans all shift than witness the devastating effects of those awful few words. But she knew Ernie's wife and kids deserved the truth and she knew they'd have questions that only someone who had been there could answer.

And that was her.

She couldn't back away from that. No matter how much she wanted to.

Much to her surprise, Alessandro again totally confounded her. He spoke softly, his accent more apparent as he gently outlined what had happened and how they'd tried but in the end there had been nothing they could do to bring Ernie back. The family cried and got angry and asked questions and Alessandro was calm and gentle and patient.

He was compassion personified.

And at the end when Ernie's wife tentatively put out her hand to bridge the short distance between Alessandro and herself and then thought better of it and withdrew it, it was he who reached out and took her hand.

It should have melted her marshmallow heart in an instant. But it didn't.

It reminded her of yesterday and Julian reaching for his father's hand and it had the opposite effect. She was furious. It felt like a red-hot poker had been shoved through her heart. She wasn't sure if it was the lack of food or the lack of sleep but she felt irrationally angry.

Was this man schizophrenic? Was he some sort of Jekyll and Hyde? How could he offer Ernie's wife, a relative stranger, the comfort he denied his own child?

He'd shown this family, this previously unknown collection of people, more sensitivity, more emotion, than he'd displayed for his four-year-old son. Yesterday she'd thought he was emotionally crippled. Grieving for his wife. Today, as they'd walked to do this, she'd worried about it again. Worried about his ability to empathise when he was buried under the weight of his own grief.

But it wasn't the case. He was obviously a brilliant emergency physician with a fabulous bedside manner. He just didn't take it home with him. To the most important person in the world. To his own child. To his son.

* * *

They left Ernie's family after about twenty minutes and Nat had never been more pleased to be shed of a person in her life. She steamed ahead, knowing if she didn't get away from him she would say something she would regret.

Alessandro frowned as Nat forged ahead. She seemed upset and as much as he didn't want anything to do with the woman who could almost have been Camilla's twin, they worked together and he knew that sudden death, such as they'd both just been part of, took its toll.

He caught her up. 'Are you okay?'

'Fine.' She repeated her response from earlier.

Except she wasn't. It didn't take a genius to figure out that something was bothering her. He grabbed her arm to prevent her walking away any further. 'I don't think you are.'

Nat looked at his bronzed hand on her pale arm. She looked at him. *Oh, Senor, you really don't want to mess with me now.* She pulled her arm away but he tightened his grip.

Heat radiated from his hand and spread up her arm to her breasts and belly. Damn it, she did not want to feel like this. Not now. She was mad. *Furious.* She sucked in a breath, ragged from her brisk walk and the rage bubbling beneath the surface.

They were standing in the corridor facing each other and it was as if time stood still around them and they were the only two people on the planet. Nat couldn't believe how it was possible to want to shake someone and totally pash their lips off at the same time.

'I'm fine.' The denial was low and guttural.

Alessandro could see the agitated rise and fall of her

chest, see the colour in her cheeks. His gaze drifted to her mouth, her parted lips enticing.

He dragged his gaze away. 'I don't believe you. I know these cases can be difficult—'

Nat's snort ripped through his words and gave her mouth something else to do other than beg for his kiss. 'You think this is about Ernie?' She stared into his handsome face, at his peppered jaw line. How could she want someone who was so bloody obtuse?

'It's not?'

Nat snorted again and she knew she couldn't hold it back any longer. 'Tell me, how is it that you can reach out and hold a stranger's hand and yet you can't offer your own son the same comfort?'

Alessandro froze at the accusation in her words. He dropped his hand from her arm as if he'd suddenly discovered she was suffering from the ebola virus. Nat watched his black ice eyes chill over as he paled beneath his magnificent bronze complexion. But she was on a roll now and she'd come this far.

'Nothing to say?' she taunted.

'Oh, I think you've said enough for both of us. Don't you?'

And before she knew it he'd turned on his heel, his rapidly departing figure storming along the corridor ahead.

She sucked in a breath, her body quivering from anger and something else even more primitive. She guessed she should feel chastised but she couldn't. If he could show this level of compassion at work, even if it was just an act, he sure as hell could show it at home.

If she could save Julian from the emotional wasteland

she'd trodden, trying to please her father throughout her childhood, then she would. Attraction or no attraction.

So, no. She hadn't said enough. Not nearly enough. Not by a long shot.

CHAPTER TWO

Two weeks later Brisbane was in the throes of an unremitting heatwave. The power grid couldn't keep up with consumer demand for ceiling fans and 24-hour-a-day air-conditioning. Tempers were short. Road rage, heat stroke and dehydration were rampant.

Even in a city that regularly sweltered each summer, the temperatures were extreme. But this was spring and totally ironic when the other side of the world battled the looming pandemic of a horrible new strain of influenza and unseasonal snow was causing general havoc.

Nat actually looked forward to stepping through the doors of St Auburn's and being enveloped in a cool blast of air. Anywhere was better than her hot little box the real estate agent euphemistically called a townhouse in a breezeless suburb blistering beneath the sun's relentless rays.

Not that it would matter soon, seeing that it looked like she was going to be evicted by the end of the month.

Nat stepped into the crowded lift on the eighth floor, pondering this conundrum yet again. She'd just transferred another heat-stroke victim to the medical ward and was returning to the department. She squeezed in and, noting the ground-floor button had already been pushed, let her mind wander to the phone call she was expecting from the realtor any time now. She would find out today whether she could get an extension on her lease.

It wasn't until the lift emptied out over the next few floors and she had some more room to move that she was even aware of her fellow travellers. Two more people got out at the fourth floor and she was suddenly aware of there being only one other person left. Big and looming behind her. A strange sixth sense, or possibly foreboding, settled around her and she glanced quickly over her shoulder.

Alessandro Lombardi stared back at her, one dark eyebrow quirked sardonically. *Hell*. She had only seen him very briefly and at a distance in the last couple of weeks since she'd basically accused him of being a terrible father. He was wearing a pale lemon shirt and a classy orange tie. A stethoscope was slung casually around his neck.

In short he was looking damn fine and her hormones roared to life.

She turned back to the panel, pressing 'G' several times as the door slowly shut, her heart beating double time.

A fleeting smile touched Alessandro's mouth as he stared at her back, her blonde ponytail brushing her collar. It was the first time he'd been close to her since her outburst a little while ago. But he'd certainly heard her name frequently enough. Julian had spoken of little else. He'd heard it so often he'd started to dream about her.

He moved to stand beside her. 'Good afternoon, Nat.'

Nat took a steadying breath. 'Dr Lombardi,' she said, refusing to turn and face him. She jabbed at the 'G' several more times—why was this lift so damn slow?

'Be careful. You'll break it.'

She could detect a faint trace of amusement in his voice but today with the heat and the eviction hanging over her head she really wasn't in the mood. She hit it one more time for good measure.

Which was when the lift came to a grinding halt, causing her to stumble against him. She heard him mutter '*Porca vacca*' as he was jostled towards her and she supposed, absently, a profanity was better than an *I told you so*.

His hand cupped her elbow and the lights flickered out. It was a few seconds before either of them moved or spoke. Alessandro recovered first.

'Are you okay?'

His big hand was warm on her arm and for a second she even leaned into him, her pulse skipping madly in her chest as her body tried to figure out what was the bigger problem. Being stuck in a lift. Or being stuck in a lift with Alessandro Lombardi.

'You know,' she said, moving her elbow out of his grasp, 'when they teach you a foreign language it's always the swear words you learn first?'

Alessandro chuckled. 'Guilty.'

His low laughter sounded strange coming from a man who had thus far looked incapable of anything remotely joyous. But it enveloped her in the darkness and made her feel curiously safe.

The lights flickered on, or at least one of them did, and Alessandro braced himself for the lift to power up and lurch to a start. When nothing happened he looked down at Nat, who was looking expectantly at the ceiling. He hadn't realised they were standing so close.

Her flower-garden scent wafted towards him and when her gaze shifted from surveying the ceiling to meet his, the urge to move closer, to stroke his finger down her cheek, was a potent force.

He took a step back. His attraction to this woman was a complication he didn't need. 'I'll ring and see what's happened.'

Nat nodded absently, also backing up, pleased to feel the solidness of the wall behind her. For a moment there, maybe it had been the half-light, his eyes had darkened even further and she could have sworn he was going to touch her. *In a good way*.

She felt as if there wasn't enough air suddenly and took some calming breaths. She wasn't the hysterical type and now was not the time to become one.

Nat listened absently as Alessandro had a conversation with someone on the other end of the lift's emergency phone. It was brief and from the tone it didn't sound like they were getting out any time soon.

He hung up the phone and turned to her. 'There's a problem with the city grid. Something to do with the heat wave. The emergency power has kicked in but two lifts have failed to start. They're working on it.'

Nat licked her lips, the thought of spending time with him in a confined space rather unsettling. Did he also feel the buzz between them or was it all one sided? 'Did they have any idea how long it might take?'

'No.'

'*Porca vacca*,' she muttered, figuring Alessandro's instinctive expletive was as good as any. In either language.

Alessandro suppressed another chuckle. He could see her gaze darting around the lift and he wondered if she was trying to calculate carbon-dioxide build-up or was looking for an escape hatch. 'You're not claustrophobic, I hope?'

Nat shook her head. 'No. I'm afraid you'll be disappointed if you're waiting for me to turn into a hysterical female.'

Was he disappointed? Certainly Camilla would have thrown her first tantrum by now, demanding to speak to someone in authority. He much preferred Nat's calm resignation. 'Good.'

Nat glanced at him briefly and quickly looked away. He loomed in the dim light and with each passing second he seemed to take up more room. 'Well, no point in standing. Might as well get comfortable for the long haul.'

She sat then, cross-legged on the floor, her back pressed to the wall. She looked up at him looking down at her and was reminded of their first meeting when she'd had the bean-bag disadvantage. He was looking at her with that now familiar coolness in his eyes.

'Sit down, for God's sake,' she grouched.

Alessandro frowned. Nat Davies was one bossy little package. He slid down the wall, planting his feet evenly in front of him, his knees bent. 'Are you always this disagreeable?'

Nat, who was excruciatingly aware of his encroaching masculinity, shot him a startled look. She opened her mouth to protest. No, she wasn't. Despite her father's desertion and the recent ending of a long-term messy relationship that would have caused the most congenial woman to become a bitter hag, she was essentially a very agreeable person.

Perennially happy. Everyone said so. She almost told him so too. But then a quick review of the twice she'd spoken to him had her conceding that his comment was probably fair.

She raised her gaze from the very fascinating way his

trousers pulled across his thigh muscles. 'I owe you an apology. For the other day. After Ernie. I was out of line. It was none of my business.'

Alessandro was surprised by her admission. It was refreshing to be with a woman who could apologise. 'You did overstep the line a little.'

Nat wanted to protest again, justify her reaction as being in Julian's interests, but he was right. 'I get too involved. I always have. The matron where I trained said I was a hopeless case.'

Alessandro smiled grudgingly. He removed his stethoscope and loosened his tie. It was already starting to get stuffy without the benefit of the air-conditioning. 'There are worse human flaws.'

He knew that only too well.

Nat stared at how even a small lift to his beautiful mouth transformed his face. Combined with the now skew tie and the undone top button, revealing a tantalising glimpse of very male neck, he really was a sight to behold. She smiled back. 'She didn't think so.'

Alessandro straightened a leg, stretching it out in front of him. He shrugged, looking directly at her. 'We'd just lost the battle to save a man's life. Death affects everyone in different ways.'

The teasing light she'd glimpsed briefly snuffed out and he seemed bleak and serious again. An older version of Julian. She hesitated briefly before voicing the question that entered her head. But they had to talk about something. And maybe he was looking for an opening? 'How long ago did your wife die?'

Alex felt the automatic tensing of the muscles in his neck. A fragment of a memory slipped out unbidden from the steel trap in his brain. Opening his door on the other side of the world to two grim-looking policemen. He drew his leg up again.

Nat watched him withdraw, startled by a twist of empathy deep inside.

Oh, no. No. No. No.

Alessandro Lombardi was a big boy. He didn't need her empathy. It was bad enough that she was sexually attracted to him. He didn't need her to comfort him and fix things too. His wife was dead—she couldn't fix that. Only time could fix that.

'I'm sorry. There I go again. None of my business.'

No. It wasn't. But he was damned if he wasn't opening his mouth to tell her anyway. 'Nine months.'

Nat was surprised. Both that he had responded and by the nine months. She'd known it was recent but it was still confronting. No wonder they were both so raw. 'I'm so very sorry,' she murmured.

Alessandro watched as her gaze filled with pity, the blue of her irises turning soft and glassy in the gentle light. He couldn't bear to see it. A sudden black fury streaked through him fast and hot like a lightning bolt from the deep well of self-hatred that bubbled never far from the surface. He didn't deserve her pity. He wasn't worthy of it. All he deserved was her contempt.

This was why he'd left England. To get far away from other people's pity. Their well-meaning words and greeting-card platitudes. Knowing that he had driven her to her death, that he alone was responsible...the hypocrisy had eaten him up inside.

Looking into Julian's face every day was more than he could stand. It was much easier not to.

He dropped his gaze. It took all of his willpower to drag himself back from the storm of broiling emotions squeezing his gut. 'Nat,' he said to the floor, before raising his face to meet hers, 'is that short for something?'

There had been a moment, before he'd looked down, when she'd glimpsed a heart-breaking well of despair. But it was shuttered now, safely masked behind a gaze that could have been hewn from arctic tundra.

He was obviously still deeply in love with his wife. It was also obvious he wasn't going to talk about it with her.

'Natalie,' she said, taking the not-so-subtle hint. 'I was supposed to be a boy.'

'Ah.'

'Nathaniel. Nat for short.'

She told the story she knew off by heart, careful not to betray how inadequate it made her feel. How she'd never felt like she quite measured up because her father had wanted a boy. 'My parents had kind of got used to thinking of me as Nat so they decided on Natalie.'

'Nathalie.' Alessandro rolled the Italian version round his tongue. 'It's pretty. Much prettier than Nat.'

It certainly was when he said it. His accent made a *th* pronunciation shading it with an exotic sound plain old Nat never had. Coming from his lips it sounded all grown up. No girl-next-door connotation. No one-size-fits-all, unisex, if-only-you'd-been-a-boy name.

In one breath he'd feminised it.

And right then, sitting on the floor in the gloom of a broken-down lift, she could see how women fell in love at first sight. Not that she was quite that stupid. Not any more. After Rob she knew better than to get involved with a man who was in love with another woman. Even a dead one.

But raw heat coated her insides and she squirmed against the floor to quell the sticky tentacles of desire.

'I prefer Nat,' she dismissed lightly, brushing at imaginary fluff on her skirt.

Alessandro dropped his eyes, watching the nervous gesture. It was preferable to the vulnerability he'd seen in her unmasked gaze.

'Ah, yes, Nat. Nat, Nat, Nat. I hear that name so often at home these days I'm beginning to think you must have magical powers. I think you could give Harry Potter a run for his money.'

Nat, pleased to be off more personal subjects, laughed out loud. Right. If she had magical powers she sure as hell would have used them shamelessly to her advantage long before now. Made her father love her more. Made Rob love her more. Made them stay.

'Julian talks about me?'

Despite not wanting to, Alessandro noticed the way her uniform pulled across her chest. The way the slide nestled in her cleavage. It had been such a long time since he'd noticed anything much about a woman at all but it was becoming a habit with this bossy, talkative Australian nurse.

He sent her a tight smile. 'Nonstop.'

Nat grinned. 'Sorry.' But she really wasn't. It made her happy to think she was making a difference to the serious little boy who came to the crèche. She knew she looked out for him on her days there and her heart melted faster than an ice-cube in this damn heat wave, when his sad little face lit up like a New Year's Eve firework display the moment he spotted her.

Alessandro shrugged. 'I'm pleased he…has someone.' Even if hearing her name incessantly meant she was never far from his thoughts. Even if that transferred into the rare moments of sleep he managed to snatch during nights that seemed to last an eternity. Those few precious hours were suddenly full of her. Bizarre erotic snapshots the likes of which he hadn't experienced since puberty.

Just another reason to despise himself a little bit more. Camilla hadn't even been dead a year and he was fantasising about some…look-alike-but-not Australian bossy-boots, like a horny teenager.

'He's a great kid, Alessandro.'

Her voice had softened and he could tell she held genuine affection for Julian. He wished his own relationship with his son was as uncomplicated. When he looked at Julian he saw Camilla and his guilt ratcheted up another notch. 'I know.'

And he did know. But he didn't know how to reach a child who was a stranger to him. He didn't know how to look at his son, love his son and pretend that he wasn't the reason Julian's world had been torn apart.

Perhaps if they'd been closer…

They looked at each other for a long moment, the air thick between them with things neither of them were game enough to say aloud. A phone ringing broke the compelling eye contact and it took a few seconds for Nat to realise it wasn't the lift emergency phone but her mobile.

She pulled it out of her pocket. 'Huh, look at that,' she mused. 'Good reception. Go figure.' She looked at the number on the screen and gave an inward groan. Great timing.

It was difficult for Alessandro not to eavesdrop. It was impossible to even pretend he wasn't. There was him and her in a tiny metal box, not much light and nothing else to do. He did try to feign disinterest, pulling his pager out and deleting the build-up of stored messages, but it was obvious she was having problems with her lease.

When Nat pushed the 'end' button on her phone with a grimace he said, *'Problemo?'*

Nat sighed and stuffed the phone back in her pocket. 'You could say that.'

'Sounds like you're having trouble with your landlord.'

Nat gave a derisive snort. 'That's an understatement. I've been given two weeks to move out.'

Alessandro dropped both of his legs, stretching them out in front as he crossed his arms across his chest. 'Let me guess. You have lots of loud parties and are behind on your rent?'

Nat, aware that his legs were a good deal closer now, flicked him a *funny ha-ha* look. The fact that he was even attempting humour wasn't enough to lift her out of the doldrums.

Where the hell was she going to go? 'The owners want to move back in.'

'Can they do that?'

Nat shrugged. 'The lease is up.'

'Ah.'

She sighed. 'Yes. Ah.'

'Have you thought of buying? It's a buyers' market at the moment with the world economic situation and interest rates being at an all-time low. I bought my place in Paddington for a very good price.'

'I have bought a place. A unit not far from St Auburn's. I bought it off the plan. It was supposed to be finished two months ago but with all that winter rain we had it's behind schedule.'

'Ah.'

Nat's legs were starting to cramp in her cross-legged position so she also stretched her legs out, her modest uniform riding up a little and revealing two very well-defined kneecaps and a hint of thigh. 'I only took a six-month lease because the project manager assured me the project would be on time. Damn man is as slippery as an oily snake.'

Alessandro's gaze dropped to the narrow strip of thigh visible between her knees and hemline before he realised what he was doing. He dragged his attention back to her frowning face. 'Do you not have a man, a husband or boyfriend, who can deal with these things for you?'

If she hadn't already been annoyed at the world—heat wave, broken lift, difficult landlord—Nat might have laughed at his typical Italian male assumptions. But unfortunately for Alessandro, she was.

'I don't need a *man* to deal with stuff for me,' she said sharply.

Frankly she was sick of men. It was because of a bloody man she was in this pickle to start with. Eternal spinsterhood was looking like a damn fine alternative these days. Although the presence of a six-foot-nine Neanderthal next time she visited her half-complete unit did hold some appeal.

Alessandro held up his hands in surrender, not wanting to get into a debate about gender roles with her already looking like she was spoiling for a fight. Things were different these days, which was a good thing. And this wasn't Italy. Besides, they might well need to preserve oxygen.

'Have you not got family here you can stay with?'

She shook her head. 'All my family live in Perth. In Western Australia. I've only been in Brisbane for six months.'

'You are a long way from home, Nathalie.'

His voice was low and it slithered across the floor of the lift like a serpent, inching up her leg, under her skirt, gliding across her belly and undulating up her spine, stroking every hot spot in between. She was one giant goose-bump in three seconds flat.

The ease with which he accomplished it was shocking but she was damned if she was going to let her body do the talking. She raised an eyebrow, going for sardonic. '*I'm* a long way from home?'

He chuckled. *Well deflected.* '*Touché.*' There were a few moments of silence as they both contemplated the floor. Alessandro had the feeling there was more to the Nat Davies story. He checked his watch. Ten minutes. How much longer?

It seemed stupid to sit in silence.

'So why did you leave Perth? Was there a reason or did you have a crashing desire to see Queensland?'

Nat gave a nonchalant shrug. 'I had a fancy to see the sun rise over the ocean.'

Alessandro smiled at her flippant reply. He was pretty sure it ran deeper than that. It took one damaged soul to recognise another. 'I get the feeling there may have been a man involved?'

Nat contemplated another snappy quip but she'd never been able to pull flippant off for very long. 'There was.'

'What happened?'

Nat repeated her earlier eyebrow rise. 'I think this is where I tell you it's none of your business, isn't it?'

Alessandro nodded his head, a small smile playing on his lips. 'I do believe so, yes.' He shrugged. 'Just trying to pass the time.'

Nat regarded him for a few moments. Why did she feel so compelled to talk to him? One look at him and she lost her mind. She didn't bother to point out they could pass it just as easily by talking about his stuff because frankly she was tired of listening to men talk about women who used to share their lives.

'It became…untenable.' She waited for the barb in her chest to twist again, like it always did when she thought about Rob and their crazy crowded relationship. Her, him and his ex-wife.

Curiously it didn't.

Alessandro nodded. So they were both running away…

'So I left. I didn't plan to leave Perth but then I hadn't planned on it being so hard to still move in the same circles.'

She glanced at him, wondering what he was thinking, wondering if he empathised. Was that why he'd moved to the other side of the world? To escape the memories that were there, waiting around every corner? 'When the property settlement came through I just…left. Took my half and relocated.'

Alessandro nodded. 'That took courage.' He knew how hard it was to up sticks.

'Yeah, well, it doesn't seem so brave now, does it?'

Alessandro crossed one outstretched leg over the other at the ankles. 'Do you have a plan B?'

'The rental market in Brisbane is tight. I only need a couple of months but no one's going to be keen to rent to me for such a short time.'

Alessandro nodded. He'd tried to get a short-term lease so he didn't have to rush into buying but there'd been nothing available and he'd taken the plunge and bought instead.

'I don't really know anyone well enough to crash with them for long periods of time, apart from Paige who I went to school with in Perth. She works in Audiology and part time in the operating theatres at St Auburn's. I stayed with her for a couple of weeks when I first arrived but her husband walked out over two years ago and she has a three-year-old with high needs. I can't impose on them again.' She shrugged. 'The short answer is, I don't know. But something will show up. It'll work out, it always does.'

As soon as the words were out the lights flickered on in the lift and the air-conditioning whirred to life. Nat laughed. 'See?'

Alessandro smiled, picking up his pager and stethoscope off the floor as the lift shuddered and began its descent. He vaulted to his feet and held out a hand to her. She hesitated for a fraction and then took it. He pulled her up, the lift settling on the ground floor as she rose to her feet, causing her to stumble a little.

Nat put her hand against his chest to steady herself, aware that his other arm had come around to help. She copped a lungful of something spicy and for a brief dizzying second she considered pushing her nose into the patch of neck his skew tie had revealed to see if she could discern the exact origin. His lips were close and his gaze seemed to be suddenly fixed on her mouth and all she could think about was kissing him.

His heart thudded directly below her palm and the vibrations travelled down her arm, rippling through every nerve ending in her body, energising every cell.

The lift dinged and saved her from totally losing her mind. 'Oops, sorry,' she said, pushing away from him, uncharacteristic colour creeping into her cheeks.

The doors opened and a small crowd of maintenance people as well as department staff were there to greet them, clapping and cheering.

Nat risked a quick glance at him, dismayed at the heat she saw in his eyes again. Her blush intensified. She high-tailed it out of the lift without a backward glance.

Alessandro had not long been home with Julian early that evening when the doorbell rang. He opened it to a middle-aged woman and ushered her in. Debbie Woodruff was the tenth applicant for live-in nanny he'd interviewed.

He had no intention of the crèche being a long-term solution for Julian. Yes, it was open 24 hours a day and Julian seemed to like it there, at least when Nat was on anyway, but he'd already been dragged halfway round the world. His son deserved stability. And that was one thing he could give him.

Debbie seemed very nice and was plainly well qualified. Julian was polite, as always, saying please and thank you as Camilla had taught him, eating carefully, playing quietly. But he wasn't enthused. And Alessandro had to admit he wasn't either.

He wasn't sure what he wanted. Someone to love Julian, he guessed. Not for it just to be another job. A pay cheque. What his son needed was a mother.

His mother.

Guilt seized him as he saw Debbie out. The one thing Julian needed the most, and he couldn't give it to him. It was his job. He was the father. He was supposed to provide for his son.

Alessandro entered the lounge room. Julian looked at him but didn't smile or acknowledge him. He sat next to his son and wished he knew how to bridge the gap. Wished his father had been around to be a role model for him, instead of the distant provider. Wished he hadn't let Camilla distance him from his own son.

He looked down at Julian, who was watching television. 'Did you like her?' he asked.

Julian turned and looked at his father. 'She was okay.'

Hardly a glowing endorsement. 'Have you liked any of them?'

Julian shrugged, looking at him with big, solemn eyes.

'Who do you like?' he asked in frustration.

'Nat,' Julian said, and turned back to the TV.

Of course.

Great. Nat, who couldn't mind her own business. Nat, who spoke her mind. Nat of the lift. Nat of the zipper. Nat, who he'd dreamt about every night since they'd met.

Anyone but her.

Alessandro looked down at his son and sighed. Julian wanted Nat. And that was all that mattered.

Nat it was. That he could do.

CHAPTER THREE

ALESSANDRO spotted Nat at the dining room checkout the next day and hurried towards her. He was just in time to hear the waitress say, 'Eight dollars and twenty cents, please.'

He fished out his wallet and handed over a twenty before Nat had even zipped open her purse. 'Take it out of this,' he said.

Nat felt every nerve ending leap at his unexpected appearance. She glanced back at him, her heart doing a funny shimmy in her chest at his sheer masculinity. She frowned, both at her unwanted response and his motivation to pay for her lunch. 'Thanks. I pay my own way,' she said, presenting her own twenty.

The waitress looked from her to Alessandro and Nat couldn't help but notice that when he wanted to, Alessandro Lombardi could indeed pull a hundred-watt smile. His face went from darkly handsome, deeply tortured widower to blatantly sexy, Roman sex god. His curved lips utterly desirable.

After another stifling night with only a fan that seemed to do nothing other than push the hot air around and little sleep, it was especially irksome.

He pushed his money closer. 'Keep the change,' he murmured.

Nat rolled her eyes as the waitress practically swooned as she reached for his crisp orange note. She stuffed hers back into her purse, picked up her tray in disgust and left him to it. Within seconds she could sense him shadowing her.

'Italian women may think it's charming to be taken care of but I don't,' she said, steaming ahead to a table that overlooked the rose gardens St Auburn's was famous for. 'So don't pull your macho rubbish with me.'

Last time she'd let a man pay for her, she'd been sucked in to wasting five years of her life on him.

Alessandro pulled out her chair for her as she angled herself into it and ignored her glare. 'I wanted to talk to you about Julian. I thought the least I could do was buy you lunch while you listened.'

Nat eyed him across the table. She folded her arms. She was damned if the man didn't already know her Achilles heel. She'd spent the morning with Julian and he hadn't seemed any worse than normal. Not that that was much reassurance. 'Is he okay?'

Alessandro's gaze was drawn to the way her crossed arms emphasised the shape of her breasts. She was in crèche clothes today—shorts and T-shirt—and he noticed how her shirt displayed their full, round shape to perfection. He wondered for the hundredth time how they'd feel in his hands. In his mouth.

Damn it!

That wasn't why he was here. He was here for Julian. Not for himself. But it was fair warning that gave him pause. Nat would be very distracting should she be crazy enough to agree to his plan.

'Of course,' he dismissed, annoyed at himself. Seeing her confusion, he hastily added, 'I just wanted to ask you something.'

Nat opened up her packaged egg and lettuce sandwiches and took a bite, intrigued despite herself. 'Ask away.'

If anything, he looked more tired than she'd ever seen him. His hair look more tousled, like he'd been continually running his hands through it, and the furrows in his forehead were more prominent.

'How come you work at both the crèche and the hospital?'

She quirked an eyebrow. Not quite what she'd been expecting. 'You have to ask me that after Ernie?'

He regarded her for a moment. 'So it's a self-preservation strategy?'

'I prefer to call it a happy medium. Too many hospital shifts and I get burnt out. But I miss it if I'm away too long.'

'The best of both worlds?'

She shrugged. 'I like to temper the Ernie days with the Julian days. Both workplaces let me have permanent shifts. No weekends, no night duty. Two days at St Auburn's gives me my hospital hit, keeps my hand in, let's me know I'm alive. Three days at the crèche restores my sanity. It keeps me Zen.'

Alessandro considered her statement. How many years had it been since he'd felt Zen? Definitely not for the last five years at least. Definitely not with her keeping him constantly off balance. 'Do you have child-care qualifications too?'

She narrowed her eyes. Why did this suddenly feel like a job interview? 'I've done my certificate and have a child health qualification.' She cracked open the lid on her can of soft drink and eyed him over the top as she brought it to her mouth and took a swallow. 'Why?'

Alessandro noticed the sheen to her lips and the way her tongue slid between them, lapping at the lingering moisture. He wondered what guava-and-mango-flavoured Nat tasted like.

Inferno! Concentrate, damn it!

He cleared his throat. 'I think I have a solution to your eviction situation.'

Nat felt his gaze on her mouth as if he had actually pressed his lips to hers. Her eyes dropped of their own volition to inspect his. They were generous, soft. Lips made for kissing, made for whispering.

'Oh, yes?' she said cautiously, dragging her attention back to his eyes. Eyes that told her he knew exactly where hers had been.

'You can stay with me.' He watched her pupils dilate and her glance encompass his mouth once again. 'And Julian.'

The canteen noises around them faded as his suggestion stunned her. Live under his roof? A man who, fully clothed, grim faced and utterly inaccessible, made her heart flutter like an epileptic butterfly? What the hell could he do to her in his own place, where the pretence of professionalism didn't exist? Where he'd be all relaxed and homey and...wearing less. What did he wear to bed? She had the feeling he'd be a nothing kind of guy.

'Just until you're unit is built, of course.'

Nat blinked as her mind shied away from images of Alessandro in bed. Naked. 'But...why? I barely know you.'

Alessandro shrugged. 'I have the room, you need a place. And you'd be doing me a favour, helping with Julian. I haven't been able to find a suitable live-in nanny and Julian adores you.'

She frowned. 'You want me to be a…nanny? I already have a job. Two, actually. Which, by the way, I love.'

Alessandro shook his head. 'No. I don't expect you to give up your jobs. Julian can still go to the crèche but he could go and come home with you, which means he wouldn't have such long days there. And he wouldn't have to go on weekends and when I'm called in at night.'

Nat listened to his plan, which sounded very reasonable. So why did it seem so…illicit?

'I'd pay you, of course. And it would be rent free.'

Of course. Nat reeled, her brain scrambling to take in his offer. She looked at him all big and dark and handsome and completely macho Italian with the added grimness that made him heart-breakingly attractive. She didn't know much right at this second but she did know saying yes to Alessandro Lombardi was a very stupid idea.

'No.'

Alessandro's brows drew together. 'You've had another offer?'

Nat contemplated lying. But it really wasn't her way. Already her cheeks were growing warm just formulating a falsehood. 'No.'

He shrugged. 'Then it's settled.'

Nat looked at the haughty set to his jaw and bristled at his arrogant assumptions. 'No.'

'I don't understand. What's the problem?'

The problem was that Alessandro Lombardi was a very attractive man. The mere thought of sharing a living space with him was breathtakingly intimate and already her pulse raced at the thought. She knew enough about herself to know she had a soft heart. And he was still in love with his dead wife. And she wasn't stupid enough to get herself embroiled in that kind of scenario again.

'Ah,' he said as she averted her eyes from him. 'You worry about what people will think? You have my word I have no ulterior motive. I have no…' He searched for the right word, looking her up and down with as much dispassion as he could muster. 'Agenda. Your virtue is safe with me.'

Because it was. His attraction was just physical, a combination of libido and abstinence. Easily tamed.

Nat felt his gaze rake her from head to toe and obviously found her wanting. She felt about as attractive as a bug. One of the really ugly ones. It wasn't something she was used to. 'Gossip does not bother me.'

'Then what?'

She stared at him exasperated. The man was obviously not used to hearing no. 'I don't have to account to you, Alessandro,' she said testily, placing her packaging back on her tray and rising. She wished she had any other reason for turning him down other than his irresistible sex appeal.

But she had nothing. 'I'm sure you're quite unused to hearing the word no. I'm sure you just snap your fingers and women fall all over themselves to do your bidding. But I'm not one of them. The answer is no. Just plain no. No equivocations, no justifications. Just no. Get used to it.'

Alessandro couldn't believe what he was hearing. She was right, once upon a time he had been a finger snapper but that had all ended with Camilla. She turned to leave and he reached across, grabbing her arm. 'Wait. I'm sorry, Nathalie, I didn't mean to be so…'

Nat shivered. She didn't know if it was from his touch or the way her name sighed from his lips like a caress. She turned back. He seemed so perplexed and she felt her anger dissipate as quickly as it had risen. 'Italian?'

Alessandro smiled and dropped his hand. 'You have knowledge of Italian men.'

'I lived in Milano for a year. A long time ago now.'

Ah, that explained her grasp of his language. 'There was a man there?'

Nat gave a wistful smile. She'd lost her virginity in Italy. She'd been eighteen and hopelessly enamoured. 'A boy. It didn't last long. I was a little too…independent for him.'

He nodded. 'So you know we're not very good at asking for things.'

A shard of a memory made her smile broader. 'I don't know. I seemed to remember he was very good at asking for some things.' It had been a heady few months.

Alessandro gave her a grim smile, inordinately jealous at the tilt of her lips and the far-away look in her eyes. 'I meant help. Italian men like to be…men. Yes?'

Nat returned to the present. Yes. She did know that.

'I need help with Julian. We are not…close. Since his mother died…it's been difficult. He doesn't let me in… he's very unhappy.'

Nat swallowed at the raw ache in his voice. It clawed at her soft spot. 'His mother just died, Alessandro. He's grieving, just like you. He's allowed to be unhappy. There would be something wrong if he wasn't. He needs time.'

Alessandro shut his eyes briefly against the pity he saw in her gaze, her words stabbing into his soul. If only she knew. 'I can't bear to see him like this. He likes you,

Nat. He smiles, laughs when he's around you. I miss hearing him laugh.'

Nat felt helpless, trapped by eyes that were deep black wells of despair. She'd seen him with his son, maybe had judged him harshly. Too harshly. At least he seemed willing to try. At least he wanted to reach out to Julian.

'Please, Nathalie. If you don't feel you can for you, please do it for Julian.'

His plea was so heartfelt it oozed past every defence she had. She stood staring hopelessly at him, like a rabbit caught in headlights. Knowing she should run like the wind but powerless to do so.

Alessandro saw the compassion in her eyes and knew he'd touched her, could see that he'd struck a chord. 'He needs a woman's touch, Nat. A mother.'

His words stuck in her tightened throat, dragging her out of the compassionate quicksand she'd been sucked into. A mother? She shook her head. He was wrong. Didn't he know that children needed their fathers too? That without their father's love they grew up only half the person they could be? Always wondering. Always yearning.

Damn it—she'd known them for a fortnight. She didn't owe this man anything. Or his little boy. They weren't her responsibility. He wanted to take the easy way out? Use her so he could remain emotionally distant? So he didn't have to try? A substitute mother? He wanted her to be his enabler? She wouldn't. Julian needed his father, just as she had needed hers, and she would not let Alessandro shirk his duties as her father had shirked his.

He had to find a way through this himself. A way to connect with his son. One day he would thank her for it.

She took a deep breath, gathering her courage, breaking away from the spell he'd woven with his beautiful accent and his tragic gaze. 'Children need their fathers too.'

And she turned and walked away, not looking back. She had to protect herself. Alessandro and Julian were a delightful package, right up her bleeding-heart alley. Too easy to fall for.

She'd barely recovered from her last relationship. A man who had claimed to love her yet all the while had still been entangled with his ex-wife. She knew how vulnerable her heart was and she'd be stupid to repeat that mistake again.

So she didn't turn back, even though she could feel his gaze boring a hole between her shoulder blades. Even though her marshmallow centre blazed hot and gooey, berating her for her callousness, urging her to turn around.

It was time to protect herself for a change. Long past time.

Alessandro was more aware of her than he'd ever been when he picked Julian up from the crèche at five that afternoon. It was one of the first days he'd managed to get away on time and Nat was still there. In fact, Julian and Nat were sitting at a table doing a jigsaw puzzle.

It was hard to look at her and know that he had laid himself bare to her, taken a leap of faith, and been rejected. He supposed he was as proud as the next man, maybe prouder. He certainly didn't make a habit of asking anyone for help. He certainly wouldn't again.

He strode towards them, stopping a few feet away. 'Come, Julian, it's time to go.'

Nat's gaze travelled all the way up to the forbidding planes of Alessandro's regal face, etched with lines of tiredness, his beautiful mouth a bleak line. He barely acknowledged her, barely acknowledged his son. He obviously hadn't taken her rejection well.

But she had no intention of letting him take his disappointment out on her or his son. She climbed out of the low kiddy chair and stood. 'Julian, matey, why don't you go and get the picture you drew for your papa today?'

He nodded a silent assent and she watched his unhurried pace as he made his way, slump-shouldered, to his open wooden locker. No welcoming embrace for his father, no jubilant tearing around at the thought of going home. She glanced at Alessandro and caught him also tracking his son's movements.

'He drew a picture especially for you,' she murmured.

Julian hadn't seemed overly excited when she'd suggested that he draw a picture of Papa at work but, then, excited just wasn't a state he ever seemed to inhabit. But he'd attacked the picture with vigour and had spent a long time getting it right, choosing the colours carefully, brightening up the background. And when he'd showed it to her she could see pride and accomplishment in his dark little eyes, so like the ones in front of her.

Alessandro pulled his gaze back to her. 'That's nice.'

Nat cringed at the politeness of his tone but refused to be swayed. She was offering him a chance to bridge the gap with his son. 'You want to know how to connect, Alessandro?' She kept her voice low. 'It's not that hard. Smile at him, touch him, praise him. Show some affection.'

Alessandro felt each suggestion slice into him. If only it was that simple. Camilla was dead because of him. Could any amount of affection make up for that? How could Julian ever forgive him? He clenched his jaw, refusing to comment. Nat could not possibly understand what they'd been through.

He was conscious of her beside him—silent, judge-mental—as Julian made his way back to them. He stopped in front of them and held out the picture. Alessandro took it. He didn't want to, he wanted to throw it aside and sweep the boy into his arms, but the memory of Julian's stiff little stance from months ago still clawed at his gut. He couldn't bear two rejections in one day.

Alessandro's gaze went instead to the picture. It was done in crayon. The background was red and purple and quite cheery. The sun shone in one corner and there were trees with possums. The detail was remarkable.

He was in the foreground, nothing more than a stick figure with a stethoscope around his neck, his mouth a grim slash in his otherwise nondescript face. An adult, maybe Nathalie, had written across the bottom in neat teacher handwriting—'*My papa is a doctor. He works very hard.*'

Alessandro gripped the page hard. *That was it?*

Nat was too busy watching Julian to notice the play of emotions across Alessandro's face or the way the paper tore slightly beneath the vice-like grip of his fingers. The little boy's expression was heart-breaking. He was looking up at his father with such hope, his face full of anticipation.

'That's wonderful, Julian,' Alessandro forced out through the chokehold around his throat.

As Nat watched, Alessandro patted his son on the head and Julian's face broke into a broad grin, happy for even that tiny crumb of affection. Not that Alessandro noticed, his gaze still firmly fixed to the picture.

She couldn't believe what she was seeing. She suddenly wished she'd let Julian do rock art so she could beat Alessandro around the head with it. What the hell was the matter with him? Couldn't he see his kid was crying out for love, dying to be swept up and showered in his father's adoration?

It was like her childhood all over again. Once her father had moved on to his new family it hadn't seemed to matter what she'd done, he'd never seemed to notice. And it had hurt—man, had it hurt.

Alessandro dragged his attention away from the picture, his heart heavy. 'Come on, Julian. Get your stuff, it's time to go.'

Nat shook her head. That was it. She couldn't stand watching this…farce of a relationship any longer. Alessandro was obviously clueless. Someone had to teach him how to be a father. And regardless of every flashing light blaring at her, regardless of the attraction that simmered between them, she knew she had to be the one.

She just couldn't witness Julian's emotional isolation one second longer. She couldn't bear him to go through what she'd been through. It was like an arrow through her heart.

'Can I move my stuff in on the weekend?' she asked as Julian's lacklustre pace obeyed his father's instructions. 'There isn't much. Most of its in storage.'

Alessandro was wound so tight it took a couple of seconds for her question to penetrate the barbed wire he leashed his thoughts with. His head snapped around. Had he really just heard what he thought he'd heard? Her gaze was open, steady. It took him all of about two seconds to realise she was deadly serious.

Suddenly the tension that had been holding every muscle taut since she'd rejected him earlier, since Camilla had died, since before then even, since their hasty nuptials, relaxed. It was as if she'd taken bulk cutters and hacked through barbed-wire in one fell swoop.

Everything was going to be all right.

Alessandro nodded. 'That would be most suitable.' He delved into his pocket and handed her a card. 'My number.'

Nat took it hesitantly. For someone who had just got precisely what he'd wanted, she couldn't tell the damn difference. His gaze was carefully masked but she saw the flare in his pupils at the same time she felt a corresponding thrum in her blood as their fingers brushed.

The intensity frightened the hell out of her. 'This is purely business,' she said, lowering her voice. 'Nothing but convenience.'

Alessandro didn't have to ask her to explain. He got the subtext loud and clear. Her husky voice, the slight tremble in her finger tips, the brief widening of her eyes. He knew she was as tuned into their vibe as he was. He bowed slightly. 'Of course.'

He opened his mouth to elaborate further, to assure her, as he had that morning, that her virtue was safe, but Julian joined them and Alessandro nodded at her briefly, said, 'Until tomorrow,' and bade her goodbye.

Nat looked at the card, the pads of her fingers still burning, and wondered what the hell she's got herself into.

Nat pushed the doorbell to the enormous house on a Saturday morning that was already proving to be another scorcher. Her hair fluttered as a warm breeze whipped through the shady portico. She felt jittery but forced herself to concentrate on the wind's caress.

The door flung open and Julian stood there, his curls

bouncing slightly as his body trembled with what she could only describe as excitement. Or the nearest thing she'd ever seen in this little boy.

'Nat!' he exclaimed. His dark eyes, so like his father's, literally sparkled as he shifted from foot to foot. 'Papa told me this morning you're coming to live here.'

Nat couldn't help be infected by his barely suppressed enthusiasm. 'Just until my house is finished, matey.'

He grabbed her hand and dragged her inside. 'I hope it never finishes,' he declared.

'Gee, thanks.' Nat laughed as a cloud of cool air enveloped her, instantly dispelling the heat and stroking her exposed arms and legs with icy fingers. She looked up and saw the recessed vent in the ceiling. Ducted air-conditioning. She closed her eyes against the pleasure.

Bliss—instant bliss.

Her eyes fluttered open as Julian again tugged at her hand and she looked around at the large entrance area dominated by white walls, white tiles, white carpet and a large white staircase. She could see boxes left and right in her peripheral vision.

'Come on. I'll show you my room. You're right next door.'

'Julian.'

Julian dropped her hand as Nat glanced up to find Alessandro lounging in a doorway directly to her left, a mug in hand. He was wearing a snug white T-shirt that emphasised the rich golden colour of his skin and every muscle in his chest. His trendy khaki cargo-style shorts rode low on his hips. His feet were bare.

The man had a rumpled look about him, his hair tousled, his jaw unshaven. He looked like he hadn't slept very much and that she could relate to. She'd been awake half the night regretting her decision.

He held her gaze through thick dark lashes and she felt a rush of warmth to places that not even the air-conditioning could cool down.

'Don't crowd Nathalie.'

She opened her mouth to tell him not to call her that. She couldn't live under his roof if he was going to caress her name with his lips like that every time he addressed her. But she saw Julian's excitement ebb and decided to drop it. For now.

'I would love to see your room. Then I have a surprise for you.'

Julian smiled at her and grabbed her hand again, pulling her towards the ugly monolith that passed as a staircase. She could feel Alessandro's eyes on her as they ascended and forced herself to walk, not run.

Alessandro tracked her path up. She was wearing her standard attire of shorts and T-shirt. Neither were particularly risqué. The mocha shorts came to mid-thigh, the T-shirt was neither low cut or excessively clingy. But there was something about the sway of her hips and the bob of her ponytail that tightened his groin.

Hell. He pushed off the wall and headed straight for the coffee pot.

Nat couldn't believe the clinical wasteland Julian and Alessandro lived in. It was all white—everywhere she looked—and littered with unpacked boxes. Most of the five upstairs bedrooms, two lounge areas and what she presumed was a study were practically bare—except for a few essential pieces of furniture and, of course, the ever-present boxes.

Julian's room wasn't much better, with a bed, a bedside table with a lamp and a couple of books spread on the floor.

There was no colour, no bright quilt or curtains. In fact, there hadn't even been any curtains hung at all. Which made the white of the room even starker as the bright sunlight pushed through the glass.

Maybe Alessandro's wife had been one of those minimalist freaks?

She must have betrayed her feelings because Julian said, 'We haven't got round to unpacking yet. Papa's been very busy.'

Nat's heart nearly broke at the defensive tone and his worried frown. She gave him a bright smile. 'That's okay. I'm here now. I can help with that stuff.'

Julian brightened. 'Your room is next door.'

They went in and she plastered a huge smile on her face as Julian looked at her for any signs of dislike. The room, like Julian's, had a bed and a bedside table. No curtains. But it did have a vent in the middle of the ceiling and it was blissfully cool. 'It's perfect,' she said.

They were walking out when Julian stopped in the hallway and turned to face the end. 'That's Papa's room.'

He pointed to the closed door like it was a forbidden kingdom. Nat bit back her disapproval. Man, Alessandro was clueless. A far-away room dominated by a closed door? What the hell did he think his son, his four-year-old son, would read into that?

She really did have her work cut out for her.

Nat gave his shoulder a squeeze. 'Want that surprise now?'

Julian looked up at her and nodded enthusiastically, a wide grin firmly in place. She smiled back at him and they made their way downstairs.

'Wait here, it's in the car.' Nat injected a conspiratorial note into her voice.

She was back at the door in a minute—thankfully. The heat seemed even worse after the cool ecstasy of Alessandro's house. She stuck her head round. Julian was waiting there, anticipation lighting his dark features.

'Shut your eyes,' she requested. 'Hold out your hands.' Julian obeyed instantly. 'No peeking,' Nat warned as she adjusted the package in her arms and passed it gently into Julian's waiting arms.

Julian eyes flew open. 'A cat.'

He looked at Nat with utter wonder and squeezed the animal close, rubbing his face into her soft fur. Flo purred appreciatively. In his excitement he even forgot about the weird stiltedness between him and his father and called out to him.

'Papa, Papa, look, a cat. Nat has brought her cat.'

Alessandro appeared in the same doorway as before. Great. A cat. He regarded it warily. Pinocchio had been Camilla's cat and had positively hated him.

'You didn't say anything about a cat,' he murmured, keeping it low for his son's benefit. Not that it mattered. Julian was totally preoccupied by the ball of fur purring like an engine in his arms.

Nat raised an eyebrow at his disapproving frown. 'You're allergic?'

'No.'

Ah. 'If the cat goes, I go.'

Alessandro sighed. He believed her. And how could he deny his son the obvious pleasure? 'The cat's fine. Just keep it out of my room.'

Nat didn't think that would be much of a problem. Flo wasn't one for wasting her time on people who didn't care for her. Especially not when there was a little boy who was obviously going to dote on her.

They watched him for a few moments. 'I trust your room is to your liking?' Alessandro enquired.

To her liking? That was a bit optimistic. 'It's fine. Thank you.'

Alessandro had heard the word *fine* enough in his marriage to know that coming from a woman's lips it didn't always mean fine. *'Problemo?'*

Nat hesitated. But, hell—she had to live here. 'Is there a reason for all the white?'

Alessandro frowned. He looked around. He supposed it was a bit stark. 'No. There's plenty of colourful things— paintings, rugs and so on in the boxes. I just haven't had a chance to unpack yet. This is the first weekend I've had at home since I started at St Auburn's.'

'So you won't object to me adding a bit of…colour, then? I can unpack the boxes if you like.'

'I don't expect you to do that,' he dismissed.

She shrugged. 'It's the least I can do for free rent.' And it wasn't good for Julian to live in such a cold space, devoid of warmth.

He looked at his son, still talking to the cat like a new best friend. 'You're here for Julian, not to be a housekeeper.'

She shot him a pained expression. 'Alessandro, if I have to live in this white palace for even a day, I'm going to go snow blind. Please let me do this.'

Alessandro gave her a grudging smile. Funny how he hadn't really noticed it until she'd pointed it out. 'As you wish.'

Frankly, if she could make Julian this happy in just a few minutes she could paint rainbows all over the house and sprinkle it with glitter.

CHAPTER FOUR

ALESSANDRO and Julian helped her carry her meagre belongings up from the car. Alessandro withdrew the minute the job was done and she had to admit to being relieved. His presence in her room was too…dominant and she found herself questioning her sanity—yet again.

Julian hovered while she unpacked, leaping at the chance to help her distribute her bits and pieces around the room. Then Flo entered the room and he sat on the floor with the cat nestled in his lap, happy to just observe as he petted the purring animal.

A lava lamp brightened things up considerably in the stark room, as did the orange and russet bedding. Her Turkish rug covered most of the hideous white carpet and Impressionists prints along with her much-loved Venetian masks added colour to the walls. Finally she looped some rich purple gauzy fabric she'd bought in China along the curtain rod, letting it drape haphazardly over the bare window.

She stood back and admired her work. Not bad for an hour's work. At least the room no longer looked like the inside of an igloo.

'What do you reckon?' she asked Julian.

Julian beamed at her, raising Flo to his face and stroking his chin along the top of her soft head. 'It's… beautiful,' he sighed.

Nat laughed. The awe in his voice was priceless. 'Do you think you could do this to my room? Make it like my old one? Before Mummy died?'

Nat felt her heart lurch in her chest at his matter-of-fact words. She scanned his face for signs of distress or grief but found none. Instead, he was looking at her as if she were Mary Poppins and had done it all with a snap of her fingers.

'Sure,' she replied. 'We'll go through the boxes tomorrow and see if we can find all your stuff.'

Nat heard Flo's half-hearted protesting miaow as Julian bounced on his haunches and squeezed her a little too tight. His eyes sparkled and he looked like a normal excited four-year-old.

And she knew in an instant that coming to live under Alessandro's roof had been the right thing.

'Right. Well. I'm starving.' She looked at the slim rose-gold watch that adorned her wrist. Midday. She saw Julian yawn in her peripheral vision and his eyes drift shut briefly as he continued to rub his chin against Flo's head. They'd been having such fun she'd forgotten he was only four and still needed his afternoon sleep.

She realised he would need lunch before going down for his nap. 'Boy, look at the time! Let's get something to eat.'

Julian followed her down the stairs, Flo bundled up in his arms, purring loudly as she wallowed in cat heaven. He led her to the kitchen and Nat braced herself to face Alessandro again. He was working on a laptop at the dining table, which was through an archway to the right off the massive gourmet kitchen gleaming in all its stainless-steel and white-tiled glory.

Alessandro looked up from the recent on-line health alerts from the Australian government concerning the spread of the deadly swamp flu which, due to international travel, could easily be on Australia's shores before they knew it. If he was going to be treating cases of it in his emergency department, he wanted to be forearmed.

Julian was smiling and chatting away and Nat's cheeks were all pink as she conversed with Julian. 'I trust you've settled in?'

Nat nodded, her gaze settling on his broad shoulders. 'Yes, thank you. Julian and I are going to attack his room tomorrow.'

Alessandro nodded. 'As you wish. I'll locate his boxes and take them up there in the morning.'

'Thank you.'

His gaze held hers, boring into her, like he already knew her, and she suddenly felt out of breath. A lock of hair fell across his forehead and her fingers tingled with the desire to push it back. She could actually see herself doing it in some weird slow-motion flash. Except he didn't have a shirt on. And neither did she.

Nat dragged her gaze away and nervously looked around for something to do. Anything. The stainless-steel fridge was right there and she reached for the door with relish. 'I was just going to make some lunch for Julian and I before he goes down for his nap.'

She stared in the fridge unseeingly for a moment while her pulse settled and her knickers unknotted. 'Shall I make you something as well?' she twittered.

'There's not a whole lot there, I'm afraid. I really need to do a proper shop.'

Nat blinked as the contents, or lack of them, slowly came in to focus. She blinked again. *Now, that was the understatement of the year.* She turned to him. 'What have you guys been living on?'

Alessandro shrugged. He hated shopping. Camilla had always taken care of that. Nothing had been right since she'd gone. 'I usually just pick up a few bits and pieces after work every second day or so.'

Nat pursed her lips. 'Hmmm.' She shut the fridge and glanced briefly at Alessandro. She located the pantry and found it similarly devoid of food. It was obvious they'd just been living from day to day. Was the man totally clueless? Didn't Alessandro know that kids needed a sense of permanency, long-term planning to feel secure? Especially ones whose whole lives had just fallen apart?

'Looks like we go shopping after your nap.'

Julian beamed. 'Can I ride in the trolley? Mummy used to let me ride in the trolley.'

She glanced at Alessandro and saw him visibly pale, his face possibly the grimmest she'd seen yet. She supposed he only used a basket to shop for his bits and pieces and that would seem rather boring to a four-year-old.

Her heart ached anew for both of them. Julian was too young to understand the things that his father was struggling with. 'Yes, you can ride in the trolley. Maybe Papa would like to come with us?'

Nat watched as both father and son tensed. Julian turned hopeful eyes on hers before he looked away, rubbing his chin along Flo's head, and she had to stop herself from going to him and pulling him close.

Alessandro watched in despair as his son fell silent and his little shoulders stiffened. He'd hoped if he didn't push, if he gave his son room and space, that Julian would turn to him eventually but hearing the word *Mummy* fall from his lips had been like a knife plunging deep into his gut and twisting mercilessly. Maybe his son would never let him closer? Maybe Julian also blamed him for Camilla's death?

'I have these journals to catch up on,' Alessandro said, turning back to his lap-top.

Nat stared at two downcast heads. So alike but so disconnected from each other. For a second she felt helpless, but not for long. These two needed intervention and it seemed the universe had decreed she was the one to do it. And she wanted Julian to be close to his father. She wanted to give the little boy the gift of the father-child relationship. She didn't want Julian growing up feeling somehow not whole, as she had. She would never wish those feelings of isolation on anyone, never mind a small child.

But it was plain neither of them were going to make it easy. *She sure had her work cut out for her.*

Alessandro followed the sound of chatter and his nose into the kitchen around five o'clock. The smell of garlic and basil, the aromas of his childhood, and Julian's laughter drew him and he was powerless to resist.

Nat and Julian were cooking. Julian was sitting on the bench next to the cook top, a large metal spoon in hand, stirring something in a saucepan as he fired a hundred questions at Nat. He could see the backs of her long legs, the outline of one very cute derrière and the swish of her ponytail as she chopped and talked and dipped her finger into the saucepan, savouring the taste.

'More salt, Julian.'

Alessandro watched as Julian picked up the salt grinder and handled it as well as a four-year-old could be expected to. He was concentrating hard, his little pink tongue caught between his teeth. It was awkward and he dropped it. Nat was quick, though, and saved it from landing in the pot.

'That's fabulous, Juliano.'

It was on the tip of his tongue to reprimand her for using the Italian form of his name. Despite Camilla insisting it appear on his birth certificate, she actually hated it and had insisted their son be called the anglicised version. But right now he couldn't deny how good it was to hear his son's name being pronounced in the way of his ancestors.

And Julian was smiling at her, swinging his legs as they dangled over the edge of the counter. He was enjoying himself and Alessandro didn't have the heart to spoil that.

'Something smells good.'

Nat faltered as he announced his unexpected presence. She felt every molecule in her body stand to attention. Her nipples jutted against the lacy fabric of her bra, as hard as bullets. Julian's chatter ceased instantly and she noticed his legs stopped swinging in her peripheral vision.

Alessandro noticed it too but steadfastly ignored it as he pushed into the kitchen. 'What are you cooking, Julian?' he asked.

Julian shrugged. 'Spaghetti. The proper stuff. From Milano.'

Alessandro's heart nearly stopped at the perfect way Julian pronounced Milan. He'd always hoped any child of his would be bilingual but Camilla had been adamant.

'Ah.' Alessandro kept his tone light. 'The proper stuff tastes best.'

Camilla hadn't been much of a cook. She'd normally bought pre-prepared food from exclusive delicatessens or supermarkets. Julian had certainly been the best-fed toddler in London, with gourmet treasures bestowed on him every day. When they'd entertained it had always been catered.

But not only had Nat filled his fridge and his pantry and their lives in just half a day but she'd also filled his kitchen with incredible aromas. His stomach growled and he absently realised he was hungry. He couldn't remember the last time he'd eaten for any other reason than as fuel to keep his body going.

When he'd given her his card to go shopping that afternoon he'd imagined she'd buy enough food to get them through the week, but she'd gone way beyond that. He'd helped them unpack and had been amazed at the items she'd considered necessities.

She'd apologised profusely for the amount she'd spent. He had shrugged it away—money wasn't any impediment for him. Besides, when you'd lost all that he'd lost, it truly meant nothing.

Nat felt rather than saw Alessandro lounge a hip against the bench not far from her. She could also sense that the lovely homey atmosphere from a minute ago had vanished. Julian was tense and she couldn't bear to see a four-year-old so…stiff.

Flo chose that moment to rub against her legs and miaow loudly. *Bless her!* 'Julian, sweetie, would you like to feed Flo?'

Julian brightened. 'Could I?'

'Of course. You know where her bowl is in the laundry and you know where the little sachets of food we bought for her today are. Maybe your papa could help you open one and he could show you how to feed her?'

Nat glanced at Alessandro, praying he'd take the bait. The long journey back to each other had to start with one step.

Alessandro considered her for a moment. Tendrils of hair had escaped her ponytail and framed her face in almost angelic frothery. 'Good idea,' he said, holding her gaze for a moment longer before skirting her and approaching his son. He grabbed an unprotesting Julian under the arms and swung him down to the floor.

'Where's this food, then, Julian?'

Nat kept stirring, not daring to turn around or interfere in any way. Their conversation was hardly natural—in fact, it was so stilted she wanted to cry—but they had to start somewhere. She was relieved though when Julian called Flo and they both left the kitchen. Her shoulders were aching and she slumped a little as the tension left the room and headed to the laundry.

Five minutes later, though, he was back. He didn't have to say a word, she could just feel the hairs of her nape standing to attention. She turned and saw him watching her from the doorway, all dark and brooding, his shadowed gaze heavy against her chest. 'That was quick,' she murmured, turning back to the spaghetti.

'He seemed much more interested in the cat.'

She stirred the sauce. 'That will fade. Give him time.'

Alessandro approached. This was a great angle but he preferred her front. Her open gaze, her perfect mouth. He turned as he reached the bench so his backside leant against it, facing in the opposite direction from her. 'It smells great.'

'Thank you. I figured I couldn't go too far wrong in this house with some pasta and sauce.'

Alessandro allowed a ghost of a smile settle on his lips. He turned so his hip nudged the bench and he was on his side, facing her. 'May I?'

Nat nodded. She stepped back a pace as Alessandro quickly dipped his finger in the sauce. She watched fascinated as it disappeared past his lips, his mouth slowly revealing a totally clean finger.

Damn. It was good. Almost as good as her dilated pupils as her eyes had followed his actions. 'Hmm,' he murmured, licking his lips to savour the residue as he held her gaze. 'You've done this before.'

Nat took a second to pull her body back into line but her voice was still annoyingly husky. 'My host mother in Milano taught me her secret family recipe for Napolitano sauce.'

Ah. Definitely the aromas of his childhood. 'You don't have to cook, you know. Or clean. Or unpack boxes.'

Pleased to be back on firmer ground, she nodded. 'I know. But I enjoy it. It's not much fun cooking for one. I usually don't bother, I'm afraid.'

In truth she missed cooking. And all the other homey things about being a couple. She'd loved cooking for Rob, they'd loved cooking together. It felt good to be doing it again. Even if it this wasn't any kind of cosy, lovey-dovey relationship.

His gaze on hers was intense and rather unnerving in his grim-faced way. She broke their connection, looking down into the saucepan and giving it another stir. 'I still think it's missing something,' she muttered as she tried to collect herself, blunt herself to his wounded charm.

She dipped the spoon in, blew on it out of habit and

brought it to her lips, sipping the rich sauce and not tasting it at all. His eyes were still on her and he was making her nervous. Her hand trembled and the spoon tilted, spilling some of the lukewarm sauce down her chest. It landed on the soft swell of cleavage just visible above the v of her neckline.

Her eyes flew to his, startled by the occurrence. His gaze had already sought it out, tracking the slow trek of the sauce as it unhurriedly made its way south. He licked his lips, involuntarily, she thought as his heated look enveloped her in a raging stupor.

All she could do was watch as he openly stared. Her nipples were the only things moving, scrunching as his hot gaze lapped fire at her skin.

Alessandro could no more have ignored the dictates of his body than flown to the moon. He wanted to taste it, taste her, so badly he couldn't think of anything else. 'I'm good with ingredients. Let me try.'

His voice was like sludge oozing over her and she didn't stop him, just shut her eyes as his head lowered and his mouth closed over the swell of her breast as his tongue lapped at the sauce.

Someone groaned. Was it her? Or him? Looking down at his dark head, she had an insane urge to bury her fingers in his hair, hold him there. Arch her back. Beg for more.

Alessandro felt a strange spiralling out of control as Nat's ripe flesh almost flowered beneath his tongue as he ran lazy strokes over the tempting swell. She tasted sweet and spicy and very addictive. Elicit. Heady.

'Nat, is it okay if Flo goes outside?'

Alessandro lifted his head as if he'd been zapped with a cattle prod, moving away a few paces as Julian's voice called to them from the other room. What the hell was wrong with him? He had his head in the cleavage of someone he barely knew when his wife hadn't even been dead a year.

Julian's mother.

'Sure it is,' Nat called. She'd spun back to face the cook top, desperately trying to ignore how her skin still flamed where Alessandro's mouth had been.

Julian entered the kitchen, oblivious to the ragged-breath adults, Flo in his arms. 'She ate up all her fish and milk but I think she wants to play.'

Nat turned to face him, plastering a smile over the confusion storming her body. 'Of course she does. Flo loves the great outdoors.'

Alessandro gripped the bench at her blatantly husky tone. 'Not too long, Julian,' he said tersely, distracted by his stupidity. 'Dinner isn't far away.'

Nat saw the confusion in Julian's eyes at his father's harsh tone and watched as he bit into his bottom lip. 'It's okay,' she said gently. 'I'll call you when it's ready.'

Julian nodded, looking deflated, and slumped off. She turned to Alessandro to chide him for his reaction. Yes, she understood where it had come from, but Julian was only four. Except he was gone. Nothing but air where he'd been. She looked to the right in time to see the broadness of his shoulders as he strode out the archway and out of reach.

Nat stayed in the lounge room till late, watching television that night, too keyed up to sleep. Julian had long since gone to bed and Alessandro, who, apart from a brief appearance to help them search for another knife, fork and plate in the mountain of boxes and eat his dinner, had taken his laptop into his equally barren study and not come out.

A light movie was on and Nat had a headache from forcing herself to concentrate on it and not on what had happened in the kitchen earlier. But force herself she did. What had occurred could never occur again. There was no point building castles in the air with a man who was obviously still so messed up over his dead wife that he hadn't even been able to look at her.

No matter how much he stirred her pulse and her senses and every feminine instinct she had. It was time to rely on other instincts—survival instincts.

The movie ended and she reluctantly made her way to bed. Alessandro's door was open at the end of the corridor, she noticed, but doggedly diverted her attention from it. She checked on Juliano, half expecting to find Flo still curled up with him, but the warm spot where the cat had obviously recently been lying was vacant. She pulled up his covers and turned out his lamp.

She wondered into her bedroom, expecting to see Flo stretched out on her bed. But, no, the cat wasn't anywhere in the bedroom. She knew she wasn't downstairs because she'd just come from there.

'Flo?' she whispered into the darkened hallway, sticking her head out of her open doorway. A distant miaow turned her head in the wrong direction and Nat stared down at the partially open end door. She knew without a doubt that Flo was in Alessandro's bedroom.

Keep the cat away from me. That's what he'd said. *Oh, hell!* She'd done enough damage for one day—she needed to get Flo out.

She tiptoed down the hallway. The thick carpet muffled

her footsteps perfectly, she just hoped it also stifled the hammering of her heart. She was sure Alessandro was still in his study, so it was just a matter of sneaking in, grabbing Flo then getting the hell out.

As she drew level with the doorway she whispered, 'Flo,' again. The damn cat miaowed contently and Nat thought seriously bad thoughts about her pet for a moment or two. She gingerly poked her head over the threshold. A low lamp threw a small glow around the room but otherwise the room was empty. Flo sat in the middle of Alessandro's bed, cleaning herself on his espresso-coloured bedding.

'Flo,' she whispered, half scandalised, half scared out of her wits. She did not want to be there but she knew Flo well enough to know that she wasn't going to voluntarily leave—not until after she'd groomed herself anyway.

'Flo,' she whispered again, more loudly, moving closer, trembling too much to notice the minimalist quality of the rest of the house carried through to his bedroom, which had equally sparse furnishings. 'Come here—now! Alessandro will not be amused.'

Flo stopped her fur licking momentarily and regarded Nat with half-closed eyes before stretching her leg in the air and cleaning it with long firm kitty strokes from her little pink tongue.

Nat almost screamed in frustration, knowing she was going to have to climb onto Alessandro's enormous bed and retrieve the recalcitrant cat.

She was two paces away from the bed when a door behind and to the left of the bed suddenly opened and a semi-naked Alessandro appeared before her. His hair was wet and the only thing stopping him from being totally naked was one white towel riding low on his lean hips.

She didn't mean to ogle but she also couldn't look away. The soft lamp bathed his body in a beautiful bronze glow and, backlit by the en suite light, his face looked more dark, more dangerous than ever.

Her mouth dried in an instant. 'Oh…er, sorry. I didn't know you were…Flo came in.' She pointed to the guilty party like a lawyer holding up exhibit A in a courtroom. The guilty party purred loudly into the tense silence. 'I was just trying to…retrieve her.'

Alessandro hadn't had a woman in his bedroom in a long while. And especially one he'd not long licked Napolitano sauce off. She was wearing the same clothes and the memory came back to punch him in the gut. The taste of her skin, the whimper that had gurgled from her throat, her uneven breath.

He stuck his hands on his hips to quell the surge of lust and the urge to do something more…productive with them. Whether she knew it or not, and he suspected she didn't, her gaze on him was frank and he could feel himself reacting under the towel.

They really needed to clear the air—before he totally embarrassed himself. 'I apologise for this afternoon.'

Nat shook her head, trying desperately hard not to think about that afternoon while he'd stood before her in just a towel. Avoidance was looking good right now.

'I gave you assurances that your virtue would be safe.'

'Don't worry about it,' she dismissed, her voice practically a squeak.

Alessandro shook his head. 'No. I mustn't…I can't… get involved. My wife…I think it best if we just forget it. It…won't happen again.'

He raked his hand through his wet hair, hating how disjointed he sounded. Hating how the possibilities between them could never be explored. She was nodding at him vigorously and he was pleased she understood.

'You have my word, Nathalie.'

And that's where it all fell part for her. He couldn't call her Nathalie and not expect her to melt into a puddle. Not the way he said it—like a sigh, like a whisper from the devil.

A startling urge to cross to him and whip his towel away was so strong she could actually see it in her mind's eye. Thankfully Flo chose that moment to miaow loudly and spring up from her reclining position, rubbing herself against her owner.

Thank god for kids and animals—where would they have been today without either of them? *Naked on the kitchen floor. Going at it on his bed.*

She blinked.

'Of course. It was just…' She stroked Flo's fur as she cast around for something to say, some syndrome or insanity plea to blame it on. But with him nearly naked before her, her brain wasn't functioning that well.

'Impulsive.' She picked Flo up and squeezed her tight. 'You're right, it won't happen again.' She backed out slowly. 'Sorry,' she said again. 'About the…' She gestured to his nakedness but couldn't bring herself to say the words. 'Anyway…'

And with that rather inarticulate ending, she turned on her heel and fled the room.

CHAPTER FIVE

THE next morning Alessandro and Julian were up when Nat wandered downstairs. She'd heard the muted noise of the television a little while ago but had lain in bed, wide awake, putting off the inevitable. She'd felt hot and restless all night, despite the air-conditioning, images of Alessandro's perfect flat abdomen and the hot lick of his tongue taunting her through elusive layers of sleep.

The very last thing she wanted to do was face him again. But after a while she knew being a coward wasn't the answer either and she hauled herself out of bed, and showered and dressed to face the day.

Alessandro looked up from his bowl of cereal when she entered the kitchen. He was shirtless and his hair was rumpled. He looked tired, his eyes bleary, like he'd slept even less than she had. And yet still he looked better than any man had a right to.

She really, really needed to talk to him about wearing a shirt.

She gave him a bright smile and kept her eyes firmly trained on his chin. 'Where's Julian?'

Alessandro, who'd stopped chewing in mid-mouthful,

swallowed. Nat looked fresh and earthy, her hair loose around her shoulders, her cheeks pink. She was wearing a sundress that sat wide on her shoulders with thin straps that tied in bows and a scooped neckline that drew the eye.

He dropped his gaze back to his bowl. 'Watching television.'

Annoyed at his shirtless state, she advanced into the kitchen and headed for the coffee pot. 'Why aren't you in there with him?'

'I asked him if he wanted me to watch with him and he said no.'

Nat shook her head. 'Don't ask next time.' *Hell, it wasn't rocket science.*

Alessandro frowned at her grouchy reply. 'I'm trying not to push him too hard.'

She opened her mouth to tell him that it was okay to push a little in some situations but Julian bustled into the room and she tore her gaze from Alessandro's.

'Nat! Oh, Nat! You're here. You're really still here!'

Julian launched himself at her, throwing his arms around her legs and squashing his cheek against her thigh. She laughed as she hugged his little body to her legs. 'Of course, silly. I can't leave until my house is built!'

She grinned and ruffled his hair, glancing at Alessandro. He was watching them, his face grave and brooding. Her smile slowly disappeared. Was it hard for him to watch Julian being affectionate with another woman? Someone other than his mother? Did it emphasise his loss even more? Did it twist the knife just a little bit deeper?

She peeled Julian off her. 'I'm making toast—do you want some?'

Julian clapped his hands. 'I love toast!'

Nat busied herself with Julian, chatting away as they shoved slice after slice of bread into the toaster. When they were done she carried it over to the central station where Alessandro was apparently reading a journal. She helped Julian climb onto the stool opposite his father and then plonked the loaded plate in the middle. She topped up their coffees and sat down next to Julian.

'Toast,' she said, not quite looking at Alessandro. 'Eat up. We made enough to feed an army.'

Julian giggled and she grinned down at him but all the while she was hyper-aware of Alessandro and she almost sagged against the counter when his long bronzed fingers reached for a slice. She'd felt his gaze, heavy and intense, on her the entire time they'd been at the toaster and it had been unnerving.

Nat wished she knew what he was thinking behind the brooding mask. Was he remembering what had happened in this kitchen only yesterday or her unscheduled visit to his room last night?

If only she knew.

For his part, Alessandro had been trying *not* to think about what would happen if he pulled one of those little bows sitting snugly atop her shoulders. How easy would it be? Just reach out and tug. Would her whole dress just slide off?

Sitting opposite him, the bows in his direct line of vision taunted him even further. He wasn't following the conversation and was surprised to find he'd somehow managed to pick up a piece of toast and eat it. He tuned back into the chatter when he became aware that both Julian and Nat were looking at him expectantly.

Well, Nat was anyway. Julian was looking wary and the

sparkle in his eyes was gone. 'I'm sorry,' he apologised looking from one to the other. 'I wasn't listening.'

Nat gave him a reproving look. 'I was just assuring Julian you were going to help us with the boxes today. Get his room decked out.'

Alessandro looked at Julian. His son didn't seem too enthused by the idea. He was sitting painfully straight in his chair, like a little soldier. 'Ah…well.' He glanced at Nat whose brow had furrowed and then back at his son who seemed to be holding his breath. 'I do have some work to catch up on.'

Nat glanced down at Julian whose bottom lip wobbled and then sharply at Alessandro who was staring down at his journal. She glared at his head but it remained stubbornly downcast. 'Julian, why don't you see if Flo wants a piece of toast?' She scooped up the last cold piece. 'Take it out to the laundry and break it into small pieces.'

Julian squirmed down off the chair enthusiastically and skipped out of the kitchen. Alessandro watched him go.

Nat took a deep breath and gently put down her coffee mug. 'What the hell is wrong with you?' she demanded. 'I just offered you the perfect opportunity to spend time with your son.'

Alessandro gave her a hard look, his eyes chilly. 'He doesn't want me to help. I'm not going to force myself on him.'

Nat got off her stool and stormed over to the coffee pot, pouring herself another. She turned to face him, leaning against the bench, pleased to be far away from his naked chest.

'Sometimes you have to push, Alessandro. He's four. Sometimes children need to be led. You two have to meet in the middle, start doing things together, and this is a perfect place to begin.'

'And what if it has the opposite effect? What if he can't handle what's inside, what if it brings up stuff he was just getting over?'

His eyes were dark and troubled. His frustration and resistance filled the space between them and Nat suddenly understood that this might not be about Julian at all. 'Ah. I understand what this is really about.'

Alessandro snorted. *He was pleased somebody did.* Nothing had made sense for quite a while now. 'Oh, yes?'

'I know that what's in those boxes may be hard to deal with for you. They're your memories. Of your wife and the life you had with her, the one you left behind. But they're his memories too, Alessandro. He's on the other side of the world, far away from everything that's ever been familiar to him. Even his relationship with you is different now. He needs his things around him. And not just in his bedroom but all around him. And he needs to feel like this is home. Not some temporary, half-lived-in dwelling.'

She drew breath for a moment then plunged on again. 'You wanted me to help. You wanted him happy and laughing again. Well, it starts here, Alessandro. And you need to be part of it. You might be surprised what he can handle.'

Alessandro blinked. Maybe she was right. Maybe this was more about him? Maybe the boxes were a bridge too far for him at the moment and he'd been resisting them because of the emotions they were bound to stir? The guilt had been too much to bear as it was.

But if it helped reach Julian...

He stood. 'Okay, sure. That makes sense.'

Nat, who'd open her mouth to strengthen her argument, firmly closed it. He picked up his mug and moved towards her, heading for the sink, his abdominal muscles shifting enticingly with each footfall. She told herself not to look but it was compelling scenery. She gripped the mug hard in case she reached out and touched.

He paused at the sink and drained the contents of his mug. Nat's gaze followed his movements, admiring the glide of his bronzed skin over toned muscle. He placed his mug inside the bowl and it wasn't until he was facing her that she realised he was saying something.

Nat dragged her gaze from the strip of hair that arrowed down from his belly button. 'Huh?'

Alessandro felt desire slam into him right where her eyes had been, as if she'd lapped at his belly button with her tongue. She was looking at him, her eyes slightly glazed, and for a moment they just stared at each other. Her bows taunted him and he curled his fingers into his palms.

'I said when do you want to start?'

Nat's brain grappled with the simple sentence, her annoyance growing. Oh, for crying out aloud, it was just a chest! No reason to lose her mind. Every man had one. Rob had had one. Except, of course, she'd never felt this inexplicable primal swell of lust at the mere sight of Rob. Not even in the beginning.

'Soon. A few minutes.' She pushed away from the bench, the need to get the hell away from him becoming imperative. 'And for God's sake,' she snapped, annoyed at him. And herself. 'Put a shirt on.'

Alessandro stared after her as she stormed out, pleased she and her damn bows were out of sight. Even if his erection wasn't.

* * *

Fifteen minutes later they were all sitting on their haunches in Julian's stark room with one of the two boxes marked *Child* in front of them. Alessandro took a deep breath before taking a Stanley knife to the packing tape.

Nat could see he was nervous. Hell, so was she. After all, Alessandro could be right—what if this whole thing backfired and Julian couldn't handle the memories? What if it upset him too much? If he became inconsolable? But she knew, deep down, that whatever the emotional fallout, father and son needed this.

His biceps drew her gaze, bunching and moving beneath his sleeves as he opened the flaps. She shut her eyes against the temptation—obviously a shirt made little difference to her wandering gaze.

Alessandro opened the box and there, on top, sat Julian's old rabbit.

'George!' Julian snatched up the rather forlorn-looking creature that had obviously seen better days and gave it an enthusiastic hug. 'I missed you, George!'

Watching the reunion, Alessandro felt utterly dreadful. Julian could have had George weeks ago. He hadn't even been aware that the toy had been packed. Or even noticed that Julian had been without him until Nat had prompted him that day at the crèche.

What kind of a father did that make him?

He glanced at Nat and she smiled at him and nodded. 'What else have we got in here?' she prompted.

Julian clung to his rabbit and peered into the box expectantly. They pulled out clothes and toys and books and colourful wall hangings and an exquisite mobile of stars and moons. They were made of brightly coloured glass that formed a whirlpool of colour when the pieces twirled.

'This is beautiful,' Nat gasped as Alessandro lifted it from the box. She could tell it was hand-made, the craftsmanship patently obvious.

'Nonna gave it to me.'

Alessandro looked at his son as Julian reached out and pushed one of the stars with a finger. He smiled. 'That's right.'

His mother had brought it in Murano when she'd been visiting relatives in Venice. He remembered how Julian would lie on his back for ages as a baby in his cot and watch the constellations swing above him in a kaleidoscope of colour.

Julian looked at his father and clutched George tighter. 'Can you hang it above my bed like in London?'

Alessandro expelled a breath he hadn't even realised he'd been holding. It was probably the first time Julian had directly addressed him for anything remotely personal. He nodded. 'Of course.'

They spent a couple of hours putting things to rights in Julian's room, hanging and placing, father and son interacting properly for the first time. And when they'd finished, the room was hardly recognisable. It actually looked like a child lived in it instead of a robot.

There was one thing left in the box and Nat reached for it. It was a box of fish food. She held it up and raised her eyebrows at Alessandro. Julian looked at it and held out his hand for it.

He turned to his father. 'It's Gilbert and Sullivan's food.'

Alessandro looked at the tin. He had bought the fish for Julian's third birthday. Julian had thought he was

Superman. Camilla, however, had not been impressed. She certainly hadn't mourned their passing.

'You had fish?' she addressed Julian.

Julian nodded. 'Daddy bought them for my birthday. But they got sick and died.'

'Ah.' Poor kid. His mother had died, his fish had died and he'd had to leave his cat behind. She waited for tears or withdrawal but he seemed quite matter-of-fact. She glanced at Alessandro. He seemed more affected, the ghost of a smile she'd glimpsed a moment ago gone.

Alessandro's heart thudded in his chest as he contemplated taking the next step forward. 'I can buy you some more,' he offered tentatively.

Julian's face lit up. 'Really?'

'Really.'

Nat felt a lump lodge in her throat at the fragile connection that was being built in just two hours between father and son. Sure, there was a long way to go but it was a start. Alessandro glanced at her and smiled. Actually smiled.

And despite her resolve to keep some distance from him, she grinned back like an idiot.

A couple of days later Nat was working triage when her friend Paige walked through the doors, cradling her listless-looking three-year-old daughter McKenzie. The child looked pale, her limbs mottled.

Paige had been through the wringer in the last few years. McKenzie, a twin, had been born at twenty-seven weeks. She and her twin sister, Daisy, had been very frail and while McKenzie had defied the odds, Daisy had died after a four-month, uphill battle.

It had been a devastating time, compounded by her husband leaving shortly after and McKenzie's chronic health issues. Paige looked tired and pinched around the mouth, her brow furrowed. A far cry from the vibrant woman she'd known back in Perth.

Nat didn't know how she kept going. Not only did she care for her high-needs daughter but she also had to work part time as Arnie, her ratfink ex, refused to pay for anything more than he absolutely had to.

'Paige, what's wrong?' she asked.

'It's McKenzie. I think she's got another chest infection.'

Nat heard the tremor in her friend's voice and ushered her into the privacy of the small triage room. Paige looked as if she was at breaking point and Nat knew her friend, who was running on pride alone, would hate to break down in front of an emergency room full of strangers.

Paige sat in a chair, hugging McKenzie close. She turned beseeching eyes on Nat. 'She's due to have her operation next week, Nat.' She rocked slightly, choking on a sob. 'It took me eighteen months to get her off oxygen and two years to get her to ten kilos and we've had to postpone it three times. Not again, please not again.'

Nat gave Paige's shoulder a squeeze. 'Hey, one step at a time, okay? Let's get her seen to first, huh? I'll just take her temp.'

Paige looked at Nat as she placed the digital thermometer under an unprotesting McKenzie's arm. She gave her friend a watery smile. 'Sorry. Of course. It's just I don't know if I can take much more of this. Thank God for Mum and Dad or I would have gone mad years ago.'

Nat laughed. Paige's parents had been a terrific support after Arnie had abandoned their daughter. 'You're doing fine, Paige. Just fine.'

The thermometer beeped, confirming an alarmingly high temp. 'When did you last give her something for her fever?' Nat asked gently.

'Just before I got in the car,' Paige said.

Nat placed a stethoscope in her ears and listened to McKenzie's chest. It sounded like a symphony orchestra conducted by a tone-deaf conductor inside her chest— wheezing, squeaking and crackling away. She slipped a saturation probe onto McKenzie's toe and the number only read 90 per cent. Paige looked at Nat and worried her bottom lip with her teeth.

'Come on. Come through and I'll get Alessandro to look at her.'

Paige stood. 'I hear he's excellent.'

Nat nodded, avoiding her friend's gaze. 'The very best.'

Nat set Paige up in a cubicle and placed a set of nasal prongs on McKenzie's face. The child, well used to the plastic in her nose and too sick to care, didn't protest. Nat used a low-flow meter to set the oxygen at a trickle. She smiled at Paige, her heart going out to her utterly exhausted friend. 'I'll be right back.'

Nat found Alessandro in the cubicle they used for eye patients. It was set up with a special microscope for high-powered viewing of the eye. She'd triaged Bill Groper fifteen minutes ago after a workplace accident had seen boiling fat splashed into his eye.

Alessandro was leaning forward in his chair, his feet flat on the floor, his legs wide apart to accommodate the low table the microscope rested on. He was staring into the eye-pieces, examining his patient's eyes. Bill sat opposite, his chin on the plate, looking in from the other side.

She noticed immediately how the position emphasised

the broad expanse of Alessandro's back and how it tapered down to narrow hips. One strong leg, bent at the knee, was positioned slightly out to the side and the dark fabric of his trousers pulled across his thigh, outlining the slab of muscle she knew, from living in close proximity, defined his upper leg.

She waited for him to finish, knowing that Paige needed time to pull herself together and McKenzie's condition would benefit from the supplemental oxygen.

'You certainly did a good job of it, Bill,' Alessandro murmured. 'Bull's-eye on your cornea.' He pulled away from the eyepieces. He noticed a figure in his peripheral vision and felt his abdominals contract. He didn't have to turn his head to know it was Nat. His body seemed to have a sixth sense when she was around.

'Never do anything by halves, Doc.'

Nat felt a similar awareness and sensed rather than saw his momentary eyelid flicker, which told her he knew she was there. It was probably imperceptible to most, but after a few days of cohabitation and an almost electric awareness of him, she was coming to know all his cues—both obvious and subtle.

Alessandro continued with his patient. 'It's not too bad, though, only superficial by the look of it. Some antibiotic eyedrops should work like a charm.'

Nat lounged against the doorframe and waited. She was used to him ignoring her now anyway. It was a policy they'd both adopted. And as far as it went, it wasn't such a bad idea. There was an attraction there. He knew it. She knew it. It hummed between them like a palpable force, like powerful magnets irresistibly drawn to each other.

But acknowledging it out loud was just plain dumb when neither of them was going to do anything about it. So they were polite. They addressed each other when required and worked together with utter professionalism. In short they carried on as if nothing had ever happened.

Like he'd never licked Napolitano sauce off her chest.

Alessandro stood and Nat spoke. 'Excuse me, Dr Lombardi. I have a patient you need to see.'

Alessandro looked at her fully then and gave her a brief nod before turning back to his patient. He held out his hand and shook Bill's. 'I'll send someone in with some drops for you.'

Nat stepped back from the doorway as Alessandro headed towards her. She could see tension in his shoulders as the looseness with which he'd shaken Bill's hand disappeared and his face drew back into grim lines.

'Three-year-old ex-twenty-seven-weeker. Twin one. Twin two died at four months of age.'

She fell into step beside him, ignoring the lurch of her cells, and launched into the standard summary she'd give any doctor she was handing over to. Here at St Auburn's she was a nursing professional and she would be professional if it killed her. Even if she did want to find the nearest vacant room and tear all his clothes off.

'Chronic neonatal lung disease, oxygen dependent for first two years of life, recurrent chest infections, failure to thrive. I think she's brewing another infection. Febrile. Sats ninety on room air. Bilateral chest crackles. Listless. Cool peripherally and mottled.'

Alessandro nodded as they walked. 'What was her birth weight?'

Nat struggled to keep up with Alessandro's stride,

which seemed to lengthen with each footfall. 'Twelve hundred grams.'

'How many days ventilated.'

'Twenty.' The answers to his spitfire questions were well known to her but his emotionless firing of them was irritating.

'Which cube?'

'Eleven,' she said as they drew level with the central nurses' station.

Alessandro nodded. He could smell that flower-garden scent he was becoming so familiar with and, as usual, he had the craziest urge to bury his face in her neck. It didn't seem to matter how fast he walked, he couldn't outrun it. 'Chart?'

She handed the thick file to him but kept hold of it. Alessandro frowned at her. *'Problemo?'*

'Paige is that friend of mine I told you about in the lift that day. She lost a baby, her husband walked out and she's dealing with McKenzie's fragile health. McKenzie's implant operation has been postponed three times in the last year and she's supposed to go in next week for it and that probably won't happen now so Paige is…a little emotional at the moment. Just…I don't know…' She looked at his grim face. 'Smile or something.'

He clenched his jaw and, ignoring her jibe, cut straight to the chase. 'Implant?'

'Sorry,' Nat dismissed, letting go of the chart as she realised she'd left out a vital part of patient history. 'Cochlear implant. McKenzie's profoundly deaf.'

Alessandro looked down at the bulging chart and then back at her. 'Are you coming?'

He didn't wait for an answer and Nat followed him in.

The harsh screech of the curtain as he snapped it back didn't bode well and she castigated herself for irritating him just prior to seeing Paige.

Alessandro's gaze encompassed the mother and listless diminutive little girl, hearing aids firmly in place. He gave Paige a gentle smile. She looked utterly exhausted. She looked like he'd felt for the last year and he felt an instant surge of empathy. 'Hello, I'm Alessandro,' he said, and signed it too.

Nat's eyes bugged, as did Paige's. 'Oh. You sign?' she exclaimed.

Alessandro gave a self-deprecating shrug. He had learned the English sign language when he'd moved to London which he believed was similar to what they used here. 'In a fashion.' He smiled. 'I have an aunt in Italy, who's profoundly deaf. I spent a lot of time there as a kid. She was like a second mother to me. My cousin Val, her son, is a renowned cochlear implant surgeon in London.'

He signed as he spoke without giving it conscious thought. Not that McKenzie cared or could probably even understand his mixture of sign language but it was second nature to him when he was in the company of a deaf person.

Nat shook her head, marvelling at the change in Alessandro when he was with a patient. He was great with McKenzie, getting her X-rayed, admitting her for intravenous antibiotics when the films revealed bilateral consolidation and quickly and efficiently placing a drip.

He was especially good with Paige, chatting about sign-language differences and asking her about the scheduled operation. He was like a different man.

Involved. Animated. Connected.

Now, if he could just be more like that at home she could walk out of their lives in a couple of months knowing it had all been worth it.

Even if it meant having to go to bed every night with a fire in her belly and a buzz in her blood that wouldn't quit.

CHAPTER SIX

ON FRIDAY Nat was sitting on the quiet mat at crèche with Julian and another boy, Henry. She was trying to encourage a friendship between them. Henry was a nice kid who had been trying to engage Julian for a little while now with not much success.

It wasn't that Julian didn't like Henry—she could tell he did. But he still shied away from other kids, preferring to keep to himself or follow her around. Julian was more than happy to play and talk with Henry as long as she was there as well.

Henry had brought in some photos of his family holiday to New Zealand and they were going through them. There was a beautiful shot of Henry and his mother. He was sitting in her lap, facing the camera. She had her arms crossed across his front, pulling his back in tight to her chest. They were looking at each other, she looking down, Henry looking up and laughing. A massive mountain gave the background some perspective.

Julian took the photo reverently, being careful to only touch the corner as he'd been taught. 'Is that your mummy?'

Julian didn't take his eyes off the photo and the look

on his face was heart-breaking. It suddenly struck Nat that there were no photos of Julian's mother anywhere. She'd been so distracted by the starkness of the never-ending white, so snow blind, she hadn't even thought about that.

Goodness, her mother had practically set up a shrine to her father after he'd gone. Despite the fact that he'd deserted them. But she'd been determined to maintain contact, to keep his memory fresh for Nat's sake.

Pity her father hadn't tried as hard.

But there wasn't even a framed picture for Julian to put on his beside table. No family portraits hung on the wall. Come to think of it, not even Alessandro had pictures of the wife he so obviously mourned. Not in his office or his bedroom. It was almost as if she never existed at all.

Was it too painful for him to even look at her? Was his grief still that profound?

And why did the thought depress her so much?

She made up her mind to ask Alessandro about it tonight after Julian went to bed. It seemed to have become her role to ask the hard questions. To be the bad guy. It certainly hadn't taken her long to realise that as much as Alessandro wanted to reach his son he was still floundering and relied heavily on her to facilitate it. They both did. She was like the buffer between them, the referee, and her ruling was final.

Alessandro seemed more than happy for her to take up where his wife had left off. Be some kind of substitute mother to Julian. And she knew that was about his grief more than shirking his duties, that he'd been knocked sideways and was groping in the dark. But she wasn't living with them so Alessandro could hide from his son, to maintain his emotional distance.

She was there until her unit was built and in the meantime she was in Julian's corner. He was a four-year-old child and, God knew, he needed someone in his corner.

Surely there were pictures somewhere? Even one? Alessandro might find it too painful to contemplate but watching Julian now it was obvious he yearned for that connection. If he was to ever recover from his tragic loss, he needed to be able to openly grieve and he needed his mother's life, her existence, to be acknowledged.

'And next Grandma Poss and Hush went to—'

'Hobart!'

Alessandro chuckled. 'For?' he prompted as he turned the page.

'Lamingtons!'

Julian just couldn't seem to get enough of this damn book—it was their second time through tonight. He seemed to forget everything as the story unfolded. About Camilla. And being dragged halfway across the world. And the stiltedness of their relationship.

At the moment Alessandro was propped against the head of his son's bed, his legs stretched out in front, his son cuddled into his side, Julian's curls tickling his chin.

Nat had been right. This was a special time of the day.

But as happy as he was, it was moments like this that the vile sting of regret was at its most potent. He'd been so busy in London, so involved with his career, with making consultant, that he'd let Camilla drive a wedge between him and Julian.

His guilt at entering into the marriage for all the wrong reasons had convinced him his strained relationship with Julian had been his due. Some kind of cosmic payback.

But, then, he'd never imagined his son would be mother-less and he would have the sole care of his child.

A virtual stranger…

'Nat bought me a lamington yesterday.'

Alessandro absently rubbed his chin against Julian's soft curls, savouring the texture and this time together. Soon the book would end and Julian would become awkward with him again. Three nights ago Nat had insisted that bedtime was a special time and bedtime stories were a father's role and firmly shoved the book at his chest.

Julian had pouted and begged her to do it but she had just smiled at both of them, kissed Julian goodnight and left them to it. And now here they were, both enjoying the night-time ritual.

Enjoying going to another world far away from their own and all its baggage.

'Did she, now?' he said good-humouredly. 'Did it make you invisible?'

Juliano giggled. 'No. But it tasted dee-licious.'

Alessandro smiled to himself as an image of delicious Nat with Napolitano sauce oozing a tempting streak down the swell of her breast rose in his mind. Not what his son had meant but he couldn't think of a better description.

Had a woman ever tasted so sweet?

Not that it mattered. It wouldn't matter if she tasted like fairy floss, cinnamon doughnuts and dark chocolate gelato all rolled in one. He was paying penance and Nat, who'd no doubt been sent by the devil to tempt him, was definitely off limits.

Nat could hear a low murmuring of voices as she collected her pyjamas from beneath her pillow. A high-pitched giggle carried easily, followed by a deeper, richer baritone that seemed to slither into her room on serpent's wings.

She smiled at the baby steps of progress. Demanding that Alessandro be proactive was doing the trick. She tiptoed down the short distance of hallway between her room and Julian's, unable to resist taking a peek. The sight that greeted her was heart-warming. Father and son stretched out on the bed in the way of father and sons the world over.

Alessandro was still in his work clothes. But he'd taken his tie off and loosened the top two buttons of his duck-egg-blue shirt. His feet were still encased in his socks. He looked relaxed for a change. Younger, even. Devoted, certainly.

Also hot, sexy and virile. What was it about seeing a big man with a small child that was irresistibly attractive?

Julian's little body was curled up, knees to chest, snuggled into Alessandro's side. His small hand rested on his father's shirt, making it seem positively diminutive against the sheer size of Alessandro's chest. He was looking at his father as he read the story like he could leap tall buildings in a single bound.

No one watching this scene would guess at the strange relationship that had existed between the two of them. The stilted politeness, their mechanical interactions, the distance. Right now it was as it should be and her foolish soft heart practically over flowed with joy.

She tiptoed away, a small smile curving her soft mouth, knowing that things were looking up and she was part of it.

An hour later, Nat, her heart thudding in her chest, knocked on Alessandro's office door. It wasn't shut, just pulled to, but, still, it was a barrier she didn't feel comfortable breeching without an invitation. He shut himself away every night after Julian went to bed. The relaxed man who lay with his son disappearing the second he walked out of Julian's room.

His message couldn't have been clearer—back off. Keep out. He'd said they should pretend it had never happened and he was hell bent on leading by example.

She heard his soft '*Entrato*' and hesitated briefly, girding her loins for the forthcoming battle. One thing she'd learned very quickly had been that Alessandro was an intensely private man. She didn't think he'd take too kindly to her entering these particular waters. He didn't talk about his wife, he hadn't even let her name slip. Nat had no way of knowing how he'd react to the photo issue.

But she'd made a commitment to herself that she would raise this with him, for Julian's sake, and she wasn't going to back down. She took a breath and pushed open the door.

He was sitting in his black-leather, Italian-designed swivel chair. His computer was on. Open textbooks cluttered the surface of the desk and the floor around his feet. Piles of medical journals, some open, littered the area as well in some kind of order…she guessed.

The rest of his office was still stark. The walls were bare and the whiteness was harsh in contrast to the cluttered desk area. She made a note to attack those boxes this weekend. Surely Alessandro wanted familiar things around him too? Maybe he'd appreciate a photo of his wife for his desk?

He'd changed out of his work clothes into his pyjamas. Boxer shorts, the soft clingy kind often seen on models, not the loose, silky ones. They came to mid-thigh and revealed more than they covered. As did a snug-fitting white T-shirt. He'd avoided being 'undressed' around her, for which she was most grateful.

The occasional glimpses she'd caught of him *sans* shirt had been hard enough.

His hair was damp as if he'd not long been out of the shower. A soft lamp spread a glow around the office and settled against the angles of his face, emphasising the richness of his bronze complexion and shadowing his mouth. He looked dark and dangerous and breathtakingly good-looking.

Her very first thought was to turn around and run.

Alessandro raised an eyebrow. 'You wanted something?'

Nat swallowed. His voice was a low purr, like Flo's—on steroids. *God help her, she did.* She wanted him like she'd never wanted a man before. Not even Rob. She shut her eyes against the image of her and him going for it in his big old chair that flashed briefly through her mind.

No! They couldn't do this.

When she opened them again his dark gaze netted her in its web. It was if he knew exactly what she'd been thinking.

Alessandro flattened his bare feet in the carpet so he wouldn't leave the chair and cover the short distance between the two of them and snatch her into his arms. Nat's gaze had licked all over him and become all heat and steam and he suddenly felt like he was sitting in a sauna or a hot spring. He kept his gaze trained on hers despite the compelling tug to let it wander down over her cleavage and further to her long bare legs and feet he could see in his peripheral vision.

Inferno! This was crazy. 'Nat?'

His voice was steely now, pulling Nat back from temptation. 'I wanted to talk to you about…' she swallowed '…something.'

Alessandro's gaze took in her mouth as she talked and

her nervous throat bob. The strange urge to stroke a finger down the ridge of her windpipe, place kisses along it, came upon him and he curled his hand around the arm of the chair, anchoring himself. 'Okay. So talk.'

Nat nodded, still uncertain how to go about asking the question. 'I was wondering if…' He was staring at her mouth and she couldn't process anything. She took a second. Probably best to just say it. 'You had any photos of your wife?'

Alessandro's gaze flicked back to her eyes in an instant. He felt the tension that was never far way come back into the muscles of his neck. 'What for?'

Nat heard the note of foreboding, the no-trespassing inflection in his wary voice. And the urge to flee became an imperative. Her heart beat loud enough that she felt sure that Alessandro must be able to hear it. 'I thought it would be nice for Julian to have a picture of her on his bedside table. Maybe one of them together?'

Alessandro stiffened, an immediate denial rushing to his lips. They'd made real progress this week. He couldn't bear to see Julian return to the practically mute little boy he'd been in those few days and weeks after Camilla's death.

His son was moving on, he didn't want to take him back. 'I think that would make him unbearably sad again.'

Nat steeled herself to be the bad guy again. 'His mother's dead, Alessandro. He's allowed to be sad.'

Alessandro shook his head. She didn't know how hard it had been. 'It's too awful to watch.'

Nat nearly gave up then and there. The anguish in Alessandro's voice cut her to the quick. But she knew enough child psychology, as should he, to know he wasn't doing his son any favours. 'You can't protect him from that. It's healthy to be sad, to cry, to grieve. You can't fast-forward this bit by pretending she didn't exist.'

Alessandro's head snapped up. 'I'm not doing that,' he denied, ice lacing his voice and turning his obsidian eyes flinty.

Alessandro's fervent denial flared out at her like a striking snake. 'There's not a single photo of her anywhere, Alessandro,' she persisted, keeping her voice even and gentle. 'You loved her. She was the mother of your child. I know it's hard for you to have reminders of her around —'

Alessandro's snort interrupted her. 'You have no idea.'

Nat frowned, surprised at the derision in his voice but ploughed on anyway, not sure she'd ever be brave enough to say it again. 'He's four, Alessandro. You know I'm right. Put aside the father, the husband, for a moment and think like a doctor. Like the good doctor you are. You know I'm right. You know this is good grief resolution strategy.'

Alessandro cursed her for being right. 'And what if I can't look at her?' he demanded.

How long had it been since he'd looked at Camilla's face? Conjured her up? He'd been trying so hard to banish the years of baggage he'd steadfastly refused to imagine her at all.

Of course, he didn't have to look too far for a reminder. But funnily enough, the physical similarities between Nat and Camilla didn't strike him any more—hadn't since that first meeting. They were two different women in so many ways. Too different to be mistaken as the same one.

Nat swallowed. She felt his pain all the way down to her toes and felt dreadful, pushing. 'I'm not asking you to commission a six-foot mural on one of these god-awful walls. Just a photo for Julian's bedside table. So he knows she existed and she loved him and she's looking over him.'

Alessandro wished it was that easy. Could he look at that photo every time he entered his son's room? Could he look at it and not feel the knife twisting a little deeper?

He looked at Nat's earnest face and sighed. Hadn't she been right about everything else? Hadn't she helped him reach out to his son already? Of course he could do it, if it helped his son mourn.

'There are framed photos,' he sighed. 'A few. In one of the boxes.'

It had been his intention to get around to putting them out. In their house in London, photos of her, of them, as a family had been everywhere. They'd been so hard to look at afterwards. The hypocrisy had been torture. And frankly he'd been enjoying the emotional freedom.

Nat felt her heart sink at both the defeat in his voice and the thought of having to search through the remaining mound of boxes. Whoever the packing company had been, they'd done a lousy job. Most of them were marked miscellaneous so the photos could be anywhere.

But it was a start, a concession. And there was no rush now that Alessandro had consented—they'd find them some time in the next few weekends and with Alessandro on the same page it would be a good avenue to open discussion. And in the meantime they could sound Julian out about the idea.

She noticed how tired he looked and suppressed her natural soppy-female instinct to go to him. She wanted to put her arms around him, hug him, give him a place to rest his head. But she knew it would be a mistake. The urge to comfort might be her motivator but she doubted it would stay that pure for long.

'Thank you. This is the right thing to do, Alessandro.'

Alessandro heard the note of genuine belief in her voice. She stood in his doorway, oozing certainty and confidence. God, he felt so out of his depth sometimes. And yet here she was in her T-shirt and shorts, all perfect and Zen and centred, telling him it was going to be all right.

He wished she'd come nearer. He wanted to put his arms around her, bury his face against her belly. Absorb some of that Zen she had going on. Maybe feel her hand sifting through his hair. 'I hope so,' he murmured.

Nat was almost paralysed by the longing she saw in Alessandro's gaze. Was it desire to connect with his son or just plain old desire?

Desire with a capital D?

His eyes roamed over her and her skin felt like it was on fire. The room had become a furnace, heat roaring between them. She opened her mouth to say something but, as if he knew he'd already given away too much, he swivelled the chair back around to face his desktop monitor.

She stood in the doorway for a few moments, staring at the back of his chair, trying to catch her breath. This was a good thing. Something happening between them would be dumb—way dumber than Rob. He was doing them a favour.

And one day, she had no doubt, she'd truly appreciate his resolve. But right now a long lonely night stretched endlessly ahead.

Nat woke in the wee small hours to Flo miaowing and nudging her. Rain drummed on the colour bond roof. She wasn't surprised. The day had been humid and a storm had been brewing as she'd climbed into bed. She stroked Flo, lying there for a second just enjoying the noise and luxuriating in being dry and snuggled beneath the covers. But Flo persisted with her nudging and Nat reluctantly got up.

'All right, bossy-boots. I know you like to frolic in the rain, you crazy cat.' She picked up a purring Flo. 'Come on.'

Familiar now with the layout of the house, Nat made her way downstairs in the dark and opened the laundry door for Flo to go out. She watched the cat bound into the rain and grinned. Silly animal—giving up a dry warm bed snuggled into a doting little boy to chase a few raindrops around.

Nat shut the door, knowing Flo would be happy out there for hours. She stopped and grabbed a drink of water in the kitchen and headed back to the stairs. A chink of light from beneath the office door caught her gaze. Good grief! Alessandro was still up?

She knocked lightly on the door and waited for his gruff '*Entrato*' but nothing. She pushed it open slowly, expecting him to swivel around with an annoyed look on his face. Instead, he was bent forward in his chair, head on desk, amidst the clutter of textbooks, his eyes closed.

'Alessandro?' she whispered, approaching carefully. He didn't stir and she stood for a moment just looking down at him. His black hair fell across his forehead, disarmingly innocent, just like Julian's did when he slept.

But the dark growth shadowing his jaw and his softly parted lips were one hundred per cent adult.

It was a shame to wake him—he always looked so tired. In fact, even asleep he looked utterly exhausted. But he'd have a hell of a sore neck in the morning if he stayed like this.

'Alessandro,' she called again as she gave his shoulder a gentle shake.

Alessandro startled, sucking in a breath and sitting bolt

upright as he dragged his body out of the sticky depths of slumber. His hand automatically went to the twinge in his neck as his brain scrambled to get up to speed.

Nat standing in his office. Nat standing really close in his office. Nat wearing some clingy T-shirt dress thingy with no bra standing close in his office.

'I'm sorry,' he murmured, struggling with the urge to drop his gaze to the bounce of her unfettered breasts in his peripheral vision. 'I must have fallen asleep.' He used both hands to rub his neck for fear of where they'd go if they weren't occupied.

He had a red mark on his cheek where it had been stuck to a textbook and Nat had a crazy urge to stroke it. 'What are you doing up so late?' she whispered. She wasn't sure why she was whispering. It just seemed appropriate in the dead of night.

Alessandro shrugged. 'I've been working on St Auburn's readiness for pandemic status should the dreaded swamp flu reach our shores.'

'It's two-thirty in the morning,' she chided. 'The swamp flu can wait. Go to bed. Get some sleep.'

Alessandro let his hands drop. If only if was that easy. 'I can't sleep,' he murmured. 'I never sleep.'

Nat felt his weariness, his anguish, right down to her toes. He looked totally wretched and her instincts cried out to comfort him. 'Oh, Alessandro,' she whispered.

She didn't give a second thought to moving closer, sliding one hand behind his neck and one into his hair, cradling his head, pulling it against her belly. 'I'm so sorry.'

Alessandro's arms automatically encircled her waist, drawing her closer. He shut his eyes as he leaned into her, his face pressed into her nightshirt. She smelled like soap and rain and flowers. And he wanted her. 'I'm tired. I'm so tired.'

'Shh.' She cradled his head and rocked slightly. 'I know. I know.' Because she did know. She knew what it was like to grieve the end of a relationship. To lose someone close.

He pressed a kiss to her belly and looked up at her. She was so beautiful. Her eyes were shimmering pools of empathy, her skin was glowing and her mouth was beckoning. He wanted to crawl into a nice, big warm bed with her and stay there for ever. 'Nathalie.'

Nat shook her head. She knew that look in his eyes. Knew for damn sure it was reflected in hers. 'Don't call me that.' Her voice shook. She hated how husky it sounded.

He rubbed his chin against her stomach. 'Why? It suits you.'

Her abdominal muscles rippled beneath his stubble as if he had licked them and deeper down other muscles stirred deliciously at the way he'd sighed her name. Her hand drifted down from his hair to his face. She rubbed gently at the red mark on his cheek with the back of her hand. 'Because I like it too much.'

They stared at each other for the longest time. They didn't move. All that could be heard in the small office was the rain on the roof and the staccato rhythm of their breathing. It was Alessandro who made the first move, applying pressure through his arms, bringing her down onto his lap, their heads close. Their lips closer.

Nat didn't protest, mesmerised by his eyes, by the desire that gleamed there. That they could be cold like black ice one moment and warm like sable the next. She wasn't supposed to be here, doing this, but she also knew she was utterly powerless to resist. She could almost feel his mouth on hers, taste it, and she wanted it so badly anticipation hummed through her system.

Alessandro's hand crept up, brushed against her shoulder and moving along the line of her collar bone until it was cradling her nape, four fingers lodged in her hair, his thumb stroking her jaw. He exerted slight pressure inching her closer. Their mouths nearer.

'*Bello*,' he murmured. He was past caring about restraint and all the reasons why kissing Nat, taking her clothes off and having her right here, right now, was a bad idea. All he knew was that in amongst all the bad things in his life at the moment this felt inextricably right.

That he suddenly felt more awake, more alive than he had in a long time. A very long time.

His hand drifted down to her neckline, coming to rest where the material scooped low on her breasts. She shut her eyes as her nipples responded to the blatant arousal. She watched fascinated as he dropped his head and kissed her not far from where the sauce had landed not even a week ago. His lips practically sizzled against her skin and she arched her back involuntarily.

'Nathalie…'

She barely had a chance to whimper before his mouth brushed against hers. Light. Gentle. A whisper of what was to come. 'Alessandro.' She wasn't sure if it was a warning or an invitation.

But it was definitely surrender.

Her hands snaked around his neck at the same time and their lips met again. Not gentle now. Not light. Deep. Deeper. Open mouths and questing tongues feasting on each other like starving beasts. She could hear his moan and felt its seductive stroke deep inside her before it travelled all the way to her toes.

Her head spun as the kiss spiralled out of control. She broke away for a second, dizzy and out of breath. Alessandro looked at her with a passion not even his hooded eyes could conceal. His lips were moist from her ministrations—full and beckoning.

She'd done that to him. Made this man look at her with eyes that devoured her, that branded her. She should be scared by this level of intensity but, God help her, she wanted more.

Alessandro rubbed his thumb across the soft swollen contours of her mouth. She had him on her lips. Them. And he wanted to be back there. Their mouths joined. To be joined even more intimately. To taste her more intimately. To be inside her. 'You're so sweet,' he whispered.

'So are you,' she murmured, before slamming her mouth back on to his.

He met her ardour, surpassed it. His hands tangled in her hair, holding her captive, making escape impossible. Not that she wanted it. She could feel he was hard for her, his cotton boxers and her position on his lap giving his impressive arousal nowhere to hide.

She squirmed against it, wanting to feel it pressed against her more intimately, not just the back of her thigh. She wanted to touch it, damn it. Without breaking the kiss, she manoeuvred herself until she was straddling his lap, her nightdress riding up her thighs.

Thank God for quality Italian furnishing.

The big leather chair accommodated her most adequately and she wasted no time grinding down against him, seeking the pleasure, the relief she knew he could give her.

He broke off the kiss on a groan, his breath outdrumming the rain. 'Nathalie.' She was beautiful, bits of her blonde hair wisped free from her ponytail and somehow, despite the experienced movements of her hips, she looked down at him with a wide-eyed wonder that could almost border on innocent. 'I want to see all of you.'

Without asking, his hands snagged the hem of her night-dress, lifted it up and dragged it off over her head. She was totally naked apart from a very inadequate scrap of lace. Her breasts fell free and he was mesmerised by them. They were as beautiful as he'd imagined, and God knew he'd imagined them often enough. Full and firm with nipples the colour of mocha.

He brought his hands up from her waist until they were full of her. They felt heavy in his palms and her peaked nipples dragged deliciously across the sensitive skin there. '*Inferno!* I want to taste you.'

And then, with one arm around her back, he swept her close, his mouth latching onto the nearest offering. He sucked hard on her nipple and Nat cried out, clutching his shoulders as her world tilted and spun.

His tongue rasped against her peaked flesh. It lapped and licked and sucked and rolled around the entire elon-gated peak. And just when he thought she could take it no longer he released her and she almost fell against him. But he steadied her with his arm and opened his mouth over the other one.

'Alessandro!' She wasn't sure if she was begging him to stop or egging him on further—all she knew was she was swirling like an autumn leaf in the wind and they hadn't even got to the main event.

Alessandro released her nipple, satisfied to see it wet and puckered from his ministrations. 'I want you.'

Three little words. Not the three words most women want to hear but Nat couldn't have cared less. She'd heard those words and they'd been an empty promise. Right now she needed this. Alessandro. A man who wanted her with an intensity she doubted she'd ever known.

But even so. There were some logistics that needed sorting. She battled with her breathing. 'Condoms?' she panted.

Alessandro shook his head. 'Are you on the Pill?'

She nodded. She could feel the ridge of his erection pressing against her and she was desperate to feel it inside. 'Of course. But it's about more than that, Alessandro.'

His arms tightened around her. Damn it. He knew that. 'I've had sex with one woman in the last five years.'

She looked into his eyes, warm like sable still, and saw the yearning and desperation that had got her into this chair in the first place. He wanted her. But he was telling her he was safe and, God help her, she'd die tonight if she had to leave this room unsatisfied. 'Same with me.'

'Good.' Alessandro returned his attention to her breasts and she grabbed his shoulders as lust slammed into her gut.

Barely thinking straight, she reached down for him, finding him bigger and harder and thicker than even she'd imagined. He moaned into her mouth and she felt a surge of warmth between her thighs as her body prepared to take him.

Alessandro pulled away as she manoeuvred him out of his material prison and her hand finally found bare skin.

'Nathalie…' he groaned, leaning his forehead against her chest. 'I don't think I'll last very long if you touch me like that.' He looked up into her face. 'It's been a long time.'

Nat squeezed his girth, her hand luxuriating in the

velvety glove sheathing the core of solid rock. He snatched in a breath and expelled it on another groan and she smiled down at him. 'Good. We can do slow later.'

And she lowered her head, opening her mouth over his, feeling him surge in her palm as his tongue thrust inside her mouth. She felt his hands squeezing her buttocks, dragging her closer, and she rubbed herself against his naked length, aroused beyond all rational thought.

There was no planning now. She was just moving to a rhythm as old as time. She needed to feel him inside her and without conscious control she was lifting over him, pushing the crutch of her knickers to one side, and then his head was nudging her entrance and she didn't even pause before her hips moved instinctively down as his moved instinctively up.

She cried out as he filled her more than she'd ever been filled before. She vaguely heard him calling her name but a pounding in her blood, like jungle drums, was taking over and she moved to their beat.

Alessandro groaned, hearing the drums too, and moved again, pulling her close, one arm still around her back. He kissed her lips, rained kisses down her neck, took a puckered nipple in his mouth, all the time obeying the throb in his blood, the rhythm in his head.

Nat held Alessandro's head to her breast, hanging on for dear life as the beat became a canter and then a gallop. 'Alessandro!' she cried.

Alessandro barely heard her above the tempo pulsing around him. It was inside, thickening his blood, and around them, pressing them closer with invisible hands. His loins moved to its beat, surging and thrusting into her hot, tight core.

Nat felt the drums rise to a crescendo and she knew she was going over the edge. 'Alessandro, I can't…Oh, God, I can't stop it.'

'Nathalie,' he roared, throwing his head back against the leather headrest, clutching her hips. He thrust one last time as the rhythm peaked and he along with it.

For a moment neither of them moved as the drums crashed to total silence and they both became airborne. And then Nat moaned and bucked, her nails digging into his shoulders as pleasure, so deep, so profound, rained down on her.

And Alessandro joined her, thrusting his hips, pumping up into her, riding the wave of his own orgasm, driven by the echo of the drums still spiking his blood and milked by her wild abandon as she bucked and rode him to completion.

And when it was over she collapsed against him and he gathered her close and he knew without a shadow of a doubt that having Nat Davies come to stay was the best thing he'd ever done.

CHAPTER SEVEN

AFTER not knowing the pleasures of a woman's body for a long time, Alessandro was insatiable. They'd made love another twice that night before Nat had slunk back to her own bedroom. And then every night since. Alessandro would put Julian to bed, read to him and then he would pounce again, no matter where she was. The kitchen, the shower, the laundry, the lounge. A week later there were very few places in the house they hadn't done it.

Thank goodness Julian slept like the dead.

It never crossed Nat's mind to refuse Alessandro. She'd been around long enough to know that the magic they'd made that first time didn't come along very often. And, anyway, her body betrayed her at every single turn. All he had to do was look at her and she practically self-combusted.

Why deny herself this little oasis of pleasure? As long as she took it at face value, remembered it was about two convenient bodies finding a little mutual gratification for a finite period of time, she'd be fine. She was an adult. There was nothing wrong with that.

For once in her life she was making a decision with her head and not her poor, easy heart.

And it felt liberating.

Plus there was something compelling about Alessandro's love-making that was addictive. He was so…driven. Intense, like the rest of him. Desperate, almost. When his body covered hers it felt like he was trying to absorb her into him. He wasn't satisfied with quick and easy and rolling over and going to sleep. They made love for hours each night until sheer exhaustion took over.

And his attention to detail was amazing.

Nat doubted she'd ever been so thoroughly bedded in her life. It was like by reaching for the maximum level of pleasure he was hoping to purge the grief. Not just sideline it. He was still hurting and it was if he'd found the perfect antidote for it—her body. And that was okay too. If her gratification helped him heal, who was she to argue?

And then there was the flow-on effect to Julian. The sex was making Alessandro more relaxed. He didn't seem so grim. He was more…laid-back. He smiled more. Laughed. And Julian was slowly becoming less serious, less wary in return.

They were careful, of course, to keep their relationship from Julian. Nat was always back in her bed by five a.m. It was hard and getting harder, especially when Alessandro was so warm and vital, his big arm tucked around her waist, his bigger body curled around hers.

And at that hour of the morning he was usually raring to go again with another treacherous seduction muddling her senses.

'Stay longer,' he'd whisper. His accent always seemed more pronounced when he was sleepy and it stroked seductive fingers along her pelvic floor.

Nat would smile as his lips nuzzled her neck, his hands

kneaded her breasts and his erection brushed her belly. The temptation to stay was great. 'Julian,' she'd murmur.

'He never wakes before seven, *bella*.'

Which was true, but Nat knew it was best not to be found together. Choosing to snatch these moments with Alessandro was fine—she was an adult. Julian was a boy who dearly needed a mother and who plainly adored her. And that wasn't fair. What did four-year-olds know of adult games? Adult relationships? It wasn't right to confuse him any more when his world had already been turned upside down.

So she dutifully dragged herself out of her lover's bed, out of his possessive male embrace, every morning. And even when he looked up at her with a sexy half-smile and smouldering sable eyes that told her more than words what he wanted to do to her, she still turned away.

But it was getting more and more difficult…

Alessandro had tried to not let their chemistry spill over into their work and for the most part it was successful. She only worked two day shifts a week in the department and usually it was on the triage desk so it was easier to avoid direct contact.

But today, on this crazy, crazy Friday, she'd been allo-cated to the cubicles and they seemed to have giant magnets attached to their butts. Today it was simply im-possible to ignore her and their attraction. Impossible to not be utterly distracted by her.

'Twenty-year-old female, right lower quadrant pain, rebound tenderness, hypertensive, tachycardic, febrile.'

Nat pushed the chart at Alessandro, trying to be brisk and professional in her handover. Everywhere she'd moved today his incendiary gaze had been on her and she was about ready to combust.

Not to mention the fact that despite his dark trousers, dove-grey shirt and beautiful mauve tie, all she could see was the way he had looked last night on his way back from the bathroom gloriously naked, hands firmly on narrow hips, his arousal on proud display.

Alessandro smiled. He could see the simmer in her gaze and knew exactly where her brain was. 'Which cubicle?'

'Twelve,' she said automatically, a vague part of her still clinging to professionalism while his rough command from last night to 'Open your legs' squirmed through her grey matter.

Nat felt her internal muscles twist firmly in a knot. His broad shoulders bobbed in front of her and she followed blindly, trying to catch her breath.

Alessandro greeted his patient. 'Hi. Ellie? I'm Dr Lombardi.' He held out his hand and the harried young woman shook it briefly, grabbing her side with a grunt as she let go. 'Nat's been telling me you have some pain.'

'Yes,' Ellie agreed. 'The odd niggle the last day or two but worse this morning. And by the time I got to work it was unbearable.'

Nat watched as his attention turned solely to his patient. He questioned her closely before methodically examining her. Even in significant pain she could see how Ellie responded to Alessandro's calm professionalism. She was scared but somehow he managed to reassure her.

Alessandro returned his gaze to Nat. She was looking at him with admiration and respect and even that went straight to his groin. 'I'll call for a surgical consult. In the meantime I'll write up some morphine and let's draw some blood, Nurse Davies.' He handed back the chart and deliberately let his gaze fall to her mouth.

Nat's lips parted involuntarily as she took the chart. It felt as if he'd physically touched them. She reached for the bed rail and cleared her throat. 'Certainly, Dr Lombardi.'

And then he was gone from the cubicle and she was left staring after him, her lips tingling, her brain scrambled.

'Do you think I can get that morphine now?'

Nat dragged her attention back to her patient. Ellie was grimacing and clutching the sheet tight. 'Oh, sorry, of course. I'll be right back.'

Nat exited the cubicle determined to keep her mind on the job. 'Imogen,' she called seeing her boss. 'I need you to check some morphine with me.'

Imogen followed her into the room where the narcotics were stored. She inserted the key into the locked metal cupboard as Nat smothered a yawn.

'Are you not sleeping well?' Imogen asked as she reached for the boxes of morphine. 'You yawned all the way through handover this morning and you look like you haven't slept in a week.'

Nat busied herself with writing in the dangerous-drugs register to hide the sudden rise of heat to her cheeks. She was sleeping very well indeed. When she and Alessandro finally succumbed, they slept the deep sleep of the sexually sated. It just so happened that it only amounted to a few hours each night.

It had certainly been well after three last night before they'd worn themselves out. 'I'm fine,' she murmured.

Imogen removed a morphine ampoule and they counted the remainder. Nat drew up the injection as

Imogen signed the register then they left the room together and entered cubicle twelve.

Imogen smiled at the patient. 'Can I have your full name, date of birth and any allergies, please?' she asked.

Ellie prattled off the requested information as Imgoen and Nat checked it against her patient number in her chart and on the medication form. Satisfied they had the right patient, Imogen departed, leaving Nat to administer the needle.

'Thigh or bottom?' she asked.

'Oh, God, I don't care,' Ellie groaned. 'You can stick it in my eyeball as long as the damn pain goes away.'

Nat smothered a smile. 'I think your thigh will be easier,' she said, exposing her patient's leg. 'You don't have to move.' Nat prepped the area with an alcohol swab and delivered the morphine in a matter of seconds.

By the time she'd done another set of obs and drawn the blood Alessandro had requested, Ellie was already feeling relief. 'Better?' Nat asked.

'Oh, God, so much better. Thank you.'

The curtain flicked back and Alessandro poked his head in. 'Surgeon will be here in twenty minutes.'

Both the women nodded and Alessandro disappeared again, flicking the curtain back in place.

Ellie looked at Nat. 'That man is totally dreamy. He can park his Italian leather shoes under my bed any day.'

Nat laughed, understanding the sentiment totally. She felt a surge of female pride, like that of a lioness, that Alessandro's shoes were firmly parked under her bed. Or hers under his, anyway.

'Seriously, seriously gorgeous,' Ellie babbled. 'You could just eat him with a spoon, couldn't you? He doesn't have a ring—is he married?'

Nat suppressed the sudden urge to turn on her patient and growl *Back off, sister* as a sudden shard of jealousy sliced through her. Her patient was smiling like a goon and her voice was a little slurred. Nat reminded herself it was the morphine talking.

'Drugs have obviously kicked in, then,' Nat said, forcing lightness into her voice. 'I'll be back with the surgeon. Here's your bell if you need me for anything.'

Nat stepped out of the curtain and took a few deep breaths. Alessandro looked up from the desk at the same time her gaze fell on him and he blasted her with a dose of heavy-lidded heat. Every cell in her body leapt to attention.

'Nat, I've just put a Mrs Rothbury into cube ten,' Imogen said as she bustled by.

Nat dragged her eyes off Alessandro but not before she noticed a small smile touch his beautiful lips. 'Right. Cube ten. Check.' And she turned away without daring to look at him again.

It was like that for the rest of the shift. Wherever she was—he was.

Smiling at her with those private eyes as she handed over the twenty-six-year-old male who had accidentally ingested sterilising tablets instead of aspirin.

Brushing his fingers against hers as she handed him the chart of the forty-nine-year-old-woman who was having an allergic reaction to an unidentified substance.

Watching her intently as he moved his stethoscope around the chest of a twenty-year-old-male complaining of shortness of breath.

Grabbing her hips and lingering a little too long as he passed behind her in the cramped confines of a lift as they transported a thirty-six-year-old female who had suddenly gone blind in her right eye to CT scan.

And calling her Nathalie every chance he got.

By the time she was halfway through her shift, Nat's body was humming with desire like a damn tuning fork. He was everywhere and each hour cranked the anticipation up another notch. She doubted they'd get any sleep at all tonight.

Just after lunch Nat opened the curtains to cube nine and greeted her next patient. Seventy-two-year-old Mr Gregory, a five-year prostate cancer survivor, was complaining of hip pain. 'Hello, Mr Gregory, my name's Nat. Pleased to meet you.'

Her patient gave a loud hoot. 'Ron, please. Mr Gregory reminds me of my teaching days and as much as I loved it I'm damned pleased I'm not doing it any more.'

Nat laughed. He was a sprightly guy, tall and snowy-haired with crinkles around his eyes like he enjoyed a good laugh and clear blue eyes that contained a wicked sparkle.

'Ron it is.'

'Sorry to be such a damn nuisance. Bloody GP's making a fuss about nothing.'

Nat could hear a strained note in his voice and sensed that beneath all the sparkle and bravado Ron was a worried man. 'Better to be safe than sorry.'

'Hmph!'

Just then Alessandro pushed back the curtain and entered, and Nat felt the wild clenching of her stomach as his presence filled the cubicle. His gaze on her was brief but no less cataclysmic before turning his attention to his patient. 'Mr Gregory, what seems to be the problem today?'

Nat tried to listen to the examination but it was kind of hard to hear over the roar of her hormones. Even the way he doctored was sexy. He listened, he didn't assume or begin with preconceived opinions. He put his patients at ease. He let them talk and gently herded them back with a pertinent question if they wandered off track.

Alessandro put the stethoscope in his ears and Nat helped Ron get into a sitting position so Alessandro could listen to both back and front.

'I see you're not married, missy,' Ron said as he dutifully breathed in and out. 'Are young men blind these days or just plain stupid?'

Nat laughed. She was conscious that Alessandro needed Ron to be quiet and also that he could hear every word magnified through the bell of the stethoscope. 'Good question.'

'Or maybe you're just holding out for a more mature gent? Very wise. Take my generation, we know how to treat a lady.'

Nat laughed again. She was used to patients flirting with her, particularly men of Ron's age. She knew the drill. It was a bit of harmless banter to pass the time and take their minds off their problems. And if it helped distract Ron for a while then it would have served its purpose.

'What do you reckon, missy?'

'Well, now, that depends. What subject did you teach?'

'English.'

'Ah.' Nat sighed. 'I had the hugest crush on my high-school English teacher.'

'I see you're a woman of very good taste.'

Alessandro frowned as he finished listening to Ron's chest and eased the man back down. His patient was openly flirting with Nat and it was frankly annoying.

'He used to quote poetry all the time. I think I was a little in love with him.'

'Poetry? I can quote you poetry. Who's your favourite? Shakespeare? Shelley? Browning? Wordsworth?'

Nat tapped the man's wedding ring. 'Oh, and what would your darling wife say to that?' she teased.

'Ah, well as long as it was Shelley she'd probably forgive me. She's a sucker for Shelley.'

Alessandro blinked as Nat laughed and patted her patient's hand. A surge of undiluted jealousy spiked his bloodstream and he suppressed the urge to pick up Nat's hand and move it away from Ron's vicinity.

'We'll get an X-ray.'

Nat looked up, startled at the steely note in Alessandro's voice. Gone was the incendiary stare and the soft smile on his full lips. His mouth was a bleak slash and the planes of his face looked harsh and forbidding once again.

'I'll organise it.' He nodded at Ron. 'Excuse me.'

Nat frowned as they watched Alessandro leave. 'He's a bit of a grumpy old so-and-so, isn't he?' Ron dropped his voice an octave or two and gave her a sly wink.

Nat gave him a weak smile. 'I think he's just a little distracted.'

She did a set of obs on Ron, chatting with him a bit more about his heyday as an English department head. Then Nat excused herself, assuring Ron she'd be back shortly. Ellie was going to Theatre to have her appendix removed in half an hour and she needed to get her prepped and her pre-med given.

She headed to the small linen cupboard that was situated halfway down the main corridor that ran behind the cubicles for a theatre gown and hat. Alessandro strode towards her from the opposite direction. His powerful thighs made short work of the distance as he stalked closer.

His eyes commanded hers and held fast. She felt like he'd hypnotised her and she was powerless to resist as they moved inexorably closer. Even though his face was grim and his beautiful mouth, capable of such eroticism, looked almost savage.

They drew level and she frowned at him. 'Are you okay?'

Okay? He felt unaccountably not okay. A cold fist was lodged under his diaphragm as a primal emotion he couldn't put his finger on dripped icy poison into his bloodstream. He felt edgy and…tense. Like he needed to prowl. Or maybe go and hunt something…

Alessandro looked around the corridor. Satisfied no one was watching, he grabbed her arm and pulled her into the nearby linen closet, shutting the door.

Nat pulled her arm out of his grasp, jostling her even closer in the tiny room usually only meant for one person. She glared at him as the stuffy air, heavy with the smell of starch, tickled her nostrils.

'You like to flirt with other men?' he rasped.

Nat blinked. His accent sounded more pronounced and, glowering down at her, his gaze as glacial as black ice, he'd never looked more Italian.

'He's seventy-two, Alessandro,' she grouched, not quite believing she was having this conversation. 'He's worried, scared the cancer has come back. He needs someone to look at him as a person, not a chart number or a medical condition. It's harmless.'

Alessandro understood what she was saying. Hell, he even empathised. With any other nurse he would have applauded it. But not her. When she did it he felt the caveman deep inside roar to life. She was his. And he didn't care how crazy it was.

Without hesitation he backed her against the shelves, hands imprisoning her shoulders, and swooped his head down. Their lips met with a sizzle and his mouth opened wide, his tongue thrusting inside her already welcoming mouth. When she responded with a moan he pressed his body against hers harder so she was in no doubt that he desired her and she was his.

He pulled away as abruptly as he had pounced, taking a step back which was as far as the confines of the room would allow. His ragged breathing mingled with hers and filled the space as each stared at the other and caught their breath.

'Don't flirt with anyone, *bella*. I don't like it.' And then he turned, opened the door and left.

Nat reached for the shelf behind her as her knees wobbled and she practically swooned. She should be furious at such liberties. At such Neanderthal behaviour. But she didn't think she'd ever been on the other end of such a blazing kiss and frankly she was too turned on to do anything other than stare at the empty space and grin stupidly.

Nat was slightly preoccupied when she picked Julian up from the crèche that afternoon. Alessandro's kiss still blazed a tattoo on her lips and all she could think about was the coming night.

'I think he's coming down with something,' Trudy commented. 'He's been so much more interactive lately but today he was really quiet. He didn't eat much at lunch and he feels a little warm. We have had a couple of kids here coming down with flu.'

All thoughts of the night fled as concern rose to the fore. Nat placed her hand on Julian's forehead. He did feel a little on the warm side. She knelt beside him. 'Are you not feeling very well, matey?'

Juliano shook his head. 'I feel sore all over.'

His usually bright little eyes looked dull and his cheeks were flushed. 'Are your ears sore?'

Juliano shook his head. 'No.

'Your throat? Does it hurt to swallow? When you eat?'

He shook his head. 'No.'

It did sound like he was coming down with flu. She just hoped it wasn't the dreaded swamp flu that was all over the news. Not that they'd had any cases in Australia to date.

'Come on. We'll get you home and give you something for the fever. Papa can look at you when he gets home, okay?'

Julian brightened a little and Nat's heart did a little flip. It was gratifying to see that, even unwell, Julian was looking forward to seeing his father. They *were* making progress.

They arrived home half an hour later after stopping at the chemist to buy some medication for Julian's fever. Nat administered a dose and ensconced him in front of the television with Flo and strict instructions to stay settled.

Half an hour later Julian was in the kitchen, Flo in tow, seemingly back to his old self.

'I'm hungry.'

Nat quirked an eyebrow. 'You better now?'

Juliano grinned. 'Yep.'

Nat smiled. She hoped so but she wasn't convinced—it could just be the medication talking. Alessandro came home two hours later and she got him to check his son out. He looked in Julian's ears and down his throat and listened to his chest anyway.

'It all seems okay.'

Nat nodded. Alessandro's gaze bathed her in flame and it was hard to concentrate on anything other than him and what she was going to do to him when they were alone later.

By the time Julian was ready for bed a couple of hours later he was feeling warm again and looking a little subdued. She administered some more medicine which he took before Alessandro swept him up in his arms and carried him to bed.

Her heart gave a painful squeeze as Alessandro strode up the stairs with him. The way Julian's skinny little arms clung to his father's neck made her heart sing. They seemed like any other father and son and it was equal parts satisfying and, strangely, sexy.

Nat had a quick shower in her en suite, her thoughts bouncing from Julian's state of health to the thawing of relations between father and son to the smoulder in Alessandro's gaze that caused her skin to tingle everywhere as she scrubbed it.

She dressed in her pyjamas—a pointless exercise—and wandered out into her room at the same time Flo wandered out. Some kind of sixth sense alerted Nat to where her pet was heading. The cat didn't like to intrude on father/son time and seemed to have developed a fascination with Alessandro's bed—not that she could blame Flo.

'Flo,' she growled.

Flo ignored her, disappearing from sight. Maybe it was her mistress's scent, so ingrained in the sheets, that attracted her so strongly. Or maybe it was just some primal recognition of pure animal lust. Whatever the reason, Alessandro hadn't warmed as much to Flo as he had Julian.

AMY ANDREWS 131

She couldn't hear any of the usual giggles or excited interaction coming from Julian's room as she followed Flo's twitching tail down the hallway. Julian was obviously not his usual self.

'Flo,' she whispered at the cat as she crept into Alessandro's room to find her pet casually licking its leg in its favourite spot—the middle of Alessandro's huge bed.

At least the room was looking more lived-in now than the first night Flo had strutted her way in. They'd all gone through boxes marked *Master* last weekend and personalised Alessandro's room. Julian had been so excited when they'd come across a piece of pasta art he'd done for his father the previous year. When Alessandro had hung it in pride of place on the wall opposite his bed, his little chest had puffed out like a rooster's.

'Flo,' she said again, hands on hips, her low voice holding a note of warning as the cat continued to ignore her. 'You know you're not allowed in here, madam. Alessandro will not be impressed.'

A fine lifting of the hairs on the back of her neck alerted her to his presence a second or two before his arms encircled her waist and she was pulled back into the hard muscles of his front.

'Alessandro doesn't care as long as you're in here too,' he growled in her ear, applying pressure through his arms so she turned to face him.

Nat's breath caught in her throat as his gaze ate her up. There was wildness there, a level of desperation she'd not seen before, not even the first time.

'I've been thinking of you all day, thinking of doing this.'

He didn't give her time to process that. Time to even

suck in a breath as his mouth opened over hers and devoured every atom of oxygen in her lungs. He walked her backwards as she clung to him, dizzy from desire and hypoxia. And then his hands were plucking at the hem of her nightdress until somehow she was relieved of it and then his shirt was pulled out of his trousers and half his buttons were undone.

As they collapsed against the bed her hand had made short work of his zip and she could feel the heavy weight of his erection in her hand. His stubble scratched the soft flesh of her neck as he made his way down and she was parting her legs wider to cradle his hips, urging him closer.

'Alessandro!' She wasn't sure if she wanted him to slow down or go faster. Her mind was a blank. An empty space devoid of any thought, filled only with his scent and the sound of his out-of-control breath.

His mouth closed over a nipple and she cried out, almost convulsing with desire. His hands pushed at her knickers as hers plucked at his trousers. As soon as he had access he entered her and she dug her nails into his back, gasping as he slid home, stretching her, filling her, making her feel more female, more powerful, more helpless than she'd ever felt before.

He pounded into her with frenzied strokes, like a man possessed, and all she could do was cling to his shoulders as each jab built her to a crescendo of lust that contracted her muscles and energised every cell, innervating them to an excruciating awareness.

Alessandro felt the first jolt of his orgasm and crushed her close, burying his face in her neck. The sensation seemed to come from his very soul and he groaned and cried out her name.

Nat wasn't sure when it finished. It seemed to go for ever, suspending them on some plane that floated high even as it faded. It was almost as if she'd lost consciousness and wasn't aware of anything other than him until he grew heavy against her and her body moved involuntarily, protesting the weight.

He rolled off and somehow in the post-coital haze he managed to pull down the bed sheets and relieve them of their barely intact clothes. And then he was surrounding her again, spooning her, pulling her into him, pressing kisses into her neck, touching her breasts and between her legs. It was slower, lazier but Nat felt the heat building again quickly and gave herself up to the moment.

Several hours later, not long after they'd fallen into an exhausted sleep, Nat woke to a strange noise. Her eyelids flicked open and despite the pull of slumber she was suddenly instantly alert. Her heartbeat boomed in her ears as she strained into the apparent silence.

The she heard it again. A cry.

Julian!

Careful not to disturb Alessandro, she eased off the bed and groped around for her nightdress. Finding it discarded near the door, she threw it on and headed to Julian's room.

The muted glow from the illuminated fish tank by the window silhouetted Julian's tiny frame as he sat up in bed. 'What is it, matey?' she crooned.

'I've been sick,' he sobbed.

Nat, her brain still cloaked in slumber and her bones still heavy from sexual malaise, reached for the nightlight and snapped it on. Julian's hair was mussy from sleep, his face flushed. She could smell the acidic aroma of vomit and noticed the soiled bed linen.

She sat on the bed beside him and put her arms around his shoulders, noting immediately how warm he felt. 'It's okay, matey. Let's get you cleaned up and give you some more medicine.'

She helped him out of his soiled shirt and groped in his drawer for another. She picked him up and carried him into her en suite where she'd left his medicine just in case it was needed in the night. She administered the medication and then wet a washer and wiped his flushed face.

His fever now seemed to be accompanied by a runny nose and a slight cough. He denied a sore throat and ears and she resigned herself to shelving plans for a day at the beach and spending the weekend nursing him through flu. She carried him back towards his room but he clung to her neck and she didn't feel comfortable leaving him all alone in his bed when he was obviously miserable.

It didn't seem proper to take him into hers. She glanced at the open doorway at the end of the hallway. A memory from her childhood assailed her. She'd been seven and ill from something she couldn't remember now. But she could remember her mother bringing her into her parents' bed and how she had snuggled into her father. He had patted her back and curled his big arm around her and she had felt so safe and secure and loved. She'd felt like he'd held the cure for cancer in his palm.

It had been just before he'd left them and Nat cherished that memory like it was gold. Sure, her mum had always showered her with TLC when she was sick but without her dad and his big old arm there, she'd always felt a little less loved.

Nat didn't give it another thought. Everyone wanted to feel they were loved when they were sick. It was just…human. She crept into the room and onto the bed and laid Juliano next to his father.

Alessandro stirred and reached for her before he realised the situation. He half sat up and frowned. 'What's wrong?' he whispered.

'Julian's been sick. I think it's flu.'

Alessandro's first instinct was to refuse. Camilla hadn't believed in Juliano sleeping in their bed and her iron-clad opinions were ingrained.

Nat could see the indecision on his face. 'He's four years old. He needs you, Alessandro,' she said gently. 'There's no better place than Papa's bed when you're sick.'

Alessandro looked down at his son. Julian was looking up at him with dull eyes, a kind of hopeless despair giving them an added misery. He smiled down at him. *'Naturalmente il mio piccolo bambino, viene al Daddy.'*

Nat smiled. Her Italian may have been rusty but she knew enough to know Alessandro had consented, and by the look on Julian's face, he knew it too. Alessandro lay down on his side, wrapped an arm around Julian, pulling his little body close. He rested his chin on his son's head.

Alessandro's eyes drifted shut as did Julian's, but not before he'd tucked his hand in his father's. Nat sat and watched them for a few moments, her heart filling with an emotion she didn't want to investigate too closely.

They looked like father and son, like a family. Alessandro, the big protective patriarch, dwarfing Julian whose hand clung tight to his father's. Julian looked how she must have looked all those years ago safe in her father's embrace.

Content, secure, loved.

She sighed and eased herself off the bed, taking one long, last, lingering look before creeping out of the room. Even as she yearned to join them.

CHAPTER EIGHT

IT WAS amazing the difference a few weeks could make, Nat thought as she sat at a distance and watched Alessandro and Julian build a sand castle together down close to the shoreline. They'd spent the day at Noosa, swimming and playing beach cricket and eating fish and chips at one of the trendy little cafés that lined the board-walk.

There'd been a subtle shift ever since Julian had been laid up with flu for those two days. Whether Julian had been too sick to find the energy required to stay aloof or whether it'd had been Alessandro's complete attentive-ness, they'd come out of it much closer. It was like a bond had been forged—newer and stronger.

And they'd blossomed under it, opening to each other a little more each day. Chatter and laughter filled the house now instead of stilted conversation and the loud buzz of longing.

Julian smiled at his father. Sat next to him on the lounge. Sought him out to tell him things. He looked for hugs and went eagerly into his father's embrace. He'd lost that taut little set to his shoulders. The wary, defeated look that had haunted his features.

And Alessandro stopped looking a hundred years old.

It was heartening to witness and Nat just knew, as the sun beat down on her shoulders, that they were going to be okay. Sure, there would be moments when their grief and sadness would come upon them again, blindside them, but at least now they looked like they'd turn to each other for comfort and support.

At least they'd stopped looking to her for guidance.

'Nat! Nat!' Julian yelled, popping his head up from his all-fours position, waving an arm at her. 'Come and look at what Papa and I built!'

Nat smiled and rose. She'd deliberately taken a back seat over the weeks, pushing the two of them together at every opportunity. It did her heart glad to see father and son doing things together. To see Julian acting like a normal four-year-old. To see Alessandro looking less and less haggard.

But as she walked towards them, their dark, downcast heads together again, beavering away a bit more on their creation, she couldn't deny the tug at her heartstrings and the deep-seated yearning that rose in her chest. She knew it was good, as it should be, but she suddenly felt on the outside. Lonely.

'Isn't it great, Nat?' Julian enthused as she drew level with them.

Nat felt tears prick her eyes and was glad of her sunglasses. It was great on many, many levels. 'It's totally awesome,' she agreed, ruffling his hair.

Alessandro smiled up at her and winked. He was in a sun-shirt that clung to his torso like a glove and boardies that hugged his butt and thighs like a second skin.

'Have I said that's a great bikini yet?' he asked.

Nat gave a half-laugh despite her heavy heart. 'Once or twice.'

His lusty eyes laughed at her and stole her breath. They looked like the smoothed, flattened black pebbles on the beach, warmed by the sun and utterly inviting. She wanted to push him back against the sand and have her way with him. He was easily the best-looking man on the beach.

'Papa and I are going to collect some shells. Can you make sure no one knocks the castle down?'

Nat dragged her shaded gaze away from temptation. She took a breath. Excluded again.

But it was good—so good they were doing stuff together. That Julian wanted to do spend time with his father now, looked to his father first. A few weeks ago he would have wanted her. So this was good.

She swallowed. 'Absolutely, I shall guard it with my life.'

'Come on, Papa,' Julian said as he picked up the bright blue bucket and marched towards the lapping ocean.

Alessandro vaulted upwards his gaze tracking his son's meandering path. 'You'd better wear that bikini to bed tonight,' he murmured, before moving off to follow Julian.

The next day they were all making popcorn in preparation for a movie afternoon. Alessandro and Julian had walked down to the video shop in the morning and chosen a couple of Disney classics.

'Ah, I think that's enough butter, don't you?' Nat laughed as Julian drenched the popcorn.

'Spoilsport,' Alessandro teased, and then gave his son a wink. 'Come on, matey, let's go watch the movie.'

They brushed past Nat, who was momentarily paralysed by the teasing note in Alessandro's voice and the way his sex appeal boosted into the stratosphere when the smile went all the way to his eyes. The fact that he seemed to have adopted the endearment 'matey' for his son was also rather…touching.

The doorbell rang, momentarily distracting her from her ponderings, and she absently called out, 'I'll get it.'

Quite who would be calling on a Sunday afternoon she wasn't sure. Maybe it was the little boy next door? He and Julian were the same age and she had told his mother that he was welcome any day for a play.

The entrance hall was warm and welcoming now with a large colourful rug breaking up the glare of the all-white tiles. Two large paintings decorated the walls on opposite sides and a hall mirror that had come from the ceramic ovens of the Amalfi coast hung by the door.

Last night Julian had helped his father hang a wind chime they'd bought in Noosa. He had passed tools to his father like a scrub nurse would to a surgeon and afterwards they'd stood, necks craned, Alessandro's hand on Julian's shoulder, admiring their handiwork.

The beautiful baby-pink mother-of-pearl discs, brittle and fragile, had cost a small fortune. But Julian had loved how they cascaded like a chandelier. And they certainly gave the entranceway a touch of mystique.

Nat opened the door. The person standing there was far removed from a little boy and very definitely Italian. He was tall and bronzed like Alessandro with an easy grin that emphasised killer dimples and a wicked glint to his brown eyes that would have put a pirate to shame.

So this is what Alessandro would have looked like had grief not hardened his features and permanently furrowed his forehead. The grin on the stranger's face quickly faded and Nat realised that not only was he staring at her rather fixedly but he was also frowning.

'Can I help you?'

As if he knew he'd been caught staring he recovered quite well and shot her a dazzling smile. 'Er…hi? I think I might have the wrong house. I'm looking for Alessandro Lombardi.'

The accent was like Alessandro's too and there was a similarity to this man that told Nat he was some sort of relation. She tried to ascertain his age. His face was smooth, unlined save for a few tiny crows' feet around his eyes, no doubt from laughter and, unlike Alessandro's, his hair was totally devoid of grey. A younger brother, maybe? Did Alessandro have brothers?

Bad time to realise she knew nothing about him. For crying out loud, she still didn't even know his wife's name.

Nat smiled back and held out her hand. 'No, you've got the right place. I'm Nat.'

The man shook it, smile firmly in place, his gaze studying her face intently. It wasn't creepy but it was disconcerting. Maybe he was surprised to find Alessandro shacked up with a woman so soon after his wife's death?

She opened her mouth to explain, feeling unaccountably depressed as their hands disconnected. But what exactly could she say? She turned her head and called out, 'Alessandro!' He could explain. Maybe he knew what the hell they were doing.

Alessandro appeared in a few seconds, his face lighting up like she'd never seen before. 'Valentino! *Il mio cugino! Così buon vederlo!*'

Nat understood enough to know the stranger's name was Valentino and they were cousins. She watched as the men embraced and Alessandro kissed both of his cousin's cheeks. It was surprisingly sexy. She'd always loved that about Italian men. The way they so openly expressed their affection, no matter which gender.

That just didn't happen in Australian society. And she couldn't help but feel it was the poorer for it.

They laughed and clapped each other on the back and then embraced again. Nat was jealous of their easy affection and she looked away as if she was intruding on an intimate moment.

'Valentino, I'd like you to meet Nathalie.' Alessandro looked down at her. He could see the confusion in her gaze and he smiled at her. 'Nathalie, this is my cousin, Valentino Lombardi. All the way from London via Roma.'

He clapped Val on the back again. Considering they'd practically grown up together, it was wonderful to see him. Val had emailed last week to say he would be in town some time in the next month for an interview but he hadn't expected him so soon.

'Nathalie.' Valentino reached for her hand and kissed it. 'It's a pleasure to meet you.'

Nat blinked at the old-fashioned greeting. She got the feeling that Valentino Lombardi was an incurable flirt. Had she not been totally immersed in Alessandro, she might have even been charmed. But Valentino seemed like a boy in comparison. More like Julian than Alessandro. Too…carefree. Too…casual for her tastes.

'Come in, come in.' Alessandro ushered his cousin inside. 'Julian will be dying to see you.'

As if he'd been called, Julian suddenly appeared. 'Uncle Val?' He looked at the person in the doorway for a second, not quite believing who it was. 'Uncle Val!'

'Juliano!' Valentino held out his arms and the little boy ran straight into them. *'Il mio ragazzo caro, meraviglioso vederlo!'*

Julian hugged his uncle's neck tight. 'I missed you, Uncle Val.'

'And I you, *bello bambino.*'

'I'm not a bambino,' Julian denied hotly.

Valentino roared. 'Of course not. *Scicocco me!*'

Nat watched the family reunion, feeling even more on the outside than ever. 'I'll just go and put on a pot of coffee,' she murmured, pointing in the direction of the kitchen and taking her leave.

Alessandro and Valentino watched her go. Valentino turned shrewd eyes on his cousin. 'Alessandro, *che cosa state facendo?*'

Alessandro looked at Val's furrowed brow. *Good question.* What the hell was he doing? *'It' indennitia di s.'*

Val rocked Julian in his arms. 'Fine?' He raised his eyebrows. 'She's the spitting image of—'

'Conosco che l'fare di m,' Alessandro interrupted. He did. He did know what he was doing.

'Fate?'

Was he sure? Yes, he was. 'She's nothing like…' Alessandro couldn't say her name. Not in front of his son. *'You il ll vede,'* he explained.

And Val would see. Alessandro knew it would only take his cousin a few minutes in Nat's company to see she was nothing like Camilla. Not remotely. He didn't see the physical resemblance any more. He couldn't even remember the last time it had struck him.

They moved into the lounge and Val stayed for the afternoon, drinking coffee and beer and reminiscing. Alessandro felt a familiar spike of jealousy as Julian sat so eagerly, so naturally on Val's lap. He'd always adored his Uncle Val.

It had taken for ever to build up the same rapport with his son. But, then, he supposed Julian had always associated wild and carefree Uncle Val with fun and good times. And Julian, beneath everything that had happened, beneath the sadness and grief, was still a four-year-old boy.

And Uncle Val's lap was only temporary. Before too long his son switched places and had crawled onto his lap, content to listen to Val from the shelter of his father's arms. Alessandro looked over at Nathalie, his gaze triumphant, and she smiled back at him with understanding eyes.

He doubted they ever would have got where they were without her.

Nat left them to it as much as possible. It was another of those family-type events that were important to Julian. Important to them both to bond as a family, and she didn't want to intrude. Of course she caught snatches of conversation as she came and went, both in English and Italian, and it was obvious the cousins were close.

She remembered now that Alessandro had mentioned Val to Paige all those weeks ago. Was it Val's mother who was the deaf aunt he'd mentioned? The one he'd spent a lot of time with growing up? His second mother?

She guessed that explained their affection.

At one stage she caught the tail end of a conversation about women. Alessandro had obviously asked if there was anyone special in Val's life. Along with a hearty laugh, he got this response. 'The word is full of beautiful women, Alessandro. Why limit yourself to just one?'

It was pleasing to see Alessandro shake his head.

She asked Valentino to join them for tea but he excused himself citing jet-lag and the need to prepare for his interview in the morning. Alessandro and Val made plans to meet for lunch tomorrow.

As they stood to say their goodbyes Alessandro's pager beeped. He took it off his belt. 'Looks like we've just had our first confirmed case of swamp flu.'

Nat winged an eyebrow. 'Where?'

'Victoria.' He embraced Val again, doing the very European double-cheek peck. 'Do you mind if Nathalie sees you to the door? I really need to ring work.'

'It will be my pleasure.' Val grinned.

Alessandro glanced at him sharply as Nat headed for the door. Valentino, much like his name, was an incorrigible flirt. But this woman was off limits. Val was charming and despite there being only six months between them, used his younger years and baby face to his advantage. '*Recidi*, Valentino,' he growled low but steady.

Val looked at Alessandro's flinty obsidian eyes and nodded his head slightly. '*Naturalmente.*' And he followed Nat out of the room.

Valentino joined her by the door momentarily and she smiled at him, holding out her hand. 'It was nice meeting you,' she said.

Val took her hand and once again turned it over and kissed it. 'Thank you, *bella*.' He released her hand and looked at her for a long moment. 'Alessandro and Juliano are doing well. Much better than the last time I saw them. You're good for him, I think.'

Nat blushed at the speculation in his gaze. 'Oh, no, it's not like that. I'm just…helping out until my place is built.'

Val gave her a small smile and bowed. '*Arrivederci.*'

And then he was gone but she was left in no doubt that Valentino Lombardi hadn't believed her for one single moment.

Nat and Julian were sitting on the lounge, watching the television, when Alessandro rejoined them. 'Is it bad?' she asked.

'No.' Alessandro shook his head and sat beside them. Julian automatically crawled into his lap and he unconsciously opened his arms to accommodate his son. 'Fit, healthy forty-year-old male. But there'll be more.'

Nat watched the easy affection between them and her heart swelled. 'Had he been travelling?'

'Yes. He's just got back from South America. They're chasing down his fellow passengers and his other contacts now.'

Thanks to geography swamp flu, a mutant form of influenza A, had, until today, been kept from Australia's shores. But it had been declared a pandemic by the World Health Organization and there were protocols that had to be followed.

Julian's thumb had crept into his mouth and he giggled at something on the television. Alessandro rubbed his chin against his son's hair, his arms momentarily tightening around his little body. 'It was good seeing Uncle Val again, yes?'

Julian's thumb slipped out as he turned and looked at his father. 'Oh, yes. I love Uncle Val. I like being called Juliano.'

Nat watched Alessandro's smile slip a little and prayed he'd tread carefully. The first day they'd met he'd reprimanded her for using the Italian version of his son's name, citing his dead wife's preference for it to be anglicised. She could tell then it hadn't been his choice but he was just trying to stick with the wishes of the woman who had given his son life.

'You like that, *il mio piccolo bambino*?' Julian nodded enthusiastically. 'You know Mummy liked you to be called Julian.'

Nat held her breath. She'd rarely heard Alessandro talk about Julian's mother with him. Occasionally, as they'd emptied the boxes they'd come across something and Julian had mentioned his mother. Nat had encouraged it, had encouraged Alessandro to facilitate it. After all they should be able to talk about the woman they both loved so dearly. But neither seemed keen to talk openly.

Using the 'm' word now seemed like another good step forward in their relationship. Julian nodded. 'I know. But I like Juliano better.'

Alessandro raised his eyes to Nat. They looked like polished river stones—black and glassy with emotion. She could see the rush and tumble of feelings there as they swirled around. Would he insist on sticking to Camilla's dictates or would he follow his son's lead?

Alessandro looked down at his son, his heart stretching in his chest, growing bigger, like a balloon ready to burst. He'd expected tears, withdrawal, a return to the sadness at the mention of Camilla. Not a matter-of-fact reply.

'I can…' He hesitated and looked at Nat. She nodded at him and he continued. 'I can call you Juliano too, if you like.'

Both Alessandro and Nat held their breaths this time as they hung on Julian's reply. The boy simply nodded, said 'Okay', stuck his thumb back in his mouth and returned to watching the television.

Alessandro let out his breath. He looked at Nat who was blinking back tears. She smiled at him and he wanted to pull her close, put his arm around her and snuggle her in beside them, feel her head drop onto his shoulder. But Nat's very sensible insistence that they keep their relationship from Julian…*Juliano*…stopped him.

So he smiled back at her instead and mouthed, 'Thank you.'

Alessandro's elation didn't last long. By the time he'd finished reading to Julian—*Juliano!*—he was seething with frustration. It shouldn't be this hard to call his son by the name he had been christened with. It shouldn't feel so unnatural. He wanted to kick things, yell, shake his fist at God.

He wanted Nat. He wanted to tumble her into bed, pound into her, make all the thoughts that circled endlessly in his head, like vultures around prey, go away. She'd help him to forget, if only for a few hours. She always helped him forget.

Nat was coming out of her shower when Alessandro grabbed her, pulling her naked body hard against his, lowering his head to claim her mouth in a kiss bordering on savage. She responded instantly, twisting her head to give him all he needed, clutching at his shirt for purchase as the power of the kiss almost knocked her backwards. She gave way to his questing tongue, opening to him, and he growled triumphantly low in his throat.

He pulled back slightly, his breathing harsh, his hands kneading her bare buttocks. 'I need you. Now.' He was so close his lips brushed hers with every word.

Nat could feel his hardness even through the layers of his clothes and her eyes practically rolled back in her head as she fought the urge to rub herself against him like some half-crazed feline. He was so close and the smell of him, the taste of beer on his breath, his mere presence was intoxicating. She could barely think for the pheromones that were clogging her senses as their chests heaved in and out, loud in the quiet of the house.

But she knew something was wrong. He'd been so happy earlier, had gone into Juliano's room with a spring in his step. And now he was looking at her with trouble tainting the lust and desire.

She pushed against his chest. 'What's wrong, Alessandro?'

Alessandro's arms tightened around hers momentarily and then he sighed and stepped back. Damn her for being so shrewd. He raked a hand through his hair as his gaze raked her body. Despite his inner turmoil she was butt naked in front of him and he wanted her. 'Nothing,' he dismissed, reaching for her.

Nat stepped to the side, evading his touch. 'Alessandro.'

He heard the warning note in her voice despite the mesmerising sway of her breasts as she moved. Then she shook her head at him, rolled her eyes, reached for her nightdress at the end of her bed and threw it on over her head.

'Better?'

Alessandro shot her a grudging smile. 'No.' She sent him a reproving look and crossed her arms. He sighed and felt for the edge of her bed as he sat down. 'It feels so strange calling him Juliano. And it shouldn't. *Inferno!* He's half Italian, for goodness' sake. It should come naturally.'

He felt suddenly impotent, despite the raging hard-on in his pants. Pushing off the bed, he stalked around the room. Damn Camilla and their screwed-up relationship.

He turned to face Nat, rubbing at his forehead. 'He was christened Juliano.' He dropped his hand. 'Camilla insisted on it.'

Nat stayed very still. Camilla. So that was her name. She frowned. 'So why Julian?'

Alessandro snorted. Because it was just one of the ways Camilla had screwed with him, made him pay. But he couldn't say that to Nat because as far as she was concerned he was still in love with his wife and what kind of a man did it make him to admit he wasn't? Admit he'd never loved her in the first place?

He sighed. 'It's a long story.'

He looked sad and defeated and she felt dreadful that he'd gone from being so happy to deeply troubled. Had Valentino's arrival dredged up old, painful memories?

'Can we please just go to bed? I want you.'

Nat's stomach clenched at his blatantly sexual request. She'd hoped he'd take this opportunity to get some stuff off his chest but just because he finally uttered her name it didn't mean he was going to open up about Camilla.

A stronger woman would have pushed harder. A stronger woman would have insisted they have it out for once and for all. But the way he expressed his desire, the way he looked at her with those wounded eyes, she knew she'd give him anything. She pulled the nightdress up over her head and opened her arms to him.

Much later in his bed, Nat lay draped down his side, her head on his shoulder, his fingers absently running up and down her arm. Sleep hovered around them in a post-coital haze that was both energising and paralysing at the same time.

She rubbed her cheek against his shoulder, revelling in its warmth and their combined aroma. Her hand was resting on his belly and she trailed her fingers up his chest. 'Val looked at me very strangely this afternoon when I opened the door.'

'He was probably trying to work out how available you are,' Alessandro murmured. The mere thought punched him in the gut, even though he knew the real reason his cousin had given her such a strange look.

'You seem close.'

Alessandro smiled. 'We grew up in the same village. Our fathers were brothers. My parents, they were very…passionate people…they argued, a lot. They split up and got back together and split up and got back together. They were up and down like yo-yos. I would get shuffled to Aunty Rosa's when things were in upheaval. Which was often. It didn't matter that she was deaf or had six kids of her own, she always took good care of me. She and my uncle had this totally different relationship. Ben adored Aunty Rosa.'

'Did you have siblings?'

'No. Just me. Which was probably a good thing.' Even though as a kid he had yearned for siblings like Val. Someone to share the burden. 'My father finally left for good when I was fourteen and my mother really fell apart. We both moved in with Rosa after that.'

Nat heard the dull ache in his voice and felt it all the way down to her soul. She rolled on her stomach and propped her chin on Alessandro's chest. 'Did you miss your father?'

Alessandro dragged his gazed from the ceiling to mesh with the warm welcoming glow of hers. 'Not really. I barely knew him. He travelled with his work a lot. He wasn't exactly a hands-on father. He left it up to my mother mostly. And then when he was home they were usually arguing.'

Nat's heart broke for him. Her own memories of her father, before he'd walked out, couldn't be any more different. Maybe that explained Alessandro's clumsy fathering. No solid role model. Maybe he too had left it up to Camilla.

'I'm surprised you married at all with that kind of history.'

Alessandro looked away from her knowing eyes, his fingers stilling on her arm. If only she knew. It had never been his intention to marry. He'd been more than happy playing the field and having a damn fine time doing so. His childhood had cured him of the romantic notion of finding 'the one' and he'd been merrily working his way through the rest.

And then Camilla—clever, sexy, cool-as-ice Camilla—had fallen pregnant. Deliberately.

He looked back at the ceiling, his fingers resuming their feather-light strokes. 'You sound like you talk from experience. Are your parents divorced too? Is that why you haven't ever married?'

Nat shut her eyes as he firmly changed the subject. She'd obviously pushed him far enough for one night and he'd revealed all he was going to—which was a hell of a lot more than she'd known to date. They didn't do this—talk. They had sex until they fell into exhausted slumber. Talking had never been high on their list of priorities. But suddenly she wanted to know everything there was to know.

She sighed and turned on her side again, draping her

arm across his chest, her leg over his thigh as she pondered his question. She didn't want to talk about herself but maybe if she did, he might open up some more about himself.

'My father left when I was eight.' Her words fell into the silence and she felt Alessandro's finger falter temporarily before starting up again. 'No warning. He'd been having an affair for a year and the other woman, Roxanne, was pregnant. So he just…left.'

Alessandro heard the slight wobble in her voice and tightened his arm around her. 'I'm sorry.'

Nat shut her eyes. Why after all this time was the devastation still so potent sometimes? 'It was never the same after that. I spent time with him and Roxy and the kids over the years, Mum made sure of it. I have two wonderful half-brothers. But it was like he'd moved on from me. Sure, he still loved me, I knew that, but he just stopped being a father to me, like I stopped being his responsibility.'

Nat swallowed the lump that had lodged in her throat. It had been a long time since she'd thought about this stuff. 'He had his new wife and his boys and I was just always…an afterthought. The old love and affection we had was gone. He became withdrawn from me, emotionally distant, and I always felt like—still do, I guess—that I had to prove I was still worthy of his love.'

It didn't take Alessandro long to figure out why Nat had felt such an instant rapport with Juliano. When he looked back now at the distance between him and his son not that long ago he cringed. Thankfully she'd been here to show them the way.

'It must have been hard for you to watch Julian…' Alessandro shook his head. '*Juliano*. In the beginning.'

Nat nodded. 'I could see the way he looked at you with such longing and it reminded me of the way I used to look at my dad after he'd left. I know the situation was different with you two, that grief was involved, but…'

'It's okay,' Alessandro assured her. 'I knew we were in trouble, I just didn't know how to fix it.' He kissed her forehead. 'And then you came along.'

Nat smiled and snuggled closer. 'Super-Nat to the rescue.' Alessandro chuckled and her heart filled with the sound of it. 'Pity I wasn't so good at fixing my own problems.'

'Is this about the man you talked about in the lift that day? You said it had become untenable.'

Nat nodded. 'He was newly divorced when I met him and that was probably my first mistake. But he was so sad, so knocked around by life and so kind and caring and he was so happy to be happy again, with me, I fell in love with him. He was endearing.'

Which was exactly why being here with Alessandro was stupidity. Alessandro and Juliano were just history repeating itself. Except it was worse. Rob and his wife had chosen to separate. Alessandro hadn't chosen for his wife to be taken from him.

'So what happened?'

'His ex-wife was in his life, our lives, a lot.'

'You didn't like her?'

'I liked her fine. But I don't think either of them ever really let go. He spent more and more time with her, making excuses to see her. A leaky tap. A family wedding. A Valentine's Day meltdown. And after years of coming second to her I just couldn't do it any more.'

'That does sound untenable.'

Nat shut her eyes, the skin on her arms turning to goose-bumps as Alessandro drew circular patterns with his fingers. It had been awful. A long slow death, hanging on, hoping things would change.

'C'est la vie.' She shrugged. 'By the end there wasn't really any love left. Just hurt. I'm over it now.' She didn't want to talk about Rob any more. Or her father. It was his turn.

'What about your wife? Camilla? How did she die?'

Alessandro's fingers stopped abruptly. He couldn't talk about Camilla. Not to her. Not to anyone. He could barely utter her name without waves of guilt pinning him down. She had no idea how much it had cost him to say her name earlier.

He shifted, displacing her temporarily, and then moved over her, settling his pelvis against hers. 'I think we've talked enough for one night, don't you?' And he lowered his head, dropping a string of tiny kisses up her neck and across her jaw.

Nat should have protested. God knew, she wanted to know everything about him but she felt her body respond to his weight and his smell and the way his mouth found all her sensitive places. And did she really want to know about the perfect Camilla and their perfect love? Hadn't she had enough of that in her last relationship?

So she didn't push him away and insist on talking. She didn't get huffy. She didn't get up and leave his bed. Instead, she shut her eyes and let him sweep her away to the place she knew he could take her.

There'd be enough time for talking when she moved out and their relationship came to an end.

CHAPTER NINE

THE following Thursday afternoon Nat led Alessandro into cubicle fifteen to examine a thirty-eight-year-old woman complaining of a sore leg. She had her nine-month-old baby boy with her, who was crying and irritable.

Alessandro smiled at the rather harried-looking woman who apologised about the noise as she jiggled the babe on her hip. 'He's picked up a bit of a cold so he's not exactly a happy camper at the moment.'

'That's okay…' he searched for the patient's name on her chart label '…Nina. What seems to be the problem?'

'I've got this really sore leg,' Nina said.

'Why don't you give the baby to Nat and hop up here so I can have a look?'

Nat smiled at Nina and the baby and held out her arms. 'What's his name?' she asked.

'Benji.'

'Come on, Benji. Let's give Mummy a bit of a break.'

The baby went willingly enough, sneezing three times during the transfer. 'Bless you, bless you, bless you,' Nat cooed, stroking the baby's warm forehead as she settled him on her hip and began swaying.

Alessandro was momentarily distracted as he watched Nat with Benji. The baby had stopped crying and was looking at her curiously as Nat's ponytail swished with the rocking of her hips. Nat chose that moment to look up at him and he gave her a lazy smile.

She looked good in her uniform. She looked good in shorts. She looked good in her nightdress. And she looked absolutely sensational out of it. He should have guessed she'd look good with a baby on her hip.

Nina, oblivious to their undercurrent, climbed up onto the gurney, swung her legs up on the mattress and proceeded to roll up her jeans. 'That's a bit of a climb, isn't it?' she puffed.

Alessandro's wandering attention returned to his patient. 'So, have you injured yourself in any way?' he asked half his brain still engaged with other thoughts. Images of Nat last night straddling him, smiling down at him.

Nina shook her head. 'My calf's been sore ever since I got off the plane yesterday.'

Suddenly Alessandro's brain snapped into laser-like focus. 'Plane?' He frowned. Painful calf. Air travel. DVT? 'Where did you fly from?'

Nina's brows furrowed. 'Perth.'

Alessandro's gaze sought the area that Nina was rubbing. Perth was only a four-hour flight, which made it less likely for a blood clot to have formed in the deep veins of her leg but it wasn't unheard of. And Nina was a little overweight.

'But I guess that was only a day after our flight from London,' Nina continued. 'Boy was that an awful flight. I was stuck in my seat the whole time with Benji needing to be fed constantly because of the cold playing havoc with his ears. He drank practically all through the flight. It's times like those I wished I'd chosen the bottle over the breast all those months ago. At least his father could have helped out.'

Alessandro's antennae started twitching crazily. Firstly, without even laying hands on her, he could see the swollen red area of Nina's calf. That didn't bode well. But secondly, and perhaps the most importantly, as far as the big picture went, was Benji's cough. It may have seemed quite innocent when Nina had walked in—just another childhood cold. But teamed with the word 'London' it was potentially much more.

Swamp flu was prevalent now in the UK as well as the Americas. The cases they'd had in Victoria had all been carried into the country through international air travel, although not yet from the UK. It was certainly causing all kinds of consternation and hot on the heels of several deaths worldwide some schools with infected students in Melbourne had been shut down as a precaution.

There'd been nothing in Queensland yet but due to the worldwide level six pandemic status there were procedures he had to follow. He didn't think for a minute that Benji had swamp flu but he knew he couldn't let them leave without making sure.

But first things first. Alessandro gently examined Nina's calf, the concentrated area of heat obvious beneath his palm. He felt for a pulse at the back of her knee and also felt for her foot pulses. 'Can you draw you toes back towards your knee?' he asked.

Nina complied, wincing as a hot arrow streaked straight to the centre of her sore calf. 'Ouch.'

'Hmm.' Alessandro urged her back against the pillow. 'I'm just going to feel for a pulse in your groin,' he said. He located the full bound easily. 'Any chest pain?' he asked, taking his stethoscope out of his ears and placing the bell on her chest.

'Nope.'

Satisfied her lung fields sounded clear, he helped Nina up into a sitting position. 'I think you may have something called DVT. Have you heard of it?'

Nina screwed up her face. 'That clot thingy? The one they do the talk about on planes?'

Alessandro nodded. 'Yes. You have the classic symptoms and your forced immobility on the long-haul flight definitely put you at a higher risk. We'll get an ultrasound to confirm the diagnosis.'

Nina looked at him, a worry line between her brows. 'I'm not going to die, am I?'

'They are potentially very dangerous but we've caught this in time and we can treat it.'

Nina looked relieved. 'So…what happens now? Do I have to go into hospital? I have three other kids as well as Benji.'

'I'm afraid it will mean a short hospital stay. We need to start you on a special intravenous drug that helps to thin your blood. And once you have therapeutic levels you go onto an oral form of the drug and you'll need to be on it for several months.'

Nina looked at Nat. 'Holy cow.'

'Can your husband get time off work?' Nat asked. 'Or do you have family to look after the kids?'

Nina nodded. 'My husband is still on holidays till next week. Luckily I have plenty of expressed breast milk in the freezer.'

Nat smiled. 'I'll refer you to our welfare worker as well. She can help with any of the logistics.'

Nina shot her a grateful smile. 'Thanks.'

'There's another thing,' Alessandro added.

Nina raised an eyebrow. 'Oh.'

'I'm going to have to test Benji for swamp flu, I'm afraid.'

Nina's eyebrows practically hit her hairline. 'Swamp flu? You think my Benji's got swamp flu?' She held her arms out for her baby and Nat handed him over.

'No. I don't think he has it. I think in all likelihood he has a common cold but I'm afraid there are certain protocols I'm governed by now because of his symptoms and the fact that he's just come from another country where the infection is prevalent.'

Benji, who was squirming and protesting his mother's tight hold, stopped as soon as Nina relaxed. 'Oh.' She kissed her son's head. 'But what if he does have it?'

'We'll start him on some special antiviral medication, which will help lessen the duration and vigour of the symptoms. We'll have to get the infectious disease team involved who'll track all contacts. The rest of your family will need to go into home quarantine immediately—just in case.'

'For how long?'

'Seven days. But we should have the test results back by tomorrow afternoon so hopefully only a day until they come back negative. You'll have to be nursed in isolation too until we know the results.'

'Hell. What a mess.'

'Yes.' Alessandro nodded. That was putting it mildly. 'But, as I say, I really don't think you've got anything to worry about. Okay?' He patted her hand and smiled. 'Let's just take this one step at a time.'

Nina's worried expression dissipated beneath Alessandro's comforting gesture and calm authority. She nodded. 'One step at a time.'

Nat and Alessandro left the cubicle a few minutes later. 'I'll call ID and X-Ray. We'll have to get a mobile ultra-sound,' he said. 'Get an urgent NPA on both of them and move them to an iso cube. Limit numbers in there and make sure anyone going in wears a gown and mask.'

Nat nodded as she prioritised his rapid requests, feeling the thrill of medicine in action. She loved working with him almost as much as she loved sleeping with him.

The next afternoon Nat was smiling to herself as she opened one of the few remaining boxes stacked in Alessandro's formal lounge area. She could hear father and son chattering away as they cooked tea together and she was looking forward to the weekend.

This time with Alessandro and Juliano had been satisfying on levels she hadn't thought possible as she'd watched their journey back to each other. And she was going to miss them when she left.

But, in the meantime, there were still boxes to get through. The progress had been slow as Nat had given priority to activities that kept Juliano and Alessandro together and focused on the future. Going to the beach, heading to the movies, taking a ferry trip on the river, playing soccer in the park.

Sure, going through the boxes was also something they did together and helped them connect. They talked about the things inside and it was interesting learning about their lives before they'd entered hers. But she was more than aware that it wasn't a task Alessandro relished—the memories, she guessed—so she found it was better in small doses.

Still, as she looked around the house she couldn't deny the sense of accomplishment. Emptying the boxes, decorating Alessandro's house, seeing it turn from an igloo into a warm, welcoming home, also helped by the flowering of the father/son relationship, had been immensely satisfying.

Something that had started out as a way to help, a thank-you to Alessandro for his generosity, had become much more. And seeing the dividends it was paying in every aspect of their lives was very special.

She settled on her haunches next to the nearest box and opened a lid, finding yet another stash of linen. Whoever the mysterious Camilla had been, she'd had impeccable taste. Egyptian cotton sheets and the very best quality hundred per cent duck-down quilts—a bit unnecessary in Brisbane but too beautiful to shove in a cupboard and ignore.

As she reached in to pull out the next sheet her hand knocked against something hard and she peered in. Something was wrapped in the sheet. She felt it—it was about the size of a large book but not as bulky. Was it the elusive photos Alessandro had assured her were in one of the boxes? She'd almost forgotten about them over the intervening weeks and all their distractions.

Nat's heart tripped in her chest as she gingerly unfolded the fabric to find the back of a photo frame staring at her. She felt nervous as her fingers advanced tentatively towards the object. Was she ready to come face to face with Camilla? Her hand shook a little as she turned it over.

She needn't have worried. It was a photo of Juliano as

a baby. He was sitting like a little chubby Buddha in a sailor suit with a little sailor hat plonked artfully on his head. He was grinning at the camera, one hand stroking a sleek black cat.

She smiled. She couldn't help it. Juliano looked so happy. Loved, content, secure. Not a worry in the world—as it should be. So different to the boy she'd first met. How unfair was it that in only a few short years after this candid snap his whole world would be turned upside down?

The resemblance to his father also struck her. Looking at Juliano, she had a glimpse at what a young Alessandro must have looked like. Dark hair, dark eyes, olive skin and cherubic lips. She traced Juliano's mouth with her finger, so like his father's. And that sparkle in his eyes. One that she was seeing more and more of in Alessandro's gaze these days.

He must have been a beautiful baby.

She dipped into the box, eager to see more, her hands finding the tell-tale signs of more frames wrapped in sheets. She pulled them out one by one, unwrapping them like Christmas presents, each one a moment captured in time, a window, an insight into Alessandro's life.

Most of the frames held pictures of a solo Juliano at various stages of his life, chronicling his four years. Crawling. Walking. His first birthday party. But there were two with other people. One with an older Italian-looking woman holding Juliano in what appeared to be a christening gown. Alessandro's mother? Or maybe his aunt? Valentino's mother?

And the other with Alessandro on the London Eye, the magnificent Houses of Parliament forming an imposing backdrop. Juliano looked about two and both he and

Alessandro were pointing at something outside the glass bubble and beyond the view of the camera. It was obviously a candid shot. Father and son had been caught in fierce concentration, not smiling, their brows wrinkled, their faces frozen in serious contemplation.

It was strikingly similar to how they'd both looked when she'd first met them. Unsmiling, serious. But there was an ease in the older photograph that hadn't been evident then. Their heads were almost touching, Alessandro's hold was loose and comfortable and Juliano's little arm around his father's neck spoke volumes about his innate trust.

Nat dragged her gaze away from the photo and put it aside, delving for more. The next several frames were academic qualifications of Alessandro's. She spent a few moments trying to decipher the formal Italian, practise her rusty command of the language. But it was too academic for her and she put them aside with a mental note to make sure this weekend they tackled Alessandro's office.

The box was almost empty now, with just two folded sheets sitting on top of some plump cushions. Without even having to look further, Nat knew these were the frames she'd been looking for. Finally she'd get to see the woman who had won Alessandro's heart and for whom he still grieved.

Oddly, she hesitated. After weeks of internal speculation about Alessandro's wife she wasn't sure she wanted to know. What if she was simply the most gorgeous creature she'd ever seen? Could her ego stand that? And yet there was a part of her that needed to know and she cursed it. Cursed her innate female curiosity. Her vanity.

What had Camilla Lombardi looked like? Beautiful, no doubt. Glamorous too, she'd bet. She couldn't see Alessandro, a breathtakingly handsome man who must have had his pick of women, marrying anyone less than stunning. Had she been dark and exotic like Alessandro or maybe a glamorous redhead with milky skin and green eyes?

She stared down at the sheets. Was she ready to come face to face with Alessandro's dead wife? The woman who'd claimed his heart. She drew in a ragged breath at how much it hurt to think of him being loved by another woman. How much it hurt to acknowledge that even when he was buried deep inside her, pounding away, his heart belonged to someone else.

Goose-bumps marched across her skin and she rubbed her arms. This was stupid! They were no more than convenient lovers and she had no right to such thoughts. And his wife was dead. Did it matter what she looked like?

She reached for the sheets and pulled them out of the box, unwrapping the first one and refusing to pay any heed to the knot in her gut. She flipped the frame over briskly, businesslike, mentally chastising her hesitancy. Her eyes instantly connected with an eerily familiar pair of blue ones.

And everything in that moment crashed to a halt. Her heart stopped in her chest. Her breath stilled in her lungs. The synapses in her brain ceased to function. The frame fell from suddenly nerveless fingers and slid off her lap. A loud rushing noise echoed in her head and she couldn't hear anything above the roar. It sounded like she was in a wind tunnel or in the centre of a tornado.

A terrible dreadful sense of déjà vu swept through her, paralysing her with its ferociousness.

It wasn't until her lungs were burning, bursting for

breath, and her vision started to blacken at the edges that her body kicked into survival mode and took over. Her jaw fell open, her lips, completely independent of her will, pursed into a tight pucker, sucking in a desperate breath.

Nat coughed and spluttered as it rushed in, abrading her oxygen-starved membranes. She fell forward, extending her arms to stop herself collapsing altogether. She hung her head, eyes squeezed tightly shut as the coarse white carpet pricked at her palms. She gripped it hard as she gasped for breath, for sanity.

She didn't know how long she sat there, fighting for stability in a world that had suddenly tilted on its axis. She panted and rocked on her haunches like a woman in labour waiting for the contractions to stop, for the pain to ease.

It felt like hours could have passed when she finally opened her eyes and the world slowly came back into focus. Camilla's clear blue eyes looked calmly back at her from the frame on the floor. A small smile hovered on the other woman's perfectly made-up lips, like she'd gotten everything she'd ever wanted in life and she knew it.

A splash of moisture fell on the frame and Nat blinked. She felt her cheeks, surprised to find tears running down her face. The same sort of face that looked back at her from the glass. Same blue wide-set eyes, same blonde ponytail, same high cheekbones, generous mouth and pointed chin with the cutesy-pie cleft.

Nat shook her head as her earlier thoughts came back to haunt her. *Did it matter what she looked like?* She couldn't believe it had only been mere minutes ago that she'd been that innocent. That she'd ever been that innocent.

She picked up the frame and stared at the familiar

contours of the other woman's face. *They could have been sisters.* Her and Alessandro's dead wife. Their resemblance was uncanny.

The knowledge punched her in the gut.

Nat climbed awkwardly to her feet, clutching the photo, her legs rubbery, numb from sitting too long in her cramped position. She stood motionless staring at the dead woman's face, feeling like her heart had been ripped out of her chest and stomped on. Feeling rage and impotence and desperation in equal measure as the awful, awful truth sank in.

She was in love with Alessandro.

In love with a man who was still so in love with his dead wife he'd chosen a look-alike replacement with no thought to the consequences.

Her sense of loss was so profound not even the sobs that were choking her chest, threatening to strangle her, could find an outlet. She could hear a low kind of keening and knew it was coming from her, but didn't seem to be able to stop.

It was like Rob and her father all over again. Worse. Way worse. She'd had to compete with two women in her life for the affections of men she'd loved deeply. But at least those women had been alive. Tangible. How did she compete with a perfect memory? A ghost?

And, *goddamn it,* why was she always the bridesmaid and never the bride with the men in her life? Why was she always second choice? Wasn't she good enough? Lovable enough? Her father had left her for a new family. Rob had left her for an old one. And Alessandro?

Nat heard a little voice inside her ask the question she'd never allowed herself to ask. Had always felt selfish even thinking it. *What about me?*

'Nat! Nat!'

Nat jerked as Juliano came haring into the room, jumping up and down. She hugged the frame to her chest automatically as Juliano babbled on.

'Daddy and I have cooked the tea. It's his nonna's recipe from Roma and it's so delicious.' He paused, bunched his fingertips together and kissed them for dramatic effect, like Nat had seen Alessandro do the other night in the kitchen. Normally she would have laughed but she was barely taking any of it in.

'He says as long as it's okay by you I can go and play with Flo in the back yard but I have to make sure I wash my hands afterwards before I eat dinner because that just good hygiene.'

Nat blinked, her sluggish brain catching up with Juliano's rapid chatter several seconds later. She noticed some movement in her peripheral vision and glanced up to see Alessandro lounging in the doorway in the half-light like a big lazy cat. She looked at him helplessly. Even now, even knowing what she did, even mad as hell, her body still responded to the blatant sexuality of his.

'Nat!'

Her attention returned to the excited little boy in front of her hopping from one foot to the other. 'That's fine.' She nodded.

'Yippee-ee!' Juliano took off, heading for the lounge room and calling for Flo.

Alessandro pushed off the doorframe and prowled towards her. With Juliano occupied outside he had a hankering to kiss her. Last night seemed forever ago. 'How many boxes to go now?'

Nat's heart boomed in her chest as she read the intent in

his black eyes. A part of her wept inside as she realised she'd never kiss him again. She took a step back as he advanced.

Alessandro frowned as he entered the arc of light spilling across her. She looked pale and shocked, her blue eyes red-rimmed and flashing with pain. 'Nathalie!' He took two quick steps towards her. 'What's wrong?'

Nat took another step back, moving her arm out of the way as he reached for it. He stopped and looked at her, his frown deepening.

Nat released the frame she was holding and turned it around. 'When were you going to tell me about this?'

Alessandro's gaze flicked down to the object he hadn't even noticed she'd been holding in his haste to touch her. Camilla's face stared back at him, her Mona Lisa smile taunting him. So like the woman in front of him. And yet so not.

He shuttered his gaze as the painful memories assaulted him. Their loveless marriage, the argument, the knock on the door. He stuffed his hands into his pockets. 'Ah.'

Nat felt the casual comment right down to her toes. *Ah*? He knew. No what-the-hell-are-you-talking-about? frown. No immediate this-isn't-what-it-looks-like explanation. He knew.

Oh, God—it all made so much sense now. The way Juliano had looked at her that first day like he'd seen a ghost. Followed by Alessandro's own, more subtle but definitely, looking back at it now, stunned reaction later that same day. And more recently, Valentino's double-take.

She shoved the frame at him, pushing it hard into his abdominal muscles and releasing it as his fingers closed around it. 'Is that all you've got?' she demanded. His face was the grim mask of old. She couldn't tell whether he was desperately searching for an explanation to give her or whether he just didn't give a damn.

She scrubbed at her face. 'You know, Alessandro I knew you had an ulterior motive when you asked me to stay. I knew you wanted me to be some kind of substitute mother. But I had no idea what you really wanted was a substitute wife!'

'No!' His denial was swift and certain. Yes, the evidence was damning but how could he explain to her that the physical resemblance was where the similarity between her and Camilla ended? Without going into all the sordid details? Without exposing his guilt and shame? He didn't talk about that. Not with anyone. 'You are nothing like her.'

Nat couldn't tell whether it was an affirmation or an insult. She stabbed her finger at Camilla's frozen face. 'That's not what I see.'

'Trust me,' Alessandro intoned. 'The resemblance is only skin deep.'

Nat snorted. 'Trust you?' She stared at him incredulously. 'Why should I do that? When you haven't trusted me? Hell, Alessandro, you had the perfect opportunity to tell me the night Val visited. I asked you why Val had looked at me so strangely. And you dismissed it.'

Nat shook her head, feeling an edge of hysteria building. 'No wonder you weren't keen for me to find these pictures. Why weren't you just up front with me from the beginning? Why didn't you say, "Gee, Nat, you look freakily like my beloved dead wife"?'

Beloved. She thought he was still in love with his wife. Well, of course, he castigated himself, why wouldn't she? Marriage did imply love and it hadn't even been a year yet.

Alessandro watched as tears splashed down her

cheeks. He took a step towards her, the urge to pull her into his arms, to comfort her, overwhelming. But she took another step back from him and it was like a blow to his solar plexus.

He opened his mouth to deny it, her tears clawing at his gut. But how could he say the words aloud? *I didn't love her. I didn't love my wife.* What kind of a man did that make him?

Alessandro shook his head helplessly, wanting to wipe away her despair but shying from the words he knew he'd have to use. 'It's not like that.'

His generic reply cut deep. 'God,' she wailed. 'This is just like Rob all over again. Like my father. Playing second fiddle to another woman.'

She'd bounced back from her father. She'd had the love, understanding and support of her mother and other family. And her sunny personality. And she'd come through the Rob nightmare too—a little more bloodied and battered but still with belief in herself and in others.

But she knew without requiring any deep thought or analysis that her love for Alessandro far outweighed anything she'd ever felt for Rob. The slow gentle realisation of her feelings that she'd experienced with Rob was chicken feed compared to this all-encompassing, bubbling cauldron of desire and emotion Alessandro had hurled her into and been marinating her in for these last magical weeks.

She looked at Alessandro's emotionless face. The only sign that any of this was affecting him was the clench of his jaw. 'Did you ever just want me for me?'

It was a startling thing to admit to herself. But she knew she was right. While she'd been falling in love he'd just been using her body to try and erase the memory of his wife.

Loving the one he was with.

It certainly explained his insatiability. The almost desperate way he reached for her every night. Pounding away deeper, faster, harder, like he was afraid she'd evaporate in his arms if he wasn't constantly touching her.

Alessandro flinched at her accusation. 'I think I've more than adequately shown you how much I desire you.'

She looked at him like he'd just grown a second head. Desire? He might as well have reached into her chest and ripped out her haemorrhaging heart. When you loved someone, desire was just an empty vessel. It meant nothing without love.

'Really, Alessandro? Can you honestly stand here and tell me that every night with me, every insatiable moment, it was about me and not some kind of sick reconnection with Camilla?'

Alessandro felt a rage building inside. He knew she'd been played by men but he'd never use a woman in the way she was accusing. Surely she could see that his desire for her was one hundred percent genuine? 'That I can guarantee,' he ground out. 'When I've been in bed with you there's been no one else. I'd have thought you'd know me well enough by now to know that deep in here.' He tapped her chest.

Nat's heart beat frantically beneath his fingers as if it was trying to touch them. Traitorous organ! She knocked his hand away. 'This isn't about sex, Alessandro. It's about love.'

Alessandro blanched. What the hell did love have to do with it? 'Love?'

Nat flushed. Her chest had swollen with a mix of emotions that threatened to crush her and the truth had tumbled out. She hadn't meant to blurt it like that but she was damned if she was going to back away from it now.

'Yes, Alessandro, love,' she threw at him. 'I'm sorry, I know that this wasn't about love but it happened anyway. I guess I'm not quite as callous as you.'

Alessandro raked his hand through his hair, feeling more and more out of his depth. 'Nathalie…'

Nat shut her eyes and shook her head vigorously. 'No. Don't say anything.' She couldn't bear to hear any platitudes. 'I'll be out of your hair before you know it.'

Alessandro reeled a little more. She was leaving? The thought was shocking. 'But…your place won't be ready for weeks yet. What about Juliano? You can't just up and leave with no notice. He adores you.'

Nat felt a sob rise in her throat. His son did. But he didn't. Not quite the impassioned plea she'd hoped for, even though somewhere inside she felt a surge of pride that he was at last thinking like a father. Thinking about his child even before himself.

And he was right—leaving Juliano would be heart wrenching too. She loved the boy as much as the father. But at least she knew they now had each other.

She shrugged. 'I'll tell him something has come up and a friend needs me.'

'Where are you going to go?'

Nat didn't have a clue. All she knew was she couldn't stay here another minute. She felt like she was bleeding and it was sure as hell going to make a mess on Alessandro's perfect white carpet.

'I don't know. Paige's maybe. A hotel.' She shook her head. 'Frankly, I don't care. Just away.' She backed up as she spoke. 'Far away from here.'

Alessandro reached out and snagged her arm before she could run away. He couldn't bear the idea of her gone. 'Please don't go. We need you.'

Once it would have been enough. But she was tired of men needing her too much and not loving her enough. Now she knew the true depths of love—its power, its breadth— she knew she couldn't settle for anything less.

Nat shook her head. 'No, you don't. Not any more. You two are going to be just fine.' She pulled out of his grasp, her heart breaking, her soul aching.

The phone rang and they both looked at it, suddenly becoming aware of the surroundings outside their immediate circle of misery.

'You'd better get that,' she murmured, backing away.

Alessandro ignored it. 'Nathalie,' he called after her.

Nat turned away, the desire to run from him crippled by overwhelming misery and the weight of her heart in her chest. The stairs before her suddenly seemed like Mt Everest, her room way beyond at the summit.

Alessandro watched her go. He couldn't remember ever feeling so impotent. But she was asking too much. Love? Didn't she know that he wasn't worthy of her love?

The phone's insistent peeling nagged at him and four angry strides brought him level with the infernal contraption. He snatched it off its cradle.

'Yes?' he snapped.

Nat had almost packed her bag when Alessandro strode into her room. She was crying, tears blinding her progress. Her hands were shaking and her breath occasionally caught on a sob.

'Stop packing.'

Nat gave a harsh laugh. 'Go to hell.'

'That was the ID director from St Auburn's. The baby yesterday we screened for the swamp flu tested positive. As of now we're both on seven days' home quarantine. I'm afraid you're going nowhere.'

CHAPTER TEN

THE only person remotely pleased about their enforced confinement was Juliano. Having never had his father's absolute attention for an extended period, he thought all his Christmases had come at once. He even suffered the daily nasal swabs that were couriered to and from the house with a cheerful disposition.

He was completely ignorant to the suddenly stilted atmosphere between Alessandro and Nat. He didn't notice the strained politeness or the wary avoidance of any kind of physical contact. Not even the absence of laughter or easy conversation penetrated his happy little bubble.

But Nat was excruciatingly aware of it. It was a double loss. Not just the loss of what could have been but what they'd already had. It had been a surprise for her to realise the feelings for Alessandro that had stealthily invaded her every cell were love and a particularly cruel blow to discover it at the very second it was ripped out of reach. It had become crystal clear to her in that moment they'd never be able to return to what they'd had before.

Alessandro had tried to broach the subject again that next morning but she'd cut him off at the pass with a frosty 'Don't'.

She didn't want to hear any platitudes. She didn't want to watch him tie himself into a verbal pretzel with pretty euphemisms. She didn't want to know his justifications. The truth was he had hurt her way more than Rob's or her father's rejections ever had. At least they'd declared their outside interests from the beginning.

Alessandro had been utterly disingenuous.

After three days in home quarantine, or house arrest as Nat had come to think of it, she was at screaming point. If she hadn't been young fit and healthy she might have begun to worry about the constant pain in her chest and the heaviness in her limbs. Her jaw ached from the continuous fake smile she wore and her eyes felt gritty from three nights of crying herself to sleep.

She despised the nightly ritual more than anything. But no amount of internal dialogue castigating Alessandro and his deception derailed the tears. Her mother would say they were healthy, that she was grieving and they were a painful and necessary part of the healing process, but Nat would have done anything to stop them.

She wished she could be more like Paige whose opinion of men since her husband's desertion had always made her wince. Paige wouldn't have fallen for Alessandro. Paige's heart was guarded by barbed wire and thorny bushes a mile thick. Why hadn't she done that to hers? After her father? After Rob? Wrapped it up, protected it? Why had she been lumbered with this damn eternal optimism?

Because even now, despite everything, she wanted him. Every time he looked at her with his black eyes, she felt her pelvic floor muscles shift. Every time he walked by, her nipples pebbled as if he'd brushed his hand across them. Every time he opened his mouth, she wanted to kiss it.

Despite his soul-ravaging betrayal. Despite knowing he didn't feel the same way about her. Despite knowing that every time he looked at her all he saw was his dear, darling Camilla.

She was helpless against his pull. Oh, she hated herself for it but that didn't seem to matter either. Why? Why did love have no pride?

But mostly she was worried. About her willpower. If her belly lurched just at his nearness, how was she ever going to steal herself against him? How was she going to walk out the door? How strong would her resistance be by the end of seven days? Lord knew, it had been three days now since they'd shared a bed and despite how mad she was, she wanted him on top of her and inside her with an almost crazy desperation.

What if he asked her to stay again? Would she sacrifice her integrity and stay? Like she'd stayed with Rob, hoping it would be different? Like she'd held out hope that her father would, one day, remember that he also had a daughter?

No, seven days couldn't come around soon enough. Putting on an act for Juliano was a bigger strain than she'd ever thought it would be. And it felt wrong to lie to him. She knew how it felt to find out you'd been lied to. Only too well.

On the evening of the third day she excused herself after tea. She had a headache and was feeling weary. The sleepless, teary nights were catching up with her.

'You haven't eaten much,' Alessandro commented as he inspected her almost full plate.

She stared at him, absently rubbing her bare arms that had suddenly become covered in goose-bumps. 'I'm not very hungry these days.' It was said pleasantly enough for Juliano's ears but her gaze left him in no doubt as to the cause of her poor appetite. She couldn't afford to soften her stand or let her guard down. 'Excuse me.'

Alessandro watched her go, his hands fisting in his lap. He wasn't sure whether he wanted to shake her or kiss her. It had certainly been a long time since he'd tasted her lips and her flushed cheeks and red mouth had drawn his gaze tonight like a moth to flame.

He knew he deserved her contempt. Looking at it from her perspective, his actions must have seemed extraordinarily callous. But he wasn't sure he could stand four more days of the cold shoulder.

It was like his marriage all over again. Constantly pretending everything was all right for Juliano's sake and for those outside their marriage. The stress of projecting the illusion of marital bliss had been a constant drain when it had all been a sham.

'What's wrong with Nat?'

Juliano's question broke into his reverie. He smiled down at his son. 'She's fine.' He smiled. 'Why?'

Juliano shrugged. 'She's really quiet. And she looks sad.'

Alessandro was surprised by his son's insight. They'd both been trying to carry on as normal, to protect Juliano, but he was obviously a lot shrewder than they'd given him credit for. This wouldn't do at all. Surely for four more days they could make more of an effort?

By the time Nat was halfway up the stairs waves of goosebumps were marching across her skin and every footfall jarred through aching hips and knees. She shivered and rubbed her arms, her shoulders protesting the movement. Great! Marvellous. Just what she needed—swamp flu.

Her chagrin with Alessandro vanished as fantasies of a

steaming-hot shower took over. If only her room didn't seem so far away. She held onto the rail and gritted her teeth as she hauled herself closer. After a shower she was going to bed. With a little luck she'd sleep for three days and then this whole quarantine thing would be over and she could get as far away from Alessandro Lombardi as was possible.

She entered her room, walking straight past her bed, and started pulling at her clothes, tearing them off, uncaring where they fell. Her teeth chattered as more and more of her body was exposed to the air. She stepped into the shower cubicle and flicked on the taps, shivering as she waited for it to heat up and then gratefully stepping into its fiery embrace.

But still she felt cold, so cold, beneath the spray and she reached for the taps, reducing the amount of cold water till it was practically scalding. She sighed when it finally seemed hot enough, leaning her forehead against the tiles as it seeped into her tissues, her bones, her marrow.

It had been years since she'd had flu and Nat had forgotten how truly horrible it could be. She felt dreadful. Her head ached, her joints felt like they were on fire, her throat was scratchy and she didn't need a thermometer to know she had a high fever.

As if a broken heart hadn't been enough to contend with.

Alessandro left Juliano sitting on the lounge with Flo, watching a DVD, ten minutes later. He needed to talk to Nat, whether she wanted to or not, and he didn't want little ears listening in. He heard the shower as he entered her room and his gaze tracked her path to it from her discarded clothes.

He hesitated for a moment but, hell, he had seen her

naked before. They'd showered together numerous times. Had even had hot, wet, soapy sex on more than one occasion. He was damned if he was going to tiptoe around in his own house!

He strode into her en suite, stopping in the doorway to lean his shoulder casually against the jamb. The bathroom was full of steam and even if he'd wanted to catch a glimpse of her wet naked body, the fogged glass made it impossible. 'Maybe I should have installed a sauna in here for you,' he said dryly.

Nat's head shot up and she winced as her neck objected to the sudden movement. 'Get the hell out of here, Alessandro.' She was hoping for assertive but her voice had developed a croak and it sounded more desperate than definite.

'Nothing I haven't seen before,' he drawled.

Satisfied he couldn't see her through the fog, she placed her forehead back against the tiles. 'Nothing you're ever seeing again,' she grouched.

'I want to talk to you.'

Nat shut her eyes as her head thumped. 'Yeah, well, I don't want to talk to you.'

Alessandro's jaw tightened. 'It's about Juliano. It's important. Now, we can do it out here or I can come in there but we *are* having this talk, Nathalie. Now.'

Nat heard the menace in his voice and believed him. She felt so wretched all she wanted to do was burst into tears but she'd done that too much lately as it was. She was sick of feeling weak and helpless around him. Surely she could stand it as long as they focused on Juliano? And then maybe she could go to bed and sleep for a week.

'Fine,' she muttered, flicking off the taps. 'Pass me a towel, please.' She waited a moment or two and one appeared over the top of the shower stall. She grabbed it and gave herself a brisk once—over, every joint groaning but thankful that the shivering seemed to have been remedied by the hot water.

The fogged screen didn't allow her much of a view but she could see a dark figure looming in the doorway. Nat wished she had the gumption to waltz from the shower completely naked and sail past him with utter indifference. Just to show him what he was missing out on. But she knew she didn't have the guts to pull it off.

'My nightdress is hanging on the rail.'

It too came over and she quickly pulled it on. Her knickers were outside in a drawer—she could worry about them after Alessandro had had his say.

She took a moment to gather herself and then pulled the door open, walking gingerly from the stall. A blast of cool air hit her heated skin and the hairs on her arms stood to attention. Her stomach lurched as she took in his casual stance. His tie was long gone and his top button was undone. His sleeves were rolled up to his elbows, baring strong forearms covered in dark hair. Her already wobbly knees weakened further. The overhead light glinted off his hair like moonbeams off a dark sea.

'If you're going to try and justify what you did, you're wasting your breath,' she warned as she pushed past him.

Alessandro counted to ten before he turned to face her. *No, he wasn't.* It was better this way. Let her think what she wanted. It couldn't be worse than names he'd called himself. If this was his punishment for entering into a loveless marriage, for the argument with Camilla and its subsequent domino effect, so be it.

He didn't want neither did he deserve her feelings. He'd squandered love once already and now he was paying. He didn't expect happiness.

His gaze roved over her face. Her cheeks were flushed from the hot shower. She looked all pink and fresh. He could smell soap and he wanted to pull her close and bury his nose in the place where her neck met her shoulder. He shoved his hands in his pockets.

'I told you, it's about Juliano,' he said gravely. 'He knows something is up. He's worried about you.'

The thought that Alessandro's precious little boy was worrying about her was touching. She pictured his uptight little face when she'd first met him and knew she couldn't bear to see him so solemn again.

'I was thinking today we should float the idea of me moving out at the end of the week so it's not sprung on him,' she said. 'We'll tell him the unit's finished earlier than expected.'

Alessandro nodded with difficulty. She'd made such a difference in their lives it was hard to believe she'd been in it for such a brief time. Like Mary Poppins. Juliano, who'd already been through a major loss, was going to miss her. So would he. He already missed the smell of her and her warmth plastered to his side as he lay in bed at night.

'Perhaps in the meantime you could act like we haven't been quarantined for ebola?'

Nat glanced at him sharply, each neck vertebrae groaning in protest. 'I beg your pardon?'

'Well, you haven't exactly been your usual touchy-feely, happy-go-lucky self,' Alessandro pointed out. He missed that the most. The little smiles she'd give him, the brush of her hand on his arm or his back as she went by, the quick automatic ruffle of Juliano's hair.

Nat felt another shiver quake through her abdominal muscles as her ire rose. She wrapped her arms around her middle and glared at him. 'Gee, sorry bout that. I don't know what on earth could have come over me.'

Alessandro watched a spark of anger glitter in her eyes and her cheeks redden further. 'I never meant to hurt you, Nathalie.'

'Yeah, well, you did, Alessandro,' she snapped. 'So you'll have to forgive me if I can't just shake that off and act like nothing happened.'

Her bitterness was tangible and Alessandro felt lower than snake's belly. The last thing he'd wanted to do was hurt another woman. Especially one who had come to mean so much in such a short space of time.

But, damn it, he'd never promised her anything. Certainly not love or any kind of happy ever after. Same with Camilla. She'd known the deal when they'd married. But she'd never tired of turning the screws ever tighter. The weight of his guilt was like a boulder on his chest and sometimes he felt like he could barely breathe.

He was sick of carrying around all that extra weight. He'd let Camilla pile it on him but standing in front of Nathalie he was suddenly utterly over being the guilty party. 'I never asked you to fall in love with me,' he snapped.

Nat's head was throbbing again and her body felt like one giant bruise. It hurt to talk, it hurt to think, but something goaded her on. Maybe it was the flu—she'd never been this bitchy with Rob. After years of sharing she'd just accepted that she couldn't compete with his ex and let him go. But this was like a festering wound and deep inside she knew it needed lancing.

'No, you didn't. It was just about the sex, wasn't it? And what a bonus you got in me, huh?'

Alessandro ignored the edge of hysteria. He'd never seen her so riled. But her assertion that he had just been using her body was way off base. It may not have been love but it had been more than a superficial physical liaison—of that he was certain.

'I think you know I feel more deeply than that,' he said tightly. 'How many times have I shown you these last weeks?'

Nat wasn't sure if it was the fever or his simplistic statement that caused her hysterical laugh. 'Sex?' Her eyebrows practically hit her hairline as her voice rose an octave to almost a squeak. She felt her blood surging through her neck veins and pounding around her head, flushing her cheeks further. Her head felt like it was about to blow off her shoulders.

He had to be joking! 'Sex isn't love, Alessandro. No matter how many times you do it.'

The fervour in her eyes was compelling. '*Inferno*,' Alessandro roared. She was being impossible. 'I only meant—'

'Stop it, stop it, stop it!'

Alessandro and Nat looked down as Juliano hurled himself between them. He had tears streaming down his face and was clutching Flo in his arms.

'Juliano!' Alessandro crouched down and hugged the distressed little boy in his arms. How long had he been watching them?

Nat was speechless. What an awful thing for him to

have witnessed. The poor darling had probably never witnessed a man and a woman arguing like this. She felt a rush of light-headedness as she stroked Juliano's head.

Alessandro glanced up at Nat in time to see her sway dangerously. 'Nathalie?'

She heard his voice coming from far away as her vision blackened at the edges, becoming narrower and narrower. 'Alessandro?' she whispered as she stumbled forward.

He reacted quickly, catching her before he was even fully upright. She slumped against him as if her bones had dissolved and he frowned as her heated skin scorched his. *Inferno!* She was burning up. He swept her up into his arms. 'Nathalie?' He shook her gently, her limbs swinging limply rag-doll fashion.

'Papa?'

Alessandro could hear the fear and worry wobble Juliano's voice. Nat stirred and murmured something unintelligible. 'It's okay, matey. She's just fainted.'

Alessandro gave her another shake. 'Nathalie? Are you okay?'

Nat could vaguely hear him. She sighed. It was bliss to have the burden of keeping upright taken from her. 'Damn flu,' she muttered.

'Is she sick, Papa?'

Alessandro looked down at Juliano. 'I think she may have flu.'

Juliano's eyes grew saucer-like. 'Swamp flu?'

'I'd say so.' Alessandro looked at the bits and pieces of paper, the three books and two magazines littering the surface of her bed. 'Come on, Juliano, help me get her into bed.'

Juliano also looked at the bed and then shook his head. 'No. Your bed. When I was sick you let me sleep in your bed. And Nat said there's no better place when you're sick then Papa's bed.'

Alessandro gave him a wry smile. Somehow he didn't think she'd meant it to apply to her. But he looked down into her flushed face. She looked so…still. He couldn't bear the thought of her sick and alone. Plus, given the flu's severity it would help him keep a closer eye on her. She may well hate him for it in a couple of days but Juliano was right.

He grinned down at his son. 'Good thinking, Juliano.' And he strode out of her room with Juliano and Flo trotting behind.

Juliano stayed with Nat while Alessandro went downstairs to get her some of the antiviral medication they'd been given in case one of them did come down with flu. It wasn't going to cure it but hopefully it would reduce the severity and duration. He also grabbed a couple of cold-and-flu tablets he had with his other medicines.

When he returned, Juliano was stroking Flo with one hand and Nat's hair with the other. 'She's still sleeping, Papa,' he said earnestly as Alessandro sat on the side of the bed.

He smiled at his son. 'I imagine she'll be sleepy for a couple of days.' He reached out his hand and shook Nat's shoulder gently. 'Nathalie, wake up. I have some tablets for you.' She didn't move so he shook her a little firmer.

Nat prised her eyes open even as sleep fought to tug them closed. The room was dim and her surroundings were blurry but somehow though she knew she was in Alessandro's bed. His smell surrounded her.

Their smell surrounded her.

She half sat, displacing Flo. 'I shouldn't be in here. I don't want you to catch it.' And for about a million other reasons.

'The best place when you're sick is Papa's bed,' Juliano repeated gravely.

Alessandro smiled. 'Juliano's recent flu will probably be more than sufficient immunity and I got flu in January so don't worry, I reckon we'll be fine. Anyway, it's too late now. If we're going to get it, it's already incubating.'

He opened his palms to offer her the pills and was grateful when she didn't argue any more. He passed her a glass of water to swallow them with. 'The results from your nose swab today should be in tomorrow so we'll know for sure whether it's swamp flu.'

Nat nodded wearily as she sank back into the pillows, her eyes already shut. 'Hmm,' she muttered as she drifted towards a dark abyss.

Alessandro put Juliano to bed a couple of hours later and checked on Nat again. She'd kicked her coverings off and was lying in a fairly good likeness of the recovery position, her back to the door. Her nightdress had ridden up and he could just see a glimpse of bare cheek. He'd forgotten she wasn't wearing any underwear. He strode across the room, pulled the sheet up and got the hell out.

A few hours later he came up again with some more tablets. The sheets were kicked off again but she was much more decent this time, having rolled onto her back, her clothes covering her completely.

He woke her and she roused only enough to swallow the pills and slurp down some water before collapsing back against the sheets again. He pulled the covers up and headed back to his office.

It was well after midnight when he returned to his room for the night. He was tired and couldn't avoid it any longer.

The sheets were off again when he entered and he smiled to himself. She was worse than Juliano. He left her as she was for the moment, knowing he'd pull them up when he joined her after his shower.

He lingered under the spray, his mind wandering to the peek of bare flesh he'd had earlier. It seemed like months since he'd touched her intimately. Run his hand over the curve of her bottom, had it snuggled into his groin.

Knowing she was back in his bed and had nothing on beneath her nightdress was having a predictable effect and he quickly turned the hot water off, bracing himself against the cold spray. *Inferno!* She was sick, for God's sake. Feverish and fluey. How dared he let his libido take control?

He towelled himself off briskly and threw on some cotton boxers and a T-shirt then gently eased into bed, careful not to disturb her. She was on her side again, her back facing him. He lifted the sheet over her, his hand touching her arm to gauge her temperature, pleased to find her skin was cool to touch.

Maybe she'd be spared a severe infection and recover quickly? After spending half the night scaring himself sense-less by reading swamp flu stats, he hoped so. The thought was comforting anyway and despite doubting he'd be able to sleep at all he actually drifted off with surprising ease.

He woke half an hour later to Nat's shaky voice and groping hands trailing fire down his abdomen.

'I'm s-so c-cold,' she stuttered, her teeth chattering as her body, like a biological homing device, instinctively sought the nearest source of heat.

Alessandro automatically bundled her closer, pulling her into his side, his hand rubbing up and down her arm.

Despite her shivering, she felt very hot and he knew she was having rigor.

Nat felt some relief from the cold that bit at her arms and legs and nipped at her fingers and toes as she absorbed the warmth from Alessandro's body. Her teeth chattered and she whimpered as her whole body trembled violently, shaking through already inflamed joints and her thumping head.

'Shh,' Alessandro murmured as he rhythmically rubbed her back and arm. 'Shh.'

She tried to snuggle closer. Tried to press as much of herself against him as possible, tried to become absorbed into him, into his heat, into his vitality. 'So c-cold.'

'Roll onto your other side,' Alessandro murmured.

Nat protested but he was moving and turning her gently, his hand on her hip, and with his help she rolled over. And then he was wrapping himself around her, spooning her, pulling her into his big warm chest, covering her limbs with his and plastering himself to every square inch of exposed skin.

It felt heavenly and she almost groaned out loud. She felt him kiss her hair and she nestled closer. Somewhere beneath the fever and the chills and the aches and pains she knew it was wrong but frankly she was too sick to care and as the rigor held her in its grip she'd never been more thankful to be held.

Nat wasn't sure of time and place when she woke alone the next morning. The curtains were drawn, only a few rays of sunlight finding the gaps. It took a few seconds to realise she was in Alessandro's bed and the memory of him holding her, spooning with her, in the middle of the night returned in a rush.

She looked over her shoulder to see the bedside clock. Her neck was stiff and her head felt all fuzzy, like she'd been given a lobotomy in the middle of the night and her skull stuffed with cotton wool.

Ten a.m.

'Ah, you're awake.'

Nat rolled on her back. He was standing in the doorway in shorts and T-shirt, his hair ruffled, his jaw dark with stubble.

'How are you feeling?'

'Like I've been run over by a truck.' Her mouth was dry and she licked her lips.

'Fancy some breakfast?'

Her stomach revolted at the very thought. 'Just some water.' She ran her tongue across her teeth. 'And a toothbrush.'

Alessandro grinned as he entered the room. 'Here are your next lot of pills. Why don't you take them, get up, have a shower and come back to bed?'

A shower sounded like bliss but just stretching her legs was a challenge. They felt like someone had been punching them repeatedly all night. She looked in the direction of her bedroom and doubted she could walk that far. 'I'm not sure I'm up to the trek.'

'Use my en suite. I'll get you some fresh clothes.'

He'd gone before she could answer and she was too weary to argue. It was, after all, the most sensible suggestion. And it wasn't like it was uncharted territory for her.

She shuffled to the side of the bed and slowly sat upright. A wave of light-headedness assaulted her and she shut her eyes until the dizziness passed. She downed the tablets and then stood gingerly on rubber legs, walking slowly to the shower.

Nat felt as weak as a newborn foal standing beneath the water and knew despite the luxury of the spray needling her skin she wouldn't be able to stay there for long. She leaned against the tiles, made a paltry attempt at throwing soap in all the right places and then shut off the taps.

She poked her head out of the screen and found a towel and clean pyjamas, even a pair of knickers hanging over the rail. She leaned against the vanity as she dried and dressed, her gaze falling on her toothbrush sitting next to Alessandro's.

She reached for it, catching a glimpse of herself in the mirror. She looked exactly like she felt, like a wrung-out dish mop. Pale, drawn, dark circles under her dull eyes, hair hanging limply around her face.

Her body was starting to ache again as she exited the bathroom, holding onto the walls for support. The freshly made-up bed was close but seemed light years away suddenly. She practically crawled to it and sank gratefully into its cool depths, utterly exhausted.

The aroma of clean linen filled her nostrils and on an empty stomach it was quite dizzying. She vaguely marvelled at the domesticity of it all. Toothbrushes side by side, clean sheets, her water glass topped up. If she hadn't been so weary it might have depressed the hell out of her, but it was nothing more than a fleeting thought before sleep once again sucked her under.

A few hours later Alessandro climbed the stairs to check on his patient. He'd just come off the phone from St

Auburn's, who had confirmed that Nat had indeed contracted swamp flu. Thankfully both his and Juliano's swabs were so far negative.

She was due some more tablets and he thought she might like to know. He pulled up short in the doorway when he realised Juliano, Flo in tow, was propped up on the pillow next to Nat, chatting away. Her eyes were closed but that didn't seem to be bothering him.

He opened his mouth to motion for Juliano to come away but then his son said something that rendered him totally powerless.

'Please get better, Nat. I want you to be my mummy.' Juliano stroked Nat's forehead gently. 'We love you Nat.'

Alessandro's heart thundered in his chest as his son's innocent comments. Nat stirred at that point and murmured, 'Love you too, matey,' before settling back to sleep.

Alessandro held his breath. Was she lucid? Had she heard Juliano? He wasn't sure. A roaring in his ears threatened to deafen him as his chest filled with a feeling he was becoming all too used to. Except now he knew what it was.

All that he cared about in the world was right in front of him and he'd been so blind.

He was in love with Nathalie.

He'd been so busy punishing himself for past mistakes he hadn't been paying attention to what was happening in the here and now. When Nat had mentioned the 'l' word he'd run a mile because he'd still been looking back. But looking at his son and the woman in his bed—pale and ill and the best thing that had ever happened to him—he knew they were the way forward. He knew they were his future.

If it wasn't too late.

CHAPTER ELEVEN

NAT slept for the rest of the day, waking only for water, medication and the odd rest stop. She took the news of the confirmed diagnosis with a sleepy shrug and a 'Nice to know I'm a World Health Organization statistic now'.

Alessandro was pleased for the time. It gave him time to think, to strategise. He knew he had his work cut out for him. He knew that she'd been betrayed by two men in her past over another woman and that this time round she wouldn't be so forgiving. He knew she wouldn't take any platitudes or settle for any slick proclamations.

He was going to have to tell her the truth. The whole truth. Something he'd never told anyone. What was that old saying? The truth will set you free. Maybe it would. He hoped so. Maybe it was time to get it all out in the open instead of keeping it inside and beating himself up about it.

Surely he deserved love too? Juliano certainly did. He knew he couldn't let her walk out of his life without trying. Hiding in the past hadn't done either of them any good. Maybe it was time to start looking forward, to start living for the future?

* * *

Alessandro came to bed late again that night, having gone over and over in his head what he was going to say to her once she was well enough. He was nervous, a sick kind of feeling sitting heavily in his stomach, like a layer of grease, sludgy and stagnant.

She didn't stir when he joined her and he turned on his side and just looked at her. He wanted to reach out for her, pull her into him as he had last night, but resisted. He wouldn't take advantage of her. Not when her defences had been knocked flat.

But he hoped she'd allow him to share her bed every night of his life. If he played his cards right maybe she would.

On that positive note he drifted to sleep

Nat woke with a start early next morning. Again it took a while to orientate herself as a pale finger of daylight peeked through the gap in the curtains. *Alessandro's room.* She became aware of him behind her, wrapped around her again, his strong forearm so close to her cheek she could have turned her face and pressed a kiss to it.

Had she sought him out like the previous night or had it just been a natural position for their bodies to assume? The lovers within finding a way to be together if only subconsciously?

She realised suddenly she actually felt quite good. She wriggled slightly. No aches or pains. Her headache had gone and her thought processes didn't seem sluggish. She didn't feel feverish and her throat no longer hurt. She certainly couldn't run a marathon but it seemed as if the worse had passed.

She wriggled again for the sheer joy of being able to do

so without pain and suddenly became aware of a hardness pressing into her from behind. And she knew instantly it was what had woken her, as surely as she knew her own heartbeat. The lover inside had subconsciously responded to the signal from her beloved.

'Alessandro?' she whispered.

Alessandro, who had been awake for fifteen minutes trying to quell his hard-on without waking her up, groaned behind her. He placed his forehead against her shoulder blade. 'I'm sorry, *il mio amore*. My body betrays me.'

A rush of desire slammed down low and she squeezed her legs together as a burst of heat tingled between them. He sounded in agony and she could definitely relate.

Alessandro took a deep steadying breath. 'If you let go of my arm, I'll get up.'

Nat realised his lower arm was trapped against her body. But suddenly she didn't want to release him. They'd forged a new kind of intimacy the last couple of days and she didn't want to let it go—not yet. She wanted to feel him around her, in her. Like before. Like old times.

Maybe her illness had weakened her but suddenly her blood was boiling with lust. His aroma filled her senses and the lust surged around her body, filling up every cell, every heartbeat, every breath. It was crazy, she knew, but was it so wrong to want one last moment with him to cherish for ever?

She reached behind her and slid her hand between them, seeking and finding his taut erection straining against his underwear.

Alessandro shut his eyes, pressing his forehead hard against her. 'Nathalie!' he groaned.

She gave him a fierce squeeze before burrowing past his

waistband and touching his naked length, revelling in his guttural moan that echoed around the room. He sounded like a bull elephant in rut and she could barely see she was so inflamed with need.

She grabbed his lower hand and brought it to her breast, crying out herself as he squeezed it. 'Yes!'

'Nat…' Alessandro dragged in a breath as her hand slid up and down his length, sliding it enticingly against the cheek of her bottom. 'I don't think we should be doing this now. You're not well.'

Nat shook her head as his hand rubbed against the tortured peak of her nipple. 'I'm fine. I need this, Alessandro.' She moved her hand off him to push up her nightdress and shimmy her knickers down over her hips. She pressed her bare bottom back into him, rotating it against his erection.

'Nathalie!'

She reached for him again, wrapping her hand around his girth. 'Please.'

Alessandro was seeing stars in his efforts to hold back his desire while his body betrayed him. There was so much he wanted to tell her but he couldn't now. Not in the middle of all this. She would think it was just pillow talk. Things people who didn't love each other said in bed that weren't necessarily true. And he didn't want to diminish what he had to say.

But he could show her. He could make love to her. Show her with his body, his touch, that she was more than sex, more than a substitute.

His hand left her nipple and she whimpered. 'Shh,' he said, kissing her neck. 'Just for a moment.' His fingers dragged up her nightdress so he could touch her warm vital flesh. The nipple was hard against his palm and as his other hand slid between her legs her arched back told him he'd definitely hit the sweet spot.

'Now, Alessandro. I need you in me now.'

Alessandro's hand stroked in unison. 'Slow down,' he whispered.

Nat shook her head. 'No.' She knew she was ready for him and she rubbed her hot slickness against his rampant hardness. She stretched her arm over her head, slinging it around his neck. 'Now,' she demanded.

Alessandro removed his hand reluctantly from between her legs and guided himself to where she was wet and hot for him. He nudged his head in, angling his hips at the same time she pushed back, and he slid in to the hilt.

Nat cried out at his decisive invasion, revelling in his thickness, his power. He pulled out and thrust in again as he squeezed her breast and she cried out, 'More.'

Alessandro's other hand returned to the wet cleft between her legs, her corresponding whimper travelling straight to his groin. Her hand tightened on his nape as he stroked between her legs and he dropped his head and bit gently along the length of her neck.

Her whimpers grew more frantic as he thrust deeper and stroked harder. Every frenzied noise drove him towards his own release. As she built he built too until she was trembling and clinging to him, crying out. When she shattered around him his own climax was tingling in his loins and surging through his abdominal muscles, rushing up to meet hers seconds later.

'I love you,' he called as the world fell apart around him.

Alessandro's unexpected declaration floated up to her in the surreal surroundings into which she had been flung.

Maybe he hadn't even said it? Maybe her post-feverish brain had just conjured it up in her strangely inert yet somehow gliding state. She let it pass her by, not wanting to interfere with the slow burn of ecstasy fizzing in her blood.

It seemed to take for ever to bump gently back to earth, like feathers on a gentle breeze.

'Nathalie.' Alessandro nuzzled her neck, his hand resting possessively on her hip. 'We need to talk.'

No, she didn't want to hear him trying to backpedal or justify his orgasmic slip. She just wanted to stay cocooned here for a bit longer, his arm around her, his body jammed tight against hers.

'Shh,' she whispered, tucking his arm snugly around her waist. 'Later.'

Then post-coital malaise and post-illness lethargy combined in a potent double whammy and sleep dragged her under.

It was full daylight when Nat next woke. The clock said six-thirty and her bladder was making itself known so she gently moved out of Alessandro's embrace. It was good to feel her legs strong beneath her as she padded to the en suite. Her stomach growled and she actually felt hungry for the first time in two days.

Alessandro's *I love you* played through her head as she used the toilet and then washed her hands. How could it not? She looked at her rather wan reflection, admitting to herself now how much it had hurt. Another pretty lie. Something he'd thought she wanted to hear.

Which she did, of course. But not if he didn't mean it. Not if he didn't feel it.

She steeled herself to go back out. To face him. To

excuse what had happened with a cheery smile and get through the next few days with it firmly plastered on her face. Being ill had sapped her energy. And being angry required more energy than she possessed. She just wanted it to be over now so she could leave and lick her wounds far away from the man who had inflicted them.

He was sitting on the side of the bed, waiting for her when she stepped out of the en suite. Her gaze hungrily ate up his broad shoulders and his long, bare, powerful thighs.

'We need to talk.'

Nat faltered. Wanting to prolong their nearness, to hear his voice but not wanting it at the same time. 'It's okay. You don't have to explain, Alessandro.' She looked at the floor then at the bed then at the bedside clock. 'I'm not going to hold you to anything you might have said in a moment of passion.'

Alessandro caught her wandering gaze and held it. 'I love you.'

Nat shook her head, rejecting his words, the sincerity in his gaze. 'It was a nice thing for you to say but you really didn't have to and I understand where it came from.'

Alessandro prayed for patience. 'I love you,' he said again.

Nat refused to let his words affect her. Rob had said he loved her. So had her father. Neither of them had stuck around. 'No. You're still in love and grieving for your wife. And I remind you of her. I think they call it transference, don't they?'

Alessandro pushed off the bed and stalked two paces to the window, yanking back the curtain. This was the moment of truth. He placed his fists against the window ledge, the persuasive words he'd practised yesterday completely deserting him.

All he had now was the bald truth. 'I didn't love her.'

The silence stretched as Nat tried to figure out what he was talking about. She frowned. Who the hell were they talking about now? 'Who?'

'Camilla. My wife. I didn't love her.' The words he'd kept locked inside for so long were finally out and damn if it didn't feel good. He turned to face her, leaning against the window sill. 'I never loved her.'

Nat blinked. 'What?' But the man she'd first met had been deeply mired in grief.

'You're right,' he admitted. 'You and she are very similar. I was shocked when I first met you. But it took me about two seconds in your company to realise that your physical similarities are where it ends. When I told you that you and she were nothing alike, I was deadly serious.'

Nat wasn't sure if her brain was still sluggish from her illness but she just couldn't take in what he was saying. 'I don't understand.'

'Camilla was my lover. Before we met I was having a fantastic time playing the field. I never planned to marry. You grow up with parents who fought and spent more time apart than together, you don't really see the point…'

Alessandro couldn't believe he'd ever been so stupid. 'She was beautiful and sophisticated, from aristocratic stock. Witty and charming and looked fantastic naked. All the things I looked for in a date. And then she fell pregnant. So I did the honourable thing.'

He paused waiting for the burn of bitter memories. For his internal censor to step in. But neither came.

A first.

'It was a huge society wedding and I was determined to make a real go of it. So, my life hadn't gone exactly according to plan but I knew if we worked at it, we could succeed.'

He shook his head at his naivety. 'Valentino, who, I have to say, never really liked her anyway, overheard her at the wedding talking to her best friend about how she'd trapped me. Deliberately fallen pregnant because she'd wanted to marry me. I told him he was mistaken and confronted her about it later, in the honeymoon suite.'

His lips twisted into an ironic smile. 'She admitted it. She looked straight at me and said, "*But, darling, you wouldn't have married me otherwise*." It was like the blinkers had been ripped away from my eyes and I could finally see the person Val had always seen. The cold, calculating socialite out to marry a doctor.'

Nat watched him closely as Alessandro fell silent, his matter-of-fact retelling betrayed by the turmoil in his sable gaze. To say she was horrified was an understatement. 'I didn't know,' she murmured.

He nodded. 'So I told her it was going to be a marriage in name only. Which apparently suited her down to the ground. Initially anyway. So we entered into this strange existence where we smiled publicly but slept in separate beds. And then Juliano was born and I was crazily busy at the hospital, working long hours, and she suddenly realised being married to a doctor wasn't so glamorous after all.'

He gave a stiff laugh. 'I think she thought I'd give up the emergency lark and become a Harley St specialist.'

Nat shook her head. She'd known Alessandro for only a matter of days when she'd realised he was a gifted emergency physician.

'She wanted a divorce. But she wanted me to file. Couldn't have that stain on her family's reputation. I knew

I'd never see Juliano again if I agreed. As it was, she was already using him to get to me. Don't get me wrong, she was a great mother and they had a close bond but she deliberately alienated him from me. Rationing our already scant time together. Insisting I only speak English with him. And…I let her. I felt guilty about our relationship and it was easier to give in and play by her rules. Juliano was happy and healthy and loved. And work demanded so much of me. It was easier that way. I guess I turned into my father…'

He trailed off and Nat waited for him to start again. She sensed this was something he needed to get off his chest.

'By the time she died, Juliano and I were relative strangers.'

Nat nodded. 'I noticed.' She sat down on the edge of the bed. 'How did she die?'

'A car accident. We'd argued and she'd squealed off in the flash BMW she insisted I buy for her—another guilt gift.'

Nat shut her eyes. No wonder Alessandro had looked so wretched when she'd first met him. He obviously blamed himself for Camilla's death. Guilt and remorse were powerful emotions. 'What did you argue about?'

'The divorce. What else? We didn't argue often, I didn't want that for Juliano. I didn't want him to experience the type of childhood I'd known. It was easier just to give in to her. And Camilla was much too passive-aggressive for it anyway.'

He swallowed, parched from talking and the burn of memories. 'But we rowed that day. I couldn't believe I was in a marriage like my parents'. But Camilla had a way of picking a fight.'

The ugly words taunted him to this day. 'She said she'd

taken a lover and wanted to be free to marry again. I told her over my cold dead body and that I would fight her every inch of the way. Fight her for Juliano. That she'd made her bed and she was just going to have to lie in it.'

He went silent and Nat finished the story for him. 'So she hared off in the car and crashed it?'

Alessandro nodded and her heart went out to him. She rose from the bed and went to his side, leaning her body in to him, pressing a kiss to his shoulder. 'It wasn't your fault, Alessandro.'

'I know that. Rationally, I know that. But…'

Nat nodded, dropping another kiss in the same spot. 'You've been beating yourself up about it anyway?'

Alessandro felt the warmth of her seep into him and he began to hope. 'I looked on it as my punishment. For insisting on a marriage on paper only and then for keeping her in the marriage. A marriage neither of us wanted. If I'd only forgiven her and gone on from there. Tried to make a real go of it instead of drawing the battle lines right from the start. But I was proud and angry.'

'It must have been hard.'

Yes, it had. But, then, a lot of it had been his doing.

'So you see,' he said, looking down at her, 'I don't deserve to have love, to find love. That's why I fought these feelings for you for so long. Because this isn't supposed to be my lot. And then I saw Juliano in bed with you yesterday. You were asleep and he was stroking your head and telling you he wanted you to be his mummy and he loved you and you murmured, "I love you too," and I realised that right in front of me was my whole world. You and him.'

Nat didn't remember Juliano being in bed with her but

smiled at the picture Alessandro painted. Her heart started to beat crazily as his words sank in. She wanted to believe him. But she was burned and wary.

She looked up and captured his gaze. 'I just can't get her picture out of my head.'

'I know. I should have told you earlier but I honestly didn't notice the resemblance after being in your company for just a few seconds. You were obviously like chalk and cheese.'

He lifted a finger and stroked it down her face. 'It's you I want. And not because you look like Camilla. Because you're Nat. Nathalie. Our Nat. Funny and down to earth and kind and generous and sexy, and you gave me back my son, you gave me back Juliano, and you opened my heart enough to see that maybe I do deserve a chance at love. Real love for the first time in my life.'

Nat's chest bloomed with an outpouring of the love that she'd kept firmly in check since she'd blurted it out. 'Of course you do, Alessandro. We all do.'

Alessandro saw the compassion in her gaze and dared to hope. 'Does this mean I haven't destroyed everything you felt for me?' he asked.

She smiled up at him, her heart skipping in her chest. She slipped her palm up to cradle his cheek. 'Of course not. I love you, Alessandro. I can't turn that off and on. It's a fact of life. It's who I am.'

She raised herself up on tiptoe and pressed her mouth to his. 'I will always love you.'

Alessandro grinned for the first time since he'd started talking. Then he picked her up, ignoring her squeal, and threw her in the centre of the mattress. 'So you'll stay,' he said, climbing on the bed and lying beside her on his stomach, propped up on his elbows. 'For ever and ever.

And you'll marry me and have brothers and sisters for Juliano?'

She put her arms around his neck. 'Yes, I'll stay. Yes, I'll marry you. And, yes, I'll have brothers and sisters for Juliano.' She pulled him down to seal it with a kiss. 'You want to start now?'

Alessandro grinned. 'I thought we did that already.'

A noise at the door had them both breaking apart as Juliano eyed them. 'Is Nat better now?'

Alessandro grinned at his son. 'She sure is. And guess what?' he said, gesturing Juliano over. He grabbed his son's hand and pulled him onto the bed with them. 'Nat's staying. For ever.'

Juliano's eyes grew large in his head as he looked from his father to Nat and back to his father. 'Really? Are you going to be my mummy?'

Nat beamed at him. 'Would you like that?'

'Oh, yeah! That'd be the best thing ever,' he said enthusiastically, bouncing up and down on his haunches.

Alessandro couldn't have agreed more. 'Well said, matey.' He grinned as he grabbed Juliano and lifted him in the air above his head, tickling him with his fingers, boyish laughter filling the room.

Nat laughed too as Juliano giggled and begged his father to stop. She pinched herself. She was really a part of all this. She couldn't remember every being this deliriously happy.

It couldn't get any better than this.

But it did.

VALENTINO'S
PREGNANCY
BOMBSHELL

BY
AMY ANDREWS

MILLS & BOON®

All the characters in this book have no existence outside the imagination of the author, and have no relation whatsoever to anyone bearing the same name or names. They are not even distantly inspired by any individual known or unknown to the author, and all the incidents are pure invention.

First published in Great Britain 2010
Harlequin Mills & Boon Limited,
Eton House, 18-24 Paradise Road, Richmond, Surrey TW9 1SR

© Amy Andrews 2010

ISBN: 978 0 263 87914 8

Harlequin Mills & Boon policy is to use papers that are natural, renewable and recyclable products and made from wood grown in sustainable forests. The logging and manufacturing process conform to the legal environmental regulations of the country of origin.

Printed and bound in Spain
by Litografia Rosés, S.A., Barcelona

Extract from
VALENTINO'S PREGNANCY BOMBSHELL:

Paige held up the test, barely keeping upright as the foundations of her world crashed all round her. 'It's positive.'

Valentino stared at the pink plus sign. It was a full minute before the information sank in. He was going to be a father. He smiled. And then he grinned. 'This is the best news I've ever heard.'

Paige wasn't similarly overcome. In fact, a huge block of emotion built in her chest till she thought she was going to pass out from the pressure of it. It stung her eyes and prickled her nose. She sucked in a breath. 'No, Valentino, it's not. This is the worst possible news. You have no idea.'

And she burst into tears.

**This book is dedicated to all those
bionic ear pioneers who strived to give deaf people
everywhere options they'd never had before.**

Such achievements are totally inspiring.

CHAPTER ONE

PAIGE DONALD could feel Valentino Lombardi's gaze on her from across the altar. Not even the beauty of the ceremony or the happiness in her heart for her friend, Natalie, could distract her from the intensity of it.

It caressed every inch of her body, making her even more self-conscious about what she was wearing.

The bridesmaid's dress clung to non-existent curves. The hem grazed her knee and she suppressed the urge to yank it lower. This wasn't her. This frothy, clingy, femme fatale dress with shoestring straps and low back.

Very. Low. Back.

The crimson creation didn't say busy single working mother with a high-needs child who hasn't slept an entire night through in three years.

It said Sexy. Flirty. Time for pleasure. It said the playground is open, come on in. And Valentino Lombardi, possibly the sexiest man she'd ever laid eyes on, probably the sexiest man in existence, looked like he wanted to be first to ride.

But she didn't have time. Not for flirting. Or riding. Or pleasure. Or any of those trivialities. And especially not for a man who looked like he held a PhD in trivia. There were never enough hours in the day as it was.

There was just never enough time.

She had a sudden hankering for her faded grey trackpants and her favourite oversized T-shirt back in her wardrobe at home in Brisbane. Or better still her baggy blue scrubs. She didn't like being this…on display. She felt awkward.

The heat from Valentino's gaze radiated towards her and she slid him a mutinous back-off-buddy glance. It was one she'd perfected since Arnie had walked out on her and it usually stopped a man dead in his tracks. But Valentino just grinned and gave her a saucy wink.

Great! Please, God, don't let me have to dodge this Italian Neanderthal all night.

'Can I have the rings, please?'

Paige could have kissed the priest as Alessandro's best man was given a job to do other than look at her. Unfortunately, though, his actions commanded the attention of the entire female population of the church, including her, and Paige found herself drinking in the way his exquisite suit pulled across broad shoulders and how the fine wool of his trousers outlined powerful quads and one very fine backside.

Very, very fine.

He glanced at her as he stepped back into his place and his espresso eyes told her he knew exactly where hers had been. A smile touched his lips, beautiful lips that could have been carved by one of the masters. Except they were warm and vital.

Desirable. Kissable.

There was a frankness in his gaze that stopped the breath in her lungs. She searched for something more, beyond the promise of tonight. Something deeper. A connection. Something that told her he was interested in more than getting her between his sheets. But all she found was heat and sex and lust.

Totally superficial. Like the man.

Another flashy male. All sparkle, no substance.

Still, her heart skipped a beat and she sucked in a ragged breath.

Paige hit the 'send' button and placed her mobile on the table, drumming her fingers. Her gaze returned, yet again, to Valentino as he worked the room. She tried to ignore him and her steadily growing irritation as women almost swooned at his feet but the rich sound of his easy, frequent laughter made it impossible. It reached out from across the room as if he had physically caressed her, drawing her attention like a moth to flame.

Valentino Lombardi was not a man you could ignore. With his killer dimples, boyishly curly hair and Italian playboy charm, he was pure vice.

Paige's phone vibrated and she reached for it, her pulse spiking.

McKenzie fine. Sleeping well. Stop worrying.

Paige's fingers flew over the keypad. *Apnoea mat on?*

Alessandro laughed again and Paige drank the sight of him in as she pressed 'send'. He threw his head back, giving the belly laugh its full freedom, and her gaze followed the bronzed length of his exposed neck peppered with dark stubble.

Another vibration dragged her eyes back to the table. *Yes. Go and dance for crying out loud!*

Paige smiled despite the gnawing, ever-present worry.

She could almost hear her mother saying the words. But she'd never had a night away from her daughter. Frankly she didn't know what to do with herself.

Don't think I'll stay the night. If I leave after cake can be home by midnight. 'Send'.

Paige checked her watch, doing a quick calculation in her head. Yep. She could definitely make it home by then.

'Everything okay?'

Paige glanced up into the bride's face. Nat had fresh bluebells threaded into her blonde locks, which brought out the colour of her eyes and matched the crystal beading decorating the neckline of her ivory gown. Alessandro's hand rested possessively on her shoulder and Paige felt a sudden yearning she couldn't explain.

Why? She'd been where they were. Had the divorce to prove it. She certainly had no desire to do it again.

She smiled at her friend. 'Just telling Mum I might not stay the night.'

'Paige? No.' Nat grabbed her hand. 'Your parents have booked and paid for it. Including breakfast. Your mother would skin me alive if I let you leave.' Nat squeezed Paige's hand. 'It's just one night. Don't you think it's time you enjoyed a well-deserved break?'

Paige shied away from the earnestness of her friend's expression. Everyone said that to her—you need a break, Paige. But she was a mother first and foremost and McKenzie needed her. That's just the way it was. Nat would understand one day too.

The phone vibrated and Paige grabbed it, relieved to break eye contact with the bride. She opened the message and read it three times, a ghost of a smile touching her lips. She held it up to Nat.

Don't. You. Dare.

Nat grinned. 'Have I mentioned how much I like your mother?'

Paige rolled her eyes. 'Okay, okay. I'll stay.'

'Good.' Nat squeezed her hand. 'The speeches are about to start.'

A deep laugh floated towards them and Nat looked across to where Valentino was chatting with some nurses from their work. 'You should take a page out of Val's book. He's certainly having a good time.'

Paige felt her gaze drawing to him again. 'Isn't he just,' she said dryly.

Nat sighed. 'I tell you, if I wasn't utterly besotted with Alessandro and was up for a brief fling, I'd be over there too.'

'Hmm,' Paige murmured noncommittally.

'Do you know he used to date Adrianna de Luca?'

Paige gave her friend a mystified look. 'Who?'

Nat rolled her eyes. 'One of Italy's top catwalk models.' Of course he did. 'Fancy that.'

'They were in all the magazines last year.'

Paige hadn't read a magazine in for ever. Or a book. Sunday newspapers were about her limit. 'Of course they were.' Her voice dripped with derision.

Nat regarded her friend seriously. 'Not all men are like Arnie, Paige.' She looked up as Valentino laughed again and poked her elbow into Paige's ribs. 'Come on, you have to admit, he's a bit of a spunk.'

'I hope you're talking about me, *il mio tesoro*,' Alessandro interrupted, nuzzling his new wife's neck.

'But of course.' Nat smiled, turning to Alessandro, her lips poised to meet his as he lowered his head.

Paige felt a tug at her dress and was grateful for a reason

to avoid the blissful clinch she knew was happening beside her. She looked down to see, Juliano, Alessandro's four year old son.

'Where's McKenzie?'

Paige smiled at the boy. 'Juliano, you look magnificent!' He was dressed in a mini-tux and was the spitting image of his father.

With the boyishness and dimples of his father's cousin.

Juliano stood a little higher. 'Nat says I'm handsome.'

'Nat is one hundred per cent right.'

Juliano beamed. 'Is McKenzie sick?'

Paige shook her head, saddened that it was such a natural conclusion for Juliano to jump to. 'No. She's at home with her grandparents.'

Juliano's face fell. 'I wanted to ask her to dance.'

Paige's heart just about melted and she pulled Juliano in for a big hug. 'You are so sweet. I see you have your father's charm.' She glanced at Alessandro, who winked at her. 'Another time, huh?'

Nat had wanted McKenzie to be her flower girl but Paige had declined. The truth was, crowds made Paige very nervous for her daughter. As an ex-prem with chronic lung disease and poor immunity, every single person was a potential source of infection, a silver bullet to McKenzie's weak defences. It just wasn't worth the risk.

'Okay.' Juliano nodded, squirming out of her embrace. 'See ya,' he chirped, and ducked away, heading for the dance floor.

Paige watched him, smiling even though her heart ached. What would she give for her daughter to be so able-bodied, so carefree? She returned her attention to her phone and replied to her mother's text.

Promise you'll ring if there's a problem.

It took five seconds for the reply. *I promise.*

Paige texted back. *Anything at all. No matter how trivial.* She released the message into the ether and held on fast to the phone, tension tightening her stomach muscles.

She knew people thought she was too uptight about her daughter but what did they know? It was she who lived every day with the reality of McKenzie's fragile health, not them. And one thing was for certain—being vigilant had kept McKenzie alive.

With the operation only a couple of months away now, Paige was determined to keep McKenzie healthy and avoid any more delays. It had been rescheduled three times already. No more.

The phone vibrated in her hand and Paige opened the message. *I'm switching the phone off now. Go and have fun. That's an order.*

Paige smiled. She'd obviously stretched her mother's patience enough for one night. Thank God for her parents. She would never have got through the past few years without them.

A tinkling of cutlery on glass cut through the low murmur and Paige turned to see Alessandro standing. She pushed all thoughts of the world outside the room aside, determined to follow her mother's orders, and motioned for the drinks waiter.

'So,' Valentino said, topping up Paige's half-full glass with some more champagne, 'I believe it is a custom in your country for the best man and the bridesmaid to dance the bridal waltz together.'

His voice was low and close to her ear and her body

reacted as if he had suggested something much more risqué than a customary dance in front of a room full of people. It took all her willpower not to melt into a puddle. Not to turn her head and flirt like crazy.

Except it seemed like a million years ago now that she'd last flirted and she was pretty sure she didn't have a clue how to go about it. And why she would choose to do so with a man who was all glamour and sparkle, after her experience with Arnie, was beyond her.

The bitter burn of memories was never far from reach.

'That's right,' she said, refusing to look at him, focusing instead on the bubbles meandering to the surface of her champagne.

'*Eccellente*. I'm looking forward to that.'

Well, that made one of them. The thought of them dancing, his arm around her practically bare back, their bodies close, was sending her heart into fibrillation. Sitting next to him at the table, aware of his every move, every breath, their arms occasionally brushing, his deep voice resonating through tense abdominal muscles, was bad enough. Being pressed along the magnificent tuxedoed length of him? Frankly it scared the hell out of her.

She felt gauche and unsophisticated and totally out of her depth next to his man-of-the-world, model-dating perfection.

What if she stuffed up the steps? Or trod on his foot?

What if she liked it too much?

'You are worried your boyfriend will mind that we dance, yes?'

Valentino's comment snapped her out of the vision of her clinging to him like some sort of groupie as he pressed kisses down her neck. She glanced at him, startled.

A big mistake.

Thus far she'd managed not to look at him this close up. And now she knew why. This near, he was simply dazzling. Gorgeous hair the colour of midnight waved in haphazard glory, thick and lustrous with not a hint of grey. It brushed his forehead and collar and Paige finally understood the itch some women talked about to run their fingers through a man's hair.

Jet-black eyebrows quirked at her as her gaze widened to take in his square jaw line, heavy with five-o'clock shadow. His full lips curved upward and were bracketed by dimples that should be outlawed on anyone over five. His eyes, dark like a shot of the best Italian espresso, were fringed by long black lashes and promised fun and flirting.

A buzz coursed through her veins at the fifteen different kinds of sin she could see in them.

Valentino smiled at the little frown that knitted Paige's caramel brows together and crinkled her forehead. She was a most intriguing woman. Her grey eyes were huge in her angular face dominated by prominent cheekbones and a wide mouth.

She wore no eye make-up to enhance them, she didn't need to. They drew the gaze regardless. Her strawberry-blonde hair had been severely styled into a pixie cut that feathered over her forehead and would have looked boyish on anyone else but only seemed to enhance the hugeness of her eyes and the vulnerability he saw there.

She was no beauty. She certainly wasn't his usual type. He liked them curvy. Everywhere. Not rail thin like Paige. And confident. Women who were secure in their sexuality, who smiled and flirted and enjoyed life. Women who knew the score.

And yet…

There was something about her that intrigued him. Not least of all the fact that she'd been the only female in the room who hadn't clamoured to be closer to him.

'I see you texting. All night,' he prompted when she still didn't say anything. 'I figure a beautiful woman…' He shrugged and shot her his best hey-baby grin, 'it must be a boyfriend?'

Paige shook her head to clear it as Valentino's smile muddled her senses. 'I'm a little old for a boyfriend, don't you think?'

'Paige. We are never too old for love.'

The slight reprimand in his voice didn't register. Nothing registered beyond the way he'd said her name. Paige. He had drawn it out a little at the end, giving it a very European flair, and it had stroked across every nerve ending in her pelvis.

She shut her eyes. This was madness. He was just a man. God knew, she hadn't even thought about the opposite sex since her husband had walked out on her. And, besides, she just didn't have time for a man. Especially not a model-dating, Italian playboy whose interest in her would no doubt wane the minute after he had his way with her.

Which wasn't going to happen.

Even if, deep down, in a secret, hidden part of her, she wanted it very, very badly.

I am a single-mother of a high-needs child.

I am a single mother of a high-needs child.

She turned back to her champagne and took a long deep swallow, the bubbles pricking her throat as they slid down, matching the prick at the backs of her eyes. 'I am.'

Tonight, as always, Paige felt absolutely ancient.

'Excuse me,' she murmured, rising and headed for the refuge of the bathroom.

Valentino watched his cousin dancing with his new wife, a gladness in his heart that Alessandro had finally found love after the train wreck of his first marriage.

It always humbled him when he saw two people ready to make a lifetime commitment. Sure, after an early escape he'd worked out it wasn't for him, but that didn't mean he didn't believe in it for others. His parents were, after all, still blissfully married after fifty years.

He spotted Paige making her way back to the table and he was struck anew by how not his type she was. The crimson dress outlined a figure that had more angles then curves. Her breasts were small, her body one long, lean line, and she moved with purpose rather than grace.

And yet…

He rose as she approached the table and held out his hand. 'I believe it's our turn.'

Paige's heart thundered. His gaze had tracked her from all the way across the room and her heart beat as if she'd just dashed one hundred metres in less than ten seconds. She looked up at him, caution wrangling with temptation. How easy would it just be to surrender? To forget her mangled heart and the type of man who had mangled it in the first place and succumb to the invitation in Valentino's eyes?

But Paige had never been into masochism.

She ignored his hand and headed towards the dance floor.

Valentino grinned. If she thought for a moment that he couldn't read every emotion, the battle in those large grey eyes, she was utterly deluded. He followed her to the floor, his gaze glued to the elegant length of her naked spine the dress afforded him, and wondered what it would take to convince her to let her guard down.

Paige reluctantly let him shepherd her into the circle of his arms. His big hand sat low, just above her butt and just this side of decent. It was firm and hot and she felt a lurch in areas that hadn't felt anything in a very long time.

Valentino felt resistance as he tried to pull her a little closer. 'Relax,' he murmured to her temple.

She jerked her head back slightly to forcibly remove the brush of his lips from her skin. Relax? He may as well have asked her to fly to the moon. She glared at him. 'Let's just get through this, okay?'

Valentino chuckled. Paige wasn't one for stroking egos. Another factor he was finding surprisingly appealing. He'd drifted through life never having to work for the attention of a woman—ever. From his mother to his sisters and cousins, to the girls at school and beyond, he'd always had them twisted around his finger.

He was starting to realise how boring, how predictable, his life had been.

They moved to the music and Paige automatically followed, her senses infused with Valentino's clean male scent. She sought desperately for something to say to instil distance, to break the hypnotic pull of the music and his warm breath.

Anything.

'So, Valentino, Alessandro tells me you are a cochlear implant surgeon.'

Valentino smiled at her robotic question. He looked down into grey eyes that were averted to a point beyond his shoulder. That she could see over his shoulder was a first for him too. Most women he'd dated, apart from Adrianna, had been shorter. At six feet two, he still had a few inches on her but the fact that it would just take one tantalising tilt of her chin to claim her mouth was an intriguing proposition.

'Yes, Paige. Alessandro tells me you have a daughter who needs one?'

Paige stumbled at the mention of McKenzie, grateful for a moment that Valentino's body was there to lean into, to steady herself. But then aware, too aware, of the muscles beneath his shirt, the strength in his arms, the heat of him, the power of him.

'Yes,' she said, pushing away from his chest and holding herself as erect, as far away as was possible, which was severely hampered as the dance floor filled with other couples and they were jostled closer together.

'She's scheduled for two months' time.'

Curiously Paige found herself wanting to tell him about McKenzie, about her fragile health and the long road they'd both been on, but as much as she was desperate for conversation to maintain distance, the ups and downs of her life were not for public consumption.

'Is she a patient of Harry Abbott's?'

Paige's face lightened. Now, Harry, her boss, she could talk about. She could talk about him and his genius all night long. Finally she felt on solid ground. 'Oh, yes. Only the best for my little girl. Do you know him? He's an absolute pioneer in the field.'

Valentino smiled, amazed at the difference in Paige as passion filled her eyes and she came alive, her face animated. Is this what she would look like beneath him in bed? His hand tightened against her spine, inching her un-resisting body closer.

'Of course.' He shrugged. 'Everyone knows Harry.' In fact, it had been Valentino's very great pleasure to finally meet the man a couple of months back during an interview.

Paige nodded. 'He's an absolutely magical surgeon, so clever and such a fair boss. And great with his patients. He insists everyone in the audiology department knows how to sign so the patients are at ease.'

She chatted away, finally comfortable in his arms. So comfortable, in fact, she didn't notice that the song ended and another began. Or that they were now so close their bodies rubbed deliciously against each other as they swayed to the tempo.

Valentino, on the other hand, had noticed. In fact, he could barely register anything else. Her chatter faded into the background along with the music as his body responded to the subtle friction of her dress against the fabric of his trousers and the waft of frangipani and woman lit a fire in his groin.

She shifted against him as someone from behind bumped into her and he almost groaned out loud. 'Paige.'

His voice, low and throaty, snapped her out of her prattle and she was instantly aware of the chemistry between them. The ache of her taut nipples as they chafed against the fabric of her dress and his shirt. The darts of heat radiating from the fingers of his hand on her spine, shooting waves of sensation over her bottom and the backs of her thighs. The heat in her pelvis stoked by the heat in his.

Her eyes locked with his, the lust, the intent in his espresso gaze frightening. She opened her mouth again to use conversation as a weapon to repel him, to push him away.

But Valentino got in before her. 'Do you think if you talk enough you'll be able to ignore what's going on here?'

Paige's eyes widened at his insight. 'I…I don't know what you're talking about,' she denied, feeling frantic, like a mouse on a treadmill set on maximum speed.

'Paige.' Valentino ground out her name as he flattened his palm against her spine, bringing them even more intimately into contact. 'I think you do.'

For a few seconds Paige wanted nothing more than to grind herself against him. It was an urge she had to suppress with an iron fist.

The music stopped and people clapped. She used the distraction to gather every ounce of willpower and step out of his arms. 'No. I don't.'

And she spun on her heel and got as far away from Valentino Lombardi as she could.

An hour later Paige couldn't take being sociable another second. She knew it was bad form to leave the wedding before the bride and groom but she just couldn't stand being in the same room as Valentino, watching him dance and flirt, for a second longer.

She made her apologies, assuring Nat she was staying the night but pleading a headache. When the lift arrived promptly she almost pressed a kiss to its cold metallic doors. The impulse was short lived as they opened to reveal Valentino, his jacket slung over his shoulder, his bow-tie undone, leaning against the back wall.

They stared at each other for what seemed an eternity. 'Going up?' he murmured.

Damn, damn, damn. Paige entered the lift after a brief hesitation during which an errant brain cell urged her to run. But she was damned if she was going to show this man he had any power over her. She turned her back on him, keeping to the front of the spacious lift, and searched the buttons for floor twelve.

Of course, it was already lit. Great! Same floor. Next they'd have adjoining rooms! The doors shut and she clutched her bag, reaching for patience.

Valentino, afforded an unfettered view of her spine, looked his fill. He couldn't deny he wanted to see more of her back. And her front. He wanted to see her become passionate and animated again. And not about a nearly seventy-year-old surgeon who was old enough to be her grandfather. But about him. And what he was doing to her.

But she'd made it perfectly clear that any attraction was not going to be acted on. Valentino Lombardi had never had to beg in his life—he wasn't about to start.

The lift arrived at their floor and Val smiled as Paige practically sprinted from it. He followed at a more sedate pace, not really wanting to know where her room was. What if they happened to be neighbours? Would knowing she was in the next room be any good for his equilibrium? Wondering if she slept naked? Wondering if she was as sexually frustrated as he that she might help herself to ease the ache?

He shook his head. *Dio!*

Except it seemed they were to be neighbours and if her cursing and muttering was anything to go by as she rammed the keycard in her door, he was going to have to lend a neighbourly hand.

He hung his jacket over his doorknob and strolled towards her, resigned to his fate. 'Can I help with that?'

Paige slotted the card in and out several more times, wanting to scream as she twisted uselessly at the handle. She turned to him, glaring like it was all his fault. 'I hate these things.'

Val smiled. She was animated when she was angry too. Her cheeks flushed pink, her chest rising and falling enticingly, grey eyes sparkling like headlights in fog. He reached for it. 'Allow me.'

Paige didn't protest. She couldn't as his scent infused her senses. She'd done it all back at the wedding. There was no more resistance left. His fingers were sure as they slowly inserted the card into the slot and slowly pulled it out again.

Would he be that slow with her? That thorough? The light turned green and she shut her eyes as he turned the doorknob and opened her door.

'Entri.'

Paige looked into her room. Her big empty room. She flicked her gaze to Valentino's big hands with his sure fingers.

Val was surprised by her hesitation and although he couldn't see her eyes he sensed the battle from earlier had returned with gusto. 'Maybe I could join you?'

Paige felt absurdly shaky inside. She wanted to cry, burst into tears. She hadn't realised how lonely the last couple of years had been until an attractive man had propositioned her.

She looked at him instead. Saw the naked desire heat his gaze. This was crazy. 'I don't…' What? Have sex? Make love to? What could she say without sounding gauche or desperate or like a sixteen-year-old who'd never been kissed? 'Sleep with men I've just met.'

After all, it had taken her three weeks and a handful of dates to succumb to her attraction to Arnie.

'I promise you, there will be no sleeping.'

Paige swallowed hard. Both at the gravel in his voice and the sincerity in his gaze. 'I don't understand,' she said. Her throat was parched as she fought a little longer, hoping the sexual malaise invading her bones would lift. 'Any woman in that room tonight would have accompanied you here in a flash—why the hell do you want me?'

Val gave her a lazy smile as anticipation built in his gut, his loins. 'Because you're the only woman who wouldn't have.'

So she was a challenge? She supposed she should have been insulted but funnily enough they were precisely the right words for him to use. It told her she was something to be conquered and discarded, like all the others. Which, contrarily, right now, suited her just fine. She didn't have time or room in her life for the distraction of a love affair. But she did have tonight.

Obviously the only thing he was interested in.

It was win-win.

Paige pushed off the wall and without saying a word brushed past him and entered her room. She hoped it looked confident and sexy and that he couldn't hear the boom of her heart or the knocking of her knees.

She stopped in front of her bed, opened her bag, took her mobile out, checked it for messages then placed it on the bedside table before tossing the bag aside. She heard the click of the door behind her in the muted light and didn't have to turn to know that he was walking towards her. And in seconds his heat was behind her, his breath at her neck.

He said nothing as his fingers stroked up her arms. Neither did she. Nor did she say anything when his hands peeled the dress off her shoulders, baring her to her waist.

But she did cry out when his thumbs swept across her bare nipples, already hard and eager for his touch.

And when he kissed her neck.

And when he whispered her name.

Paige woke disorientated to a warm hand laid possessively low on her abdomen and a strange buzzing as a pale dawn broke through the gaps in the heavy curtains. She glanced at the clock—five-thirty. They'd been asleep for thirty minutes—Valentino had been true to his word.

The buzzing came again and movement caught her eye as her mobile vibrated and moved slightly across the surface of the bedside table. It must be a text message.

It took another couple of seconds for the import to set in. A text message.

McKenzie.

Instantly frantic, she grabbed her phone and accessed the message, her hands shaking, her heart pounding.

McKenzie woken with a slight temp. Don't worry. Everything under control.

Paige read the message three times, feeling progressively more ill. Oh, God. Her daughter was sick again and where was she? In the arms of some Italian Lothario thinking only about herself.

She leapt out of bed, ignoring the pull of internal muscles, grabbing for her clothes, furious at herself and Valentino for last night. She should have followed her instincts and gone home. Not stayed. Not let herself be seduced into a one-night stand, no matter how amazing it had been. Seduced into forgetting about the one person who meant more to her than anything else on the entire planet.

Her baby was ill. She had to get to her.

She didn't even look at Valentino as she threw her things together in record time. Or as she fled the room.

As far as she was concerned, if she ever saw him again, it would be too soon.

CHAPTER TWO

PAIGE arrived for her last day of work before her holidays at St Auburn's, with a spring in her step. She hadn't had a spring in her step for a long time but it was there today. She couldn't believe that McKenzie's operation was just three days away now. Her daughter hadn't been unwell or had a fever since the night she'd slept with…since Nat and Alessandro's wedding two months ago, and she had even put on a little weight.

Things were finally looking up. Finally going their way. All she had to do was convince Harry to let her be in the theatre to observe McKenzie's operation on Monday and life would be complete.

A butterfly flapped its wings in her stomach as she rehearsed the words again. Not that Paige really thought it would be an issue. Yes, it wasn't usual but she knew Harry well enough to feel confident that he'd overlook the rules for his right-hand woman.

Paige was actually humming as she entered the operating theatre change rooms. Dr Gloria Reinhart, the anaesthetist Harry used for his lists, was changing into her scrubs and Paige bade her a hearty good morning.

'Morning,' Gloria said, staring at Paige, an odd look on her face.

Paige frowned. 'What?'

Gloria shrugged. 'Nothing. It's just that I've never heard you hum before.'

Paige didn't need a translation. She knew she was serious. That she wasn't much fun. She came to work, ran Harry's theatre and his clinics with ruthless efficiency, not particularly caring whether she made friends or not. She didn't socialise or have time for gossip or idle chit-chat.

She was respected. Whether she was liked or not hadn't been a priority.

Paige grinned. 'Well, it's about time that changed, don't you think?'

Gloria responded with a grin of her own. 'Past time, I'd say.'

They chatted while Paige changed into her scrubs and then went in different directions—Gloria to the staffroom for a cuppa with her colleagues, Paige to Theatre four to set up for the first case.

The theatre list was sticky-taped to the door of theatre four's anaesthetic room and Paige removed it. Not that she needed it, she knew exactly which patients were being operated on today. In fact, if pushed, she could probably recite the list for the next month, even though it was next Monday's she was the most fixated on.

There were two paediatric patients on the list this morning. Children were always done first. It caused less stress for the parents, who didn't have to wait around all day worrying about their child going under general anaesthesia, and also for the children, who were often at an age where they were frightened of the clinical hospital environment and didn't understand why they couldn't eat and drink and run around.

A little thrill ran through Paige's stomach at the thought that, come Monday, McKenzie Donald would be first on this list and her spirits lifted even further. Paige couldn't remember a time when she had felt this positive. It had been a long hard three years with many a detour and road-block. It was hard to believe the path was suddenly clear.

Theatre four was frigid when she entered via the swing doors and Paige rubbed at the goose-bumps on her arms. Soon she would be gowned up and under hot lights and wistfully remembering the cold, but for now it seeped quickly into bones that had very little covering insulating them.

You're too thin.

The words Valentino had uttered that fateful night as he had lazily run his finger up her spine crept up on her un-expectedly, as they so often did, echoing loudly in her head and sounding very close in the silence of the empty theatre. So close, in fact, she looked behind her to check he hadn't actually appeared.

Nope. Just her.

She shook her head and frowned. She'd thought about the man so much in the last two months it wouldn't have surprised her to have conjured him up. She'd tried, usually quite successfully, to pigeonhole her thoughts of him to night-time only, to her dreams, but sometimes they crept up on her unawares.

She should have been insulted by his assessment of her body but one look at the heat and desire in his eyes and she'd known that he hadn't been turned off. In fact, quite the opposite—he'd wanted her badly.

It was merely a statement of fact. She was thin.

She hadn't had much of an appetite since the twins had been born prematurely. Daisy's death, Arnie's desertion and McKenzie's fragile health had robbed what little had remained. She ate only to fuel her body, with no real enjoyment when she did.

All her energy was focused on getting McKenzie to eat. McKenzie's appetite. McKenzie's nutritional needs. McKenzie's caloric requirements. Paige Donald came low down on Paige Donald's list of priorities. And, besides, things just tasted so bland.

A hoot of laugher outside in the corridor pulled Paige out of her reverie and she pushed thoughts of Valentino aside. This was daytime. Tonight she could think about him again, dream about him again. Vivid dreams that woke her in a sweat with parts of her throbbing, his name on her lips, his taste in her mouth.

She busied herself getting the theatre set up, grabbing the trolleys and positioning them correctly around the operating table, wiping them down with a solution of surgical spirits. She exited the theatre via the back door into the sterilising room. Four sterilised trays wrapped in special blue disposable cloth were waiting for her and she grabbed the nearest, along with extra drapes and gowns and two pairs of size-eight gloves for Harry and his resident.

She dumped them on the trolleys inside the theatre, ready to be opened by the scout nurse while she herself was at the sinks scrubbing up. She went back out again, selecting other bits and pieces she knew Harry would need—suture material, dressings and, of course, the actual implant device itself.

Paige turned the boxed bionic ear around in her hands.

It was hard to believe that something so innocuous could give such a precious gift. That come Monday one would be implanted into McKenzie's head. She hugged it to her chest, sending up a quick prayer into the universe.

Please let everything be okay.

She went back into the theatre, dropping the extras on the trolley. A noise from the anaesthetic room alerted her to Harry's arrival and she smiled. It was nice working for someone as dedicated as she was. Paige glanced at her watch. Now, while they were still alone, was as good a time as any to ask her boss the question.

She shoved open the swing doors with her shoulder, ready to launch into her spiel. Excited even. Except the man in the anaesthetic room wasn't Harry. He wasn't thin and a little stooped and grey-haired. He was big and broad with curls of dark hair escaping the confines of his theatre cap to brush the neckline of his scrubs. Even if she hadn't dreamt about that back every night for the last two months, the lurch low down in her pelvis would have alerted her to his identity anyway.

Valentino Lombardi looked up from the theatre list he'd been studying and turned. Neither of them said anything for a few moments as a host of memories bubbled between them.

Valentino swallowed. He'd been prepared to see her again but totally unprepared for the sucker punch to his gut as her big grey eyes, round with shock, met his.

'Paige. Bella. We meet again.'

Paige blinked. She even blushed a little as the things they'd done together made her awkward beneath his gaze. It didn't help that he filled out a pair of surgical scrubs better than any man on the planet.

She'd seen him in a tux and in the buff and now in a set

of scrubs. Was there nothing the man didn't look magnificent in? 'Valentino?'

What did he think he was he doing here? Was he here to observe? To assist? Didn't he live in Rome? Or London? Where was Harry?

Valentino saw the confusion in her gaze and shot her a lazy grin. He'd relegated their one night two months ago to a pleasant interlude and done his hardest to forget about it. But standing before him now in baggy scrubs, no make-up, her hair covered in a sexless blue theatre hat, he finally admitted he hadn't forgotten one second of their time together.

A strange unease descended on them and he couldn't bear it.

Paige's heart skipped a couple of beats and then accelerated as his low flirty voice oozed into all the places that still craved his touch. The pinkness in her cheeks deepened as she remembered where his mouth had been. Oh, God! This wouldn't do at all.

'Dr Lombardi.' Paige's voice was stern as she glared at him and regained her composure. 'What are you doing here? Where's Harry?'

Valentino laughed. So much for small talk. He regarded her for a second. What he had to tell her next would have an impact on her probably more than anyone. Harry had stressed the need to break it to Paige gently.

'I'm afraid Dr Abbott had to rush to Hobart in the early hours of this morning. His grandson was kicked in the head by a horse and is in Intensive Care.'

Paige gasped, pressing a hand to her chest. Oh, no! How awful. 'Was it Andy or Ben?' Harry's daughter and her family lived on a horse stud just outside Hobart.

They were a close-knit family despite the distance, and Paige knew this would be devastating for them all.

'Ben.'

Oh, dear, Ben was only four. One year older than McKenzie. Paige moved closer to him, needing to know more. 'How is he? Is he…has he…?'

Valentino covered the distance between them, reaching out for her, clasping her shoulders gently. 'He's critical. That's all I know.'

Paige looked at him, trying to process it. Trying to understand how fate could be so cruel to a little boy and a man who had only ever done good things. 'That's just so…awful. I can't believe it.' She shook her head to clear it, searching his espresso depths, waiting for him to tell her it was all a bad joke. 'I just can't…take it in.'

Valentino nodded. 'Yes.' What else could he say?

Paige wasn't sure how long she stood there, staring at him, trying to clear the block of confusion in her mind. But she suddenly became aware of the slow, lazy circling of his fingers against her upper arms and the clean, male smell of him. When the temptation to lay her cheek against the V of his scrub top came upon her she knew she had to step back.

Valentino released her and watched as she retreated to the nearby bench and leaned against it. 'I'll be covering Harry's patients until he's ready to return.'

It was then that the full impact of this incident hit home. McKenzie. She glanced at him sharply as her heart thudded like a rock band in her chest.

No. No, no, no.

Why? What had she done, what had McKenzie done to deserve such upheaval? The surgery had been delayed too many times already. So many things had gone wrong in her short life. The one constant had been Harry and his absolute faith that he could give McKenzie the gift of hearing that prematurity had robbed her of.

And now that was in jeopardy too. 'My daughter's surgery is on Monday.'

Valentino nodded. 'Yes. Harry mentioned that.' In fact, Harry Abbott had gone to great pains to explain to him that Paige would be understandably concerned and probably not all that happy.

Paige felt awful. She wanted to scream and rant and cry. For Harry as well as herself. Disgust built inside her too. How could she even be thinking of herself, of McKenzie, when little Ben was critically ill?

'It's okay. I'll do her surgery.'

Paige glanced at him sharply as a tense 'No' fell from her lips.

Val's jaw tightened. 'You don't think I'm a good surgeon?'

Paige had the urge to laugh hysterically. This was a truly bizarre conversation. She was having trouble keeping up. 'How do I know, Valentino? I don't know the first thing about you.'

Valentino raised an eyebrow. 'Really? I have one night that says differently.'

Paige slashed her hand through the air, rage bubbling inside that he would make an innuendo at such a time. 'You know I meant—professionally,' she snapped. 'Don't ever, ever, talk about that night again. Okay?' she demanded. 'Just don't.'

Valentino had every intention of talking about it again. In fact, standing before her, his loins stirring at the memory of them, he had every intention of doing it again. But he could see she was close to the edge and that night, for now, was better off left in the past. He put his hands up in front to calm her.

'I am a world-class cochlear surgeon. I'm head of the department in a large London hospital. I chair an international cochlear implant committee. I have performed this operation countless times on both children and adults. And…' he placed his hands on his hips '…I am a damn good surgeon.'

Paige shook her head, his arrogant stance and impressive credentials falling on deaf ears. He didn't get it. He just didn't get it. This was McKenzie.

McKenzie.

Her child. Did he think she would allow a total stranger to cut into her? Drill a hole in her head? Did he think that was an easy thing for her to consent to? Never mind allowing someone she didn't know to do it?

Still, she was torn. McKenzie needed the operation and if they delayed now, who knew how much longer it might be? Her heart broke, thinking about yet another delay for her beautiful baby girl locked into a world of silence. 'I'll wait. I'll cancel and wait for Harry to return.'

Valentino flinched inwardly, surprised that her rejection of his skills would feel so personal. He gave a stiff bow. 'Of course, that is your prerogative.'

Paige nodded. 'Yes.'

'It could be a long time,' Valentino murmured. 'Harry was talking about months, maybe a year if Ben needs extensive rehab.'

The thought of McKenzie waiting that much longer was like an ice pick to her heart. She wanted to weep and wail and beat her chest. She shrugged instead, struggling for nonchalance, the effort nearly killing her. They'd waited this long…

Valentino could see the abject disillusion written all over her face and shimmering in her big grey eyes. 'Why don't you hold off making a decision until after today? Watch me in action. Then tell me you don't want me to operate on your daughter.'

Paige couldn't believe he would think it was quite that simple. 'It's not just about that, Valentino,' she snapped. How were they supposed to have any kind of doctor/mother-of-patient relationship with their one-night-stand between them?

God, why had she been so impulsive two months ago? She was never impulsive!

Valentino regarded Paige, her implication clear. 'I will treat McKenzie like any other child who is a patient of mine.'

'And me?'

Valentino shrugged. 'Like any other mother.' Liar. He stood still, waiting for the thunderbolt.

'Oh? How many of the other mothers have you slept with?'

Valentino gave a grudging smile. 'I thought we weren't talking about that?'

Paige sighed, too weary and plain heartsick to respond properly. 'No. We're not.' She glanced at him, the epitome of cool, calm and collected, while she felt all at sea. There was still so much she couldn't wrap her head around. 'I don't understand how you're even here, now…in the country.'

'Harry interviewed me months ago. He's thinking of retiring—'

'Retiring!' Paige spluttered. 'He never mentioned retiring to me!'

'He's sixty-eight years old,' Valentino calmly pointed out.

'Yes, but…' Harry talked to her about everything. And he still had so much to give, to contribute.

'I've wanted to work in Australia for a while now,' Valentino continued, his gaze on the little frown nestled between her caramel brows. 'I think there are things I can learn here to take back home with me. I have my visa, all I need is the right job. I was attending a symposium in Melbourne—'

'"Bionic Ear in the Twenty-First Century?"' Paige enquired absently, not really caring. Harry had given a paper at it two days before.

Valentino nodded. 'Harry contacted me in the early hours of the morning and asked me to fill in. I got the five a.m. flight out of Melbourne.'

'Oh.' So they'd be working together too. This wasn't how it was supposed to pan out. None of it was. But, then, when had her life gone according to plan over the last three years? Bitterness rose like bile in her throat. Wasn't it her turn to catch a break?

Valentino pushed off the bench opposite, which he'd propped himself against, and took three paces until he was standing in front of her. 'Watch me today, Paige,' he murmured. 'Then we'll talk.'

Paige felt his husky tones wash over her, soothing the burn and the knot of worry that sat like an iron fist deep in her gut.

And before she could refute him, rebuff him again, he turned away and she watched as he exited the anaesthetic room.

So much for feeling positive. How could her day have gone to hell so early?

It took about ten minutes into the first surgery to convince Paige of Valentino's capabilities. He was, indeed, an ex-

tremely good surgeon. Efficient, steady, sure and capable.
Methodical in his approach, supremely knowledgeable,
unfailingly polite and, despite the mask and being covered
head to toe in green, devilishly charismatic.

There wasn't one nurse he didn't flirt with, including
Di Hamilton, who'd been married for thirty-five years and
had twelve grandchildren. It was obvious he adored
women and Paige watched as every female fell under his
spell.

But he was a man's man too. From the nervous surgical
resident who was assisting to the orderly adjusting the
theatre light, he won them all over, talking football and
Australian beers and the price of petrol.

They all loved him. Paige wished she could say the same.
Between concentrating on her job, the thoughts circling in
her head at a thousand miles an hour and the cataclysmic
brush of his arm or fingers as she passed him an instrument,
she was totally over him by the end of the day.

Every breath, every move, every chuckle or low request
for something stroked along her pelvic floor and took her
right back to that night. Being under him. The way he'd
felt inside her. Which only agitated her even more. She had
bigger things to worry about. Like poor Harry and his
grandson. And McKenzie.

It was like she was in a bubble with him, just the two
of them, everyone else fading into insignificance. She
knew that was the way it often was between surgeon and
scrub nurse, requiring a special kind of synchronicity. But
it was more than that and she knew it. She'd anticipated
Harry's every move in Theatre for the last two years but
had never felt this more base reaction.

She just wanted out. To get as far away from St Auburn's

and Valentino Lombardi as possible. To hug McKenzie and remember what was real in her life and what was fantasy.

When the last op was finished, Paige couldn't get out of her gown quickly enough. Thankfully Valentino had left the theatre to go and do post-op checks in the wards and she was able to breathe again. To function without a pulse that kept racing and a stomach that wasn't looping the loop. To clean up. To do her job.

She was back in the audiology department thirty minutes later, making notes in patient charts, very aware that she had the next six weeks off and conscientious enough to ensure everything was up to date on today's operative cases.

'Here you are. Gloria said you'd be here.'

Paige's heart gave a jolt and she braced herself as she looked up from her chart. He was lounging in the doorway in trousers and business shirt, open at the neck and turned up at the cuffs, looking dark and tousled and incredibly sexy.

'You have hat hair,' she commented, before casting her eyes downwards again.

Valentino chuckled, ruffling his locks. 'Yes.' He guessed that was one of the advantages to her pixie cut. Not a lot of hair there to get bent out of shape.

'I thought you might like to know that Ben's condition has stabilised a little.'

'Oh!' She glanced up quickly. 'What a relief!' She'd tried to ring Harry during the break between lists but had got his message bank. 'Thank you.'

If anyone knew what it was like to watch your child

critically ill in an intensive care unit on life support, it was Paige. Her heart went out to Harry and his family. She didn't envy them the days ahead.

Valentino nodded. 'We're all going for a drink after work. Why don't you come? I can give you a lift if you like.'

Paige ignored the traitorous pull she felt at his invitation. Was he insane? 'Sorry. I can't.'

Valentino gave her a wry smile. 'Can't or won't?'

Paige shook her head. 'Can't.'

'Who takes care of McKenzie when you work?'

'My mother.'

'I bet she wouldn't mind staying on for an extra hour.'

Paige knew for a fact she wouldn't. But that wasn't the point. She wanted to see her daughter. She missed McKenzie desperately when she was at the hospital and resented the hell out of Arnie for putting her in a position where she had to work to support them both.

Paige took in the lazy grace with which he lounged in the doorway, the charming smile on his face and those dimples, which thankfully the mask had hidden all day. What did an Italian playboy know of her mundane, hand-to-mouth, practically housebound existence?

'Sorry. I can't.'

Valentino pushed out of the doorway and sauntered towards her. He placed two hands on the desk where Paige was sitting. From his height advantage he could see the ridges of her prominent collarbones. And the unlined curve of breast which told him she wasn't wearing a bra under her modest T-shirt. 'You know you want to.'

This close he looked better still. And smelled absolutely divine. She put her pen down and plastered a bored look on her face. 'I don't expect you to understand, with your carefree, different-girl-every-night lifestyle, but I'm a mother.' She said it slowly so he understood. 'At the end of the work day I go home to my child. I even look forward to it. That's what a parent does.'

Valentino gripped the desk hard. She was wrong. He did understand. There'd been a girl once, a long time ago. And, briefly, a baby.

He frowned. He hadn't thought about Daniella, about the baby that never was, in years. He pushed off the desk lest the urge to speak about it, to tell her he did know, overcame him.

He folded his arms. 'Suit yourself.'

Paige nodded. She intended to. His dimples and his lazy lounging had gone and he was all dark brooding intensity. It was equal parts sinister and sexy. 'Hadn't you better be going?' she asked pointedly as the silence between them grew.

'I was wondering if you'd had a chance to think over McKenzie's operation?'

Had a chance? She'd thought about little else all day. And she knew she didn't have it in her to postpone again over something so petty in comparison to her daughter's deafness. Not when she had the services of a world-class surgeon and a place on his Monday-morning list.

Still, her pride, all she had left these days, made the words difficult and she hoped she wouldn't choke on them. 'Yes, I have.' She nodded, dropping her gaze to the top button of his shirt. 'I'll not be cancelling.'

Valentino regarded her for a moment. He could see how hard it had been for her to say the words. He hadn't wanted that. He'd sensed from the beginning that Paige was like a tightly coiled spring, just holding it all together. It wasn't his object to break her. Not like this anyway. 'Good. I guess I'll see you Monday morning.'

And he turned away, heading for the door.

'Wait.'

He turned back. She'd risen from her seat and was looking at him with desperation in her eyes.

'I need to ask you something. A…favour.'

Valentino clenched his fists at his sides. He could tell she was uncomfortable asking something that was obviously quite personal to someone who, apart from one frenzied night two months ago, was a relative stranger. 'Okay.'

'I want to be in there. With McKenzie.'

Valentino took a moment searching for a way to soften the instant denial that had sprung to his lips at her completely unethical suggestion. No wonder she'd looked so hesitant. 'Paige.'

'Not scrubbing in or anything. Just…there. Nearby.'

He searched her big grey eyes. Saw the worry. The anguish. '*Bella*, you know I can't allow that.'

Paige shut her eyes. This was so unfair. Harry would have. She felt like she was about to burst into tears and his endearment didn't help. She would not break down in front of him. 'Don't. Don't call me *bella*.'

'You need to be a mother on Monday,' he murmured. 'McKenzie needs you to be a mother.'

'Harry would have allowed it,' she said, defiance in her gaze.

'No, Paige, I doubt very much he would have.'

Paige swallowed hard. 'Please.'

Valentino wanted to go to her. He could see her struggle,

knew this was difficult. But he could also see she wouldn't want his sympathy. He ground his feet into the carpet. 'Don't you trust me?'

Paige bit down hard on the lump in her throat. 'Of course I do.' And she did. She knew McKenzie was safe in Valentino's skilled hands. But she'd never been apart from her, had been by her daughter's side through all her ups and downs. She couldn't let her go through this momentous surgery all alone.

'Then let me do my job. And when it's over, you can do yours.'

Paige swallowed another block of emotion welling in her throat, desperate to persuade Valentino. 'Is this about the drinks?'

Valentino stilled, her implication smarting. His eyes narrowed as he tempered his words. 'Be very careful, *bella*. I don't like your insinuation.'

To her horror a tear squeezed out before she could blink it away and she was as vulnerable and as exposed to a man as she'd ever been. Not since Arnie had walked out on her after Daisy's death had she felt so completely at the mercy of a man.

What did he want? Did he want her to beg?

That she wouldn't do.

Valentino stepped towards her as the tear trekked unhindered down her cheek. 'Paige.'

She dashed it away and held out her hands to ward him off. 'Go. Just go, damn it!'

Her words pulled him up short and as much as the doctor in him urged him closer, the man knew she was only just holding it together and the last thing she'd want was to break down in front of him.

He nodded. 'See you Monday.'

Paige waited for him to leave before flopping back in the chair and bursting into tears.

CHAPTER THREE

PAIGE was finger painting with McKenzie when the doorbell chimed on Sunday afternoon.

Who on earth could that be?

She just didn't get visitors, other than her parents and they'd left a few hours ago. And if she did, she liked to have prior knowledge, screen them first. The days of people just popping in were long gone. Even Nat knew to call first before she brought Juliano around for a play.

Paige tried to control, as much as she could without making her daughter a virtual prisoner, the numbers of people she exposed McKenzie to. The more outside contacts, the greater the risk to McKenzie's less than robust immune system. Paige knew only too well that a mild illness a normal toddler could shake off in a few days usually landed McKenzie in hospital on a drip.

She knew people thought she was a control freak but she could live with that.

'Coming,' she called as she quickly washed her hands under the tap in the kitchen. It was probably somebody trying to sell her something and with the operation tomorrow weighing heavily on her mind she really didn't have the patience for it.

She yanked open the door, mentally drawing herself up to give the person on the other side the thanks-but-no-thanks-now-go-away spiel and shut the door on them as quickly as possible.

Except Valentino Lombardi smiled down at her, dimples a-dazzling, and Paige felt her chest deflate. He was wearing faded blue jeans, a white T-shirt and wicked aftershave. His hair was damp, curls clinging to the back of his neck, as if he'd not long been out of the shower.

It made her excruciatingly aware of her own rumpled state. Baggy trackpants and a tatty oversized T-shirt falling off her shoulders and streaked with paint. 'Oh.'

Valentino quirked an eyebrow. She had a smudge of dried red paint on her cheek. He liked it. 'You were expecting somebody else, yes?'

Yes. Anybody but you. She frowned. 'How do you know where I live?' Had he been following her?

Valentino grinned. 'Alessandro.'

Of course…Paige made a mental note to call Nat and ask her not to give out her address to Italian Lotharios.

Valentino noticed the tightening of her lips. 'Don't be cross with them. I told them I wanted to meet McKenzie before the surgery tomorrow.'

McKenzie chose that moment to appear, grabbing hold of Paige's leg with her paint-smeared fingers and shyly looking up, all the way up, at Valentino. Paige shifted slightly to accommodate her daughter, her hand automatically going to cup the back of McKenzie's head.

'Ah.' Valentino smiled. He crouched down so he was at eye level with the diminutive little girl. As her chart had indicated, she was thin but her eyes were bright and intelligent. 'Here she is.' He signed as he spoke. 'Hello.'

McKenzie's eyes, so like her mother's but framed by blonde ringlets, widened for a moment before she shyly signed her greeting back.

'I'm Valentino.'

Watching McKenzie's tiny fingers form all the letters that made up her name always clawed at Paige's heart and today was no different. Had she known her daughter would be deaf, she would have chosen a much shorter name.

'Hello, McKenzie,' Valentino signed back, speaking the words also. 'I'm very pleased to meet you. You have paint on your nose.'

Paige watched as McKenzie, shy by nature, actually grinned at Valentino as he gently swiped at it with his finger. She could see the same sort of recognition in her daughter's gaze that she'd seen in other females whenever he was near. An awareness of him as a man, a purely feminine response to his charisma.

For goodness' sake, she was three years old! Did the man have to charm every female he came into contact with?

Paige drew her daughter closer, her hand firm on McKenzie's shoulder. 'Do you usually make house calls?'

Valentino grinned one last time at McKenzie and rose to his full height. Paige was annoyed. But, then, when wasn't she?

'No.'

'Then why are you here? You could meet my daughter tomorrow morning on the ward.'

Because Harry had asked him to speak with her. And he had agreed, even though he knew Paige was big trouble. Her appeal to him the last time they had been together, her pride, as tears had shone in her eyes, had captivated him.

He should run a mile. He didn't do this. He didn't get involved. Yet he'd thought of little else except her all weekend. And then there was Harry.

But not yet.

'I wanted to see you were okay. After Friday.' He held up a bottle of wine and a brown paper bag. 'I brought a peace offering.'

Paige stiffened. Did he really think she could relax over a glass of wine with him? 'There was no need. I'm fine.'

Fine she may be but all Valentino could see was a woman who was starving, both physically and emotionally. Shutting herself off, denying her body the things it needed. The things every body needed. Denial was not good for anyone.

He crouched down to McKenzie again. 'What do you say, McKenzie?' he said as he signed. 'Can I come in?'

McKenzie smiled at him and nodded, holding out her multicoloured hand. He took the little girl's offering and rose, quirking an eyebrow at Paige.

Paige glared at him. 'That was low.'

He smiled and took a step forward as Paige fell back passively, like she feared his nearness. He took full advantage as McKenzie led him into the apartment. 'You need to eat,' he said, moving past her. 'Lucky for you I've found the most amazing delicatessen near where I'm staying.' He looked down at McKenzie and moved his hands as he said, 'Kitchen?'

Paige stared at him as McKenzie pointed and then happily led Valentino to where he wanted to go. How had that happened? It was a few moments before she registered the drift of Valentino's chatter coming from the other room and the fact she was still standing like a powered-down robot in the hallway, staring after them.

She sighed and shook her head as she followed. How long would it take to get him out? By the time she'd reached the kitchen Valentino had seated McKenzie on the bench beside him, poured two glasses of wine and was supervising as her daughter distributed a variety of olives into little bowls.

She leaned against the jamb. 'Making yourself at home, I see.'

Valentino looked up at an unsmiling Paige. Her shirt had fallen off a shoulder and he could see the distinctive hollow above the bony ridge of her collarbone. He also noticed the lack of bra strap. Not that he could make out anything interesting beneath the shapeless shirt.

'McKenzie is very helpful.'

It was strangely sexy to see him in her kitchen, laughing with her daughter. His broad shoulders stretched the confines of his white T-shirt as his hip rested casually against her counter. Even more sexy was the way he signed and talked without conscious thought, as if it was completely natural.

McKenzie, noticing Valentino's interest had wandered elsewhere, turned and grinned at her mother, and Paige's heart rose in her throat. Her daughter never took to anyone this quickly. Trust her to take to a guy who, like her father, was never going to stick around.

Absently she noticed that Valentino had had the good sense to wash the paint off McKenzie's hands first.

Valentino removed the still warm baguette from the bakery bag. 'Ah.' He held it to his nose and inhaled the yeasty fragrance. *'Quello sente l'odore di buon.'*

He offered it to McKenzie to smell as well, which she did mimicking him perfectly. 'You like?' he signed, and McKenzie nodded. He located a knife in a drawer near his hip and sliced the bread into thick discs before arranging them on the plate next to the olives.

'Is there somewhere we can eat this?'

Hell!

Paige, also used to signing and speaking while her daughter was around, followed his lead. 'Will the deck be good enough for your lordship?'

He looked at McKenzie and winked. 'Perfect.'

Valentino scooped McKenzie off the bench and she skipped after her mother the second her feet touched the floor. He loaded the food and wine onto a nearby tray and followed the women through the house.

They passed through an airy lounge room cluttered with children's toys and framed photographs. Valentino's gaze fell on a largish one standing on top of the television. It was Paige with an older couple. Her parents? She was younger, her figure fuller, rounder, no angles. Her hair in a caramel bob. And she was laughing, her grey eyes lit with an easy humour.

Interesting.

His gaze returned to her as she stepped out onto the deck, her back ramrod straight, very different from the relaxed woman in the picture. Although it was lost in the fold of a voluminous shirt, he still remembered how her back had looked, long and elegant, bare to the hollow, on the night of Alessandro's wedding.

Still remembered running his fingers down the naked length of it as they had danced, and the way her breath had caught, the ragged edge to her breathing.

Heat in his loins had Valentino gripping the tray a little harder and searching for something to take his mind off how well he knew every inch of her body.

Not just her back.

'Does she know about tomorrow?' he asked as Paige indicated for him to take the seat opposite her at a sturdy wooden table.

Paige glared at him as she made room for McKenzie on her chair. 'Of course.'

Valentino ignored the steel in her voice and the seating suggestion as he sat himself at the head of the table closest to her. If he had to force-feed her, she was going to have to be within arm's reach.

'Okay,' he said, plonking the tray between them and handing her a glass. 'Do you want to tell her who I am?'

Paige took the glass automatically. It was a perfectly sensible idea. She'd put off telling McKenzie that Dr Harry wouldn't be doing her surgery until bedtime. Now, particularly as McKenzie seemed quite enamoured with Valentino, seemed as good a time as any.

'McKenzie?' Paige touched her daughter's arm. 'This is Dr Lombardi.' She spelt out each letter of his name even though she knew that at three McKenzie had no concept of spelling.

McKenzie looked at him. 'Valentino,' he reiterated, signing his first name.

Paige bristled. 'Dr Valentino,' she corrected, her voice firm, her signing slashing at the air. 'Dr Harry had to go and visit his grandson who is very sick so he can't do the operation to make you hear again. Dr Valentino is going to do it instead.'

McKenzie looked from her mother to Valentino and back to her mother. 'Dr Valentino is going to make me hear?' she signed.

Valentino looked at Paige, saw the way she nodded confidently, even though her eyes were worried.

'Yes,' she said.

McKenzie turned to look at him with her big blue eyes as serious as her mother's. After a moment she transferred her gaze back to Paige. 'Okay,' she signed, and reached for a piece of bread.

Paige blinked. That had been easy. McKenzie adored Harry. Trusted him. He'd been her specialist for over three years now, since her diagnosis in the NICU, and she loved it when he came to visit her in hospital. Paige glanced at Valentino, searching for a reason. He looked up at her simultaneously with dark espresso eyes and smiled at her, dimples on high beam.

Her stomach looped the loop. Could it be that simple?

McKenzie tugged her arm and she dragged her gaze from his. 'Can I watch *The Wiggles*?' she signed.

She nodded and said, 'Sure.'

McKenzie climbed off the chair and Paige followed her inside to set up the DVD, thanking modern technology and *The Wiggles* for their special DVDs for deaf kids, complete with Auslan interpreter at the bottom of the screen. Just because her daughter was profoundly deaf, it didn't mean she didn't like to wiggle with the rest of the toddlers.

Paige smiled as McKenzie's curls bounced and she laughed at something the red Wiggle had said. But beneath her smile was profound sadness that McKenzie couldn't even hear the sound of her own laughter. Only the prospect of tomorrow, of starting a whole new chapter, dragged Paige out of her gloom.

Valentino watched an even more subdued Paige walk back towards him. She pulled up her chair, picked up her glass and absently swallowed a mouthful of the crisp Pinot Grigio he'd chosen because it came from the area near where he'd been born in the north of Italy. There was no recognition on her face of the glorious crisp, spritzy taste.

He picked up the plate of olives and brought them close to his face, inhaling deeply. 'Hmm. Don't these smell divine?'

Paige looked at the plate with disinterest. 'I'm not hungry,' she murmured.

Valentino smiled. It was going to be fun reviving her appetite. 'Who says you have to be hungry to eat?' He picked up an olive glistening with oil and stuffed with feta and sucked it into his mouth. 'Food is to be enjoyed, *bella*. Not endured.'

Paige watched as the olive disappeared from sight behind Valentino's plush lips, leaving the merest trace of oil smeared on his lips. It was a compelling sight.

'Try one,' he coaxed.

Paige, forgetting that her daughter was nearby, suddenly knew how Adam had felt when presented with the apple. She'd bet he hadn't been hungry either. 'If I do, will you just go?'

Valentino grinned. 'Soon.' He presented the plate to her and nodded encouragingly.

Paige rolled her eyes. Anything that got him and his dimples out of her house soon was worth a try. She selected the same kind he had from the array of plump specimens on the plate. She popped it into her mouth, chewed it twice and swallowed it. 'Happy?'

Valentino tsked. 'You need to savour it, *bella*. Inhale its aroma.' He picked one up and waved it under his nose, inhaling deeply. 'Roll it around your mouth.' He sucked it in with a satisfying *phft*. 'Let it sit on your tongue,' he murmured, shutting his eyes as the salty flavour fizzled on his taste buds.

His eyes fluttered open to discover her gaze firmly fixed on his mouth. Her black pupils had dilated in the grey pools of her eyes and his breath became constricted in his lungs.

He pushed the plate closer. 'Try again.'

Paige shook her head as his low murmur wrapped seductive tentacles around her pelvis. As if seducing an olive with his mouth hadn't been bad enough. 'Are you always this bossy?' she grouched.

Valentino stared into her eyes. 'You are beautiful but you need to eat more.'

Paige let her gaze drop to the array of olives, embarrassed by his empty compliment. She hadn't felt beautiful in for ever. 'I'm just not hungry any more. Not since…'

Valentino heard the catch in her voice. Understood her silence. It may have been a tiny blip a long time ago which he'd buried beneath wine, women and song, but he understood loss a little. 'Since your daughter died.'

Paige nodded slowly as her gaze drifted back to his face. 'Alessandro?'

Valentino inclined his head. 'He mentioned it.'

He seemed so empathetic, his dark eyes soft like velvet. But how could he possibly know? 'I wouldn't expect you to understand.'

'I understand some.'

He held her gaze for a moment or two and then dropped it to the plate and picked up an olive. 'Be careful of this one, it still has its pit.' He presented it to her mouth and pushed it gently against her lips, stroking it against them. 'Don't be deceived by its plainness. The buttery flavour is truly sensational. Creamy. Seductive.'

No one was more surprised than he when she sucked it

into her mouth with no protest. She started to munch and he put his finger against her lips. 'No. Don't. Stop. It's not popcorn. Let it sit in your mouth. Savour it. Roll it around. Tell me what you taste.'

Paige was as surprised by the request as she was by the fact that there was even an olive in her mouth in the first place or that his finger rested tantalising against her lips. She pulled back slightly. 'It's just food.' She shrugged. 'It tastes like food.'

Valentino sighed and shook his head. 'Shut your eyes.'

'What?' Did he think she was mad? 'No.'

Valentino almost shook her from pure frustration. 'Just shut your eyes,' he implored, bringing a hand up to gently shutter her lids.

Paige wanted to tell him to leave. To pull away. But his fingers were incredibly slick from the olive oil and wonderfully fragrant.

'Now, tell me what you taste.'

Paige knew he wasn't going to let this go so she took a moment to tune into the olive sitting in her cheek. She pushed it onto her tongue as he had suggested and mentally homed in on the taste. 'Salty. But smooth, like thick double cream.' She opened her eyes, surprised at herself.

Valentino smiled. 'That's the spirit.' Not giving her a chance to change her mind, he reached for another. A black Kalamata marinated in herbs. 'What about this one?'

Paige closed her eyes again to block out the image of him as he inched it towards her. Her nostrils flared as it slowly moved towards her. What was that herb? Rosemary? Her stomach rumbled.

Valentino pushed the olive past lips that parted slightly at the merest touch, like a flower to the first rays of the sun.

A little burst of heat fizzed to life in his loins. The oil moistened her lips and the urge to follow the path of the olive with his own mouth was an urgent thrumming in his blood.

Paige bit into the flesh, bruising it a little, and let out an almost suppressed 'Oh' as a burst of flavour exploded against her palate. Rosemary and chives and something else. Something spicier. Her lids snapped open and Valentino was so close, so sure. Maybe the spice hadn't been in the olive at all.

'Hmm.' She licked her lips and got another burst of flavour. 'That is good.'

Valentino sucked in a breath. She had no idea. Oil still smeared her mouth and he wanted nothing more than to relieve her of it. Their gazes locked as memories of their night together were suddenly thick between them.

'That's nothing,' he said, dragging his eyes away from her face that was a delightful mix of uncertainty, confusion and newly discovered pleasure. 'You have to taste this ca-membert. It's incredible. So rich and creamy.'

He loaded up a piece of bread with the soft cheese. 'Did you know,' he said as he presented it to her, 'that you shouldn't have cheese on crackers? It should always be eaten with bread?'

Paige eyed the loaded offering coming closer and knew from the still frantic beat of her pulse she couldn't let him feed her again. She reached out and took it from him, suddenly too hungry to deny herself but not stupid enough to invite liberties that she wasn't free to give.

Valentino watched as she took a bite. 'Remember, slowly. Let it melt against your tongue.'

He watched and waited. Waited for the cheese to hit

her taste buds and for her to realise she'd been starving for too many years. When her eyelids briefly closed, he knew he had her.

'Good, isn't it?' He smiled as he reached for one himself. 'The aroma is intoxicating, yes?'

Paige had to agree. Intoxicating. Yes. Just like him. But, seduced as she was, she knew she was treading on very dangerous ground with him. Too dangerous. She savoured the bread and cheese and washed it down with a mouthful of wine that suddenly seemed to sing in her mouth.

Valentino smiled at her and she knew she had to put a stop to it. 'What are you really doing here?'

Still he shied from the information he'd come here to impart. 'I told you. I came to meet McKenzie.'

Paige raised an eyebrow. 'Really?'

Valentino made them another cheese offering each and pushed hers towards her. 'And to, how do you say, clear the air? Set the ground rules. We're going to be working together in the coming months, whether you like it or not.'

Paige stilled. Ben? She sat up straighter. 'You've heard about Ben, haven't you?' Harry had spoken with her briefly on Friday night but she hadn't been able to get hold of him since.

Valentino nodded. 'He has a significant brain injury. They don't think it's fatal but there will be considerable…deficits. They are expecting a lengthy rehabilitation period.'

Paige searched his face for the truth of it. The horrible, horrible truth of it. That's why he'd come. 'You could have rung.'

Valentino shook his head. 'I think you are very close to Harry. I knew you were worried. I didn't want to tell you over the phone.'

Paige nodded absently, knowing it was kind, appreciating it on some level. Poor, poor Harry and little Ben. A deep well of sadness opened inside her and she was quiet for a moment, her thoughts troubled.

After a while she looked at Valentino and it suddenly sank in. For the short term, he was her new boss. They were going to be working together. And he wanted ground rules.

Well, good, she had a couple of her own.

She narrowed her eyes. 'Number one ground rule. We're never going to be…' She broke off, shying from the intimacy of the word.

'What, Paige? We're never going to be what?'

Paige glared at him. He knew exactly what. Did he think she was some shy, wilting Victorian virgin? That she couldn't say the words? Her chin rose defiantly. 'Lovers. Again.'

Valentino smiled. He had to give her points for guts. 'Agreed.' He tended to keep his relationships short and sweet and this one reeked of complicated so her rule suited him.

He made another cheese and bread combo and handed it to her, gratified to see her eat it without protest. 'So let's just be friends. I'm going to be your boss. Your daughter will be a patient of mine. It wouldn't be right to be anything other than colleagues. Friends.'

Paige stared at him. He could seriously do that? 'We can do that? You and I?'

'*Naturalmente.*'

She shot him an incredulous look. 'Do you have many female friends?'

Valentino chuckled. Already she knew him surprisingly well. 'Women love me,' he evaded with a knowing grin.

Of that she had no doubt. Paige laughed in spite of it all. In spite of having an impossibly sexy man right in front of her who she knew carnally and who had just admitted his track record with women didn't usually run to friendship.

She should have been running a mile.

But being friends would certainly make the time until Harry came back to take over McKenzie's care easier. And it would make working for him a lot smoother. She and Harry worked well together not just because she respected his abilities but because she liked him.

Except, of course, Harry had ever seen her naked...

But surely she could have the same kind of relationship with Valentino? If they worked at it. They were both professionals after all.

Paige offered her hand. 'Okay. Friends.'

Valentino looked at her hand. 'In my country we're not big on handshaking,' he teased. 'We prefer to kiss.'

Paige rolled her eyes but kept her arm fully extended. 'There's a shock. Just as well we're in my country, then.'

Valentino chuckled and enfolded her hand in his. 'Friends.'

Paige nodded as a flush of heat spread up her arm and coursed through her system. Not a very good start...

The next morning McKenzie was happily ensconced in a bed in her own private room at St Auburn's. She was comfortable here, her home away from home, unworried as she watched television that she couldn't hear but engrossed nonetheless. Paige sat by her side, her heart splitting in two, her heart palpitating wildly every time she thought about her daughter's imminent surgery.

She'd wanted this. She'd wanted it for so long. But now it was here, it seemed too much. Too much for a little girl who'd already been through enough. She was jumpy and nauseous. Her empty stomach growled at her and she ignored it. She just hadn't been able to face the usual piece of toast she forced down every morning.

'*Buongiorno.*'

Paige turned to find Valentino lounging in the doorway. He wore dark trousers and a deep green business shirt with a paisley tie. He looked relaxed and confident and was like a sudden balm to her stretched taut nerves. She shot him a strained smile.

'McKenzie?' Paige touched her daughter's arm.

McKenzie looked away from the television and her face broke into a wide smile as she waggled her fingers at an approaching Valentino.

Valentino grinned back. 'Are you ready?' He signed as he spoke.

McKenzie nodded and when he held out his hand to her, she high-fived him. Valentino dropped his gaze to Paige, who was currently shredding a tissue into a million pieces. He placed his hand gently on her shoulder and gave it a squeeze. 'How are you?'

Paige bit down on her lip hard. She would not cry. She just wouldn't. She looked up at him. 'Terrified.'

He could see that. He gave her a gentle smile. 'I'm going to take very good care of her.'

Paige nodded. Too emotional to speak. Too scared to open her mouth lest she break down.

'Here,' he said, thrusting another one of those brown paper bags at her. 'I brought you some *biscotti* from the deli. It's to die for.'

Paige frowned and took it automatically. 'I really couldn't eat a thing.'

'You have to pass the time somehow. You may as well eat really good food.' He winked at her, keeping it casual, upbeat, even though he wanted to gather her close and whisper assurances in her ear until she relaxed. But he sensed she was barely keeping herself together and he didn't want her falling apart before it had even begun.

'See you after the op,' he murmured, before swaggering out of the room.

Three hours. Three interminable hours later they pushed a sleeping McKenzie, her head swathed in bandages, back into her empty room, accompanied by a nurse. Paige, who had gnawed through half of the *biscotti* out of sheer nervousness, felt all the worry fall away like the *biscotti* crumbs as she stood. Relief coursed through her, strong and sweet. Her legs wobbled and she grabbed hold of the bedrail.

Paige's breath caught in her throat as she surveyed her daughter. For a moment, lying so still and pale against the white hospital sheets, McKenzie looked like her sister. Memories of Daisy swamped her, those last horrible days rising large in her mind as an awful feeling of dread rose in her chest.

Was McKenzie even breathing?

The nurse busied herself around the bed as Paige leaned over her and pressed kisses to her daughter's face so different without her blonde curly halo. She needed to touch her, needed to know, to be sure.

'McKenzie,' she crooned.

McKenzie stirred, her eyelids fluttering open for a second. 'Hello, baby,' Paige whispered.

She dropped her forehead onto her daughter's chest, shutting her eyes, riding the surge of release as the cold, hard grip of worry slackened its hold. McKenzie's heartbeat coursed strong and sure against her forehead and it was instantly comforting.

It was well after lunch before Valentino joined them. Paige knew there was only a morning list today and had expected to see him some time in the afternoon.

'Hi,' he whispered, approaching quietly.

Paige looked up. He was wearing the same clothes as earlier *sans* tie, showing off the golden skin of his neck. She had the strangest urge to press her face to it.

'Hi,' she whispered back, not wanting to disturb a sleeping McKenzie.

Valentino crouched down beside her. 'It all went really well. In a few weeks we should be able to switch the device on.'

Paige nodded. His voice was a low murmur and she was suddenly overwhelmed by the gift his skilled fingers had given his daughter. She'd been sitting here for hours, trying not to think about it, trying to concentrate on the here and now. But Valentino had opened the door.

A rush of emotion swamped her chest and she could feel her eyes filling with tears. 'Thank you,' she whispered.

'Hey,' Valentino crooned as tears spilled down her cheeks. Her face crumpled and he pulled her head onto his shoulder. 'It's okay.'

Paige nodded as a sob escaped. Then another. For the first time in years she actually felt as if it was really, actually okay.

And she had him to thank for it.

CHAPTER FOUR

TODAY was the big day.

It was totally surreal for Paige. She walked into St Auburn's, McKenzie in tow, pressed the lift button for the fourth floor, stepped out, turned right and walked through the open doors marked Audiology.

It wasn't any different from what she'd done three days a week for the past couple of years.

Except it was. Everything was different.

Today was the day they'd know whether the operation had been a success or not. Today was the day McKenzie would hear.

A week ago Valentino had seen McKenzie for her routine two week post-op check. He'd been pleased with her progress and they'd set this date for the activation of the device.

'Hi, Paige. Hello, McKenzie.' Greg Palmer, the team's social worker, was first to greet them. He grinned at McKenzie as he signed. 'Today's the day, huh?' he said to Paige.

Paige gave him a tight smile as McKenzie went straight to the corner of the large entrance lounge to where she knew the puzzles were kept. 'Yes.'

He squeezed her arm. 'It'll be fine.'

Paige nodded as she pressed a trembling palm against her stomach. Of course it would be okay. 'I'm a little early. Is Ellen in yet?'

Greg frowned. 'I think Valentino's going to do the honours.'

'Oh.' She hadn't counted on that. Ellen was one of the two audiologists in the department and today was her day on, so Paige had just assumed...Valentino must have made room in his schedule to be there for McKenzie.

The knot of nerves in her belly twisted even tighter.

Today, if all went according to plan, was probably going to be quite emotional. And she'd cried in front of Valentino once too many times as it was.

'I think he's already in his office.'

Paige shot a nervous look towards Harry's office. *Valentino's office.* She wanted to go in, was eager and excited on one hand but scared and nervous too. What if they got no result?

'Go,' Greg urged, squeezing her arm again. 'It'll be fine.'

Paige took a deep breath and nodded. 'Come on, McKenzie,' she said, crossing the room to her daughter and crouching down next to her. 'Let's go and see Dr Valentino,' she said as she signed.

McKenzie smiled at her and took her hand and they headed for the door behind which lay a whole new life. Paige knocked lightly and entered at Valentino's command.

Valentino looked up from a pile of charts on his desk as Paige's deer-in-headlights eyes sought his. He knew all about the squall of emotions going on inside her. Had seen it on hundreds of parents' faces as the big moment arrived.

She looked tired, dark shadows beneath her incredibly huge eyes making them appear even more stark in her face. Her clothes, as usual, were two sizes too big, skimming the bony angles of her body, hanging instead of hugging. Had she eaten any of the goodies he'd had delivered to her house every day for the last few weeks?

'Paige,' he said, standing, denying the dictates of his body urging him to go to her. He transferred his attention to McKenzie instead. 'Hello, there.' He grinned. 'Are you ready?' She nodded and he signed, 'Come in.'

Paige held fast to her daughter's hand and didn't move. 'You don't have to do this. Ellen will be in soon. You have surgery.'

She didn't know why she was so resistant to Valentino switching on the implant. A few weeks ago she wouldn't have cared less had it been a trained monkey. But this man, this sexy Italian playboy surgeon, was different. There was more than a professional connection between them, no matter how they tried to avoid it.

There was intimacy. And Paige knew from bitter experience that intimacy left you vulnerable. Something she swore she'd never be again when it came to men.

She doubted it would have mattered had she not slept with him. But she had. And while he was obviously a pro at separating himself from that, standing before him now, she knew she couldn't.

Valentino shrugged. 'I had a cancellation.'

Paige frowned as she searched her memory for this week's theatre cases. 'Who?'

'Paige.' The reproach in his voice was heavy. 'You're off duty, remember?'

'I know. It's just…' Paige didn't understand why she just

couldn't let it go. Why she was resisting. 'That's why we have two audiologists so the surgeon is free to operate.'

'And miss the pay-off? This is the best part of my job, Paige. That moment when my patient hears something for the first time. It's what makes it all worthwhile.'

Paige felt humbled by his response. And petty for equivocating. Every day since McKenzie's surgery tempting edible treats had arrived on her doorstep. From flaky pastries to scrumptious pizzas to the richest of chocolates. All from Valentino.

She'd been trying to dismiss him as a charming, love-them-and-leave-them pretty boy but how could she when confronted not only with his gifts but his heartfelt words? He was a great surgeon, good with his patients, excellent with their mothers and obviously emotionally invested in the gift he gave.

After everything he'd done for her, could she really deny him the rewards?

McKenzie spied the low kiddy table strewn with puzzles and tugged on Paige's hand, dragging her into the office. Paige let an eager McKenzie go and shut the door behind her.

'Why don't you sit down with McKenzie while I get set up?'

Paige nodded and walked on wobbly legs to the table, sitting on the child-size chair beside her daughter.

'Has she had any repetition of those earlier dizzy episodes?' Valentino asked as he tapped away at his computer.

'No.' The first few days post-op Paige had noticed McKenzie would stagger a little on standing. She hadn't been concerned, knowing it was directly attributable to the disruption of the inner ear and they'd settled quickly.

Valentino pressed one last key on the laptop and glanced at Paige. 'Okay. Ready. Let me check how the wound's doing first.'

He got up from his desk and took the seat on the other side of McKenzie. He tapped her hand and when she turned to him he signed and said, 'How is your ear, McKenzie? Can I have a look, please?'

McKenzie nodded her agreement and cocked her head to allow him access. He lifted the angelic curls that covered her right ear out of the way to expose the small shaved area where he'd operated. Two weeks ago there'd been some slight swelling over the bony area behind her ear but now it looked normal. 'It's healed beautifully,' he murmured.

He let her hair flop back over the site. 'Okay, then,' he said to Paige, but signed for McKenzie's benefit. 'Let's fit the external component.'

Paige nodded, apprehension swirling in her gut. 'Dr Valentino is going to fit your new hearing aid,' Paige signed.

Not that it was the type of hearing aid that McKenzie was used to but having worn them most of her life it was the simplest way to explain it to a three-year-old.

McKenzie kept playing as Valentino fiddled with the external component, fixing it directly over the area where he'd implanted the internal part. It was a small circular unit that consisted of a microphone, a speech processor and a transmitter. It linked magnetically to the internal mechanism, which consisted of a receiver and a stimulator.

He then retrieved his laptop from his desk, and set it up at a smaller desk directly behind where McKenzie was sitting. He fiddled some more, plugging the external component into the laptop via a long cord.

'Okay, you know the drill now,' Valentino said. 'I'm going to run the neural response telemetry first. It should take about ten minutes. She won't be able to hear this.'

Paige nodded. She knew that Valentino would pick a few of the electrodes now implanted into McKenzie's cochlear to stimulate via the computer. He would get a reading back which told him that the auditory nerves had responded.

Unlike hearing aids that magnified sound, the cochlear implant directly stimulated the auditory nerves inside the inner ear.

The minutes seemed like hours as the silence in the room built. The urge to drum her fingers on the table was like an itch and she deliberately tucked her hands in her lap.

Valentino nodded. '*Buon*. Good,' he murmured. 'The nerve is responding perfectly so we know the implant's working.'

A rush of adrenaline kicked in at Valentino's confirmation and Paige gripped the table as she gave him a tight smile. She'd been having nightmares that they'd get to this point only to find the implant was a dud.

The first hurdle had been surpassed!

Valentino saw the slight sag to her shoulders and a flicker of relief light her profile, and despite the battle raging inside over professional distance he reached out and gave her shoulder a quick squeeze before returning his hand to the keyboard.

'Okay, I'll switch it on now. Yes?'

Paige nodded. This was it. This was the moment. One or two clicks of the mouse and her daughter should be able to hear sound.

Paige looked so tense Valentino wondered how much longer she could go before she snapped in two. 'It's important not to expect miracles,' he murmured gently. 'A lot of children don't react—'

'I know that,' Paige interrupted. *Just do it!*

'I know.' He nodded. 'But I'm going to go through it anyway. It's different when it's your own child.' He waited for her to protest and when she didn't he continued. 'McKenzie may not do anything at all once it's switched on. That's common. It's hard to know with little ones what they're hearing, particularly if they're pre-verbal or have been deaf all their lives as McKenzie has. They don't even know what sound is.'

He stopped and checked that Paige was with him and then continued. 'I have it on very low so sudden noise doesn't frighten her, but she could cry. That's quite a common reaction.'

Paige nodded again, pleased suddenly that Valentino had taken the time to mentally prepare her for the range of possibilities, even though she knew them back to front. The fantasy in her head was very different from what would probably happen so it was a good reminder.

'Yep. Okay.'

'This is just the first step. It's going to need several mapping sessions as well as intensive speech therapy to train McKenzie's brain to recognise the sounds she'll hear as speech and to learn to talk herself.'

Paige nodded again. 'I know.' She was prepared for the long haul.

'Why don't you sit opposite her and then we'll start.'

Paige rose and moved to the other side of the table. McKenzie, engrossed in her puzzle, didn't even notice.

Valentino clicked the mouse a couple of times. 'It's on. Why don't you try calling her?'

For a few seconds Paige wasn't capable of speech. Of anything. She'd been looking forward to this moment for the last two years and now it was here she was totally overwhelmed. Just like that. One click and a whole new world for McKenzie. It seemed like such an anticlimax. Surely it should at least be heralded by trumpets. Or angels?

A swell of emotion rose in her throat and stuck there, her heart beat like an epileptic metronome, her lungs couldn't drag air in and out fast enough.

'It's okay, Paige,' Val murmured as he watched her emotional struggle. 'Take your time.'

Paige glanced at him. He was smiling at her encouragingly and she swallowed hard. He was obviously well used to the raw emotion of the moment.

'M-McKenzie.' Her voice shook and she cleared her throat. 'McKenzie, darling, can you hear me?'

McKenzie played on, blissfully ignorant to sound or to her mother's turmoil. Paige flicked her gaze to Valentino.

'It's okay,' he said. 'Keep on going. I'll keep adjusting it louder.'

A part of Paige was desperate to gesture to McKenzie, gain her attention. This was the biggest test of both of their lives and Paige couldn't believe how much she wanted her daughter to pass. But pre-empting the process by letting McKenzie know she was speaking to her was pointless— they were after an uncoached reaction.

'McKenzie? I love that puzzle you're doing, sweetie. It's just like that one we have at home with the koalas, isn't it?'

The silence in the room reached a screeching crescendo. She raised her eyes to Valentino, her heart beating so loudly now in the utter silence she thought it might explode out of her chest. 'Nothing.'

The air of helplessness in the word was heartbreaking and surprisingly Val felt Paige's anguish deep in his gut. When had this little girl and her mother become so personal?

He shot her his most comforting smile. 'The telemetry is telling me her nerves are being stimulated. You know sometimes it can take a few weeks for kids to recognise any useful sound.'

Paige nodded, her lips pressed tightly together. She did know. But still she felt gutted.

'I'm going to try clapping.'

'Okay.' Paige tried to keep the dejection out of her voice and failed.

Valentino gave three loud claps. Paige watched as her daughter startled and swiftly turned her head in the direction of the offending noise. She gasped as tears rushed to her eyes.

She'd heard! McKenzie had really heard.

After three years of living in a world where no noise existed, McKenzie could actually hear.

If someone had asked Paige to describe the emotion threatening to suffocate every cell in her body she wouldn't have been able to. She was totally overwhelmed. It was a miracle.

A miracle!

Valentino grinned at McKenzie. 'Hello. Did you hear that?' he signed, and clapped again. 'Clapping,' he said, and did it once more.

McKenzie swivelled her head to look at her mother. The

expression on her face was one of pure wonderment. She pointed to Valentino and clapped.

Paige laughed through her tears, dashing them away with the backs of her hands. Her daughter looked like she'd just invented clapping. Like she was the only person on earth who could hear! And Paige knew exactly how she felt.

'Well, I think that was fairly definite, yes?' Valentino smiled.

Paige nodded wildly, even though her face was threatening to crumple. Her deaf daughter could hear. It was simply the most amazing thing she'd ever witnessed. Even though she'd been present through so many activations in her two years with Harry, this time it was simply incredible.

She rose from her chair and in three paces was by McKenzie's side, picking her up, kissing her face, rocking from side to side. She wanted to spin and twirl, dance like a mad thing, but was aware of the cord attaching McKenzie to the laptop.

Still McKenzie rocked enthusiastically and giggled, holding tight to her mother's neck, enjoying the ride. Paige laughed too, giddy with joy and hope, lighter than air.

'It's amazing. Amazing, amazing, amazing!'

Valentino chuckled. 'Yes, it is.'

Paige slowed and pulled McKenzie against her for a long hard hug. Valentino was watching them with a big smile, dimples on high beam. Even sitting in his chair, he looked big and broad. His long bronzed fingers rested against the keyboard.

Fingers that had given the gift of hearing to her daughter.

'Thank you Valentino. Thank you,' she said over McKenzie's head. 'I don't know how I could possibly thank you enough. Words just seem…inadequate.'

Valentino dismissed her words with a quick wave of his hand. McKenzie's reaction, Paige's reaction, had been thanks enough. He grinned at her. 'I have a great job, don't I?'

Paige grinned back. 'Yes, you do.'

McKenzie squirmed and Paige realised she was still holding her tight. 'Sorry, darling,' she said, lowering her to the floor. McKenzie went back to her puzzle as if nothing momentous had happened and Paige laughed again.

Valentino adored the sound. It was quite melodious and he realised he hadn't heard her laugh, truly laugh with joy and abandon, until now. He guessed she hadn't had a whole lot to be happy about in the last three years. He was glad to have been instrumental in it.

'I like hearing you laugh,' he murmured.

Paige dragged her gaze away from her daughter, sobering a little. He was staring at her mouth and there was intenseness in his espresso depths. Her stomach muscles undulated as if he'd brushed seductive fingers against her belly. 'It's nice to have something to laugh about for once.'

Valentino nodded. 'Shall we continue?'

Paige drew in a suddenly husky breath. 'Please.'

That evening Paige flopped down on her couch utterly exhausted. Who'd have thought excitement could wear you out? They'd spent the rest of the day at her parents' place, watching McKenzie like a hawk, engaging her as much as possible, trying to gauge the extent of her new-found ability.

On the whole there were no major changes to indicate anything had changed. McKenzie didn't seem to respond to their voices but Paige had no doubt now that would come. Towards the end of their visit, however, McKenzie did, very obviously, hear the crash when her grandfather accidentally dropped a metal bowl on the kitchen floor, turning instantly towards the sound and running to the kitchen to check it out.

They spent a hilarious hour dropping as many non-breakables on the floor as possible and revelling in McKenzie's amazed reactions. It was like watching her discover the world for the first time and Paige seriously doubted she'd ever tire of it.

There was a long way to go. She knew that. But today had been a resounding success and as she propped her feet up on the lounge, McKenzie tucked up safely in bed, Paige could honestly say she was content.

She sighed and shut her eyes, weary beyond belief but with a smile on her face. This had been an absolutely fantastic day!

The sharp peal of the doorbell startled her. Who on earth could that be at…she checked her watch…eight o'clock? She groaned. It was only eight o'clock? It felt like three in the morning.

Paige struggled out of the chair, a feeling deep down in her gut intensifying the closer she got to the door. It couldn't be? Could it?

She eyed her standard trackpants and baggy top and briefly wished she was wearing something different. More…feminine. But a spurt of irritation overrode it. She wasn't dressing to please him. And if he was going to keep turning up on her doorstep unannounced then he could take her as he found her. At least she had showered. She yanked open the door.

Valentino smiled down at her. 'Minestrone!' he announced with a flourish.

Her irritation dissipated instantly. She couldn't be cranky with him. Not after today. And he was wearing blue jeans and a snug-fitting T-shirt, his damp hair curling on his nape. 'Are you trying to make me fat?' she grouched.

He lifted the lid off the bowl and brought it close to her face. Mouth-watering aromas wafted her way. 'Yes, *tesoro*. That's exactly what I'm trying to do.'

Paige's stomach grumbled as the smell enveloped her in a warm cocoon. Every day for the last three weeks some sumptuous dish or other had been delivered to her doorstep. It seemed tonight was to be no different.

Except for the personal delivery.

'Let me guess. Mrs Agostino at the deli?'

Valentino gasped and clutched at his chest, feigning injured pride. 'Made it myself. One of my mamma's recipes.'

A man who could cook? Arnie had been the laziest man on the planet. Charming but utterly useless. She hadn't noticed it in the beginning but then their lives had taken a dive and Arnie had not risen to the occasion.

Just when she thought he was like her ex, Valentino went and did something that surprised her. Paige opened the door wider. 'Come in, then.'

She led him to the kitchen, reaching up for two bowls. She heard the scrape of glass against marble and turned to see him pouring two glasses of red wine the colour of ripe mulberries.

He held it out to her and she almost refused. McKenzie

would no doubt wake at some stage during the night, as was her usual pattern, and be up early, as bright as a button. And she was really out of practice with drinking wine. But today he'd performed a miracle and she would have drunk out of a poisoned chalice right now if he'd offered it to her. So she took it.

Valentino smiled and lifted his glass. 'To McKenzie.'

Paige shook her head. 'To you.' And she clinked her glass against his.

They ate their bowls of soup sitting on the lounge. She only half filled hers, giving Valentino the lion's share. But when she'd finished she'd wished she'd kept a little more for herself.

Valentino had been tempting her palate so much these last few weeks she was actually noticing flavours and textures again. Her appetite was hardly normal but instead of ignoring her stomach when it grumbled she actually went looking for something to put in it. Lucky for her, with Valentino's edible gifts hanging around, there was plenty of choice.

She looked longingly at Valentino's bowl. He lifted his eyes from his food and looked at her and she quickly dropped her gaze. But then she noticed how his jeans moulded to powerful quads and she remembered how they'd felt beneath her fingers and she quickly looked away. Thank God she'd had the sense to sit on the cushion furthest away from him on the three-seater after he'd chosen the single lounge chair.

'Would you like some, *bella*?'

Startled, Paige glanced at him. The look on his face was one of pure innocence, the soup bowl thrust towards her. But his eyes and the slight lift of his mouth told her he was perfectly aware of the double meaning.

'No. I'm really full.' Her stomach growled at her loudly as if in protest and she blushed as he chuckled, placing her hand on it to calm the recalcitrant beast.

She was never hungry. Or at least hunger was so inconsequential in her life; she never paid it any heed.

She grabbed her barely touched wine and took a sip. 'So, this is your mother's recipe? What's that herb I can taste? It's so fragrant but I'm afraid I'm out of touch with all things culinary.'

'Basil.' Valentino watched her as she took another sip of wine, her lips pressed against the glass. 'Fresh basil, straight from the pot. My mother always says when in doubt add basil.'

Paige smiled. When he was sitting here like this in her lounge room she could almost forget he was a smooth, seriously sexy playboy with a girl in every port. That he'd dated a supermodel. It was like he was just an ordinary Joe, enjoying a quiet evening at home.

Oh, dear. She did not like the direction of her thoughts. Next she'd be convincing herself she could change him.

Because that had worked so well with Arnie.

'Your mother's deaf, right?'

Valentino nodded. 'Since birth. Maternal rubella.'

Paige nodded slowly. 'So you've always signed?'

'*Si.* I've been signing since before I could talk. We all can.'

'All?'

'Me, my father, my five older sisters. Even Alessandro.'

Five sisters? No wonder he knew women. She'd bet her last cent he'd charmed every one of them. 'Was that hard? Growing up with a deaf mother?'

He shrugged. 'It was the way it was. I never really

thought about it. I'm sure it was a lot harder for her, having six kids to manage.'

'So you speak two languages and sign in them as well?'

'I sign in three actually. I had to learn BSL, British sign language, when I went to London and then when I came here I had to learn Auslan, although it is very closely related to BSL so that was reasonably easy.'

Damn it, did the man have to be so perfect? She folded her arms more tightly across her stomach. 'Has your mother ever expressed a desire to have an implant? She must be a perfect candidate.'

Valentino nodded absently. Paige had pulled the fabric of her shirt taut across her chest and suddenly he could see a lot more. Like she wasn't wearing a bra. Suddenly their decision to be friends was making less sense.

'She is. And I really want her to have one but she doesn't. She doesn't see that there's anything wrong with her. She has a full life, she can communicate and is quite active in the deaf community back home.' He shrugged. 'And I respect that.'

'Does that make me an awful person, then? Do you think by going down this path with McKenzie, my daughter will think that I think something is wrong with her?' She searched his face for an answer. 'Is it wrong of me to want this for her?'

Valentino frowned. He sat forward and placed his bowl on the table. 'Of course not, Paige. My mother is a firm believer in doing what you feel is best. As am I. Implants just increase options for the deaf. She would be proud of you.'

Paige felt a trill of pleasure squirm through her belly at

the thought of Senora Lombardi's approval. 'I bet she's proud of you.'

Valentino grinned. 'But of course. Tells everyone about her son the surgeon.'

Paige laughed. 'That sounds familiar in any culture.'

Valentino regarded her for a few moments. 'There it is again,' he murmured. 'That laugh.'

She grinned. 'It might actually become a habit.'

Valentino's gaze flicked to her shirt where it had fallen off one shoulder and her nipples made two points against the fabric.

Friends, friends, friends.

He returned his eyes to hers. 'Wouldn't that be nice?'

Paige sobered. Very novel. He held her gaze and it was like being sucked into warm dark mud. 'Did I thank you enough? Really, Valentino, I don't know how to thank you enough.'

He shrugged. 'It's my job. I'm just lucky to have the best job in the whole world.'

'Still…' On impulse she stood and took a step towards him. And then another, until she was standing in front of him. 'Thank you so much,' she whispered. Leaning down, she slid her hands to cup either side of his face, her fingers pushing into the luxury of his hair, and pressed her mouth to his in a brief kiss.

It wasn't meant to be sexual. It really wasn't. It was meant to be grateful and heartfelt. A thank-you kiss from the bottom of her soul.

Friendly.

Quick in and quick out.

But she should have known she was playing with fire. Because her senses were filled with him. His food offerings had awakened them to flavour and aroma and texture and she was experiencing them all—his warmth, the scratch of his stubble and the clean male smell of him—and even though she pulled out of the kiss she was incapable of moving away.

Valentino looked up at her. Her eyes had gone smoky and just before she'd covered his mouth, her baggy shirt had fallen forward and he'd feasted his gaze on her pert naked breasts.

It hadn't been something a friend would do.

He was already hard for her as he reached out and encircled her wrists with his fingers.

Paige looked down at where his thumbs ran a lazy path over her pulse points. There was a brief moment when it was possible to back off, to remember that they'd decided not to do this again. But it passed. And then she was sinking her knees into the leather either side of his thighs, straddling him, settling herself against him.

And then they were kissing. Like the world was about to end. And then her shirt was off and his mouth was on her breasts, sucking her nipples deep into his hot mouth, rasping his tongue around them as they peaked and surged against its boldness.

And then his shirt followed and she was reaching between his legs, unzipping him, touching the hard edge of him, rubbing herself against him as she freed him from the prison of his underpants.

'Oh, God,' he groaned, thrusting himself into her hand. 'Condom?'

Paige slowed.

What?

Condoms? Of course.

Her heart was racing as she tried to order her thoughts.

But then Valentino sucked a nipple into his mouth and she clung to his shoulder as her brain turned to mush.

'Condom,' he said again, releasing her thoroughly worshipped nipple.

Paige sucked in a breath, pushing her hands into his hair. 'I don't have any.'

Valentino groaned into her neck. At home he had boxes of the things. Not that he'd used one of them since coming to Brisbane. They pulled apart and looked at each other, heaving in oxygen, their chests rising and falling, sexual frustration adding to their agitation.

They looked at each other for about ten seconds and then they were kissing again, touching, rubbing, sighing, moaning.

And somehow, Paige wasn't quite sure how afterwards, he manoeuvred her trackpants off and then he was in her, thrusting up as she ground down, and they were panting and calling each other's name and it felt good and right and the consequences be damned.

CHAPTER FIVE

VALENTINO had no idea how long it took for them to bump back down to earth. It was a slow realisation. A creeping awareness of the jut of her hips in his palms, the weight of her head against his shoulder, the slight brush of her lips against his collarbone as her breathing returned to normal.

He shifted slightly and murmured, 'I guess there is one advantage to having a deaf child.' He felt Paige smile against his skin and chuckled.

Paige, malaise heavy in her bones, couldn't move. It was warm and cushioned against his shoulder and she felt as if she'd been stroked all over with a thousand velvet fingers. The fact that they were still joined and he was still hard inside her was another incentive not to move.

Although if she did this…

'Don't do that,' Valentino groaned, clamping his fingers on her hips harder, holding them still. How could he possibly still be so hard?

'What? This?' Paige undulated her hips again and felt the full length of him glide erotically against sensitised tissues.

Valentino felt his breath strangulate in his throat. 'Yes. That.'

Paige smiled again, suddenly getting a second wind. She pushed away from his shoulder, her nakedness on full display. She looked down at herself, at how wanton she was, how not herself.

She'd always hated her breasts. They'd always been small and with her weight loss even more so. But tonight they looked one hundred per cent female, the pale blush of her nipples darkening and puckering like raspberries beneath Valentino's rapt gaze.

She arched her back a little and Valentino pulsed inside her. He didn't seem to find them wanting.

Further down she could see his fingers spread wide against the angles of her hipbones, bronzed against her paler skin. She could feel them holding her firmly, holding her close, branding her. His thumbs circled lazily, stroking the sensitive skin where her hip sloped to her belly.

Lower still she could see where they were joined. Where they became one. The most intimate of connections. It was hot and slick, tingling with the remnants of their joining and the hard hot length of him still buried inside her, and Paige undulated her hips again.

This time Valentino thrust a little and she gasped. 'Hmm, that feels good,' she murmured.

Valentino shut his eyes and nodded, slowly pulling out a little and pulsing back in one more time. 'How about that?'

Paige bit her lip as the fuse sparked to life. 'Really good.'

He opened his eyes and watched as her high breasts bounced a little. 'And this?' He leaned forward and took a nipple in his mouth, his tongue mimicking the torture of the deep slow thrusting down lower.

Paige whimpered and stabbed her fingers into his hair,

grasping a fistful and pinning him there. Her hips moved of their own volition and he thrust up again as she slid down.

Valentino moaned, releasing her breast, his eyes shutting as his forehead dropped to her chest. Their bodies seemed to find a rhythm together and he was powerless to resist the pull of it. They were barely moving at all but she was tight around him, holding him inside, massaging his length with subtle flexions and slow pulsations creating a wonderfully erotic friction that stoked a furnace deep in his belly.

He slid one hand to her naked bottom, pressing her closer, and the other up her back until his hand cupped her nape, his fingers furrowing into her hair. His lips brushed her chest, her collarbone, the hollow at the base of her neck.

She whimpered at the back of her throat and he could feel her trembling. Could feel a corresponding quivering of his own muscles as a climax that had been on a slow burn ignited to full throttle.

When she gasped and threw her head back his hand slid to her shoulder and he pulled her closer still, their joined bodies slick with heat and sweat as they rocked.

'Valentino,' Paige cried, as her orgasm broke and she bucked against him.

'Yes,' he groaned. *'Quello è ritiene così buon.'*

Paige had no idea what he'd just said and neither did she care. It was low and husky in her ear and then she was sucked back into the vacuum where only they existed and pleasure was the only purpose.

Valentino looked up from fixing his clothes. Paige was dressed again and watching him with strands of passion still decorating her gaze like dewy cobwebs. She smiled at him and he realised he could get used to that look.

Kiss it goodnight every evening.

Wake up to it every morning.

His smile faded a little as a frisson of unease crawled up his neck.

Because there was no denying in such a short time he had felt a connection with Paige. Even just today, they'd been through so much. Witnessing McKenzie's reaction to his clap had been incredibly satisfying. And talking about his mother this evening had been…nice. Normal. What couples who dated did.

What couples did, full stop.

Not what he did. He didn't do couple stuff.

Not since…

And then there was what had just happened between them on the lounge. Twice.

What the hell was he thinking?

Paige picked up their bowls off the coffee table, the movement of her thoroughly ravaged body shrouded beneath her baggy sexless clothes.

It was a timely reminder that she wasn't the usual type of woman he did this with. Despite the sexual gratification shimmering in her gaze. She was a single mother with a high-needs child. She had commitment written all over her. She was a couples woman. Or at least she deserved to be.

And this was the second time they'd got naked together. It was starting to feel like something a little more serious than what he usually went in for.

He didn't have a script for that.

Not any more.

'We can't do this again,' he said.

Except all he could think about was doing it again. Stripping those godawful clothes away and doing it in every room in the house.

And then maybe come back and do it all again tomorrow. *No. No. No.*

Paige blinked, setting the dishes down. Okay.

She knew he was right, of course but, deep in her heart a little dent appeared. She shrugged with as much nonchalance as she could muster. 'Of course.'

Valentino blinked. Well, that was easy…

In his experience women didn't usually take those five words all that well. 'I don't really do anything serious,' he explained, not really understanding why he felt the need to clarify things. 'And I think it's a bad idea for colleagues to get too involved.'

Paige suppressed a laugh. He hadn't been too worried about it thirty minutes ago. But he was certainly running now! Looked like the playboy had reached his end game.

Well, that was okay. Or it would be. This had only ever really been one thing. A thank-you kiss that had got way out of control.

Just as well, though, she hadn't expected anything from him. That Arnie had hardened her heart to romantic nonsense and that she didn't have the time or the energy for someone else in her life. How many women had he devastated with that turn of phrase? She could well imagine how some dates would not take it so well.

'I agree.'

Valentino nodded, his hands on his hips, waiting for the *Oh* that usually came in this part of a conversation he was especially good at.

It didn't come.

He decided to explain further. 'I think we're adult enough to accept this for what it was.'

Paige suppressed a smile. 'It's okay, Valentino. I understand. Neither of us do this.' She gestured back and forth between them. 'I can't and you choose not to. It's fine.'

He opened his mouth to protest her assessment but he couldn't. He did choose not to. Since Daniella.

This was what he did. This was what he was used to.

'So…colleagues? Friends?'

She quirked an eyebrow. 'We're back to that again, huh?'

'You think you can't do it?'

'Oh, I can do it.' Did he seriously think she had time to sit around pining after him? She stuck her hand out. 'Can you?'

Valentino regarded her outstretched fingers. Remembered how they'd felt digging into his back. 'But of course.' And he clasped her hand in his and gave it a firm shake. 'I'll see you at the clinic tomorrow.'

Paige followed his broad back to her front door. He seemed to take up all her hallway and as some internal muscles protested her movement she was reminded of how big he was everywhere.

Valentino pulled the door open, paused and turned. 'What if there are consequences?'

Paige regarded his serious face with a sinking feeling. Somehow, even without the dimples, it looked as sexy as hell. She didn't like the direction of his thoughts.

Paige sighed. 'It'll be fine.' She hadn't had a proper period since the twins had been born. She doubted she'd even ovulated regularly the last two years due to her borderline weight.

She probably had the fertility of a panda.

'It's…safe?'

She knew what he was asking and it was an assurance she felt one hundred per cent comfortable with giving, even though they both knew, as medical professionals, no time was one hundred per cent safe. 'Yes. It's safe.' Still, she found it difficult to meet his gaze and she looked out at a point beyond his head, to the darkness of the street.

Valentino reached forward and lightly grabbed her chin, directing her gaze back to his. He fixed her with a stare. One that told her he meant business. 'I want to know, Paige. If…'

The mere thought of it was so painful Paige couldn't even contemplate it. She certainly was clueless to the slight edge of menace in his tone, to the fierce light in his eyes. Even mentioning it without actually saying the word was enough to fracture the surface of her heart and she shut her mind to it, blocked it like a force field.

'It'll be fine,' she repeated, before stepping back, causing his arm to fall by his side.

There would be no pregnancy.

Valentino regarded her for a moment or two longer before delivering a slight bow and disappearing into the night.

The next few weeks flew by. Life was fuller, crazier than normal. Further mapping sessions of McKenzie's implant and twice-weekly speech therapy chewed up her remaining three weeks at home.

But the rewards were amazing. After a few days it was evident that McKenzie heard just about everything and it was like witnessing the world being created all over again, seeing her wonderment of it all.

Instruments in the toy box that had merely moved in the past now made noise. The drumstick did more than bounce off the taut surface of the bongos—it actually bonged. The tambourine did more than shimmy—it rattled. And the sleigh bells tinkled.

But not just that. The doorbell chimed. And the plughole sucked and gurgled greedily as the water swirled away. And the television talked to her. The Wiggles talked to her! Every sound was new and amazing.

In the beginning she'd caught McKenzie just looking at objects that created noise, as if expecting them to get up and produce sound completely unaided. But she'd caught on quickly and no object was safe.

Her speech had also come on. In just a few weeks she already had a handful of words. Paige had never dared hope for the day that she would hear her daughter say 'Mummy'. But she had. And it had simply been the best moment of her life.

McKenzie still signed as she spoke—they both did— and Paige wondered how long it would be before her verbal communication skills were such that they out-stripped her signing vocabulary. They would always need to sign as McKenzie was still deaf without her external device so it was vital to keep up their signing vocabulary as well.

And, anyway, being bilingual was such a skill— Valentino being a classic example—it would be a shame to lose it.

Before Paige knew it, it was time to go back to work, which she did reluctantly. Every minute with her daughter as she discovered a whole new world was precious and Paige resented having to surrender any of them.

Sure, McKenzie was in good hands with her parents but that didn't stop the gut-wrenching emotion she felt as she kissed her daughter goodbye three mornings a week. The only consolation was she still got to see McKenzie when she came in for her speech therapy and she made sure she scheduled her daughter's appointments for the days and times she was on the clinic.

There had to be some advantages when you ran the show.

Three weeks in and everything was back running like clockwork. The op had been successful, intensive therapy had been instituted and the care arrangements clicked smoothly back into place. And McKenzie hadn't been sick in months. There was even some roundness to her face for a change, although Paige didn't hold too high a hope for cracking the twentieth percentile any time soon.

She and Valentino had even managed to find a happy medium in their relationship. She'd expected it to be awkward at first, like the day they'd first met again after that fateful night, but they'd both been invested in making it work. And he was great with McKenzie, who had also learnt to say 'Dr Valentino' very quickly.

Finally there'd even been encouraging news with little Ben, who'd been transferred out of Intensive Care and admitted to a specialist acquired brain injury rehab ward.

Things were great for once. All the planets were aligned. The gods were smiling. Life was good.

And then it all went to hell.

The last day of her third week back started as an ordinary day. Nothing remarkable. Until she was standing in neck-to-toe green, masked and hatted, waiting for Valentino to finish drying his hands and gown up, and a strong urge to go to the toilet gripped her bladder.

She frowned as she mentally suppressed the urge. For goodness' sake, she'd already been three times this morning already. Once when she woke up, once when she got to work and just prior to scrubbing up. How on earth could she possibly want to go again?

And, anyway, she couldn't just walk out of the theatre and go to the bathroom. She was scrubbed, sterile. It would require degowning and then rescrubbing and regowning, and with theatre times tight they didn't have the luxury of running on the whims of her bladder.

She gritted her teeth and ignored it, holding the cuff of Valentino's glove open ready for him to thrust his hand straight in.

'Thanks,' he murmured as he repeated the process on the other side.

Paige could tell by the smile in his eyes that his dimples would be flashing beneath the mask. Normally that would be exceedingly distracting, despite their determination to keep things asexual, but today, as her bladder twinged again, it didn't even rate.

She clamped down on the sensation, trying for mind over matter as the three-hour operation stretched in front of her. There was no physical way her bladder could be full again.

She'd had a glass of water with breakfast and that had been it. Years of working as a scrub nurse had taught her not to drink tea or coffee prior to commencing surgery for just this reason.

It wasn't physically possible to have anything in her bladder. Surely?

Maybe she had a urinary tract infection? But no. It hadn't stung or burned at all. Fever? She did feel hot but she was swaddled in a gown, under bright operating lights and holding her muscles so tight she was probably over-heating every cell in her body.

Or maybe it was some kind of delayed cystitis from that night a few weeks ago? Valentino's arm brushed hers and for a sweet second she was back on his lap again.

Ten minutes later, though, she knew she couldn't hold on any more. She was actually crossing her legs beneath her gown. 'Darren can you scrub in, please?' she asked, hoping the discomfort in her abdomen wasn't detectable in her voice. Darren was one of the two scout nurses on for the theatre today.

Valentino, who was just preparing the drill, stopped and looked down at her. 'Everything okay?'

She nodded as she passed him the next instrument. 'Fine.'

The five minutes it took for Darren to wash his hands, re-enter the theatre, dry his hands and gown up felt like an hour as her bladder stretched to painful proportions. 'Excuse me for a moment,' she murmured stepping back from the table and degloving and degowning as quickly as possible without looking like her underwear was on fire.

She made it to the bathroom in record time and had never been more pleased to sit on a toilet in her whole life. So when the sum total of fifteen mils was forthcoming Paige was totally unimpressed.

What the hell?

After a further ten minutes of sitting was no more pro-ductive, Paige finally gave up. She washed her hands in the sink, inspecting her face in the mirror. The hollows beneath her cheekbones seemed more pronounced in the harsh fluorescent light. Maybe she did have a UTI? One that just involved frequency? Or maybe a kidney stone was blocking the neck of her bladder, only allowing a dribble through at a time? A painless one?

Hell, maybe she was the only woman on the planet to be in possession of a prostate gland?

She shook her head and watched her reflection follow suit. Maybe it'd be okay. Maybe it wouldn't happen again. Maybe she was going crazy and she should get back to work and stop worrying about something that was probably nothing.

She hurried back to the theatre, washing her hands again before donning a mask and pushing through the swing doors. Valentino and Darren both looked up as she entered.

'You want to scrub back in?' Darren asked.

Paige shook her head. She didn't want to risk it. 'You keep going. I'll scout.'

Which ended up being a wise decision. Paige spent the entire day in and out of the toilet. She may as well have stayed at home for all the help she'd been. And when the last patient was wheeled out of the theatre to Recovery she'd never been more pleased to clock off in her life.

She changed into her civvies, grabbed her handbag out of her locker and hurried back to Audiology to update the day's operating charts. The department had shut for the day and was deserted, for which she was grateful as she steamed into her office and made a quick phone call to her G.P.

This situation was ridiculous and needed remedying as soon as possible. She was put on hold straight away and Paige tapped her foot.

'I knew I'd find you here.'

Paige startled a little as she looked up to see Nat beaming at her from the open doorway.

'Hi.' She smiled back, gesturing for her friend to enter.

'Oh, sorry,' Nat whispered, plonking herself in the chair opposite. 'I didn't realise you were on the phone.'

'It's okay. I'm on hold. What's up? You look like you just won a million bucks.'

Nat grinned. 'Better. I'm—'

Paige held a finger up as the receptionist came on the other end. 'Just a sec,' she said apologetically. 'Hi, yes, my name's Paige Donald. I was wondering if Dr Mantara could squeeze me in this afternoon?'

Paige listened as the receptionist explained it was impossible and tried not to scream her frustration down the phone. There was no point in shooting the messenger. She took an early morning appointment the next day instead and hung up.

Nat crinkled her brow. 'Everything okay?'

Paige sighed. 'I don't know.' She looked at her friend. They'd been close during school but life had pulled them apart again until the last few years. Paige just hadn't had the time or an excess of emotional energy for the type of friendship most women valued. She didn't realise how isolated she'd become until right now as the urge to unburden took her by surprise.

'I think…' She hesitated, unused to sharing such private matters. 'I think I have a UTI.'

'Okay.' Nat leaned forward, placing her elbows on the desk. 'Why don't you start at the beginning?'

Paige told her about the day and the inconvenient frequency symptoms. 'It has to be a UTI, right?'

Nat regarded her for a few moments. 'You're not…? Could you be…pregnant?'

It took a few seconds for Paige to compute what her friend had said. And she laughed. 'Don't be ridiculous,' she dismissed. And then she sobered as a cold hand clutched at her gut. No way. She couldn't be. Surely?

Nat watched a procession of emotions march across her friend's face. 'Are you sure? I thought you and Valentino might be getting—'

'Quite sure,' Paige interrupted, her heart booming like church bells in her chest.

Nat didn't think Paige looked overly convinced. She reached into her handbag. 'I just happen to have an extra one of these.' She placed a packaged pregnancy test on the desk and pushed it towards Paige.

Paige looked at it like it was a venomous snake. She could not be pregnant. Could not. An image rose unbidden in her mind. Daisy's tiny white coffin covered in pale pink roses.

Even now it had the power to paralyse her.

'You know it's the first thing the GP's going to do anyway,' Nat murmured. 'Might as well save her the effort.'

Paige nodded, knowing Nat was right. She looked at the test again, a sudden thought occurring to her. 'Just happen to have this huh?'

Nat shrugged. 'I bought one of those two-in-ones…in case.'

Paige could tell from her friend's face that she'd already used the first one and was trying really hard to be sensitive to Paige's situation in the face of her own good news. 'Does this mean congratulations are in order?'

Nat nodded and then grinned. 'You're the first one to know.'

Paige grinned back, even though inside she felt bleaker than a Bronte moor. 'That's fabulous, Nat.' She leaned forward and gave her friend a big hug. 'Alessandro and Juliano will be over the moon.'

'They'll be ecstatic,' Nat agreed. 'I've been trying to get hold of Alessandro for the last two hours but he's not answering. I just had to tell someone.'

Paige smiled. 'I feel honoured.'

They chatted for the next few minutes about due dates and morning sickness until Nat's phone beeped with a message from Alessandro. 'He's at home.'

'Well, what are you waiting for? Off you go,' Paige teased. When Nat hesitated she said, 'I mean it, go. I'll be fine.'

Nat stood. 'You will do the test, won't you?'

Paige eyeballed it, remembering the last time she'd done a pregnancy test. The joy. The hope. She looked away. 'Yes.'

'I'm going to ring in the morning and check on you.'

Paige rolled her eyes. 'Yes, ma'am.'

Nat leaned down and gave her friend a quick squeeze. 'I'll see you tomorrow.'

The room seemed preternaturally quiet after Nat left. There was just Paige and the test and her heart beat ticking loudly in the silence like the doomsday clock.

Her fingers trembled as she picked it up and turned it over and over. She couldn't do pregnant again. After Daisy had died she'd vowed to never make herself vulnerable like that again. She couldn't stand nine months of living on the edge, being paranoid about things going wrong, demanding scans every week, thinking the worst should there be no foetal movements for a minute, an hour, a day.

Giving birth in a haze of anxiety, constantly testing the baby's hearing, driving herself insane at the slightest sniffle.

Oh, God. What if it was twins again?

And what about McKenzie? Her child, the one she already had, needed her. There was no time for another.

Certainly not for two. There was no spare time to give at all.

She just couldn't do it again.

'Are you going to take that or just stare at it?'

Paige didn't have to look up to know Valentino was standing there. He sounded annoyed.

He could get in line.

'I have a UTI,' she said, raising her face defiantly.

Even glowering at her from the doorway he looked magnificent and her breath caught in her throat. His hair was all messy from the cap and his top two buttons were undone. In another time and place, having his baby would have made her very happy indeed.

'Is that why you kept leaving the theatre today?'

'Yes,' she said testily.

'So why bother with that?'

She shrugged. 'Just pre-empting my GP.'

Valentino's heart beat a crazy tattoo in his chest. What if she was pregnant? What if his baby was already growing inside her? 'What if it's positive?'

Paige felt her stress levels rise a notch. 'It won't be.'

'What if it is?' he insisted.

'It isn't.'

Valentino wanted to shake her. Years ago he'd known briefly what it was like to have created life before it had been snatched away. He was surprised now at how fiercely he still wanted it. 'So go and prove me wrong.'

Paige swallowed. She should. She knew she should. But at least here and now, with the test tucked safely away in its packaging, she could believe in her denial. Once it was out, once the test had been done, it became a whole different proposition.

She stood. 'Fine.' It had been twenty minutes since she had last gone and the urge had returned with a vengeance. May as well get it over and done with. Then at least she could discount pregnancy and get on with having the right tests done.

Valentino stood his ground as she brushed by. He would not be shut out the second time around. 'I'll wait in the lounge.'

Paige's legs felt like wet noodles as she made her way through the lounge area to the staff toilet. Her hands shook as she undid the packaging and it took her several attempts before she was able to liberate it. Between her nerveless fingers and the vibrations of her heartbeat she was frightened she was going to drop the damn thing in the loo!

She doubted very much that Valentino understood the potential impact of this test. How could a footloose, fancy-free, playboy bachelor understand the full implications? For him it was no doubt a test of his virility. Proof of his manliness.

But for her? It was a whole different proposition.

Still, regardless of that, it did need to be done so she took a deep breath and managed to eke out enough urine to do the test.

And even before the little plus appeared somewhere inside she knew.

'Well?' Valentino asked as she appeared back in the open lounge area.

Paige held up the test, barely keeping upright as the foundations of her world crashed all round her. 'It's positive.'

Valentino stared at the pink plus sign. It was a full minute before the information sank in. He was going to be a father. He smiled. And then he grinned. 'This is the best news I've ever heard.'

Paige wasn't similarly overcome. In fact, a huge block of emotion built in her chest till she thought she was going to pass out from the pressure of it. It stung her eyes and prickled in her nose. She sucked in a breath. 'No, Valentino, it's not. This is the worst possible news. You have no idea.'

And she burst into tears.

CHAPTER SIX

WHATEVER Valentino had been expecting it hadn't been this and confronted with her emotional state, he felt at a loss. 'Hey,' he crooned, stepping forward and putting his arm around her shoulders.

Paige shrugged his arm away and moved back. 'Don't touch me,' she half snapped, half sobbed as she wiped at her face with the heels of her palms. 'That's what got us into this mess in the first place.'

'It's not a mess, Paige,' Valentino said gently. 'I'm really okay with this.'

Paige felt a bubble of hysteria rise in her throat to join the mix of other emotions. 'How lovely,' she said sarcastically.

'I'm just saying—'

'Do me a favour,' she interrupted. 'Don't say anything, okay?'

Valentino wisely followed her advice, standing silently, his fists curled by his sides while tears poured down her face. She was in shock. She needed a little time to wrap her head around it. He understood that. But as far as he was concerned, he'd been primed for this moment for a long time. Ever since his ex-fiancée had come into his hospital half-dead from a botched back-yard abortion.

Yes, since then he'd taken precautions to avoid it but whether it was his Italian pride or his legendary uncle status, he'd always known deep down that he wanted to be a father.

And he would move heaven and earth to make sure this child, his child, had everything it ever wanted.

Paige didn't know what to do with herself. Valentino had sat on one of the lounge chairs and was regarding her with his steady brown gaze. 'How can you be so calm?' she demanded. Her cheeks felt hot and she knew she must look a mess. Her nose was running and her face was no doubt an ugly, blotchy mess.

Valentino shrugged. 'I don't see the point in hysteria.'

Oh, really? As far as she was concerned, this was precisely the moment for hysteria. 'Why?' she asked, raking her hands through her hair. 'Why did you have to come along and ruin everything? I was perfectly happy the way I was.'

Valentino was prepared to talk about it, he was even prepared to argue and to cope with more tears, but he wouldn't sit here and listen to her lie to herself. 'I think we both know that's not true.'

Paige choked on a sob. What did he know about her life? 'Are you calling me a liar?'

'I'm just calling it like I see it, Paige.'

Paige's lips twisted into a bitter grimace. 'Oh? And what do you see? This should be interesting.'

'I see a woman whose world was torn apart. One who's going through the motions but can't get any enjoyment out of life. I see someone who's physically and emotionally starving.'

Paige shied away from the truth that resonated in his words. 'I'm eating,' she said, completely exasperated.

'Great. So your stomach is full but what fills your emotional well, Paige?'

'That doesn't matter,' she dismissed.

Valentino snorted. 'Of course it does.'

'Well, what fills yours, then, Valentino?'

'Vivaldi.' It was sterner than he had meant it to come out but her stonewalling was frustrating in the extreme. He continued in a gentler tone. 'A letter from my mother. The first time a patient hears sound. Children laughing. Bruschetta. The way a woman's waist curves out to her hip. *Swan Lake.*'

Hell, did he think she had time for ballet? 'What? No raindrops on roses?'

'Paige.' This was no time for deflection. 'The point is I can take enjoyment from the world around me. When was the last time you did that? When was the last time you rejoiced in being alive?'

Paige fleetingly thought about those few seconds of dread that she woke with every morning and quickly pushed them aside.

'Oh, for crying out loud,' she snapped. 'I don't have time to get my emotional well filled.' She suddenly felt overwhelmed by everything and sat in the lounge opposite Valentino. 'I'm the sole parent to a high-needs child. I certainly don't have time for another baby. That wouldn't be fair to McKenzie.'

'You don't think McKenzie would like a brother or a sister?'

Paige rubbed her brow. 'I'm sure she would. I'm also pretty sure she'd like a unicorn. Unfortunately she doesn't get a say.'

Valentino chuckled but, as he had just stated, she didn't

find any joy in it. She turned beseeching eyes on him. 'I'm tired, Valentino.'

'I'll be here. I'll help.'

Her gaze turned quickly incredulous. How long would it take an Italian playboy surgeon with an international reputation to grow tired of playing house in little old Brisbane? She hardened her heart to his pretty words. Arnie had also promised he'd help. Promised he'd be here until death parted them.

Obviously he'd taken Daisy's death as a literal translation. Their daughter hadn't even been in the ground a week when he'd left for good. She couldn't go through that kind of heartbreak again. She just couldn't.

'And when London calls? When Harry gets back?'

Valentino hadn't thought that far ahead. 'Then you come with me.'

Paige felt the broken edges of her heart grate together. 'No, Valentino. I won't. This is my home. It's McKenzie's home. And whether you like it or not, we are a package deal. I'm not going to uproot her when she has years of therapy left.'

'They do have speech pathologists in other parts of the world.'

Of course they did but Paige had vowed never to blindly follow a man again, like she had Arnie. 'She trusts the St Auburn's team. Has built a relationship with them.'

He shrugged. 'Children adapt.'

Paige glared at him. Spoken like a true egotist, used only to looking after himself. Not a responsible father who put the needs of a child first. 'So let me get this straight. You want me to up sticks and follow you around the world with your child without any mention of us? Of our relationship? Do you even love me, Valentino?'

Valentino could see the stormy uncertainty in her gaze, the earnestness. He looked away. Love? *Dio!* He was too busy trying to come to terms with becoming a father. 'I don't think that's relevant.'

Paige's head spun at his quick dismissal of the fundamental human emotion. 'How is it not relevant, Valentino? Do you expect me to follow you around like a puppy dog, hoping you can squeeze your child in between your work and dating catwalk models?'

Valentino stood, the scorn in her voice stabbing like a stiletto between his ribs. '*Dio!* No, I have more respect for you than that. We would marry, of course.'

Paige blinked up at him. If that was a proposal, it sucked big time. Not to mention it was utter insanity. 'What?'

He hadn't given any of this much thought but now it was out there he knew it was the right thing to do. 'We'll get married.'

'You just told me that love wasn't relevant and now you want to marry me?' Try as she may, Paige couldn't rid her voice of its high squeaky quality.

It had been a long time since Valentino had thought about love. About those three little words. But he did remember how callously they could be used. How empty they could be. 'Did you love your husband?'

Paige frowned. 'Yes. Of course.'

'How'd that work out for you?'

Paige gasped. If her legs had been feeling remotely solid, she would have stood up and slapped his face.

Valentino could see he'd shocked her. Hurt her. He hadn't meant to be so insensitive. He sat. 'I'm sorry, that was unthinking of me.'

She was sitting hunched forward in her chair and he

reached across the space between them to squeeze her arm but Paige moved back out of his reach.

'Yes, it was.'

Valentino regarded her solemnly for a few moments. 'I don't have all the answers yet, Paige. I'm just saying we can work them out. We have time.'

Except the thought of going through it all again, of growing a baby inside, loving it, wanting it, was just too much for her to bear. Her head throbbed in unison with her heart. It was just all too overwhelming.

She stood. 'I can't think straight any more. I have to get home. Mum will be wondering where I am.'

Valentino nodded. 'Of course. Will you tell them about the baby?'

Paige frowned, her mind too full to think straight. 'Of course. Eventually.'

She shuffled her feet awkwardly for a moment. Valentino's head was downcast. This had no doubt thrown a huge spanner into the works for him too. And even though he'd just made the most preposterous suggestion she'd ever heard, she kind of got where it came from. This whole thing was completely unexpected.

She had the strangest urge to gather him in close and lay his cheek against her belly where their baby grew. Instead, she brushed past him with a quiet 'Goodnight'.

Valentino grabbed her hand as she went by. She looked down at him and he fixed her with imploring eyes. 'You won't do anything…rash, will you?'

His meaning was clear and her first reaction was anger. Did he seriously think she would go off behind his back and terminate his baby? Or that she'd go off riding a wild bronco or throw herself off a cliff with only a bungee cord around her ankle? But there was a plea in his gaze that reached right inside her gut and she realised he was as vulnerable, as unsure as she. He had as much at stake as she did.

It seemed natural then to follow through on her earlier impulse and move closer. She buried her hand in his hair and urged his cheek against her stomach.

'Of course not. I won't do anything without talking to you first.'

Valentino shut his eyes as her fingers sifted through his hair and her aroma filled his senses. Her words were utterly sincere and he didn't doubt her. 'Thank you,' he murmured, turning his face to press a kiss against her belly where his child nestled.

Paige shut her eyes as the innocent gesture constricted her throat and breathed fire into her belly. She wished she could give him what he wanted. But what about when it conflicted with what she wanted?

What about her?

'I need time to think. I have to go,' she said, wriggling out of his hold and striding away without looking back.

After a fitful sleep, Paige woke the next morning with only the craving to eat everything in her pantry trumping the dire urge to empty her bladder. She couldn't remember the last time she'd woken with biological matters taking such urgent precedence.

Usually she had to fight herself out of a thick shroud of grief that seemed to pounce in her sleep, making her limbs weak and dampening her mood, steeling herself to face the day for McKenzie's sake. But this morning she was so hungry none of that registered. She would have eaten the sheets had she been tied to the bed.

The devastating fact of her pregnancy, the thing that had had her tossing and turning all night, seemed to pale in comparison to her hunger. She felt like a grizzly bear coming awake after a long winter's hibernation.

The doorbell rang as Paige passed it and she checked her watch. Seven-thirty. A little early for her parents to be here. McKenzie, unusually, was still sound asleep. Paige had checked on her twice already.

She opened the door to find Valentino standing there. He looked good, even for someone with bloodshot eyes and hair that appeared to have been raked all night. It was on the tip of her tongue to tell him to leave then she spied the brown bakery bag under his arm at the same time a waft of yeasty goodness reached her nose.

'Oh, God,' she said, grabbing the bag, her mouth watering already. 'Come in,' she ordered, turning on her heel as she opened the bag and the warm sweet smell of freshly baked croissants hit her olfactory system.

Valentino blinked as Paige disappeared as quickly as she had appeared. He looked at the space where his offering had been and was now gone. He'd been expecting many things this morning. More tears. More anger. Recriminations.

Certainly not this.

Hunger was a good sign, yes?

He found her in the kitchen, tearing chunks off a croissant and stuffing them into her mouth. She was making short work of it. It was compelling viewing as flakes of pastry stuck to her lips and she made little noises of pleasure at the back of her throat as each morsel hit her taste buds.

In fact, he was rather turned on.

When Paige opened her eyes Valentino was the first thing she saw, leaning casually in her doorway. She wasn't sure if it was the morning light or the sugar rush but he looked pretty good there.

'Do you own anything that's not ten sizes too big?' he mused.

'Sit.' She gestured to the stool opposite, ignoring him as she stuffed the last piece of her croissant into her mouth. She turned and retrieved some plates from the cupboard behind her and placed a croissant on each one, pushing his towards him.

She nodded at the side counter. 'Coffee percolator if you want one.'

Valentino would rather never drink coffee again than settle for the stuff that Australians euphemistically called coffee. 'Not even if I was dying,' he said dryly.

Paige laughed. She actually laughed at the disdain on his face. 'Snob.' And then she tore some off her second croissant and devoured it. 'God, this is so-o-o good,' she sighed, licking her fingers.

Valentino temporarily lost his train of thought. Watching her eat was gastronomic pornography. 'Your appetite has returned, I see.'

She nodded. 'I'm so-o-o hungry. I'd forgotten how good things taste,' she said around another mouthful.

'Pleased I could be of service.' He made a mental note to bring a wider array of tempting goodies every time he called in. Which hopefully would be often.

Valentino watched her choose a third croissant, bringing it to her lips, opening her mouth but stopping before she took the first bite. 'Oh, I'm sorry. This is yours,' she said, placing it back on top of the bag.

Valentino chuckled. 'Take it.'

'No, no.' Paige shook her head even as the flaky pastry called to her like a mermaid luring sailors onto the rocks.

He picked it up and held it out. 'I wouldn't dream of depriving you, *bella*.'

Paige winced and hesitated. 'I'm being a pig, aren't I?'

Valentino shook his head. 'I could watch you eat all day,' he murmured, and passed the croissant slowly beneath her nose. 'Besides, you're eating for two now, remember?'

Paige made a grab for the pastry on his second pass. Not even the reminder of her predicament, their predicament, overrode her stomach's demands. Maybe the decision she'd come to in the wee small hours made everything a little easier.

She sank her teeth in, the flakes of soft, velvety pastry melting as they hit her tongue. 'Mmm,' she sighed.

Valentino waited until she finished, not wanting it to end but knowing they had things to discuss. 'We need to talk.' He pulled a tissue out of the box on the counter top and passed it to her, knowing he wasn't going to be able to concentrate with delicate flakes clinging to her gorgeous mouth.

'Sorry,' she apologised, licking at her lips, desperately playing for time now her stomach was satisfied. What had seemed thoroughly reasonable at 3 a.m. didn't seem so reasonable with Valentino sitting in her kitchen. 'I bet it's everywhere.'

Valentino almost groaned as her pink tongue ran back and forth very thoroughly over her lips, picking up stray flakes. Then she dabbed at her mouth with the tissue like a proper society matron. Like she hadn't just done a good impression of the cookie monster or licked her lips like a porn star.

'So,' he said, trying to wrangle his thoughts and the ruckus in his underpants back under control. 'The baby. You said you needed time to think. I don't know about you but I've thought of little else since yesterday afternoon.'

Paige nodded. This was it. She only hoped he understood. 'I can't have this baby, Valentino. I just can't.' She held up her hand as he opened his mouth to protest. 'Please, just hear me out.' She shifted off the stool. 'I want to show you something.'

Valentino followed Paige into the lounge room, his anger simmering. If she thought he would sit by and let her decide the outcome for their baby then she was sorely mistaken. Despite evidence to the contrary only a minute ago, he felt so impotent. He would not let another woman take from him what was also his.

'Sit down.'

He sat and watched her, his thoughts swirling and brooding inside like a gathering storm. She opened a cupboard beneath some bookshelves and pulled out what appeared to be a photo album. She stood for a moment, running her forefinger over the front cover before turning back towards him and sitting down next to him.

Paige passed him the album, her hands trembling. Her eyes locked with his. Her fingers kept hold of the object, lingering, reluctant to surrender it even when she knew it would help him to understand.

'I've never shown this to anyone before.'

Valentino nodded. He could see her qualms swirling like encroaching fog in her big grey eyes and he felt her resistance when he tried to take the album from her. He could see the struggle and what it took for her to finally release it to him.

'I am honoured,' he murmured.

His gaze fell on the window cut out of the cover. It was a close-up of a tiny baby, eyes closed, crisscrossed with tubes and wires. The only way to even tell its sex was from the tiny pink knitted cap that fitted snugly over its head. The little girl was clasping an adult finger in the foreground. It dwarfed the little babe's arm, giving true perspective to its size.

'This is Daisy, yes?'

Paige nodded. 'Yes.'

Valentino hesitated, even though she'd yielded the album to him. 'May I?'

Paige took a deep breath and nodded. Valentino opened the cover slowly, as if he'd just been handed an incredibly old parchment, and she was touched by his reverence.

Her gaze fell to the pages. There, first up, was a picture of Daisy at four hours old. And three years rushed out at her, sucking her straight back into the tumult. The anguish.

'They were twenty-seven-weekers, yes?'

Paige nodded as he continued his reverent journey through the album. 'Daisy was nine hundred grams. McKenzie was twelve hundred.'

Ah. That explained a lot. Premature babies born under one kilo had the odds truly stacked against them.

'It's a beautiful album,' he commented as each picture chronicled Daisy's battle and ever-increasing medical support. The pages were pale pink and decorated with pretty stickers, silky ribbons and baby-themed cut-outs. Every effort had been made to present Daisy as a baby, a precious gift, cherished and loved.

'My mother made the album for me after…'

Valentino didn't push her to complete the sentence. 'It's a good idea. She obviously took a great deal of care with it.'

Paige nodded. 'Mum's very good at craftwork. She does all her own stationery and cards.'

Valentino flipped the pages over, taking great care to linger over each photo with the reverence it deserved. Towards the end they became more medicalised. There were more tubes than baby.

'She had several chest tubes, I see.'

'She kept blowing pneumothoraxes towards the end. Her chronic neonatal lung disease was so bad she didn't respond to any treatment and they just couldn't ventilate her.'

Valentino didn't say anything. What was there to say? It must have been agony to watch. In fact, it was written all over Paige's face in the photos. The album wasn't just a timeline of Daisy's life but a startling map of Paige's grief.

'They withdrew treatment?'

'Yes. She'd suffered so much.' Paige reached out and traced Daisy's face with her forefinger. 'We couldn't ask any more of her.'

The 'we' soon became evident as Valentino turned to the second last page. A photo of a blond man looking down at Daisy, his hand resting against her ever-present woollen cap, jumped out at him. 'Your husband?'

Paige nodded. 'Arnie.'

'He…left?'

'Two days after Daisy's funeral.'

Valentino gripped the edges of the album. How could he do that? How could he walk away from his grieving wife and his other child? What kind of a man did that? 'Do you have contact with him? Does McKenzie see him?'

Was that one of the other factors that Paige had to consider? Was she still carrying a candle for him? The thought struck deep in Valentino's chest. Surely not?

Paige snorted. 'The only correspondence I've had from Arnie since the day I begged him not to leave me has been through his lawyer when the divorce papers arrived.'

Her voice was laced with bitterness and Valentino knew without a shadow of a doubt that it was Arnie he had to thank for Paige's less than flattering opinion of men, the brick wall around her heart. But at least she seemed well and truly over him.

Valentino flipped to the last page. He felt Paige tense beside him and he could see why. It was a very raw photo, difficult to even look at without feeling as if he had intruded on something truly intimate. A snapshot full of utter human misery. Painfully private.

Paige was holding a swaddled Daisy. She was free of all her tubes, her eyes swollen and closed, pink cap pulled snugly over her head. Her mouth was a straight line, the lips colourless, her skin deathly pale. The caption in stickers read 'Rest In Peace Our Precious Daisy'.

Paige was crying in the photograph as she looked down at her daughter with such anguish, clearly distressed. Like she'd give anything in that moment to bring her daughter back. Trade places even. The look said, Don't go, I haven't had the chance to get to know you yet.

Completely desolate was a good description and Valentino felt it right to his very soul.

'She was just too little,' Paige whispered. It had been a couple of years since she'd seen this photo. Tears burned at the backs of her eyes and then welled up and spilled over.

'She fought the good fight,' Valentino murmured.

'She did. She fought for so long.'

Valentino heard the sob catch in her throat and put his arm around her, tucking her head against his shoulder.

He closed the album and let Paige cry until her tears ran out.

Paige wasn't sure how much time had elapsed when she pulled away from him. She was just grateful he'd let her cry. He hadn't tried to tell her not to upset herself or be brave for McKenzie, as Arnie had. He'd just been there.

She used her baggy sleeve to dry her face. 'Do you see why I can't go through another pregnancy? I can't lose another child, Valentino.'

Valentino knew he had to tread carefully here. That just because Paige's fears weren't necessarily rational, it didn't mean they weren't real to her. 'I understand why you don't want to be emotionally vulnerable again. You've been through a lot in the last few years.'

Paige nodded, pleased to see he understood. 'Don't you see?' she reasoned. 'If there is no baby then there's no chance of what happened to the twins happening again.'

Valentino took her hand. 'But there is a baby, Paige. Do you think terminating a pregnancy doesn't count as losing a child?'

'It's…it's different,' she said defensively.

'No, it's not.'

Paige looked at him sharply. Just when she'd thought he understood. 'Is this a religious thing?'

Valentino's brow crinkled. 'What?'

'You're Italian. I know it's frowned on there…'

Valentino was trying to hold onto his temper but it was fraying rapidly. 'This has nothing to do with religion. It's my child, Paige. My. Child. I have rights too and if you think I'm going to allow you to terminate this pregnancy, you're very wrong.'

Paige was surprised to feel the depth of his convictions

blast towards her. The vehemence in his speech. The fierce light burning in his gaze. But it didn't mean he could dictate to her.

'Why?' she demanded. 'Why do you care so much? This whole thing smacks of commitment, of long term. I'd have thought you'd be running a mile.'

Valentino knew her assessment was justified but it stung anyway. He stood and strode to the glass doors that overlooked the deck.

'You thought wrong.'

CHAPTER SEVEN

PAIGE flinched at the steel in Valentino's voice. But as he continued to stare out of her windows, his hands buried in his pockets, she sensed there was more to his insistence then she knew.

'Is there something you're not telling me?'

Valentino could hear his heartbeat pounding like surf in his head. He hadn't spoken her name in years. But if ever there was a time to open up, this was it. Paige had just shared a part of her life that was intensely private. Maybe it was time to share his?

'There was a woman.' His voice was husky and he cleared it. 'A long time ago.'

Paige stilled. Ah. 'I see.'

Valentino turned. Where did he even start? 'We were in love. Or at least I thought we were. I was first year out, an intern, back home. She was a fashion design student. She was…beautiful.'

It was a surprise how much it hurt to hear him talk about a woman in such hushed, awed tones. And even though he was looking at her, Paige knew he'd gone somewhere far away.

'She was twenty-one and she had all these curves and this gorgeous long hair…'

Valentino stopped and Paige didn't need to join the dots to know the woman must have been a stunner. She suddenly felt plain and unattractive with her short hair and angular frame.

What had Valentino seen in her?

'I was completely besotted. I proposed within two months and she leapt at it. Bought her this magnificent rock because she just had to have it. We went to lots of parties, made the society pages. She bragged about marrying a doctor to all her friends and revelled in the kudos.'

He paused for breath and Paige spoke for the first time. 'What was her name?'

Valentino fought his way back from the past and Paige slowly came into focus. 'Daniella.'

Once even the mention of the name had sent him a little crazy but he was surprised at how unaffected he felt, standing here today.

What on earth had he seen in her? Looking at Paige now, an intriguing woman with depth and layers, he just couldn't figure it out. Daniella had been terribly superficial. Yes, she'd been young but all she'd cared about had been clothes and shoes and the trendy new bars in town. He could admit now that conversation had been terribly dull. He'd just been too in lust to see it.

'Then I took her to meet my parents. The whole sign-language thing freaked her out, I think. And when I started to talk about setting a date and planning a family, she ran a mile. She had a career and a social life. How could she possibly fit into her designer wardrobe or drink champagne at glamorous balls with swollen feet and no waist? What if we had a deaf child?'

Paige heard the bitter edge to his voice. 'Ah.'

Valentino nodded. 'I was devastated.'

'Of course. First love is always the hardest.'

Despite having dated on and off throughout her twenties, Arnie had been her first love. She'd fallen for him hard and married him in a rush. His desertion when she'd needed him most had cut deep.

As, obviously, had Daniella's. Suddenly his playboy rebound love-life made sense. He'd evidently been trying to forget Daniella's callousness. Who was she to judge how he dealt with his loss? Just because she'd withdrawn completely, it didn't mean it was the right way to cope.

Was there a book of etiquette somewhere that explained how you were supposed to act when your whole world fell apart?

Valentino's mouth compressed into a tight line. 'There's more.' He hesitated. How did he say something he'd never truly voiced to anyone before? 'Six weeks after we broke up I was working night shift in Emergency when Daniella was rushed through the doors. She was haemorrhaging heavily. She'd had a back-street abortion.'

Paige gasped. She hadn't expected that. 'Oh, Valentino.' She got to her feet, crossed the short space between them and placed her hand on his arm. 'I'm so sorry.'

He captured her gaze. 'She didn't tell me she was pregnant. She didn't ask me for help or bother to find out what I wanted. She just went and took my child from me.'

She closed her eyes against the anguish she saw in Valentino's. She knew how it felt to have a child taken from you. No wonder he'd been so vehement with her. It must be like Daniella all over again. 'You wanted to keep the baby?'

Valentino gave her a hard look. 'I wanted the choice. I wanted to be consulted. Included.'

Paige nodded. 'That was wrong of her. To act without consulting you.'

'Damn right.'

'She was young and scared,' Paige said gently.

'So was I,' he said. 'But I'm not now.'

Paige sighed and returned to the lounge. She raised pleading eyes to him. 'Valentino, please don't make this more difficult for me than it already is.'

'You want me to make it easy for you? I won't.'

He strode towards her, dropping to his knees beside her. He grabbed her hand and pressed it to her belly. 'Feel that. Inside there is our baby. He lives and he grows. He has a heartbeat and every right to be born. He's going to have my dark wavy hair and your beautiful grey eyes and he's going to be healthy and perfect and we're going to love him.'

Paige shook her head from side to side. Damn him. It was ridiculous to think she could feel the baby move but she could have sworn tiny flutters danced beneath their joined hands. And suddenly she could picture him.

Him! For crying out loud!

Just as Valentino had described him. Perfect in every way. A unique blend of both of them.

And she knew she couldn't do it. Not to Valentino. Or herself. Or the baby. A baby she already loved more than life itself. As she had loved Daisy and McKenzie from the second she'd known about them. Who was she kidding? She could no more deny this tiny life growing inside her than fly to the moon.

And looking at Valentino's tormented face, she knew she couldn't hurt him either. Not like that. Not like Daniella had.

Her gaze fell on the album beside her and she touched Daisy's cheek with heart-breaking reverence. 'Chances of delivering early again increase in subsequent pregnancies.' She glanced at Valentino with huge eyes. 'I'm scared,' she whispered.

'Don't be. I'm not going to let anything happen to our baby.'

And for a crazy moment she believed him.

The next day Valentino arrived on her doorstep, bearing freshly baked blueberry muffins. And an engagement ring.

'Dr Valentino!'

'Well, good morning, young lady.' Valentino crouched down, signing as he spoke. He could just make out the external component of the implant attached to the side of her head and mostly hidden by her gorgeous curls. She was wearing a pink tutu and fairy wings, which looked even sweeter on her diminutive frame.

'*Osservate molto abbastanza oggi.*' Although he spoke in Italian he signed in English so she knew she was looking very pretty today.

'We're having breakfast,' McKenzie signed with a flourish.

'That's good.' Valentino grinned. He opened the bag and let McKenzie peek inside. 'I brought muffins.'

'McKenzie, darling?'

Valentino stood as an unfamiliar voice came closer. It sounded older. Paige was obviously not alone.

'Oh. Hello, there.'

An older woman with Paige's big grey eyes blinked curiously at him. He recognised her from the photo on the television. 'Hi. I'm Valentino,' he said, holding out his hand.

'Oh, yes.' Paige's mother shook his hand. 'You're the surgeon who took over from Harry. You did McKenzie's surgery.'

Valentino smiled. 'Yes.' McKenzie slipped her hand into his and he watched as the older woman's shrewd gaze followed the movement.

'I didn't realise you made house calls?'

Valentino saw the teasing sparkle in her eyes and chuckled. 'Only for my special patients,' he said, grinning down at McKenzie and signing for her benefit.

'I'm Adele, Paige's mother.'

'Very pleased to meet you.'

And he was. Adele was a fine-looking woman. Tall, like her daughter, she'd aged well with graceful laughter lines around her eyes and mouth. But what struck him the most was her aura of contentment. Adele obviously lived well and laughed a lot. She looked healthy and robust and mischief danced in her eyes. She reminded him of his own mother.

'Would you care to join us for breakfast?'

Valentino held up the bakery packet, pleased to have bought a few extras. 'I brought muffins.'

'I'm sure they'll be welcome. My daughter seems to have found her appetite at last.'

She gave him a speculative look before turning on her heel, and Valentino smiled as he and McKenzie followed her.

'Look who I found lurking in the doorway,' Adele announced as she stepped onto the deck.

An older man looked up from several newspapers he appeared to be reading at once. He looked at Valentino over the top of bifocal glasses with a startled expression. Paige looked up from buttering the last slice of toast.

'Valentino!'

She wanted to say this really had to stop but he looked all sexy in his casual chinos and open-necked shirt and infinitely male and his dimples screamed lazy Sunday morning.

But this really had to stop.

Adele could see the indecision on her daughter's face. 'He brought muffins,' she said, digging Valentino in the ribs.

Valentino smiled to himself and held out the bag exactly as Adele had no doubt hoped he would. 'Blueberry,' he said. 'Warm. Just out of the oven.'

Paige relented. How could she still be hungry after an omelette stuffed with mushrooms, cheese and bacon and three pieces of toast? 'My favourite.'

Adele relieved him of the packet, placing it in the centre of the table, and walked around to the empty chair beside Paige and pulled it out for him. 'Sit here, Valentino.'

As a well-adjusted Italian male, Valentino had a healthy respect for mothers and wasn't about to argue with one who would hopefully soon be his mother-in-law. But before he sat he stretched his hand across the table towards the man he assumed was Paige's father.

'Hello, sir. I'm Valentino Lombardi. Pleased to meet you.'

Paige's father half stood as he accepted Valentino's hand in a firm, brief shake. 'McKenzie's surgeon? Don Eden.' He looked over his glasses at his wife as he reclaimed his seat, speculation in his gaze. 'Didn't realise you blokes made house calls.'

Valentino grinned as Adele winked at him. 'Coffee?'

'Valentino would rather eat dirt then drink our heathen

colonial coffee,' Paige said around a mouthful of muffin. 'Is that a fair summation?'

Valentino chuckled. She had crumbs on her lips and it was most distracting. It was sexy, watching her eat with such gusto. He wondered how she'd look eating something gooey, like ice cream. In bed. With no clothes on. 'More than fair.'

'Oh, I don't blame you,' Adele said. 'Nicest coffee we ever had was in Italy, wasn't it, darling? Where are you from exactly?' she asked.

They chatted for half an hour about Italy and travelling and McKenzie's implant. Not that Paige contributed much. After eating two muffins she dropped her head back against her chair and shut her eyes, letting the morning sunshine warm her skin.

She didn't want to encourage him, she didn't want him too cosy with her family. Just because she'd agreed not to do anything rash, it didn't mean they were one big happy family.

Despite his assurances of support, Paige had been burnt before.

It was pleasant conversation but Valentino was charming her parents and it was strangely irritating. As good as he was to look at, as amazing as he smelled this morning—like bakery and sunshine—she wished he would just go.

Valentino found his attention drifting as he chatted with Adele and Don. He was hyper-aware of Paige beside him all loose and relaxed in her chair. She was wearing her usual baggy clothes but whether it was the angle of her body or this particular view he couldn't help but notice how fuller her breasts seemed. How they formed two firm, high mounds against the thin fabric of her shirt and bounced when she shifted in the chair.

He wanted to nuzzle her neck, let his hand drift to one of those very enticing mounds.

Dio!

He came here for one thing and one thing only. He rose, needing desperately to get away and get his mind back on the game plan. 'Excuse me for a moment.' Valentino stood. 'Paige, your bathroom?'

Paige gave him directions and, despite wanting him to leave only seconds ago, she suddenly felt bereft without him. She steeled herself for the grilling she knew was to come.

Her mother went first. 'I like him.'

'You don't know him.'

'I'd known Arnie for two minutes and knew I didn't like him.'

Touché. She glanced at her father smiling at her mother, his dimples blazing. 'You've always been a sucker for men with dimples.'

Adele ignored him and looked at her daughter. 'So have you, darling.'

Had she? When she looked back over her life prior to Arnie the few boyfriends she'd had had indeed all been blessed with dimples. 'Dimples do not maketh the man,' Paige grumbled.

Adele smiled at her husband. 'I would have to disagree with you there.'

Paige shook her head, humbled as ever by her parents' enduring love and affection for each other. 'Well, you would.'

'I'm just saying that I think he's good for you.' Adele reached across the table and squeezed her daughter's hand. 'Isn't it about time you declared a truce on the men of the world? They're not all like Arnie, darling.'

Paige wondered how her parents would feel if they knew that this Italian Lothario they were so enamoured with had impregnated their daughter. Neither of her parents were keen for her to have any more children given what had happened with the twins.

Before she could speak, Valentino's voice drifted out to them and three pairs of eyes sought him out. He'd stopped to talk to McKenzie.

McKenzie had grown bored quickly with the adult conversation and had asked for 'Wigga' and Paige, who didn't like her watching too much television, hadn't been able to refuse. Hearing her daughter say actual words was sweeter than the sweetest music in the world and seeing her dance now she could actually hear the music was endlessly thrilling.

They watched as Valentino took McKenzie's hands and danced around with her. McKenzie giggled as he lifted her off the floor and twirled her round, his dark hair almost black compared to her lighter hues. She clapped as he put her down and said, 'Again.' And Valentino complied, his easy laughter rich and deep.

Laughter you could drown in.

And her broken, fractured, battered, stomped-on heart just about melted in her chest.

'Oh, my,' Adele said, her hand fluttering to her chest.

Paige dragged her gaze away from the endearing sight of Valentino—a large, virile, Italian man his hands dwarfing McKenzie's torso—twirling her daughter—a little pink fairy girl—round and round. It was exceedingly sexy.

She blasted her mother with an impatient glare. So he was good with children. Arnie had been great with kids. Had been over the moon about the pregnancy.

But look how quickly he had turned his back when it had come to the crunch.

'You've won a heart there,' Don commented as Valentino rejoined them on the deck.

Valentino shrugged. 'I have ten nieces and five nephews back home. Children like to dance in any language, I think.'

'That they do,' Don agreed.

'Actually, sir,' Valentino said. 'I'm glad you're both here.' He looked at Paige, who frowned at him. 'My cousin Alessandro tells me its tradition here to ask, permission of the woman's parents to marry her. So—'

'What?' Paige stood up, effectively cutting Valentino off. Had he gone mad? 'I'm not marrying you, Valentino. I told you that yesterday.'

Valentino reached into his pocket and pulled out a velvet box. He opened it and placed it on the table in front of her.

Paige blinked. The simple square-cut diamond nestled in the satin and dazzled in the direct sunlight. It was simple and beautiful and perfect. Every woman's idea of an engagement ring right there before her. And she wanted to put it on her finger so badly it itched. Instead, she reached down and pushed the lid shut.

'I said no.'

Don and Adele looked at the box and then at each other. 'It's pretty traditional to have the woman's consent first,' Don joked, and Adele dug him in the ribs with her elbow as she fought a smile, mashing her lips together hard.

'Which he doesn't have,' Paige said adamantly.

'Paige, I can't allow our baby to be born outside marriage.'

Paige felt the air around her evaporate. 'Valentino!'

Valentino frowned as Adele gasped and turned to Paige.

'Baby?' she demanded.

Valentino raked his hand through his hair. She had said she was going to tell them. 'You haven't told them about the baby?'

Paige shut her eyes and slowly sat down. 'No,' she said, utterly defeated. 'Not yet.'

Adele looked at Don. 'That explains the appetite.' She turned to her daughter and gave her hand a squeeze. 'Are you okay, darling?'

Valentino could see the worry in their eyes as Paige's parents looked at her with concern. They were no doubt apprehensive about their daughter going into premature labour again.

'A little shocked actually, Mum. And ravenous.'

'Maybe that's a good sign?' Adele suggested. 'You couldn't keep anything down with the twins.'

That was true. She'd actually landed in hospital on a drip twice. 'Maybe.' Paige nodded. But the truth was she was still scared witless about the pregnancy. And she didn't have to look at her parents to know they were too.

Valentino observed the byplay intently. He could see the prospect of a second pregnancy for Paige didn't just affect her and him. That her parents had been a major support for Paige and they were understandably concerned.

'I'm not going to let anything happen to Paige or the baby. You have my word.'

Adele gave a sad smile and squeezed her daughter's hand again. 'I believe you. But for now I think we'd better leave you both alone to talk this through. We'll take McKenzie out to the park.'

Paige nodded. 'Thanks.'

Paige's parents rose and Don held out his hand to

Valentino. 'It was nice meeting you. And I appreciate that you want to do the right thing by our daughter.' He dropped his hand after a brief shake. 'It's been a tough few years for all of us. It hasn't been easy as a father to watch Paige go through what she's been through. I trust you understand our less than enthusiastic response.'

Valentino nodded. 'Of course.'

Paige was grateful that Valentino waited till they had all departed before he spoke again. 'I'm sorry. I didn't know your parents were going to be here this morning.'

Paige picked up the velvet box and held it out. 'That didn't seem to stop you.'

Valentino ignored it. 'I'm serious about this, *bella*.'

'So am I.'

'You are carrying my child. It's the honourable thing to do. My duty. My mother would disown me if I didn't do the right thing.'

Duty and honour. Two things that Arnie hadn't been big on. Still, they weren't the words a girl wanted to hear when talking marriage. Arnie had said he loved her and couldn't live without her.

That had worked a treat.

Fortunately she was somewhat more evolved now, her heart hardened to flattery. But there was no way she was making the biggest commitment of her life based on anything other than love. And as she'd vowed to never be so stupid again, she just didn't see how it could work.

Paige placed the box back on the table. 'Listen to yourself. This shouldn't be about what's honourable. About duty. This is a long-term commitment. You are not a long-term guy.'

'I am now.'

Paige gave him a reproving look. 'Are you telling me

that the first time you laid eyes on me you knew I was the girl you wanted to marry?'

Valentino didn't think it wise to tell her exactly what he had been thinking that day at the wedding. Suffice to say it had come to fruition a few hours later. 'Love at first sight is not a sound basis for marriage.'

'Maybe not, but it's a good place to start. What about Daniella? Didn't you take one look at her and know?'

Valentino frowned. 'I was twenty-four. I'm pretty sure I wasn't thinking with anything north of my belt. It was lust, not love.'

Maybe it had been lust with Arnie too? Maybe she hadn't fallen in love after all. Maybe his flashy, blond good looks and his total adoration of her had blinded her to the real man beneath.

'And it didn't work out. Neither did you and Arnie. So maybe approaching marriage like this is the best way to go about it. We don't have to get married straight away, we have time to get to know each other.'

'My mother would say we should have done that first.'

He shrugged. 'So would mine.'

Paige smiled despite her heart pounding in her chest as she prepared to ask the next question. 'Just say I agree to getting married…what happens when you do meet the one and you're trapped in a marriage with me? Do you expect me to be okay with it? Do you expect me to sit back and watch you break our child's heart when you leave me for her? Not to mention McKenzie's heart? Would you fight me for custody?'

'*Il mio dio!* I haven't thought about any of these things.'

Paige tried not to let his avoidance of the answer have an impact on her. 'No kidding!'

Valentino's jaw tightened. 'There will be no other women.'

'What about sex?'

Valentino frowned. 'What about it? I thought you liked having sex with me?'

Paige didn't think her liking it was really the issue. That was a no-brainer. 'If you think I'm going to risk this pregnancy by having sex during it, then you really are crazy.'

Valentino rubbed his forehead. He hadn't thought about that aspect of it. *'No problemo,'* he dismissed.

'You seriously expect me to believe you can go without sex for that long?'

Arnie had cited lack of intimacy as one of the reasons he was leaving and she'd known their defunct sex life had frustrated him. But she had been exhausted, being at the hospital all day and worried sick about the twins, watching Daisy grow steadily more ill. She'd been emotionally numb and physically disconnected from her body, and sex had been the last thing on her mind.

And, besides, it hadn't felt right, enjoying herself while her children were in Intensive Care, fighting for their lives.

Valentino smiled at her incredulity. He should have been angry with her sexist assumption that he was incapable of going without. But he wasn't. 'You don't think,' he said, his voice dropping an octave as his gaze dropped to the interesting mounds he could now make out beneath her baggy T-shirt, 'I'm imaginative enough to be able to satisfy you in other ways?'

Paige swallowed and to her dismay her nipples hardened in blatant response to his ogling. Her breasts had been sore and tight and uncomfortable but they seemed to flower beneath his gaze.

She was temporarily speechless.

Valentino caught her gaze and chuckled as she folded her arms across her chest. Good, he had her attention. 'I don't want to be excluded from the pregnancy, Paige. I want to be around to feel the baby move and kick, to see your belly grow. To help out when you're not feeling well. To get you ice cream and tomato sauce when you wake up with a craving at three o'clock in the morning. I want to get to know McKenzie as well. I'm going to be in her life too.'

Paige wanted to shut her ears to the cosy picture he was painting. A flash of McKenzie and Valentino dancing flitted through her mind, the look of adoration on her daughter's face as she'd clung to his neck crystal clear.

How could she expose McKenzie to him, like he was asking? Have her love and adore him when, try as she may, she couldn't believe he was going to stick around.

Especially if something happened to the baby.

Yes, he was telling her he would but he'd spent the last decade of his life constantly moving on from one woman to another. Did he seriously expect her to believe he could reverse what by now must be fairly ingrained behaviour?

'And what if something happens to the baby—?'

'I told you nothing would happen,' he interrupted.

She held up her finger. 'Just go with me here on this, okay? Something happens and I go into labour again at twenty-eight weeks or even less and the baby dies. There's nothing keeping us together after that—there's certainly not love. Are you going to tell me you're going to stick around? Or will you run when it all becomes overwhelming because, trust me…' Her voice wavered. 'It will. What happens to McKenzie then?' Or to her, for that matter. 'It'll be devastating.'

Valentino ran a hand through his hair. 'It won't happen.'

'Goddamn it, Valentino,' she snapped, banging her fist on the table. 'What if it does?'

'You're dealing in a lot of what-ifs.'

'Yeah, well, I have to, I'm her mother, I have to protect her. That's my job.' To say nothing of protecting herself.

Valentino's jaw clenched. 'I make you a solemn promise. I will not walk away.'

'But it would be easier for you to go if we didn't marry. If there was no wedding ring holding you here.'

It was Valentino's turn to slam his hand down on the table in frustration. '*Dio!* Listen to me. I. Will. Not. Walk. Away.' He punctuated each word with a vicious finger stab at the table.

For what it was worth, she believed him. Right now, at this moment, his conviction was palpable. But Paige knew that life cold throw you curve balls and things could change in a heartbeat.

She also knew this was getting them nowhere. They needed a compromise, something to break the stalemate. 'You want to get to know me? Us? Then let's just do that for now. I'm not going to stop you from being involved in the pregnancy, Valentino. I will include you as much as possible.' She picked up the box again. 'Let's spend some time together first and then…' she pushed it across the table to him '…we'll see.'

Valentino picked up the box. Paige looked conciliatory and certainly a lot less exasperated. It was a good compromise. She was so skittish, so hurt from her ex, he suspected if he pushed too much she'd never agree. Maybe he'd have to play it cool for a bit. Prove to her he could be the man she needed him to be.

'So it's not a no? It's a maybe later.'

Paige nodded, even though she knew deep in her heart she would never marry again. 'That's right.'

Valentino examined the box for a few moments and then put it back in his pocket. 'I'm going to keep asking.'

And she was going to keep saying no. She smiled at him. 'I wouldn't expect anything less.'

CHAPTER EIGHT

AND he did. At the end of every week together he asked her again. And at the end of every week she said no. Then they started all over again.

They fell into a routine. He came for tea one night a week after McKenzie was in bed. Paige insisted they wait till her daughter was asleep. She knew how easily McKenzie loved people and she didn't want her becoming too attached.

On Sunday mornings he joined the whole family for breakfast. It seemed less intimate with her parents there as a buffer to his charisma and charm and Paige had to admit she looked forward to it. If for nothing else than to taste what amazing culinary offering he brought with him.

And, of course, they saw each other at work three days a week. Although Paige and Valentino were scrupulous about keeping it strictly professional. No one in the department had an inkling of their private affairs, which was exactly what she wanted.

Paige had also insisted that they tell no one about the baby, including McKenzie, not until she'd passed the twenty-eight-week mark at least. To her surprise, Valentino agreed. As he had with the McKenzie-in-bed rule. It seemed he didn't want to do anything to upset her.

He treated her with kid gloves. Was attentive and sweet. He fed her tempting, delicious creations at every opportunity and made her laugh. Apart from his weekly proposal he didn't push her into any decisions or even try to make a pass at her, despite how alarmingly she wanted to feel his lips on hers again.

It was an urge that grew with each week of pregnancy into an almost unbearable craving. Forget ice cream with tomato sauce! Her hormones went into overdrive as she entered the second trimester and Valentino looked more and more edible.

But he seemed immune to her vibes. It was like he'd decided her body was a temple for his baby and that she was no longer a woman that he'd kissed and made very thorough love to on two very long nights. She was a mother now. A sacred vessel.

She should have appreciated it. And she did. By and large. But sometimes she just wanted to grab him and smack a kiss on that full sexy mouth so badly she could barely see straight.

When she started to feel the baby move at 16 weeks he came over twice a week for tea and spent all day Sunday with them. Which was harder on the raging libido but involved him more, for which he was very grateful.

And Paige really kept him as involved as possible without them actually living under the same roof. He attended the weekly ultrasounds and all the doctor's appointments. When it came to discussing the best course of action to prevent another premature labour, she involved him in all the decisions and even looked to him for advice.

Dr Erica de Jongh, the obstetrician, was confident that although Paige was at an increased risk of having a second premature labour, it was highly unlikely she would this time round because the risks factors from her first pregnancy did not exist in this one.

For a start, there was only one baby and from the weekly ultrasounds they could see their baby boy was growing normally, unlike Daisy who had always been small for dates and suffered from borderline intra-uterine growth retardation.

Erica saw no reason for intervention, fully confident that Paige would go to full term. It was only the patients who went into premature labour for no apparent reason that she tended to treat more aggressively in subsequent pregnancies.

And even though it was true that Paige would never be entirely relaxed, both she and Valentino had confidence in Erica, who specialised in high-risk pregnancies and were happy with her care and her treatment plan. And each week as their little boy grew and did all the right things and there were no signs of trouble, they were more and more encouraged.

The day she turned twenty-two weeks Paige was joined by Valentino in the scrub room as she was nearing the end of her three-minute hand wash. It was their first case of the day.

'So,' Valentino said, wetting his arms and applying the liquid surgical scrub, 'twenty-two weeks today.'

Paige could see the smile in his eyes and knew his dimples would be dazzling beneath his mask. Still, they'd agreed not to talk about it at work. 'Not here,' she murmured.

Valentino chuckled. 'I'm just making conversation.'

Paige rolled her eyes at him. 'It's a nice day is conversation. We need more rain is conversation.'

'Ah.' Valentino shrugged, his arms soaped to his elbows. 'Blame it on my command of the English language. Subtleties are harder to pick up on.'

Paige laughed. Valentino spoke perfect English. He certainly understood subtleties and nuance just fine. 'Poor Valentino.'

As she ran her hands under the water for one last rinse the baby kicked her hard and high as if he objected to Paige teasing his father. She gasped, the motion of her hands freezing as her breath was momentarily stolen by the strength and suddenness of it. She leaned over a little, her hands still elevated above the sink.

Valentino frowned, his hands also ceasing their activity. 'Paige? Are you all right?'

Paige nodded as the baby continued to tap-dance in her womb. 'I think this baby's going to play soccer for Italy.'

Valentino grinned. 'It kicked?'

'Oh, yeah. I think he's awake and ready to party.'

It took Valentino all of two seconds to decide his next course of action. He abandoned his scrub and reached for her belly, soaped arms and all.

'Valentino!' Paige gasped as his hands made wet imprints on her blue scrubs. She looked over her shoulder. 'They're expecting us inside.'

He ignored her. 'Where?' he asked, shifting his hands around, waiting for the tell-tale movement beneath his palm, desperate to be part of this moment with her. He would never tire of feeling his son move. Her scrubs were an annoying barrier and he ran his hands under the hem until his soapy fingers touched bare belly.

Paige gasped again, quieter this time, her teeth sinking into her bottom lip as she concentrated on keeping her arms sterile and remaining upright while his asexual touch spread sticky tentacles to places lower. Much lower.

He'd felt her belly before. But never skin to skin, always through her clothes. His warm, slippery hands were completely methodical and thorough as he slid them all over her small bump, searching for movement. It was crazy. There was nothing intimate about it at all and yet her nipples hardened and rubbed painfully against the fabric of her bra.

'Valentino…' Even to her own ears it sounded husky and aching. Not that he seemed to be listening, intent on awaiting the baby's next move.

She was about to give him the whole this-is-entirely-inappropriate spiel but then the baby kicked again, another hard jab, right where Valentino's hand was, and he laughed, looking up at her with joy in his eyes, and she forgot about what was appropriate. He turned a few more loops for Valentino's benefit and Paige watched his downcast head, his dark hair visible beneath the semi-transparent fabric of his theatre hat.

'This is just the best feeling in the world, isn't it?' Valentino asked, looking up at her.

Paige smiled and nodded. It was hard not to be infected by his enthusiasm. Even though she could only see his eyes, his joy and excitement were plain to see. He held on for another minute, rubbing his hands around the rise of her abdomen.

Paige, her arms having practically drip-dried by now, shifted slightly. 'I think the show's over.'

Valentino's gaze returned to hers. Her grey eyes had gone

all smoky and he became very aware that he was touching her quite intimately. Still, the ripe swell of her felt good beneath his hands. Sexy. Right. He hadn't touched her bare stomach since the night they'd conceived his son and he suddenly realised he missed touching her.

He'd spent so much time trying to distance himself from Paige as a woman that he'd forgotten how good her skin felt. He withdrew his hands as if he was back in fifth grade, being rapped over the knuckles by the nuns.

'Sorry.'

Paige wobbled as his hands left her belly and she ground her clogged feet into the floor to stop herself from pitching forward. She tugged a deep breath into her lungs and nodded at his hands. 'You'd better start again.' Then she flapped her arms to dispel the last drips from her elbows and headed for the theatre doors.

That Sunday Valentino accompanied McKenzie and Paige to the riverside markets and then they met Adele and Don for brunch at South Bank. It had been months since McKenzie had come down with a sniff or a fever and Paige, at the urging of her parents, had decided to risk an outdoors expedition.

And she was pleased she had. The weather was glorious and McKenzie had been in absolute heaven. She'd worn her external device but, unused to crowds, the background chatter combined with the cool river breeze played havoc with the sensitive external microphone and overwhelmed her quickly. Paige removed it after the first ten minutes and she was much happier.

McKenzie had come along in leaps and bounds with her language skills over the last few months and it was a joy to watch her grow and develop now sound and speech were a part of her world.

It was midday as they got up to leave, passing the lunch crowd on their way out. Paige was feeling quite weary from all the walking around and couldn't wait to collapse on her lounge and veg out for the afternoon.

McKenzie tugged on her sleeve and Paige looked down. Her daughter was pointing at the large, white modern Ferris wheel that was a smaller version of the London Eye and could be seen from all over South Bank. Paige groaned. She'd forgotten she'd promised McKenzie a ride.

'We'll take her,' Adele said, giving her daughter's arms a squeeze. 'Valentino, drive her home. She looks exhausted.'

Paige felt torn. 'Are you sure?'

'Of course,' Don assured her.

Paige reluctantly agreed and watched her daughter skip off quite happily with her parents. Then Valentino whisked her away and had her ensconced on her lounge within twenty minutes, including a quick stop at his favourite deli.

'Mmm, that feels good,' Paige groaned as she slipped her shoes off and lay down on the squishy leather.

Valentino smiled at the pleasure in her voice, which he could hear all the way from the kitchen. He arranged a fat slice of tiramisu on a plate and picked it up, along with two forks.

'This is just as good,' he announced as he carried it into the lounge.

He lowered himself onto the edge of the coffee table closest to her head, immediately noticing the way her hand rested low on her belly, emphasising her bump. His baby was just there and he was surprised by the urge to link his hand through hers.

His gaze drifted higher and was drawn to the way her shirt pulled taut across her chest. Her belly wasn't the only thing that was burgeoning—her breasts seemed determined to keep pace.

He swallowed. Up until he'd laid his hands on her belly the other day he'd been doing just fine with keeping his distance. Treating Paige as the pregnant mother of his child. Affording her the right amount of reverence and respect. But that smoky look in her eyes had stayed with him and ever since his thoughts had been less than... reverent.

'Tiramisu for two,' he said, dragging his gaze back to her face.

Paige could smell the coffee and chocolate before he even sat down, reviving her somewhat. 'Mmm, smells delicious.'

Valentino passed her a fork and watched as she struggled into a semi-upright position. It was on the tip of his tongue to tell her to stay put, that he'd feed her, but the images that rose to his mind were far from respectful and he feigned interest in the dessert as things shifted and moved interestingly.

He held the plate forward and watched as she attacked the cake with gusto, loading up her fork and stuffing it into her mouth. Her pink tongue lapped at excess cream on her lips and her sigh of bliss went straight to his groin.

'Mrs Agostino is a goddess,' Paige groaned.

Mrs Agostino wasn't alone there. Paige had put on weight and there was a healthy glow to her fuller cheeks. Watching her eat was a divine experience.

She loaded up again and slipped the airy creation into her mouth. She looked at Valentino to share her bliss and noticed he wasn't eating. 'You're not joining me?' she asked, around a mouthful of cake.

Valentino's gaze fell to her mouth decorated in crumbs and cream. *Dio!* Was she trying to kill him?

Paige stilled her chewing and swallowed her mouthful as the direction of his gaze registered. Her lips tingled beneath the intensity of it. Maybe he wasn't as immune to her as a woman as she'd thought? She felt a surge of feminine hormones power into her bloodstream and arched her back a little. The corresponding rounding of his eyes made the move worth it.

'Valentino?'

Val dragged his gaze away from her breasts. 'Sorry. What? Oh, no, thanks. Here.' He thrust the plate at her. 'You have it.'

Then he shifted off the table and went and sat in the single lounge chair furthest away. It was still a sin to watch her eat but at least he'd removed himself from the temptation of leaning forward and using his tongue as a serviette.

'Mmm, that was amazing,' Paige said a minute later, scraping the last crumbs off the plate before placing it on the coffee table. She should be full but nothing seemed to fill her up these days. She had three years of sparrow appetite to make up for and her stomach was accepting the challenge with gusto.

'Now, if only my feet didn't ache so much, everything would be perfect. Honestly...' she looked at Valentino '...you'd think a theatre nurse would be used to standing.'

Valentino chuckled. 'We walked a lot.' Now she'd stopped eating he felt on a more even keel. He moved across to the end of her lounge. 'Here,' he said, slapping his lap. 'Pass me that moisturising cream. I'll give you a foot massage.'

Paige regarded him for a moment. He looked cool and calm and totally in control again and she wondered if she'd imagined that mad moment when he'd looked at her like she was on the menu. Maybe her hormones were also playing havoc with her eyesight?

Anyway, she wasn't about to pass up a foot rub when her feet were throbbing so she grabbed the cream and handed it to him then shuffled down the lounge till she was almost completely horizontal, her head resting on the arm, and placed her feet in his lap.

Valentino soon discovered there was no such thing as an even keel with her as her heels and her painted red toenails created instantaneous mayhem in his trousers. Praying for strength, he lifted one into his hands and shifted the other to the relative safety of his thigh.

Desperate for something to do other than look at her, he got right on the job, squeezing some cream onto his palms and then smoothing it onto her foot.

'Oh, my God.' Paige's head lolled back against the arm. 'That is so-o-o good,' she groaned as aching muscles responded to his light touch.

Valentino's fingers temporarily forgot their job as her breathy appreciation caused paralysis of everything but the activity in his pants.

'Don't stop,' she groaned, wiggling her toes.

Reaching for sanity, he willed his fingers to continue.

'Maybe you should give up work?' Valentino suggested in a bid to give himself something else to think about other than inching his hand higher up her leg.

Paige lifted her drowsy head. 'Erica seems to think it's okay to continue. She'll let me know if she thinks I should pack it in.'

'I know. I'm just saying you're exhausted and you're only going to get more tired as the pregnancy progresses.'

'I'm fine,' Paige murmured, her eyes drifting shut as Valentino rubbed her instep and her head lolled back. 'Besides, I can't afford to give up work this early.'

He kept his gaze firmly on her toes with the red nail polish. 'I can support you.'

Paige was too chilled out to be affronted. 'No.'

'Paige—'

Paige smiled at the wounded Italian male pride she heard in his voice. 'No. If I need your help, I'll ask.' She lifted her head from the arm. 'Okay?'

Valentino didn't dare look at her. Her voice was all light and husky—he didn't need to see her looking all loose and relaxed and blissed out. 'Fine.'

'Good,' she murmured, dropping her head back. 'Now, please just keep doing what you're doing.'

So he did. The job would have been a lot easier, however, had Paige remained silent. But every time his fingers strayed to a new part of her foot she gave an appreciative moan and it shot his concentration to pieces. He continued through sheer grit alone and steadfastly refusing to look at anything but her feet and what his fingers were doing.

And not thinking about what they'd like to be doing.

Paige hovered on a blissful plane a few inches off the lounge as Valentino's deep steady strokes soothed all the aches away. She watched him through half-closed lids, diligently concentrating on the job. He hadn't taken his eyes off her feet once. Not even when he'd offered to make her his kept woman.

Anyone would think he was a professional masseur, for crying out loud.

Just looking at his bronzed hands on her pale skin was building a fire deep down low. The deep press of his fingers sent streaks of sensation from her foot up her instep to her inner leg and on to her entire body. She was melting into a puddle of desire, a boneless mass of longing.

It was wrong on so many levels. She'd told him this wasn't going to happen. But she wanted him more at this moment than she ever had.

And he was being Mr Professional.

Paige squirmed her body to ease the ache inside and pressed her palm to her belly for some outside fortification. How was she going to get through the next weeks without jumping his bones?

The squirm was his limit. He'd been fine till she'd moved but things jiggled in his peripheral vision and he couldn't stop himself from turning his head and looking his fill.

Her hand rested on her belly in a pose he'd seen more and more often these last few weeks since her tummy had popped out. Her habit of wearing baggy clothes and her baggy scrubs had allowed her to hide it from others, but he knew. He'd felt it.

He knew.

She was wearing a skirt that was too big, its folds hiding her legs all morning, but lying horizontal the folds fell away and the skirt very neatly outlined thighs that had filled out beautifully over weeks of feeding her the most tempting food he could find.

Paige popped her head up. 'Hey,' she protested quietly. 'You stopped.'

Valentino looked down at his stilled hands, surprised. 'I'm sorry.' His gaze returned to her hand splayed down low on her stomach. He wanted to see it. He wanted to gaze on his child growing inside her. 'Can I…can I look?'

Paige's breath stuck in her throat at his intense gaze. He looked so unsure. Valentino, who always looked so sure of himself. She could have no more refused him than have got her boneless body up off the couch. She locked her gaze with his and slowly inched the fabric of her shirt up her abdomen until she was exposed to his view.

Valentino sucked in a breath at the sight of her small round belly. His child grew there. 'You're beautiful,' he murmured. 'May I?'

Paige nodded and watched as his hands left her feet, slid up the sides of her legs, over hips that were less angular these days and onto her stomach. Her muscles contracted beneath his hands as he pushed the waistband of her skirt down slightly and they moved to cradle his child.

Valentino leaned forward and Paige widened her legs to allow him better access, and when he dropped a string of kisses across the swell of her belly her eyes blurred with tears and her fingers speared into his hair.

His tongue found her skin, laving her belly, and she felt the erotic scrape of his three-day growth deep down inside. When he dipped into her belly button she cried out.

Valentino looked up from his ministrations, his chin resting against the rise of her stomach. Her lips were parted and her smoky eyes glazed. Not taking his eyes off her, his hands moved slowly up, pushing her shirt as they went. When they found the lace-enclosed mounds of her breasts she shut her eyes and arched her back and Valentino swiped his thumbs over the taut peaks of her nipples.

Her whimper was soul-deep satisfying and he wanted to kiss her mouth so badly he was moving before he knew it, rising on his knees, looming over her, dropping his head closer and closer to her moist parted lips.

And when she raised her head to shorten the gap there was no holding back. Her mouth was sweeter than he remembered and the moan deep in her throat as she parted her lips widely, inviting him in, mingled with his.

He couldn't get enough of her mouth. Or the curve of her neck or the sweet spot behind her ear. His hands pushed aside her bra cups and she arched her back, pushing herself harder into his palms.

He dropped his head to suck a taut bud into his mouth and her swift indrawn breath was harsh in the silent room. He released it and looked down into her flushed face, her lips moist and ravaged from his ministrations.

Paige's breath sawed in and out of her lungs as she burnt up beneath his incendiary stare. She wanted him in her so badly she could almost feel him.

But.

'We can't…' Actually, technically, they could. Erica hadn't forbidden it at all. But Paige didn't want to risk anything.

'I know.' He nuzzled her neck. 'Move over,' he whispered. 'Lie on your side.'

Paige gave him kudos for having a plan. She was beyond such things. But her body knew what it wanted and eagerly followed his instructions. And then they were on their sides facing each other and Valentino's mouth was plundering hers and his hands were roaming over her breasts and stomach and pushing the waistband of her skirt lower, lower, and repeating the process with her underwear.

Her hands had a mind of their own too as they plucked at Valentino's shirt, pulled at it, lifted it over his head. Then reached for the clasp and zipper of his trousers, making them seem flimsy as she quickly undid them. His erection strained against his underwear and she pushed it aside too.

'*Dio!*' Valentino groaned into her neck, and shut his eyes as her hand enclosed him, squeezed him.

'You feel so good,' Paige murmured, milking the length of him.

'So do you,' Valentino gasped, his mouth closing over a dusky nipple as his hand found its way between her legs.

When his mobile rang it took several seconds for either of them to even hear it over the beat of their hearts and the heaving of their breath.

Valentino lifted his head and Paige pulled him back to her. 'Ignore it,' she whispered.

But Valentino had a separate ring for family members so he knew it was one of his sisters. He did a quick calculation in his head, surprised to find he was capable and also realising with a sinking feeling it was three in the morning back home. He knew they wouldn't be ringing at that time for anything trivial.

He pressed a hard kiss to Paige's mouth and then laid his forehead against her chest. 'I'm sorry. I have to get it. It's one of my sisters.'

Paige almost wept when he rolled away from her, adjusting his clothes and fishing in his back pocket for his mobile. She certainly wasn't capable of movement.

Definitely not capable of fixing her own clothes as her blood pounded like the ocean through her head and the room spun merrily around.

Valentino flipped his phone open and turned his back to her. She looked rumpled, dazed, her mouth glistening, her nipples engorged, her belly round with his child. He could smell her all around him and she looked thoroughly seduced. The temptation to end the call and turn his phone off was far too great.

'*Ciao.*' It was harsher then he'd meant it to come out but, really, his sisters had always had a sixth sense for interrupting at very inappropriate moments.

Paige listened absently to the conversation in Italian she didn't understand. It was brief and something was obviously wrong as Valentino's voice grew urgent and his words quickened.

He snapped the phone shut and turned back to her. Paige was still lying on the lounge, clothes skew, belly on proud display. She looked utterly sexy and he'd give anything to rewind time and delay the phone call.

'I'm sorry. That was my sister Carmella.' He raked a hand through his hair. 'My mother has been in a car accident not far from where we live.' He shut his eyes briefly as his sister's hysteria clawed at his gut. 'They're flying her to Rome for exploratory surgery.'

In the face of Valentino's wretchedness the sexual fogged evaporated and Paige pulled herself together. 'Oh, Valentino!' she gasped, climbing off the lounge, yanking her shirt down and adjusting her skirt. 'Is she all right?' she asked as he opened his arms and drew her close.

'I don't know. No one knows anything at the moment. I…have to go.'

Paige felt the blow to her heart immediately. She pushed away from his chest and plastered a resolute look on her face. 'Of course you must. Go. Go now.'

Valentino was torn. He couldn't believe in a few short months a woman had become just as important as his family. 'Come with me.'

Paige blinked. What the…? Had the haze of lust fried his brain cells. 'I…can't. I can't just up and leave. I have McKenzie and work and—'

'It'll just be a few days, maybe a week, until I know. Your parents—'

'No,' she interrupted, dismayed at his lack of understanding. 'I'm not leaving McKenzie.'

Valentino tensed, taken aback by her rejection and struggling to appreciate her reasons. 'Fine.'

'Valentino,' she said, stepping towards him, reaching for him. How had they gone from the heights of sexual dizziness to this? 'You know this isn't possible.'

A nerve jumped in his jaw and he flinched as she touched him. 'Anything's possible.'

Paige dropped her hands from his chest. 'No. That's what I've been trying to tell you. You can drop things and just leave. Like right now.' Like he no doubt would for the rest of their lives. Would he want to take their baby too? 'I can't.'

Valentino could feel irrational anger simmer in his blood. He grasped her by the upper arms. 'Marry me.'

Paige could feel the bite of his fingers peripherally only. She knew this was coming from a deep well of concern for his mother but it didn't make it any less difficult to deal with.

If only things were different…

But they weren't.

Paige shifted against the restraining bands of his hands. 'No. Go to your mother. Go home.'

It took a few seconds for her words to sink in and he released her, rubbing at her upper arms, smoothing where he had hurt her. 'I'm sorry,' he said.

Paige linked her arms around his neck and gave him a fierce hug. 'It's okay. Now go.'

Valentino pulled back slightly, slammed a hard kiss against her mouth and then turned away.

It wasn't until she heard the front door shut that Paige realised the awful truth. She loved him. Loved a man who didn't love her back. And there was nothing she could do about it but keep it to herself and never let him know.

CHAPTER NINE

Two weeks later Valentino lay horizontal in his business-class seat, wide awake, somewhere over the Pacific Ocean. The lights in the cabin had been turned down low and most sensible travellers were using it to grab some shut-eye. They'd be landing in Brisbane in just over four hours.

But he couldn't sleep.

He was impatient for the plane to fly faster, to get there sooner. He needed to see Paige. To tell her that he loved her.

It was something he'd known the minute he'd walked out of her door that momentous afternoon and had kept to himself for two weeks. Well, not strictly to himself. He'd told his mother about the baby and she'd demanded to know about Paige. She'd asked him point blank if he loved her and he'd been able to say yes with utter conviction.

But he hadn't been able to confirm Paige's feelings for him to his mother. The truth was he just didn't know how she felt at all. She'd been keeping him at a distance, protecting her damaged heart for the entire time he'd known her. Valentino just didn't know if she'd ever allow herself to fall in love again.

Sure, there was something between them. He knew that. There was a strong physical attraction. He sincerely doubted whether they'd ever be able to keep their hands off each other for any length of time. And there would always be their son.

But he wanted to be more in her life than just the father of their child. A part-time parent. Someone to scratch the itch when it got too much to bear for both of them. He wanted to love and cherish her. Introduce her to his family as his bride. He wanted to grow old with her.

He'd come a long way since his infatuation with Daniella. The young love he'd felt for her was lightweight compared to this heavy feeling in his chest. It had been impulsive and superficial. Skin deep.

What he felt for Paige reached right down to his soul. It was complex, multi-faceted. Messy and complicated. Especially in comparison to the easy, carefree time with Daniella. But maturity was a wonderful thing. He now knew sometimes good things didn't come easily. Sometimes they had to be fought for.

And if that's what it took then he'd do it, because he most certainly knew his life would be empty without her by his side.

Paige rubbed her back absently as she sat in her office chair and updated the charts from the day's surgery. It was hard to concentrate when her mind kept drifting to Valentino and the fact that in two weeks she'd received three lousy texts.

One had been to say his mother had undergone an emergency splenectomy and was doing well. The next had come four days later to say she was being discharged and he was staying another week or so. And the last a couple of days ago, which had informed her he'd be back soon.

She'd been worried sick about him but he hadn't answered any of her calls or returned any of her messages. He couldn't have been any clearer about her lack of importance to him if he'd opened his mouth and told her.

And it hurt.

Worse than with Arnie. Way worse than with Arnie. Because she'd been an infatuated, blind fool with him but she'd walked into this one with her eyes wide open and the door to her heart firmly shut, but she'd opened the damn thing anyway. Flung it wide open despite her misgivings. And not just her heart but McKenzie's heart too. She was the worst kind of fool.

Another tightening sensation gripped her belly and she had to stop what she was doing and rub at it. She'd been having irregular Braxton-Hicks' contractions on and off all day, no doubt aggravated by standing in a cold theatre in hard clogs.

She'd panicked earlier in the day when the first one had hit in the break between theatre cases and she'd rung her obstetrician in a state of absolute dread, fearing the start of another premature labour.

Not that it felt like it had with the twins at all, just an occasional tightening, but at only twenty-four weeks and with her history, any little niggle was cause for fright.

After asking succinct questions, Erica had assured her they were Braxton-Hicks' contractions, which were perfectly normal. Not having had any before her first pregnancy had come to a rather early finish, Paige was ignorant to what they felt like, although she'd heard pregnant women and mothers talking about them frequently.

Erica had talked her through the things to watch out for and by the time Paige had hung up the panic had receded and she'd got a grip. Braxton-Hicks were a perfectly normal sign of a perfectly normal pregnancy. They were a good thing. She was going to have a normal pregnancy and deliver at a normal time.

She picked up the pen and starting writing again.

'Paige?'

Her hand stilled in mid-word and her heart contracted as her gaze flew to the doorway. Valentino stood there, taking up all the space, looking as sexy as ever in a haggard twenty-four-hour-flight kind of way. Rumpled clothes, jaw heavy with stubble, bleary eyes and unruly hair.

Actually, he looked like hell.

Good.

She stifled the urge to get up and run to him. No matter how her arms ached to hold him and her heart bled, she would not debase herself with him any more. He'd made it perfectly clear where she stood.

'Valentino,' she murmured, her fingers strangling the pen. Another Braxton-Hicks came and she frowned as it gripped her belly hard, much closer and stronger than any of the others. How long had it been since the last? 'How is your mother?'

Valentino saw the wariness in her eyes. The frigid coolness of them. It hadn't been the welcome he'd expected. Not that he'd known what to expect but the way they'd left things he'd hoped for a little more warmth. Maybe even pleasure lighting those expressive grey pools.

Her shuttered look certainly wasn't conducive to confessing his undying love. 'Fighting fit again. Not much keeps her down for long.'

Paige nodded, her jaw cramped with the effort of keeping her voice evenly modulated. 'Good to know. I'm pleased she came through it well. It must have been worrying for all of you.'

Valentino frowned at her formality. He didn't want this. He wanted to sweep her up and lay her down, see how much her belly had grown in the interminable two weeks he'd been away. Kiss it. Kiss her. Tell her how much he loved her. 'Is everything okay?'

Her shoulders tensed. 'Fine.'

Valentino walked into her office and stood in front of her desk, hands on his hips. He was so tired. All he wanted to do was lie down with her, fall asleep with his hand on her belly. 'You seem…upset.'

A bubble of rage combined with another sharp pain spurred her into standing. She was so angry with him the Braxton-Hicks was secondary. Was he seriously that obtuse? 'Upset? Why on earth would I be upset?' she snapped. 'You don't answer your phone or return my calls. You could have plunged into the ocean days ago for all I knew.'

Paige hated how she sounded. Like a spurned lover, or, in his case, a discarded girlfriend. But she couldn't stop as the pain gripping her belly increased in length and intensity.

She glared at him. 'I was worried sick about you.'

Valentino was unsure whether it was a good thing or a bad thing that she was mad. She'd been worried about him? Did it mean she cared? 'I texted you.'

Paige slammed her hand against the desk. 'Three times! Three lousy times in two weeks? You profess to want to marry me, for us to be a family together, yet you can't even ring me when you get there to tell me everything's okay? You text me?'

Valentino blinked, taken aback by her fervour. It was true he hadn't rung. But that had been deliberate. He'd known that the minute he heard her voice he would have told her he loved her and he hadn't wanted that for her. Not over the phone.

He'd wanted to say the words face to face. So, no, he hadn't rung. But he'd dialled her number a hundred times and listened to her messages over and over again, wishing she was by his side.

And then there was the other side of it. If he'd told her he'd loved her and she'd rejected him or, worse, panicked and run, he would have been a half a world away, unable to do anything about it. At least face to face she couldn't run or hide.

'Nothing to say?' she snapped. 'Damn it, Valentino, I—' Paige broke off as another pain assailed her down low, doubling her over. She gripped the desk with both hands.

Valentino rushed to her. 'Paige!'

Something was wrong. 'Help,' she cried, clutching Valentino's sleeve. That hadn't felt like a normal, natural Braxton-Hicks. That had felt exactly like it had with the twins when her membranes had ruptured at twenty-eight weeks and she'd been eight centimetres dilated. Exactly.

'I think I'm in labour.' And she burst into tears.

Valentino stared at the top of her downcast head, his arm going around her back, supporting her against him.

No.

No, this could not possibly be happening. He'd told her it wouldn't. He'd told her he'd look after her.

Paige turned a tear-streaked face to him. 'I'm only twenty-four weeks. We have to stop it.' She grabbed the front of his shirt. 'We have to.'

Valentino fought a tidal wave of emotions. The woman he loved was in distress, fighting pain and a bunch of demons. And his baby, his son, possibly also in distress, was too young to survive.

But he couldn't afford to let the wave sweep him up and carry him out to sea. She needed him. So did his son.

'We will,' he said, grim determination in his eyes as he swept her up into his arms.

'What are you doing?' she cried.

'Taking you to A and E. I'll call Erica to meet us there.'

Valentino's long strides took them quickly through the lounge and he deposited her gently into the wheelchair they always kept in the department. Paige's anguish tore at his gut but he blanked it out as he pushed her to the lifts, using his mobile to call Erica.

'Have your membranes ruptured?' Valentino asked.

'No,' Paige wailed.

He relayed it to Erica, listened for another moment and then snapped his phone shut. Another contraction hit as they entered the lift and Paige cried harder, reaching back for his hand. 'Its okay, Paige, just breathe. Erica's ten minutes away.'

The ride in the lift was the longest of his life and by the time he wheeled Paige into St Auburn's chaotic accident department he was running on sheer adrenaline.

Nat was the first person they saw. Her initial look of welcome quickly turned to alarm as she took in the situation. She knelt beside the wheelchair. 'Paige! Whatever is wrong?'

Valentino answered for her. 'She's twenty-four weeks pregnant and having contractions.'

Nat blinked. 'Pregnant?'

'Yes,' Valentino snapped. 'Pregnant. Erica de Jongh is on her way.'

Natalie didn't need any more information. She didn't reprimand her friend for lying to her on the phone all those months ago when she had rung to check on her. In thirty seconds a blubbering Paige was in a cubicle and being transferred onto a gurney.

'I'll just get the CTG,' Nat said, ducking out of the curtains.

Paige, who was lying on her side, her back to Valentino, had curled herself into a ball and was sobbing quietly. Valentino couldn't bear to see it. 'Paige,' he murmured, placing his hand on her shoulder and applying gentle pressure to get her to face him.

'Go away,' she choked out, giving her shoulder a violent shrug. 'Just go away, Valentino. It'll save you the effort later.'

Her anguished insult hit him square in the solar plexus. 'I'm not going anywhere,' he said, pulling at her shoulder again.

Paige felt a block of rage like molten rock wedge in her chest as she flung herself back to face him. 'I told you. I told you this would happen again and that I didn't want to get close to another baby, to love another baby.'

She half sat, wiping at her streaming eyes and nose. 'But, no, you said it'd be fine, you said it wouldn't happen. You…' she poked him viciously in the chest '…made me go along with it. You…' another poke '…made me want him.'

Valentino's heart broke at her torment. 'Paige, we don't know what this is yet.'

Paige shook her head violently. 'I do.' She knew deep in her bones. 'I. Do.'

Valentino tried to take her hand but she snatched hers away. 'We discussed this contingency with Erica—'

A contraction gripped her and Paige's gasp interrupted him. She tried to breathe but was crying too hard at the same time. It eventually eased and then Nat came in with the CTG machine and hooked the belt around her bump. She squeezed Paige's hand. 'Erica will be here really soon.'

Paige watched the curtains fall back into place as Nat left. She looked at Valentino, so strong and positive, and felt weary, old beyond her years. 'I can't do this again, Valentino.' Paige heaved in deep breaths. 'Do you hear me? I can't do it. I don't have enough strength for this.'

'Yes, you do, Paige. You are the strongest woman I know.' He brushed at her fringe. Her face was all red and blotchy, her nose and eyes were streaming and he cupped her cheek, using his thumb to wipe at her tears. 'Look what you've been through already. Look how you survived. You're a survivor.'

Paige angled her head and leaned her face into his palm and her eyes, two more tears squeezing out and trekking down her face. 'Why can't something just go my way for once?' She opened her eyes and straightened her head. 'You told me it would be okay,' she whispered. 'I trusted you.'

He placed his other hand on her face so he was cupping both cheeks. 'You can trust me. I'm not going to let anything happen. We'll get an ultrasound and if it is preterm labour then you'll go on nifedipine and the labour is going to stop and you're giving up work and going on bed rest and I'm going to support you and feed you and pamper you and this baby will go to full term and then we're getting married because I love you and we're going to Italy for a honeymoon and we're taking the kids.'

Paige was feeling so churned up she found it difficult to follow his stream-of-consciousness speech. She wasn't even sure if she heard him right. But the conviction in his words was strong and she so wanted to believe him.

And had he actually said the L word? She sniffed and said, 'What?'

Then the curtains snapped back and Erica arrived, pushing a portable ultrasound machine and looking calm and efficient and in control. Valentino squeezed her hand and they and their future faded away as the immediate danger to their baby took precedence.

'How are you doing?' she asked both of them as she switched on the machine and fiddled with some dials.

'Lousy,' Paige admitted.

Erica nodded. 'You?' she asked Valentino.

'Scared witless.'

Paige looked at him, startled. He hadn't seemed in the least bit afraid. He'd been commanding and confident and had got her to A and E and arranged for Erica to be here and told her everything was going to be okay. He'd been the epitome of cool, calm and collected, especially in the face of her histrionics.

Erica nodded again. 'Normal, then.' She inspected the graph readout the CTG had traced.

Her face gave nothing away but that just made Paige even more frantic. 'It's bad, isn't it?'

Erica looked her in the eye. 'It's showing regular strong contractions. But the baby's heart rate is steady and there are no decelerations. He doesn't appear to be in any distress. Let's have a look first, okay?' She placed a condom over the trans-vaginal probe and squirted warmed lubricant on it.

Paige grabbed Erica's sleeve. 'Please tell me it's going to be okay.'

Erica glanced at Valentino then back to Paige. She shook her head. 'I don't know yet, Paige. But I will in a second. Let's be sure, okay?'

Paige felt a hot tear escape out the corner of one eye and tried not to tense as she drew her knees up and Erica inserted the probe beneath the sheet. Valentino squeezed her hand and dropped a kiss on her shoulder, which made her tear up even more.

An image flickered on the screen and she shut her eyes tight, turning her head into Valentino's shoulder. She couldn't bear to watch.

After what seemed like minutes Paige couldn't take the silence any longer, convinced Erica was trying to find a way to tell her she was almost fully dilated again. She glared at Erica. 'Well?'

Erica flicked a switch and the sure and steady beat of their baby's heart filled the cubicle. Paige broke down at the glorious sound. It seemed so strong but Paige knew at twenty-four weeks their son was so very, very fragile. Too young to be in the outside world.

Erica removed the probe and switched off the machine. She looked at Valentino, his arm around Paige, who was weeping quietly. 'The good news is you haven't dilated at all.'

Paige clutched at Valentino's sleeve as the news sank in. He kissed her head and for the first time since she'd realised she was in labour, Paige felt a ray of hope.

'But. You are fifty per cent effaced.'

Valentino knew both effacement—shortening and thinning of the cervix—and dilatation were required for the baby to be delivered. 'So, it's definitely preterm labour?'

Erica nodded. 'I'm afraid so.'

Paige was incapable of anything as she went from fragile hope to the walls crashing around her. It was happening all over again. She was going to give birth to Val's baby soon. Too soon. A hundred memories of Daisy and McKenzie when they had first been born floated before her.

And her son was going to be even earlier. A whole four weeks of crucial development time.

'So what's the plan?' Valentino asked.

'Oral nifedipine regime to relax the uterus and hopefully stop the contractions, even if it's only for a few days to give us time to administer some steroids to mature the baby's lungs.'

Valentino nodded. 'And then?'

'Hospital for a few days, monitoring blood pressure and regular ultrasounds to check on the cervix.'

He nodded again. Nifedipine's normal use was as an anti-hypertensive and had only been used regularly in an obstetric drug in relatively recent times. Paige's blood pressure would need close monitoring. 'And then?'

'If we can stop the contractions, home on twice-daily tablets and lots of bed rest. If she makes it to thirty-six weeks we take her off the medication and let nature take its course.'

Valentino's methodical medical mind prioritised and sorted. 'So, the worst-case scenario is that we buy a few days. The best case is we go to term?'

Erica nodded. 'Spot on.'

Paige was taking none of it in. She was numb now. Numb all over. There were no more tears left. Flashes of three years ago bombarded her—the twins on life support,

Daisy's tiny white coffin, Arnie walking away—as she tried to reach a mental place where she could shut down her emotions and deal with the next few days, maybe months if Valentino's child was a fighter.

Juggling McKenzie and watching Valentino become ever more distant.

A sob caught in her throat.

'Paige!'

Valentino's voice invaded her thoughts and the mental place moved further out of reach. She looked at him as if seeing him for the first time.

'Leave me alone,' she whispered.

Valentino could see her withdrawing before his eyes and he wanted to shake her. *Dio!* He would not let her give up. This wasn't a battle he could fight on his own, neither could his son. She had to believe it was going to be okay too. 'No.'

Paige had started to recede again and his insistent denial dragged her back. 'What?'

'I said no.'

Paige shook her head. He truly didn't understand how much of her had died inside her last time. 'Just do what needs to be done,' she muttered. He said he loved her? Then he could do that for her.

Valentino looked hopelessly at Erica. 'What do I do?'

Erica gave him a grave smile. 'What she asked you to do. Do what needs to be done.'

Valentino glanced at Paige, so near and yet so far. 'Okay, then.'

Paige swallowed pills and lay passively as they put in an IV and gave her a steroid shot and took her blood pressure endlessly. She didn't feel the belt of the CTG strapped to her abdomen or notice the contractions slowing and then stopping or Valentino's bedside vigil when she was finally transferred to Maternity.

Inside her head she was in a warm dark place with her babies—McKenzie and Daisy and her little boy—and she was singing them a lullaby and as she drifted to sleep they were all happy.

Two hours later Erica strode into Paige's room to check on her patient. She headed straight to the constant readout on the graph paper. 'They've stopped,' she murmured.

Valentino nodded, too exhausted from his flight, which seemed a million years ago now, and worry about Page's mental state to truly appreciate the deep well of joy and sheer relief of his son being okay.

They'd dodged a bullet.

Erica looked down at him and gave his shoulder a squeeze. 'She'll be all right,' she murmured. 'Paige has been through a lot. It's just her way of coping. She'll be a different person when she wakes.'

Valentino nodded but his heart felt heavy as Erica left. He'd been so excited about the baby—his son. About becoming a father. About the things they'd do together. He truly hadn't considered the mental implications for Paige. She'd tried to tell him she couldn't cope with another poor outcome and he'd swept all her objections aside, promising her hearts and rainbows.

He'd been an arrogant man.

'I'm sorry,' he whispered at her sleeping profile, looking still and pale in her white hospital gown against the white hospital sheets.

He'd been so wrapped up in being in love with her and their joyful future he'd forgotten how truly badly love could hurt.

Paige's arm slipped off the bed and she jolted awake with a gasp. Valentino jolted awake too. 'What is it? Are you okay?' he asked, lifting his head off the bed where it had fallen an hour ago. He stood and loomed over her, blinking bleary eyes and fighting a thick fog of fatigue.

Paige took in the room and the drip and tried to remember what had happened. Her mouth was dry and she had a headache. She looked at him with frightened eyes. 'The baby?' Had they taken the baby?

She reached for her belly, expecting flatness and to feel pain from an incision.

'It's okay,' Valentino soothed, placing his hand on top of hers. 'He's still there. Feel him,' he urged, running the flat of her hand around her bump. 'Erica managed to stop the contractions.'

He pushed aside the bedside chair and checked the nearby growing pile of graph paper. 'Nothing,' he said. 'Not one single contraction.'

Paige's heart banged in her chest. Dared she even hope he was telling the truth? 'Really?'

Valentino smiled. 'Really.'

'So…it's going to be okay?'

'Erica's encouraged by your uterus's rapid response to the medication. You'll need to stay on it but…'

Paige couldn't believe what she was hearing. The last thing she remembered she'd been preparing herself for the worst. 'I'll take a truckload of the stuff if that's what it takes.'

Valentino chuckled for the first time since he'd landed. 'Two a day should be enough.'

Paige laughed as Valentino resumed his chair. His chin rested on his hands and he looked utterly exhausted. His stubble was longer still and his clothes more rumpled. His hair looked as if it had been raked to within an inch of its life. 'You should go home,' she murmured. 'You look totally exhausted.'

Valentino rubbed his chin against the sheets and it rasped into the silence. 'I'm not leaving,' he said. 'I'm never leaving.'

Paige swallowed. She believed him. The man had seen her at her lowest ebb and was still here. Arnie had never been good with her tears and hadn't been able to cope with her grief. He certainly would have been at a loss with her withdrawn state.

Valentino had just taken it in his stride.

'I'm sorry about earlier. I don't know where I went…I totally freaked out.'

Valentino slid his hand back to her rejoin hers nestled against her belly. 'You went where you needed to go. It's okay.'

Paige gave him a small smile and yawned as her eyelids fluttered shut.

'Go to sleep,' he urged. 'I'm staying right here.'

Paige nodded but something niggled at the back of her mind as she drifted off. Three seconds later she was wide awake and sitting bolt upright, her heart in her mouth. 'McKenzie!'

Valentino squeezed her hand. 'She's fine. She's with your parents. I've been giving them regular updates.'

'Really?' she demanded, her pulse still racing.

'Really,' he assured her, reaching his arms up to push gently against her shoulders. 'Go to sleep.'

Paige complied as her heart rate settled and her breathing became deep and even, yet still something niggled.

Paige wasn't sure how much time had elapsed since she'd last woken up but she could see a slight pink hue lightening the sky through a gap in the curtains.

Her gaze drifted to Valentino's sleeping face. For the first time he actually looked his thirty-seven years. A lock of his luscious hair had fallen forward and was kissing his eyelid. It was such an endearing picture her heart filled with her love for him. She forgot all about being mad at him earlier.

What did that matter now? He had been her true hero tonight and she loved him completely.

And suddenly she was able to put a finger on that strange niggly feeling from earlier as memories from yesterday afternoon rushed back. He had told her he loved her too. And today, at the breaking of a new dawn, after a night of miracles, she was going to embrace it and choose to be happy.

Paige advanced her finger slowly and gently lifted the stray lock back into place. He murmured and stirred and then opened his eyes.

She gave him time to focus. 'Good morning,' she whispered.

He licked his dry lips and smiled. *'Buongiorno.'*

She smiled back, her toes curling at his husky morning voice and sexy accent. 'You told me you loved me.'

Valentino stilled for a moment and searched her face. She seemed relaxed. Happy even. 'Yes.'

'Did you mean it?'

'Assolutamente.'

Paige smiled, not needing a translation for that one. 'And when did you have this particular epiphany?'

'About ten seconds after I left your house to go to the airport a fortnight ago.'

Paige laughed this time. 'I think that was about when I had mine.'

Valentino's heart stopped briefly before skipping madly in his chest. He slid his hand to her belly. 'Really?' he murmured.

She nodded, holding his hand close. 'Really.'

'It was before that, though. The moment I fell in love with you. I just didn't realise until much later.'

Paige quirked an eyebrow, intrigued. 'Oh? When?'

'That night at the wedding when you looked so confused as to why out of all the women at Alessandro's wedding I wanted you.'

Paige frowned. 'Why then?'

'Because you truly didn't know how beautiful you were and that, my darling…' he lifted her hand off her stomach and kissed it '…was utterly endearing.'

She could feel her cheeks turn pink. 'I think for me it was when you promised me there would be no sleeping.' Valentino chuckled and she grinned. 'That was a great line. You'll have to teach it to our son when he's older.'

Valentino felt his chest expand. Their son. 'So you're not going to fight me any more? You'll marry me?'

Paige nodded vigorously and snuggled his hand back against the swell of her belly. 'And the four of us will honeymoon in Italy together.'

Valentino grinned. It sounded like bliss. 'I brought this with me from the airport.' He reached into his pocket with his spare hand and pulled out the velvet case he'd produced all those months ago. He presented it to her. 'Will you wear it?'

Paige slipped her hand out of his and flipped open the lid. The diamond glittered beneath the dim overhead light. 'Just try and stop me,' she murmured as she freed it from its satiny cushion and slipped it on. 'See?' She turned it around to show him and he rose slightly and pressed a gentle kiss against her mouth.

'Perfect. Just like you.'

'Just like us,' she whispered. 'Just like him.' And her hand rejoined his as she kissed him back.

EPILOGUE

'HE'S perfect. Perfect in every way,' Valentino mused, peeling back the wad of wrapping in the crook of his wife's elbow to reveal his one-hour-old son Ferdinando Lombardi.

Paige smiled as her little boy slept. She couldn't agree more. She was exhausted from a fifteen-hour labour but somehow still too elated to sleep. Erica had taken her off the nifedepine a week ago and their son, after wanting out at such an early stage, had finally decided to make an appearance seven days later, weighing a very healthy three and a half kilos.

'Can we come in?'

Paige looked up to see her parents and McKenzie waiting impatiently in the doorway.

'McKenzie!' Valentino smiled and held out his arms to her.

She rushed into the room. Don and Adele followed at a slightly more sedate pace. Slightly.

Valentino swept McKenzie into his arms and plonked her on the side of the bed. 'Are you ready to meet your little brother?' he said as he signed simultaneously.

McKenzie squirmed with barely suppressed excitement. 'Yes,' she said.

Paige smiled, still in love with her daughter's voice as she turned her son around.

'This is your brother, Ferdinando,' Val murmured, signing as well.

McKenzie looked at him as if he were a baby unicorn she'd found in an enchanted forest, her eyes big and round. 'Nandi,' she said, and leaned forward to kiss the tip of her sleeping brother's nose.

'Looks like he's already acquired a nickname.' Adele beamed, reaching forward to gently touch her grandson's tiny fingers.

Valentino chuckled. 'I like it.'

Paige made way for McKenzie to snuggle into her side and they all gazed on her newborn son's perfection.

'Thank you,' Valentino mouthed after a few moments, interlinking his hand with hers.

'Thank you,' she whispered back.

0910/03a

BACHELOR OF THE BABY WARD
by Meredith Webber

New to Jimmie's Children's Unit, anaesthetist Kate Armstrong is desperate not to fall for the sexy surgeon Angus McDowell – because she knows he'll be impossible to forget! But Angus' son has other ideas… All *he* wants is Kate to be his mummy…!

FAIRYTALE ON THE CHILDREN'S WARD
by Meredith Webber

Dear Santa, I've just learnt I have a daddy called Oliver, who works with my mummy Clare at Jimmie's Children's Unit. All I want is for my family to be together by Christmas Day! Love, Emily (aged 9¼)

PLAYBOY UNDER THE MISTLETOE
by Joanna Neil

Heartthrob Dr Ben Radcliffe is back in town and A&E doctor Jasmine knows she should stay well away, but it's impossible! As the snow starts to fall the village has their fingers crossed that the mistletoe at the village dance will work its Christmas magic!

OFFICER, SURGEON…GENTLEMAN!
by Janice Lynn

When Dr Amelia Stockton sees dashing naval surgeon and old flame Cole Stanley on board her ship, her heart calls mayday! Cole is aware of the Navy's 'no relationship' policy! But when it comes to the beautiful Amelia, rules are made to be broken!

On sale from 1st October 2010
Don't miss out!

Available at WHSmith, Tesco, ASDA, Eason and all good bookshops
www.millsandboon.co.uk

0910/03b

Medical Romance™

MIDWIFE IN THE FAMILY WAY
by Fiona McArthur

Emma has built a beautiful life for herself and her little girl in Lyrebird Lake. Gianni has come to the lake for a whistlestop tour, but is soon enchanted by the beautiful Emma. Will he be able to leave when he discovers she's expecting?

THEIR MARRIAGE MIRACLE
by Sue MacKay

Doctor Fiona is about to face Dr Tom Saville, her new boss – and the husband she hasn't seen for years. They were separated by heartbreak, but is Tom's incredible smile enough for Fiona to find the courage to take this second chance at happiness…?

On sale from 1st October 2010
Don't miss out!

Available at WHSmith, Tesco, ASDA, Eason and all good bookshops
www.millsandboon.co.uk

Spend Christmas with
NORA ROBERTS

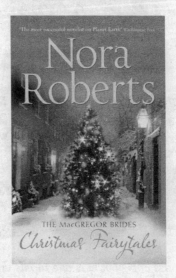

Daniel MacGregor is the clan patriarch. He's powerful, rich – and determined to see his three career-minded granddaughters married. So he chooses three unsuspecting men he considers worthy and sets his plans in motion!

As Christmas approaches, will his independent granddaughters escape his schemes? Or can the magic of the season melt their hearts – and allow Daniel's plans to succeed?

Available 1st October 2010

www.millsandboon.co.uk

2 FREE BOOKS
AND A SURPRISE GIFT

We would like to take this opportunity to thank you for reading this
Mills & Boon® book by offering you the chance to take TWO more
specially selected books from the Medical™ series absolutely FREE!
We're also making this offer to introduce you to the benefits of the
Mills & Boon® Book Club™—

- **FREE home delivery**
- **FREE gifts and competitions**
- **FREE monthly Newsletter**
- **Exclusive Mills & Boon Book Club offers**
- **Books available before they're in the shops**

Accepting these FREE books and gift places you under no obligation to buy, you may cancel at any time, even after receiving your free
books. Simply complete your details below and return the entire page
to the address below. You don't even need a stamp!

YES Please send me 2 free Medical books and a surprise gift. I
understand that unless you hear from me, I will receive 5 superb new
stories every month including two 2-in-1 books priced at £4.99
each and a single book priced at £3.19, postage and packing free. I
am under no obligation to purchase any books and may cancel my
subscription at any time. The free books and gift will be mine to keep
in any case.

Ms/Mrs/Miss/Mr _____ Initials _____

Surname _____
Address _____

_____ Postcode _____
E-mail _____

Send this whole page to: Mills & Boon Book Club, Free Book Offer,
FREEPOST NAT 10298, Richmond, TW9 1BR